Athaliah

The Samaritan Woman

Don Rasmussen

Athaliah

The Samaritan Woman

© 2023 by Don Rasmussen

ALL RIGHTS RESERVED

ISBN 978-0-9993750-6-8

For information:

MASTER PRESS

3405 ISLAND BAY WAY, KNOXVILLE, TN 37931

Mail to: publishing@ masterpressbooks.com

Dedication

This book is dedicated to all those who started life with dreams of success in making great achievements: the satisfaction of fulfilling their dreams of love and meaningful relationships, but instead found loneliness, deception, and pain, only to become heartbroken, roaming aimlessly in a world of emotional devastation with no way out.

I have a vivid hope that in reading these words, the will of God will be accomplished for those who seek restoration and emotional healing. Jesus said, "I am the way, the truth, and the life" (John 14:6). And, in saying this, He expresses His power as God to give us abundant life, joy, and fulfillment emotionally and spiritually.

Believe in Him. Take Him by the hand and witness the discovery of a life full of abundance that He has in store for you.

᠅

Contents

PART I

CHAPTER ONE

The Plan

"Chara, I'm afraid. Will I ever be healthy again?"

"Athaliah, what a silly question; of course, you will. Look, you are already walking around, gaining strength by the day. You are eating better, and your complexion has returned."

"I know, but I don't feel like I am better. I still don't remember anything that happened to me. Why am I so weak and sickly?" she pressed.

"You worry about what you can't see. Your mind can't understand it, because you can't remember what happened, that's all," Chara said, with feigned conviction. "It makes you use the energy you don't have, and it eats you up. You would do much better if you could get your mind off it."

In a moment of inspiration, Chara stood, "I have an idea. Why don't we go to the garden and let the evening breeze soothe our hearts? You will feel better, I'm sure."

Taking Athaliah by the hand, she lifted her up. "Good, you can rest against my arm as we walk."

"I love the cool breeze here," Athaliah said, as she chose a spot near the fountain. Water gently erupted from its center, producing an almost magical mist that felt wonderful against her skin. The water babbled, reminding her of the brook where she and Benjamin loved to fish.

"You know, Chara, I have tried to remember, but I can't. All I can think of is Daniel. He promised me he would say goodbye before going away. I know he would not do anything to hurt me. I just know it."

"Don't think of that day, Athaliah. It will make you worse," Chara insisted.

"But, when I think of him, I somehow feel better. In my heart I know it wasn't him."

"You can't know for sure, and if you can't know for sure, why deny the possibility? It only makes you hide deeper inside. If you continue doing this, you will not get better."

"I do remember the first time he came to me. His eyes spoke to me. It was as though I could see right into his heart. He is a good man. That is what I am going to remember, nothing else. I know he didn't do this thing."

Resolve entered her heart as she spoke these words of assurance, "Chara, I think I am going to be better. I must be better for when he comes back. When he returns, he will tell everyone that he didn't do it. You will see," she said, confidence springing up just as the refreshing water of the fountain.

"I feel like eating," she said. "Can you bring me some dates from the kitchen?"

Chara walked toward the kitchen, gloom filling her heart. *This is my fault. I should have never let him meet her.* Self-condemnation rushed over her. She felt flush. *I must be strong for her.*

Master Obed ben Haddad saw the noticeable change in Athaliah over several weeks and was delighted.

Before leaving the house for work one morning, he said to Mara, "Action must be taken to find a husband for Athaliah. Almost a year has passed. Athaliah is better and showing little signs of trauma. She will completely mend."

Though his business enterprises filled his time, he was never far from her in his heart. He loved his daughter and would do anything to provide a good life for her.

The conflict that ate at him was the knowledge that not only was his reputation on the line, but that of his family as well. Their secret must be guarded at all costs. *We will find a way.*

He made his way to the city gate and took his usual place. This was where much of his business transactions happened. Associates from all over the city, and surrounding areas, met at the city gates to work and cement deals. Tax collectors milled among them, representing the government's interest.

"Good morning, Obed," a colleague called out, as he approached. "It's a good day to be alive, and business is promising, don't you think?"

"Yes, my friend, it is. Say, Jacob, don't you have a caravan due back soon?" Master Haddad said.

"Yes, I have been waiting several weeks. You know how it is. Nothing moves fast when one waits."

"Where did your men go this time?" Obed asked.

"They went west. I instructed my foreman to go as far as Macedonia if need be."

"That may be the reason for the delay."

"Yes, it is always a waiting game. One never knows what will happen on the trail. I have great hope in my men. They are a faithful lot. The Almighty favors me."

With a smile, Obed looked past his friend to the trail that snaked its way up the mountains from the Northwest.

"I think I can see men coming in the distance. Can you see them?"

"Oh, yes. Maybe this is my day. You might have a caravan arriving as well."

They kept their eyes on the trail, as camels appeared around a bend in the distance, casting up dust with every step along the well-worn trail.

"It looks like several caravans are coming together."

A group of businessmen gathered to watch the advancing procession. It could take hours for the travelers to arrive. Camels were not known as the fastest mode of transportation, especially when they came laden with goods.

Conversations flourished. Speculations could be heard, as each man wondered if his caravan was among the approaching procession. Excitement filled the air. This was indeed a good day.

Tax collectors readied their papers and filled their inkwells. They too, would be busy today.

Some of the businessmen sent out runners to learn who was coming. "Come back as fast as you can," they told their servants.

"But don't return before you know if our men are coming."

The conversation was brisk. Excitement mounted. Men prepared for their caravan's arrival.

Shortly, runners appeared with news. Businessmen controlled their excitement, but the anticipation made it difficult.

"Master Marcos, your men are coming. They are the second group in line." Shouts of joy rang out just across the way, as Marcos' workers heard the news. Obed stood on his tiptoes to see over the crowd, wanting to see if his runner was returning. "There's my runner," Jacob shouted.

"Master Jacob, your caravan is the first in line. Master Haddad's men are behind, in the distance. I was told that they are coming."

"Good news, my friend," Obed said, as he congratulated Jacob.

"This is an important day, Obed," Jacob said. "My son, Abel, returns. He went along to learn the trade. He will be my new assistant from now on."

"That's right, you have a son. I had forgotten. You are favored," Obed said. "Passing the torch to the next generation, are you? That is good. I will do the same soon. My son, Benjamin, is almost ready to join me in my business, as well."

"We can both be proud this day," Jacob said.

The runners returned and informed their masters of their approaching caravans. For security purposes, it was a common practice to travel in groups. One by one, the caravans arrived. The area was filled with men and animals. It was a challenge to maintain order. Designated areas were provided for each caravan as they arrived, tired and trail weary. Fatigue showed on their faces, and smiles belied their exhaustion. It was good to be home.

Voices were loud, as workers milled about, unloading their beasts of burden.

"Master Haddad, your animals will be over there by the wall," one servant shouted over the crowd.

"Yes, thank you," he said, making his way to the designated area.

"Jacob, it looks like your area is next to mine," he said, looking over his shoulder.

"There is much to celebrate this day, my friend."

"We must do something to celebrate," Jacob said. "I will see to my men, and we can talk in a little while," he shouted over the hustle and bustle.

There was much to do. Merchandise and provisions had to be counted and stored.

Obed busied himself with the tasks at hand. It was approaching dark when Jacob saw him again.

"We must celebrate," he said, as he shook Obed's hand.

"Yes, by all means. I would like that."

"Why don't you bring your family over to my house for a celebratory feast? I will send runners to your place to inform you of the day and time."

"Excellent, thank you," Obed said.

"Oh, here is my son, Abel," Jacob said, looking past Obed.

"How you have grown, Abel," Master Haddad said. "How handsome you have become. I'm sure your father is proud of you. It is good to meet you again, after all these years. The last time I saw you was when you were knee-high to a duck."

"Thank you, Sir," Abel said respectfully. "My father speaks of you often."

Obed was visibly impressed. "How had time passed so quickly? *This young man is surprisingly handsome.*

Abel had all the right credentials: An up-and-coming businessman, a good family, and a wonderful reputation.

Why have I not thought of him before? Obed wondered.

"I will await your invitation, then, Jacob. Thank you so much, we are at your service."

That night, Obed spoke with his wife as they prepared for bed. "I have good news. I met a young man who would be perfect for Athaliah."

"What do you mean?" she asked. "I thought you already knew everyone."

"I do, but this young man has grown up. I remembered him as a child, but today he returned with his father's caravan. You remember Master Jacob? Well, he has invited us – the whole family – to his home, to celebrate his good fortune. One of his caravans returned today."

"When will he do this?"

"He said he is going to send a servant to inform us of the time."

"It is nice of him to invite us. If the whole family goes to the celebration, we will have to buy new cloaks for the children, don't you think?"

"Spoken like a true woman," he said, smiling. "But they are no longer children, my Dear. Athaliah is a lady in every way, and beautiful, if I say so myself."

"I know. Even Benjamin is no longer a child, but a man in his own right," she confirmed.

"Where do the years go?" he said, more of a lamentation than a question. "But we are favored this day. You will see."

The next few days flew by. Everything was different. No longer did Mr. Haddad sense the gloom that had been over him since Athaliah was brought home that fateful day, a year ago. There was life in his eyes. His life had meaning once again, and there was hope in his heart. His daughter no longer had to worry about her future. In his heart, the deal was already made, and sealed. His daughter would marry Master Jacob's son. All that lacked was time, and the opportunity would take care of itself.

Master Jacob's servant arrived with the anticipated invitation. To the household's joy, the date was set. Everyone knew of the pending celebration. Secretly, all the servants knew the plan. They pieced together small, overheard comments, and busily built their case. It was unusual for a young lady to pass sixteen and not be married, or at least, promised in marriage. Delighted whispers flew around the house as the servants prepared for "Athaliah's celebration."

"No, it can't be for Master Jacob's business ventures only that Master Haddad's family is invited," one cook commented to her co-worker. "I overheard them say that Master Jacob has a son. To my mind, this celebration must be so Athaliah can meet Master Jacob's son. I don't really know his family, but he is a wealthy businessman. His son might make a perfect mate for her. This is the reason for the event, nothing less," she declared.

"I do hope you are right. Athaliah needs a positive change in her life after all she has gone through."

The extent of Athaliah's illness was a closely guarded secret. Only the most trusted servants knew what truly happened and held their peace upon threat of life and limb. Athaliah herself was unaware of all the facts surrounding her illness. Her parents wanted it that way.

"Let's keep a grip on our emotions. The two in question must first meet each other," Obed cautioned Mara. "Let's not be too obvious."

Athaliah was guarded. She heard that Master Jacob had a son. How would she react to him? What would she think of him?

How can I meet someone else when I know, in my heart, that I have met someone already? She thought.

She was raised with the understanding that her parents would someday arrange her marriage, but she wanted to, at least, have a say in the matter. Her parents had to know what was best, by virtue of their maturity and experience. She was expected to consent to her their wishes. Turmoil filled her thoughts.

She wanted to fulfill the family's dreams, but she was torn. Would she ever get over Daniel? Could she get over him? Where was he? From the day of her mishap, she had not heard a word about him. Was he gone from her life forever? His caravan had returned and gone again, a couple of times. She had no news of him. Maybe she should give up waiting for him. Obviously, he must not care for her as much as he had professed.

Abel. That is the young man's name I am to meet. I will submit to my parent's wishes. I am too confused to make a proper decision.

The night of the celebration was upon them. Excitement and expectation cast their glow over the family. It was no use trying to hide the obvious.

"Let's go. Let's not keep them waiting," Obed said one last time.

"Benjamin, make an extra effort to be respectful," Mara said. "I want them to see you as I see you. They can't help but like you."

"Athaliah put on your best face and manners. You look terrific tonight," Obed said.

"Son, this is an exceptional night," Jacob said to Abel.

"Yes, Father."

"I know you are tired after that long trip, but you have had a few days to rest, and you deserve to be celebrated."

"Thank you, Father."

"You are my pride and joy, you know. I have invited a number of people here to introduce you to my world of business. You are worthy of it. You paid your dues and exceeded my expectations on the trip. You have learned things no one could teach you from books. I have brought you up for greatness – even greater than I have known.

"It was a long journey, Father."

"Now, do you remember what I told you about Master Haddad? He is a powerfully influential man."

"Yes, Sir. You and he go back many years. This is the first time you have invited him to our home, and you want to make a good impression."

"That is correct."

"You want me to be my best tonight because you want to suggest some joint ventures to him, with me at the helm."

"Right again. He is by far the wealthiest man in the region, and I think we could do some great things together if you make the right impression tonight."

"Father, don't you think he will see what you are up to?"

"What do you mean? This is business. You will see, of course, but if we work things right, he will see the wisdom of joining forces to advance us both even further in business. Synergy has its advantages. Neither of us will sacrifice anything. That is the beauty of what I am thinking. We win, and he wins. He also has a son, who will join him in a few years. Together we can be a force, the likes of which no one has seen … except for a few kings," he added.

With a side glance, he whispered, "And you will meet his daughter."

Abel said nothing.

"Son, I have worked hard to bring this night together. You will see. This is a turning point for us. This is a good night. Now, let's be ready to meet our guests as they arrive. Come down as soon as you can."

Servants scurried around the house, making sure all was in order.

"Young lady, bring some of the Jasmine flowers and place them just over there. Don't get them from the vines out front, but from the ones in the back of the house. We don't want our guests to see you working as they come in. Drape them over the top of that small stone column," the head housekeeper called out. "Hurry now. The guests are arriving soon."

Abel sat in his room, daydreaming. His father was an influential man in the community. He would do his part in making sure his father's efforts paid off. After all, this is his life as well, being the heir of all that his father possessed. Prospects were good.

The Haddad family's coachman awaited them at the front entrance of their home and helped the ladies into the family chariot. The evening breezes made the trip pleasant. The distance to Master Jacob's was not far, as the bird flies, but the winding road between farms and estates was like a snake. By the time they neared their destination, the afternoon was waning. Beautiful clouds floated across the blue sky, as the sun slid toward the western horizon. Shadows lengthened toward the east, breaking the sunlight that cast a glowing array of colors across the valley in the distance.

The Haddad family had never been to Master Jacob's home, though Master Haddad and he had worked around each other for years. It was the coachman's duty to get them there safely, and he fulfilled his job flawlessly.

Athaliah marveled at every detail of nature as it passed, enjoying the wonderment of creation. *It has been a long time since I have enjoyed such a scene.*

Benjamin reached his hands out to catch the leaves that wandered too close to the chariot, as it went along.

It was indeed a wonderful evening. Their parents sat next to each other, enjoying the ease with which Athaliah expressed herself.

"She is finally enjoying herself," Mara whispered to Obed.

"I know. Isn't it wonderful? She is back."

Master Jacob was a wealthy man. His home attested to the fact in grand fashion. Trees lined the entrance to the estate and conducted arriving chariots to the elaborate front reception area. The chariot stopped under an expansive lattice work that supported flowering vines overhead. The vines grew from established trunks, which wound their way up and around crafted columns, and joined overhead to form a thick mesh that cooled the breeze in its shade.

"Oh, mother, can you smell the Jasmine," Athaliah asked. "Isn't it divine?"

"I could sit here all night, just to take it in," her mother said.

Other guests were arriving. Some had already made their way into the reception area. A few were unknown to Master Haddad, while others were lifelong friends.

"This will be an excellent time to meet and talk business over the tables, while the celebrations take place," he said to Benjamin, as they awaited the servant to assist them.

"Always the businessman," Benjamin said, winking at his father.

"Good boy," Obed said. "You are indeed my son."

A servant approached, and offered his hand to the ladies, as they stepped down.

"Welcome. Master Jacob is expecting you. Please allow me to escort your family. Just follow me," he said, formally.

The evening was planned with attention to detail as was evidenced by elaborate hanging flowers and eye-catching adornments throughout the house. The entrance glittered as strategic lamps illuminated specific statues that lined the route which conducted the guests toward the reception and dining areas.

"Oohs" and "ayahs" were heard as the guests entered, proceeded by elegantly dressed servants. This night was meant to impress, and it did. Conversations erupted among the guests as they arrived. Men presented their wives and children to their business associates. The din of voices filled the air.

Merriment followed naturally. Wine was offered to the adults upon entering the foyer.

Master Jacob entered, followed by his son, and took a seat at the head table. His wife and other children sat comfortably at another table close by.

This was a family extravaganza for the enjoyment of friends and associates of Master Jacob. This night, the whole family would join in the festivities.

Obed was invited to sit with Jacob at his table.

"Bring your son over, and take a seat here at my table, won't you? Your family may sit at the table with my wife and children," he said, as he motioned them in the right direction.

"Welcome to my home. This is truly a delight. I get to meet your son, and the rest of the family."

"Yes, indeed," Obed said. "Thank you, so much, for the invitation to celebrate your good fortune. This is my son, Benjamin. He, too, will soon step into the business, as your son is doing."

Master Jacob took Benjamin's forearm in a mutual grasp of greeting. "This is my son, Abel, Benjamin," he said warmly. Abel greeted Master Haddad respectfully and then turned to Benjamin, greeting him in the same manner.

"I am delighted to meet you both."

"Please be seated," Master Jacob said, as he reclined at the table.

Servants quickly filled their chalices. Finger foods were offered. Brisk and delightful conversation followed.

Abel watched as Master Haddad's family took their seats at his mother's table. Athaliah did not escape his glance. *Father didn't tell me she was so beautiful.* He turned back to the guests seated at his table and avoided being seen watching the beautiful young lady at the other table. He couldn't help stealing glances from time to time when the others had their attention elsewhere.

Dancers came in, gyrating to music provided by contracted musicians. The tone of the dances was moderate, to fit the occasion. The evening was going just as planned, to the delight of all present.

Master Jacob gave a few words of greeting to all and invited them to partake in the feast as servants distributed the first course consisting of fresh, sweet fruit on elegant, silver platters. Conversation was replaced with sounds of delight, as the guests ate. Several courses followed, including pheasant, roasted to perfection, legumes, and vegetables prepared in palate pleasing sauces of herbs and spices, and complemented with choices of fig pudding, raisin fruit cake, and apple dumplings. Each time the guests thought there would be no more, another course appeared.

The unconscious desire to fill one's plate each time a new platter appeared was moderated by the self-imposed admonition to leave room for the next exciting dish. Expressions of delight confirmed the excitement of the guests, as each new course arrived.

All evening Abel expertly carried on conversations with the guests, while stealing glances at Athaliah.

"Abel, you are in exceptionally good spirits tonight," his father said.

"Yes, Father, this is a wonderful celebration. Even I am impressed."

"Please stand at my side, son."

Master Jacob clapped his hands to gather attention. When the guests fell silent, he began. Abel stood at his father's side, listening. "This is a very special night. It is our joy to have every one of you with us to help celebrate our good fortune. This is made even more special by the fact that my son, Abel, is officially joining our family business. He has proven himself, as you who accompanied him on this last venture into Macedonia know. He learned quickly, if I say so myself. The 'fruit' indeed does not fall far from the tree."

Polite, but heartfelt laughter filled the room, in confirmation.

"Tonight, I am proud to announce my son's stepping into the business world. It is my desire that he prosper long after I am gone. Son, can you say a few words?"

With respectful ease, Abel looked out over the audience.

"Thank you, Father. It is my heartfelt intent to faithfully work, not only for the benefit of our family, but for the well-being of all our workers, without whom …" He pointed to each of the workers in turn, "we could not be successful. As we prosper, each of you prospers. Thank you for your faithful work."

The fact that some of them were slaves didn't affect what he said. The seating arrangement belied the social differences, but the slaves loved their master and his family, because they were treated honorably with respect.

Applause erupted, and all stood in respectful expression of joy and pride. Impulsively, one business associate approached Abel, and shook his hand. Others followed his lead, greeting the young man warmly. The workers respectfully remained at their tables, applauding.

The obvious affection was unexpected, but not wanting to seem surprised, Abel quickly adapted, and greeted each heartfelt expression of praise. He had little time to look around as a line formed behind those who had come up first.

Master Jacob, noticing the clamor as everyone took a place in line, motioned to the musicians to fill the room with music.

As the last of the greeters showed their appreciation, Abel extended his hands in an encompassing gesture of acknowledgment and quieted the listeners as they returned to their tables.

"Thank you, thank you. You are truly a great group of friends, no matter your station among us. All of you are important in your respective areas of responsibility. This makes success possible for all. I am grateful to be a part of such dedicated men and women. Let's all work together to further the desires and ambitions of everyone. Please be seated. Please continue the celebration."

"And…that is my son, ladies, and gentlemen," Master Jacob intoned. "Welcome to the family business, son."

Again, applause resounded throughout the room.

Athaliah watched as Abel spoke, obviously impressed with his poise and grace. When his father finished speaking, he took his seat at the table once again, glancing over at Athaliah's table. For a moment, their eyes locked and held their mutual glance. They had seen each other throughout the evening, but this time was different. They felt the exchange within them. Athaliah broke the moment, and looked down, feeling her cheeks flush. She felt uncomfortable. Looking up again, she realized that Abel was still watching her. He nodded his head ever so slightly and smiled. At that moment communication was complete. There was no need for interpretation. The glance said it all.

"Athaliah, your face is so red," her mother said. "Are you all right?"

Flustered, Athaliah simply said, "It is nothing mother."

At that moment, Mara, turning to look at her husband, caught Abel's expression. She knew that look. Abel had seen Athaliah.

She could think of nothing else throughout the rest of the festivities. On their way home she was all smiles.

"My Love, I haven't seen you smile like this for a long time," Obed said, nudging her. "What happened?"

"Oh, nothing. I will tell you later," she said, placing her arm in his. "Later, my Love."

"This is good news," Obed exclaimed, upon hearing the revelation.

"Yes, indeed. Now, how do we cultivate this?"

"You leave it to me. This must be done right. I will speak with Jacob at the first opportunity," he assured her.

Athaliah could not sleep. "What is wrong with me," she whispered. "I haven't felt like this for a long time. Not since Daniel. What does it mean? Why do I feel so odd, and warm inside?"

Her mind flitted like birds that can't find a place to rest, hopping from branch to branch. Thoughts poured through her mind so fast that she could not make sense of them.

How could a person, a young man, make me feel this way? What did he do? What did he say? Say? Do? The words echoed through her mind, leaving her light-headed.

Oh, yes, I liked what he said about the workers. What did he say? "Each of you is important … we will all prosper … every position is important." That's it. He must be a kind young man, who respects others, even the workers. I like that.

Light came into her heart. *He must be kind, gentle, respectful, and caring.* Each characteristic stood out in her mind and formed a picture of this young man named Abel. *He is a good person. I like that. He was so genuine in the way he expressed his appreciation of others.*

Her heart unwittingly turned a corner. Emotions rose within her that caused her face to glow in the dark of her room. *I want to know him more.*

Falling into a fitful sleep she dreamed of Abel, the son of Master Jacob.

CHAPTER TWO

Intrigued

Abel finally fell into his bed. All the guests were gone, and the servants were cleaning up. He saw no more reason to socialize and sought solitude where no one would bother him. It had been a long day of celebration and wonder. He found comfort in the fact that his father had publicly announced his joining the business. Now he had the respect of all his father's workers and associates alike. *I will do a good job. My preparations have brought me to this place in life. I will honor my father in all I do.*

A picture came to his mind, a picture of the beautiful young lady that sat across the room from his table. *She is not only beautiful, but well-mannered, and respectful. She holds herself proudly, yet not arrogantly. I must get to know her.*

She filled his mind as he fell asleep. His dreams were continuous all night. They took him from one scene to another, changing backgrounds and places, but on each occasion, this young lady appeared. He couldn't remember her name. In every scene, he found himself searching. Realizing he was dreaming, he tossed and turned. *I must learn her name. Get back to the dream.*

She stood by a wisteria vine that engulfed a tree, smelling the beautiful fragrance, looking his way. He couldn't make out her facial details but knew it was her. He approached, only to see her run from view. He followed, interest growing in his heart. Now, he was in a different setting, but there she was. Again, she smiled before teasingly running from view. This seemed to be all she did. *Why does she torment me so?* He continued searching. Every time he found her, she moved from sight. *If I only knew her name, maybe she would wait for me.* He tried calling to her, but she only smiled and led him further. Now, she stood beside a stream, dipping her hands into the water, cupping handfuls of cool, crystal-clear water, bringing them to her mouth. *How beautiful she is. Please tell me your name*, he pleaded, as she again fled from sight. She seemed not to hear his plea. He formed the words, but they wouldn't come out as he wished. Frustrated, his interest changed to longing. He felt he must know her name. *Why won't she wait for me?*

Scene after scene followed. Always she ran, but not before smiling toward him. *Why won't she stand still, and let me know her name?* Now, he stood in a field of flowers, colors beautifully arrayed as far as the eye could see. He looked from side to side. *Such a beautiful garden this is. She must be here.* She was nowhere to be seen, but turning, he finally saw her, slowly approaching from behind. Her beauty equaled that of the flowers that surrounded her. She seemed to be one with nature. Her fragrance was intoxicating. He could not move. Her smile bewitched him. Intrigued, he simply stood, as she came nearer. She slowly stretched out her hand, and softly touched his cheek, smiling angelically. "My name is Ath…" Then, she faded from sight. *No. No. Come back. Please don't go. I must know your name.* He awoke. Frustration gripped his soul.

I must get back to my dream I must know her name. But try as he might, he was awake. The dreams were gone.

CHAPTER THREE

The Request

Abel rose from his bed, walked to the water basin that sat on a small table, and poured water from the pitcher at its side. Gathering water in his cupped hands, he splashed the cool liquid over his face and felt its invigorating freshness. It cleansed his face of the night's slumber but could not erase his thoughts of the young lady.

I must hurry down, forcing himself to gather his thoughts. *My father will be waiting for me.*

"Come, my son, breakfast is ready. You look horrible. Did you not sleep?"

Abel staggered onto the breakfast patio, his mind far away, and he didn't hear his father speak. Pulling out a chair, he plumped himself down. Placing his elbows on the table, he cupped his head in his hands. "Are you alright? His father asked.

"Mmmmm. I feel as though I never slept at all last night," he finally sputtered.

The family was seated at the table and studied him quizzically.

This was unusual for him. He was always responsible and disciplined in his actions, but this morning his mind was jumping around, seemingly incoherently, like a tormented rabbit. *What is the matter with me? The family will think I am drunk.*

"I am fine. I don't know what has come over me."

"Well, you had better find out, because I have a request of you this morning since you are now assuming responsibility in the family business," his father stated.

"Yes, Father, what can I do to help?"

"When you finish your breakfast, I would like you to investigate a matter. I have just received word that several of our camels, of the southern caravan, have returned sick. This will be good for you to get familiar with the men, and maybe find a solution."

"Consider it done, Father."

Abel alerted one of the servants to ready his horse while he prepared himself for the day's work. Making his way to the family stockyards, he focused on the task at hand – forcibly. The young lady slipped into his thoughts and he, by sheer will, tried to bring himself back to his work, with little success.

At the stockyard, he asked for the caravan's master and found him tending the affected camels.

"Master Simeon, good day to you. I hear we have a problem with some of the camels," he said, jumping from his horse.

"Yes, Young Master," Simeon said.

"Do you have any idea what may have happened?"

"We were doing well on our return trip, until we got to the last oasis, two days out. There were several other caravans already drinking at the water source."

"Did you know any of the men?" Abel asked.

"I did know a couple of the caravan masters, but there were a couple I had not met. They seemed to stay apart from the others."

"How long did you stay there?"

"We spent one night because we were eager to arrive with our merchandise, but when we gathered our animals and packed them for the next day's trek, the others who had stayed their distance were already gone."

"When did the animals get sick?"

"They did well for several hours, but then seemed to slow up considerably. It took my men great effort to make them continue without stopping every few steps."

"You have experience in these things. What do you think happened?"

"Master Abel, this is a tough business. The competition is great. I am wondering if the men from the other caravans gave something to our animals to cause them to slow up, giving the other caravans the advantage by arriving first and getting the best deals."

"That could be true. Look at how the camels seem lackluster."

"Camels never look too good, Master."

The men both laughed. Camels were the most important animal in the caravan world, but everyone knew they could be obstinate. They had a will of their own and didn't mind letting everyone know it.

"But you are right, they don't look good."

"I am going to assume they were poisoned with something that wouldn't kill them."

As Abel spoke, his mind searched for a solution. A thought came to him. He remembered the time his grandmother had made him eat something when he complained of a stomachache. *What did she give me? Oh, yes. That was it.*

"This is what you can do. We will see if it works. Ask your men to build a fire and get the embers red hot. When there is a sufficient quantity of red coals, douse them with water. Have the men take the charcoal chucks, and pound them up onto powder. Compress them into little balls. Then, feed them to the affected camels. You might have to combine them with their regular feed. Once they have eaten the balls, take them to water and let them drink their fill."

"Yes Master, right away. Consider it done."

"Good, send word as soon as you notice any results. I have other concerns at the moment, but I will be waiting for your word."

"Yes, young Master."

After running several errands, Abel returned home for lunch. His father met him as he pulled up behind the house and dismounted.

"Abel, whatever you did, it worked," his father said. "The men sent word to say that the animals have begun to mend. It worked."

"Good, Abel said," clapping his hands. "Charcoal has properties that absorb poisons. I figured that if it works for humans, it might work for animals as well."

"Good thinking, son. You are going to make a name for yourself in this business."

"Thank you, Father," Abel humbly replied. "Father, come with me to the veranda where it is cool. I have some questions I would like to ask."

They walked a little distance from the main house to a shaded area under vines that brimmed with fragrant flowers. Open to the sides, Abel and his father could sit, and look out over the majestic landscapes in the distance. Light breezes blew through the space, bringing cool, fragrant air that belied the fact that the sun's heat was all around.

"This is heaven," Jacob said, as he and Abel settled onto cushions.

"We can speak here without interruptions. Would you like something to drink, son?"

"Well, yes, father. Maybe servants could bring some cool water with lemon juice and honey in it."

Calling to a servant standing near the house, Jacob let his desire be known. In a little while, a servant girl came with their drinks in hand.

"Thank you, my dear," Jacob said. "Could you make sure no one disturbs us?"

"Yes, Master."

When the servant walked away, Abel said, "I don't know what has come over me. Ever since that girl was here, I can't help thinking about her."

"What girl?"

"You know," He hesitated a moment. "You know, Master Haddad's daughter. I don't even remember her name."

Jacob smiled. "I wondered if you had seen her. She is beautiful, isn't she?"

"She is wonderful. I have not seen such beauty in all my life."

"So, this is where your mind has been."

"I just can't help it. She appears in my thoughts, whether I want it or not. I can't say she is disagreeable to me."

"Well, son, you certainly have a good eye. Just like your father. She is from a great family."

"I have never felt this way about anyone I have seen. I can't understand it. Not that I dislike what is happening, I just never thought it would be this way."

"Son, love is a wonderful thing. There is nothing its equal. It is also something that puts me at a loss to explain. One must experience it to know it. Even then, it makes one's mind run in circles."

"I have never asked you for anything like this, and I don't know how to say it. Could you ask her father if I could see her?"

"I have known Master Haddad for many years, but I have only recently come up with the idea of working close with him. We talked a lot when our caravans returned at the same time. We have even spoken of doing business together. The reason I invited him and his family over to celebrate with us was so we could further talk about combining our efforts in some way."

"Yes. But could you ask him if I may see his daughter?"

"Well, of course. These things take time, as you know. There are customs that must be observed."

"I know, Father. You have taught me well. This girl just seems different to me in a way that causes my knees to shake. Do you think I am worthy of her?"

"Yes, my son. We need to know if she is worthy of you. You are my son, and I want the best for you."

"Thank you, Father. Will you do it? Will you ask Master Haddad if I can see her?"

"Abel, I will do it, of course. But let's keep this between us until we know more. Do you agree?"

A smile came over Abel's face that unmistakably proved to his father that he was indeed serious about this young lady.

A week passed with no word. Abel could hardly contain himself. His father came and went, giving no hint of what might have transpired. He only knew that his father and Master Haddad had done business and were making plans together. To wait seemed unbearable. Time stood still. The days lingered long past their normal length. Nights were interminable, producing dreams that only inspired impatience within him.

After what seemed to be an eternity, his father called him to the veranda.

"I have a word," he said, as Abel stood before him. "Sit, I think you will like this."

Abel waited.

"Master Haddad has consented to your meeting his daughter."

"What is her name, Father?"

"Her name is Athaliah."

"It is a beautiful name, indeed. She must be named after the only Queen that ruled in Jerusalem and Samaria. It fits her well."

"There are some conditions which you must follow."

"Anything, just tell me."

"Master Haddad is going to send an invitation to dine with his family. Along with the invitation, you will learn more about your next steps. I can't say exactly when it will arrive but be patient."

"Yes!" Abel said and slapped his knee.

"Son, this could be something good for both our families. But let's take it one step at a time. Master Haddad is a good man with a good reputation. He will protect his daughter at every step, as I would, so be patient."

"Yes father."

"This is interesting," Obed said to his Mara. "Master Jacob and I spoke this morning, and he asked if his son, Abel, can meet Athaliah."

"Oh, this is so soon. I mean, parents spend their whole life wanting their children to wed the right person, and now it is our time to make that decision," she responded.

"But, let's not get ahead of ourselves. First, we need to know how Athaliah gets along with him. I would not want to push her into a marriage she doesn't want."

"I know. I want her to be loved and cared for, as you do.

"I am thinking of what happened to her. I don't want that to be a problem…"

"I know. All you must do is instruct her in certain matters, and all will be well," he said. "There are ways."

Both knew the consequences of covering up something so egregious but found it necessary to discuss it, nonetheless.

Mara was concerned, and it showed in her face. Her eyes shifted, and she leaned on her husband's chest. "I trust you, but I am worried."

Abel busied himself with the family business, assuming his responsibilities with ease. The servants respected him, and his reputation grew among them. His father brought him up well, and he now revealed the fact with his every move and decision. He was a natural.

"Simeon, we have purchased supplies and trading goods for your next caravan trip. The men should have them in the warehouse. You should find everything you need. You know what the men need to prepare for the trip. I leave it with you."

"Thank you, Young Master. I will have everything ready to leave within two days. One of the men was hurt the other day, but he is on the mend and will be ready at that time."

"I have purchased a few food items of interest for the men along the way. They will look forward to the delights."

Abel mounted his horse and headed toward the city. He loved the refreshing weather this time of year. Mornings were cool and fresh, making him feel ready to do anything with gusto. He was eager to hear back about the awaited invitation but had work to do in the meantime.

At a point, just before the city, he nudged his horse down a winding path that took him through cultivated fields of lush vineyards. Reaching a small house at the edge of an orchard, he drew up and dismounted. A young boy came running, having recognized him as he approached.

"Good morning, Master Abel," the boy said energetically.

"Hello, David. Is your brother home?

"Yes, Sir. He is just inside. I will tell him you are here." David said, disappearing into the house.

"Well, look who came to visit," Omar said, as he came out. "What brings you here? I haven't seen you for several months," he said, jokingly.

"Yes. It has been a while. I trust your family is doing well. How is your mother? Little David seems to be doing well," he said, as he peered around Omar to stare at David, who had returned to stand behind his big brother.

"The family is well. Mother works too much, but that is to be expected."

"Can we speak?" Abel said.

"Yes. Come with me." He led Abel around the house to a veranda covered with blooming flowers and tangled vegetable vines. "Sit here in the shade."

"David, would you bring us something to drink," It was more of an order than a request. Omar's brother disappeared into the house.

"Do you remember how we used to play under these vines as boys?" Abel said. "We always seemed to get into trouble with your mother in some way."

"I do remember the time you pulled a coyote squash and tossed it at me."

"It wasn't my fault you picked another one and threw it like a spear at me."

"When mother came out and saw that half of her squash were on the ground, and bruised from being thrown around, I got the left hand of correction on my behind," Omar said, laughing.

"My mother wasn't too happy, either, to see my black eye when I returned home. You always had good aim," Abel said. "Those were the days."

"We all have to live, and learn," Omar said.

"Well, I have a proposition, Omar."

"Another one of your schemes, I suppose."

"I don't know if you know, but I have now joined my father's business."

"This is a big city, but word still gets around fast. Yes, I have heard. But how does that involve me?"

"I have something in mind, and I think you can be a great help." Omar's eyes opened as interest betrayed itself on his face.

"We can kill two birds with one stone, so to speak," Abel said, receiving the mug of fresh water that David brought.

"As I said, Omar, I am now working with my father. But I have ambitions of my own, and that is where you come in. I would like you to be my eyes and ears among the workers. We know each other better than anyone. We can make a good team. I will pay you handsomely. What do you say?"

"Well, what do you have in mind? What does 'kill two birds' mean?" He liked Abel, and would do anything for him, but he must be clear.

"Everyone respects me, and I am proud of my father's men. But I want to know first-hand details that some men might not feel free to reveal. This is where you come in. You could, as a co-worker, learn to understand each of the workers, and what they are capable of. You will report back to me personally, so I can understand how to maximize our efforts."

"What exactly do you want me to do for you?"

"I would like to bring you on as part of the security team of the caravans, to move among the workers, and learn the details of the business from that perspective. You can inform me of anything out of the ordinary, should anomalies present themselves along the way. I know you are a good worker, and that I can trust you." The last part was a good touch. Abel knew Omar couldn't resist even the smallest flattery.

"Sure, I would love the opportunity to work with you."

"And don't forget, you will bring much needed income to your mother, and make it easier on her."

"I will do it," Omar said. "When do I start?"

"I have spoken to Simeon, my father's caravan leader. He is expecting you to show up. Go to him tomorrow, and he will get you situated."

Leaning closer to Omar and looking each way to make sure no one was listening, Abel said, in a near whisper, "Now, this is what I have in mind ..."

"I am your man, consider it done. I will not let you down, my friend. Thank you for coming to me. My mother will be overjoyed to know that I have permanent employment."

"Just remember, you will be working for me, undercover, so to speak."

Obed called Athaliah to his side the next morning and beckoned her to accompany him into the garden. He put his arm around her, as they strolled among the lush trees and flowers. Sounds of bubbling water gently danced in the air when they approached the centrally located fountain.

"My dear, I have good news. I have invited Abel – do you remember him? He is Master Jacob's son."

"Father, you jest. Surely you know I remember him," she said, softly.

"You might appreciate this. I have invited him for supper tonight."

Athaliah stood to her feet. Her surprise was genuine. She didn't know what to say. Above all, she didn't want her father to see how much she wanted to hear those very words. *This is wonderful.* She was going to see "Master gorgeous" again.

"Father, if you wish, I would be pleased to accommodate him. He seems to be a good young man, with good character." *He is great. I am going to have him at my table, no less. I will see those beautiful eyes and speak of delightful things with him.*

"I believe he is, my dear. I thought you might want to know, so you can prepare yourself before coming down for dinner."

"Thank you, Father." *I will need all day to prepare. There won't be enough time. I will have to start right now. How can I get ready in time?* "Father, I thank you. I must take my leave. There is much to do."

She ran to the house, and up to her room.

Abel arrived upon his majestic steed, careful not to seem too proud. He pulled up at the front entrance, where he was met by a servant who received the horse and led it to the stables. Another servant motioned him to the door. "Follow me, sir." He was led to a beautiful waiting room, where Master Haddad was seated. As Abel entered, master Haddad stood, and walked toward him.

"Thank you, Abel, for coming," he said, formally. "It is good to have you in our home. Take a seat, won't you?" He led Abel to an ample chair and watched as he seated himself. Taking a seat next to him, he smiled.

"It is comfortably cool this evening, don't you think?"

"Yes Sir," Abel said.

"How was your ride over?"

"I enjoy riding in the cool of the evening, Sir. It was quite enjoyable."

For a few minutes, Master Haddad entertained Abel with questions of no consequence, to fill time. He responded cordially, and respectfully, keeping his composure as best he could. To be in this home with this man, whom he respected, and of whom he had heard wonderful things, naturally made him nervous, but he held his own.

At length, Master Haddad said, "Your father and I were speaking, and we both felt that since we will be doing business together, it might be nice for you to get to know our family. I need you to understand that I am not pressuring you in any way. Please, don't think ill of me if we have made you uncomfortable in any way."

Abel sat, trying to formulate an appropriate response. His silence lengthened.

Obed, normally a confident man, was off his game now. He had never entertained a young man in all his life, with the purpose with which he was now engaged. This had to be done right. He couldn't make any mistakes. Of course, his maturity and status gave him the upper hand.

"I know you have met them, but I think it is good if you get to know them better. Don't you think?"

"Yes sir. She is wonderful—" He caught himself before finishing. *Oops, now I have done it.*

Obed ignored the obvious glitch. *He is nervous. He likes her. So far, so good.* "The family will come down in a few minutes."

Before he finished, Mara arrived, and greeted Abel, cheerfully. "Good to see you again, Abel. Please feel as though you are in your own home," she said, with a welcoming smile. "Oh, here comes Benjamin."

Benjamin came in and formally greeted Abel and sat by his father.

"Where is Athaliah?" Obed asked Mara.

"You know young ladies. It takes time. I am sure she will be here momentarily," she said, glancing at Abel.

Now, Abel was outnumbered. This put him at a disadvantage, but he tried not to let this bother him. The family was pleasant enough.

Filling time, Obed said, "I see you have good taste in horseflesh. How long have you had that horse? He is beautiful." *I hope she doesn't keep us waiting too long. This could become awkward.*

"My father gave him to me a couple of years ago. Yes, he is full of energy, and doesn't like to be second when running with other horses," Abel said, with youthful pride.

"He seems to enjoy having you on his back. There is nothing better than a good, obedient horse."

"Yes sir. He is that, and more. I don't know what I would do without him."

As he spoke, all eyes turned to the door. There stood the most beautiful sight Abel had ever seen.

CHAPTER FOUR

The long Process

Abel could not believe his eyes. For a moment he struggled to keep his composure and was glad that all eyes were turned on Athaliah.

"Come in my dear," Mara said, pleasantly. "We have been waiting for you."

Athaliah saw the special guest at once and felt her face flush. She approached cautiously and greeted him formally. "Thank you for coming, Abel. It is good you have come to sit at the table with the family."

Abel stood to his feet, and responded warmly to her words, giving her a respectful bow as he did so. The moment made him feel uncomfortable. All eyes were on him, and he wanted to make a good impression, his mind busily taking in all that he saw. *I can't mess it up. I hope she likes me.*

Athaliah was nervous as well, and became flustered when she felt her cheeks burn red. *I hope he doesn't notice.* But he did.

Awkwardly, she turned to sit beside her mother, feeling the comfort of her nearness. She reached unconsciously, taking her mother's hand in hers, putting herself at ease. Smiling at Abel, she fell silent. *What should I say? What does he want me to say? Oh, he is so handsome.* Her mind worked to process the moment, trying not to be obvious, but without much success. *I wish I were dead.*

Her father, seeing her consternation, stepped in to save her. "I can see that the table is ready, and the food is hot. Shall we go to the table?" Everyone stood and followed him into the dining room.

"Abel, you may sit there on my right. Athaliah, please take your seat at his side," he said, motioning his intent with his hand. "You are most welcome in our home, Abel, and it is a pleasure to receive you at our table."

The evening passed as though in a fog. Neither Athaliah nor Abel remembered what transpired over the course of the evening, except to remember that they were the only ones seated at the table. Their attention was so concentrated that they forgot all others. Her parents attempted to bring them out of the fog, but without much success. This was to their liking, after all. This was the outcome they were hoping for. The evening went well, and the young couple responsibly undertook to learn details about each other.

Athaliah went to her room, feeling as light as a butterfly. Chara was waiting and smiled as she helped her change for bed. "I know you like him," she said. "It is written all over your face."

"Don't embarrass me, Chara. I couldn't keep my face from smiling all night. My face hurts. All I want to do is sleep, and dream. He is simply marvelous, don't you think?" Athaliah spouted. It was a question, but in her heart, she knew that it was an affirmation. "I can't get him out of my head. We sat at the same table and spoke of many things. He is just marvelous," she repeated.

"Well, you must change first, and then I will leave you to your dreams. I can't imagine who you might want to dream of."

Athaliah gave her *the look.* "I can't think of anyone better to dream of, than Abel."

"No. Really?" Chara said, feigning surprise.

Chara prepared the water for Athaliah and helped her get ready for bed. She remembered the last time she had heard Athaliah speak of a young man that she couldn't get out of her head. How much time had it been since that fateful day? A lot. *I was the reason he never showed up again. It was my fault.* No one could convince her otherwise. And no one could possibly understand the deep sense of guilt she carried for him – Daniel. The events surrounding him had changed the whole family. None of them had been the same since. Athaliah ignored much of what had happened, given her lack of memory. This caused great hurt within Chara's heart. But she was under orders never to speak of what had happened … especially to Athaliah.

Chara knew Athaliah's memory of what happened could return at any moment, but if it did, it wouldn't be because of her. This was very clear. At times she felt her life depended on her silence. She respected and honored the Haddad family, even to the point of loving them. To watch over and care for Athaliah was not work for her. It was a joy because of the deep affection she felt for them. Athaliah had come to be much more than a friend, it was as though she was a sister, and because of this, she dedicated herself to her work. But how could she love her work and at the same time feel so conflicted? It was not fair! She knew she carried a great responsibility upon her shoulders, and carried it deep within her heart, from where it could never escape. *Just don't think about it*, she told herself.

"Come, Athaliah, the water is ready. I will help you get ready for bed."

"Isn't he just divine?" Athaliah repeated.

Chara didn't know what to say. "I suppose he is good-looking."

"He is that and more." She had never seen someone so handsome. "His eyes sparkled; did you notice? I could sit and do nothing else but look at them."

"But you just met him," Chara said.

"I know, I know, he is so marvelous. I have never known anyone like him. When I saw him at his house, when his father presented him as his new business associate, I couldn't do anything but watch him. And, when he looked at me, I felt as though I was stuck to my chair. I couldn't move. But he looked at me!"

"How could he not look at you? You are beautiful. You have become a mature, beautiful woman, who could resist looking at you?"

"Yes, but he is different. He looked at me. I could feel his eyes looking at me. It was as though he said thousands of words with that look."

Chara knew Athaliah could only talk that way because she could not remember what had happened to her, and she could not allow her to recall those details. Pushing them deeper within her, Chara said, "I think you might be right. Come, you must sleep."

Abel made his way home in a silent stupor. His horse knew the way, and Abel, giving it free rein, dreamed as he rode. "Athaliah, I love that name," he spoke to the wind. His mind went over every move she had made. He didn't want to forget anything but realized that his mind couldn't think. Everything was a blur. *What is happening to me?*

Master Jacob and Master Haddad met the following morning, as they went about their respective responsibilities at the city gate.

"How did the evening go?" Jacob asked.

"It was delightful. I think the two young people got along admirably. They obviously like each other."

"Then, what do you think? Shall we proceed with the next steps?" There were cultural norms and expectations that had to be satisfied. A bride price had to be established and agreed upon between the two fathers. Obed had saved Athaliah's dowry and felt pleased with what he had. Both men planned the path that lay before them and discussed how to implement the proceedings. They spoke of a year in which Abel could prepare himself to take on the responsibility he was about to assume. The families would be proud of the arrangement. It would be a happy time of preparation for all concerned. An agreement was made about when, and under which circumstances, the couple would be allowed to meet. The parents would do their best not to be overbearing so that the couple could feel free to know each other yet restrained by moderation and propriety.

Over the next few weeks, Abel visited frequently. The couple was not permitted to leave alone to be seen in public without a chaperone. Usually, a family member was always present. One exception was Chara. She was allowed to accompany them, being a person of confidence among the family workers. Athaliah became comfortable in Abel's presence, laughing at his sense of humor, and dazzled by his intellect. Abel fell in love with Athaliah's ability of expression, and knowledge of practical things in life. Her learning in the science of mathematics astounded him. "She has a gift," he often said.

One beautiful day, Abel arrived with flowers in his hand. He had become an expected presence around the house and was welcomed by the servants.

"Come right in Master Abel. I will let Athaliah know you are here. Please be seated," the doorman said. Disappearing around the corner into another room, Abel heard a flurry of commotion, and whispered orders. Shortly, Athaliah came into view, as beautiful as ever. *How does she do that? She is always perfect.*

"Good morning, Abel. How nice to see you. It has been so long," she said smiling.

"Yes, it has, if you don't count yesterday. For me, it has been a long time. I can't get you out of my mind. I wish we could be together all the time."

"All in good time," she said as she approached him. "What shall we do today?"

He took her hand and looked deep into her eyes. "Let's walk. Can we go into the back garden?"

"It is such a lovely day. I would love to do that."

They walked through the house, across the back patio, around the fountain, and into the manicured beauty of the garden. Trees, shrubs, flowers in abundance made it a most romantic spot. It was not lost on them. They made their way down the slope and sat under a shade tree. They hardly noticed Chara, as she kept a respectable distance. She pretended not to see.

"I love this place," Abel said. "Your parents are truly to be commended for having designed it just for us. I know they had us in mind when they designed it."

She chuckled sweetly. "Oh, I am sure you are right. There could be no other reason … but, maybe they just love to come out here themselves."

"Without a doubt," he said, with a mischievous smile. "No one could enjoy this as much as we do."

"I am sure we are not the only ones to notice the lovely birds, the sweet-smelling flowers, and the delightful shade this affords. Even the fountain adds a delightful touch. It was my father's idea, you know."

"Why think of others?" Abel said. "We are here together, and it is beautiful. It is especially wonderful when you are present. Everything seems to light up when you are around. It is as though bright, shining candles are casting light everywhere you are."

"You exaggerate, but that pleases me. I am delighted." *How did I live before knowing Abel?*

"Let's walk down a little farther, shall we?" Taking her hand, he led her down the slope. A path could be lightly seen before them as they walked. When they reached a point around some bushes, she stopped and would go no further. Sensing her hesitation, he asked, "Where does this path lead to?"

"Oh, it leads to a creek, but it is too far. I haven't been down there for a long time."

"Can we go there some time?"

"No, I don't think so. I don't like to go there anymore."

"Why?" He asked. "It might be a good walk for us."

"No, it wouldn't. Let's turn around and go back."

"Whatever you say, my Love; I just love being with you."

"I love being with you, too." She smiled, and he led her back up the path.

"I think you are the kindest person I have ever met," he said, to change the subject.

"Well, thank you. You are wonderful too," she said.

"I love it when you laugh. I bet you are always the sweetest thing that ever lived."

"I am normal. My brother wouldn't think I am so sweet."

"What do you mean?"

"When we were little, I think I resented him for taking all the attention I used to get from my parents. So, I would do things to get him into trouble."

"That seems normal between siblings to me. What would you do?"

She laughed. *Why did I bring that up?* "Well, I remember playing tricks on him, at times."

"What kinds of tricks?"

She held her breath for a moment. "One time, I said, 'Ben, let's play the pushing game. It will be fun.' He said 'No.' But, I insisted. After several attempts, and much insistence, he relented. I said, 'I will go first.' Then I pushed him, just enough to make him stagger a little. Then it was his turn. He halfheartedly gave me a push and I threw myself on the floor and cried as loudly as I could. 'Mom, he pushed me.' My screams brought everyone running. They found me on the floor, holding my arm as though it were broken. Ben just stood there in unbelief. 'Mom, he pushed me hard, and made me fall.' I cried so much I impressed even myself."

"What happened then," Abel asked.

"He got into trouble, of course."

"You were bad." Abel said.

"I know. I don't know how we grew up and still love each other. He never seems to hold it against me. Ben is a good boy, or should I say, young man, now. I do love

42

him dearly."

"I also have similar stories with my sisters," Abel confessed. "Not so much now, that we are older. I remember asking Miriam to take something from my hand as I held it out to her. She opened her hand to receive it, and I let drop a little mouse. She screamed all the way into the house and wouldn't talk to me for days."

It was fun to hear the stories of their childhood. They felt drawn together in simple ways.

A few days later Abel came to visit and asked to walk with Athaliah in the garden.

"My dear, I am building a home for you. I have been preparing it ever since we met. You will love it. I want it to be a surprise for you," Abel said.

"I trust you made the kitchen large enough. Men seem never to think of that when it comes to building houses," she said.

"You will never have to go into the kitchen."

"Maybe not, but I know what women have to put up with and want the workers to have ample room to work."

"I love you," he said. "You always think of others."

"Do you know that that is what drew me to you, from the first time I saw you?" she said.

"You surprise me," Abel said. "Me?"

"Yes, the very night you spoke to the workers. You were so graceful. I noticed the way you looked upon them with friendship and consideration. You treated them with respect and not as servants. That was what caught my eye."

"You can get more with honey than you can with vinegar. My father taught me that."

"He is a good man, your father."

"Thank you, but let's get back to the subject of the house. You will love it. I have thought of every detail. Nothing is too good for my Love."

They held hands as they walked along a shady lane. Chara followed at a short distance, just out of earshot. The couple accepted the norms and didn't try to take advantage of their situation. They loved each other and wanted to do everything correctly.

"Abel, do you really love me?" Athaliah said.

"I have already told you that I love you."

"But I want to hear it again."

"Yes, I do love you. I never thought it would be like this. I feel honored to have you at my side," he said, looking into her eyes.

He didn't have words to express his true desire. He felt as though words couldn't express his real feelings.

"I will show you just how much I love you soon."

"It seems so far away," she said.

"I know. But now I have something else to tell you." She stopped in her tracks and looked at him.

"What do you mean?"

"My father wants me to take a trip."

"Do you mean we won't be able to see each other? How long will you be away?"

"I will be going with the caravan to the east. As a matter of fact, one of your father's caravans will go as well, in a co-venture."

"But how long will you be away?"

"We will be going to the City of Towers, near the Gobi Desert. There, we will trade with merchants who come in from further east. Then, we will return home."

"I can't think of how I will get along in your absence."

"I will think of you every passing moment."

"I will do the same."

They continued walking in silence. A sense of loss fell over Athaliah. *How can this be? I don't know how I can live without him, not even for a day.*

Abel felt the same way. "We must not think of the length of time, but how much we love each other. That will sustain us."

Sadness filled their hearts. "I will come back to you as soon as I can," he assured her.

Glancing back at Chara, Athaliah said, "Abel, hold me. I can't think of you being away from me. Just hold me." He took her in his arms and held her, wishing time would stand still. Once he had her in his arms, he didn't want to release her. He felt her warmth, and softness. The fragrance of her hair filled his senses. She felt his strength, and tenderness. "Just hold me, my love."

"When I return, I will publicly announce my intentions to marry you. Our new house will be completed, and my fortune will be great. My ability to support you will be recognized by everyone, and we will be able to take the next steps. I will set the date then," he said in one breath.

CHAPTER FIVE

The City of Towers

The caravans were ready for departure. The men in charge went over details with the workers to satisfy themselves that all had been thought of, and prepared. Provisions for the workers, sale items, security measures and an adequate number of tents, were packed on the camels. The camels busied themselves by making guttural noises to each other, knowing that they were being called upon for service, confirming their reputation for being obstinate, and sometimes stubborn.

Joab called the caravan leaders together. "We leave before sunup. Make sure all your men are up and ready to go. We must avoid as much heat as possible."

The joint caravan started out very early, under bright moonlight. This part of the journey was familiar to everyone, and the trails were taken with ease. Soon, the sun made its appearance over the eastern horizon. Mountains, far in the distance could be made out through the morning haze.

The road led downward, toward the Jordan River. Abel joined the caravan leaders as they followed it almost without thought, being accustomed to its twists, and turns. Dust was kicked up by each step the animals took, leaving a cloud behind them that hung in the air. Once at the Jordan River, they would let the animals drink their fill, in preparation for dryer areas ahead. The Arabian Desert lay ahead. The caravans slowly skirted the city of Damascus by a large margin.

Their destination was the City of Towers, situated on the "Silk Road," weeks of travel to the northeast. Several countries had to be traversed. Deserts, mountains, and rivers were not the only obstacles to be faced. They were only a part of what was to be expected along the way. Bands of marauders often waited in hiding to take what they could, feeling that it was much easier to steal than to do honest work.

Abel already missed Athaliah. *How am I going to live these months without her?* He busied himself by watching over his men and encouraging them. *I will have to do whatever I can to keep my mind busy.*

Chara entered Athaliah's room to help her dress and prepare for the day. Athaliah was on her bed sobbing.

"What is the matter, Athaliah," Chara asked, as she hurried over to the bed. Concern filled her heart. *Is she weeping over some memory? Could she be reverting to some hurtful event?*

"He is gone," Athaliah said, through her tears.

"My dear, yes, he is gone, but he will return. You will see," Chara said, to calm her.

"I know, but what if something happens to him. I will never see him again."

"You mustn't borrow from tomorrow. That only makes your heart hurt. You must try and think only of what you know to be true. Think happy thoughts. He is riding on his handsome horse, prancing ahead of the caravan, making sure all is well. Nothing will happen to him. Of that, I am sure."

"I wish I could be so sure. I don't know what has come over me. I have never felt so lost. I don't know what I will do without him."

"You do love him. I can see it all over you. It won't help to worry about what you don't know. He will return safely. You will see. This is a new thing for you. It is a good sign. If you really didn't love him, it would not affect you so much. What you feel comes from real love."

"Is this real love? I never thought it would hurt so much," she mumbled.

"Come, let's get you dressed. Breakfast is waiting. Then, we can take a walk to get your mind off that handsome, talented, and lovable young man.

Abel was tired. Months of travel had taken its toll on the whole troupe. When he saw the towers of the famous city come into view, his spirit was revived. In the distance, the towers stood, unmistakably. He had never seen such an impressive sight but had been told of their majesty. The city was surrounded by a massive wall. At its corners were towers that commanded a view of the whole region–eleven in all. No one could come or go without being seen by the soldiers that stood watch, day, and night. Within the walls was a gushing spring-well that occasioned the construction of the city, given its strategic position along the Silk Road. Over time, it became a landmark known to all who traveled this way.

The distance to the walled city appeared to remain the same, even after hours of travel toward it. Having seen the walls, the travelers found it difficult to understand why the city didn't come any closer. Distance was not easy to calculate. The heat made it worse. In the vastness of the region, people looked minute. The city seemed close, but, as Abel realized, it was not. It appeared to be just over the next ridge, only to have another valley or a gulch to traverse. Each new obstacle broke his resolve a little. He became thirsty and tired.

"Don't think of the distance. It is deceptive, Master Abel. Put your mind on other things. How are your horse's pads holding up?" One of his camel drivers asked. This caused him to look down at his horse's feet, one by one. The pads were still holding. Camels had hooves that made it easy to cross desert sands, horses not so much. Horse's hooves buried themselves deeper into the sand causing the animals to work harder and exert more energy. The road they followed was packed hard from much use over many years, but there were places where sand dunes dominated the region, making advancement slow, and laborious. When Abel came to the first of many dunes, one of his servants said, "Come, Master let me show you a secret."

He pulled four sheepskins out of his travel pouch and came back to Abel. "Here, I will do this." Looking around for some clumps of dry camel dung, he flattened each skin out on the ground in turn and piled a generous amount of dung on each one. Then he brought the horse and made him stand on each pile in turn, first one hoof, and then the next. He brought the corners of the skins up and tied them with leather strands around each leg. When all legs were tied in this way, the horse looked like he had camel's feet, with a much greater hoof print. "With people, these are called gloves, and with horses, they are called desert pads. Now the sand will not be such a difficulty for him, see? He won't sink into the sand as much."

"Well, one learns something new every day, it seems. Thank you," Abel said.

Abel was glad his horse was fitted in this way. His fixation on the distance to the city was broken, and he put his thoughts to more important things—Athaliah. Late that night, the travelers arrived at the gates.

"Who goes there?" someone shouted from atop the wall.

"We are merchants from Samaria, here to trade."

"Very well, I will send soldiers out to meet with you, and see your documents," the man shouted back.

The caravans stood waiting, as the appointed official opened a small door that was built into the massive city gate.

"You must wait outside the gate for tonight. I will announce your arrival to the appropriate people, and you can enter in the morning. Just take your people over and set up camp at the foot of that hill," the official ordered.

The travelers were tired after a long day on the dusty road. Servants received orders to set up tents and prepare the evening meal for everyone. Abel's men took a spot that was high enough to afford a good view of their surroundings. Joab's group sat up camp a little distance away. Other caravans were also waiting for entrance but were camped at an acceptable distance.

Abel fell onto his bed role and was asleep in seconds. His men would take care of anything left to be done. Security guards were set up around the camp, and all was well.

Joab made sure all his men were fed. The night's security detail was in place. Other groups were doing the same, and before long, the night fell quiet. Only the occasional sound of disgruntled camels could be heard, as the men settled in. Assigned watchmen assumed their positions for the first watch.

Stars filled the skies, illuminating everything, making in unnecessary to keep big fires ablaze. It was surprisingly easier to see without firelight. Coals were placed into receptacles made for the purpose and taken into the tents for heat against the high desert cold, night air. The outside fires were then banked, to keep the coals alive for morning.

Morning came all too soon. The city guards opened the gates, and the caravan leaders entered, hoping to get the best accommodations for their crews. People were everywhere, walking or running to their places of trade. The city was alive and bustling. Caravan leaders from the north, east, south, and west sat their wares out for display.

Joab and Abel had the disadvantage of having arrived late the night before, so the morning was spent getting their things out for display.

Abel's steward, an expert and experienced merchant, readied their items for the day's barters and trades. Some things had to be bought with gold or silver. Hard currency was tightly guarded and brought out only when paying for purchased items.

The stables were located just inside the city walls. Most were occupied. Servants made sure the animals had provisions. Water was in abundance, delivered to the troughs by specially made canals that carried fresh water from the artesian well that produced ample supply for the whole city. This was truly an oasis in the desert.

Just next to the stables were the bazaars, which the merchants used to display their goods. Business was brisk. Servants busily carried out items for display when available space became freed up as trades happened. In this way, an impression of abundance was maintained for those seeking to do business.

Next to the bazaars were the rooms the merchants occupied. There were single rooms for the caravan leaders. Normally, each room was guarded by security personnel. Other large communal rooms housed the servants. Bathhouses were located throughout the area for easy access, for all the classes represented.

Eating establishments were strategically placed throughout the city in abundance. Anything a merchant might want was easily acquired. Diversions of all kinds were offered to the visitors and were usually kept very busy. There were places for the rich, and places for the not-so-rich.

Abel, satisfied that his men were comfortable in their specific roles, sought out officials to fulfill his part in the negotiations. Goodwill and favor were always built with important men to insure future business opportunities. Many times, one's success depended upon, not what one knew, but who one knew. Abel had his father's gift of expression and made sure to let those he met know that he had special abilities without seeming braggadocios.

Once he knew something, right down to the smallest detail, he never forgot it; names, places events, all were at his mind's recall. In his mind, he could see ledger sheets, and recall details that others would find difficult to remember without looking at the records. As a child, one of his favorite pastimes was to have his family ask him questions on any subject, to see if he could answer them. Try as they might, he always knew the answers. *It is a gift*, his father said.

His ability to remember came in handy, right away. The trade languages were not totally unknown to him, and as the days came and went, he found it increasingly easier to make himself understood, as well as to understand those around him. His need of interpreters became progressively less. He kept his comments to a minimum at first, but branched out, as he learned. Every time he learned a new term, he found a way to use it several times before the day was over. Repeating a word in his mind was a habit he enjoyed. The people around him were amazed at his prowess. Merchants from the Far East were a noticeable challenge at first, but he advanced rapidly. He learned to take special care when negotiating with them. They seemed to have an uncanny way of extracting extra funds from those with whom they made deals.

"This is fun," Abel commented to his steward one evening. "I am having the time of my life. I do believe we are going to be able to cut our stay here by several weeks, because of the deals we have done since we arrived."

"I agree," his steward said. "Your ability surprises even me. I have watched you grow, and learn, but this is impressive. Of course, it is because you have learned from the best."

"You are the best at what you do," Abel assured him. "I do thank you for allowing me to learn at your side. My father is proud of your work and asked me to convey his gratitude."

"I enjoy my work and take delight in his favor." He said, with a respectful bow.

As they spoke Abel's childhood friend, Omar, came around the corner and stood at the door.

"Come in Omar," Abel said.

"Abel—"

"Please, do not address me so when others are present. You may say, 'Master Abel.'"

"I am sorry. Please forgive me, Master Abel. But I have some news I think you should know."

Abel could see that he was nervous. "Come over and sit. What is this about?"

Omar sat and seemed unable to form words.

"Well, what should I know? It is alright to speak in the presence of my steward."

"Master, I have overheard something. Do you remember how you told me to stay in the background, and not be overly friendly with the others?"

"Yes, I do."

When they had last spoken, Abel had given him instructions to become a shadow, and not stand out among the other servants. He was to work in security and keep an eye on the others, reporting back to Abel only. So far no one knew he was a personal friend of Abel's. That is, with the wise exception of the steward.

Only the two men knew who Omar was, and why he was present. He was to make himself useful in security and keep a low profile. So far all was well.

"Master, you know I have obeyed your wishes all this while. I enjoy my work. Last night I chanced upon several men in an eating establishment. They were telling stories, and bragging. I saw that they had been drinking, and as the night passed, their demeanor changed, and the stories got more unbelievable."

"Who were these men; were they men of our caravan?" Abel asked.

"Well, a couple of them were your men, but the others were from other caravans. I had not seen them before. Well, only one man had I seen. They all had been drinking, as I said, and they seemed unable to control their mouths."

"What were they saying?"

"Most were telling stories of escapades while on past journeys. It seems there were women involved."

"That is to be expected," Abel's steward said.

"Yes, well, as the stories got bigger, and more unbelievable, the man I had seen before, started talking about another man who used to be the head of security of his caravan."

"Did he say the man's name?"

"No. Only that that man had become the head of security when he thought the job should have been his. He seemed disturbed. Of course, being drunk, made him talk much too openly."

"This type of jealousy happens all the time. There is nothing surprising about that," Abel said.

"You are right, but I began to listen closer to his words. He, being in his state of intoxication, said he carried out a plan, and got rid of the man. Then, he said, 'I am now the head of security for my master.'"

"Did he say who his master was?"

"No, as I said, I was sitting in a corner listening. He didn't even know I was there, but I knew which caravan he was with, because I had seen him in the caravan as we traveled," Omar said. "He was the head of security for Master Haddad."

Abel quickly sat up. "Thank you, Omar. Don't say a word to anyone. As you know, Master Haddad is to become my father-in-law. I will take care of this. Keep silent and go about your work. Let me know if you hear anything having to do with this, but don't talk to anyone about it. This is an order."

"Yes, Master. I will say nothing."

"Thank you. You can go your way." Abel said as he led Omar to the door.

As Omar left, Abel returned to his chair. "What do you make of this," He asked his steward. "I think we should keep this quiet. It may be nothing, then, it could be serious."

"You are wise to say nothing for now. Let's keep our eyes on this man."

CHAPTER SIX

Guilt

Days turned into weeks. Nothing was more difficult than not knowing anything. Athaliah tried to fill her mind with other concerns, but it seemed fruitless.

"Chara, I don't know what I would do without you. You are such a good friend."

"I will always be at your side."

"Oh, I haven't thought of that. What will I do when I get married? I won't have you to help me. This is so sad."

"Well, you are right. What will you do? What will I do? Life seems to be more complicated than we thought. I didn't know things would be so difficult when we became grown-ups," Chara said. "What will we do?"

"I must speak with my father. He will know what to do. I will ask him to let you live with me in my house. I don't think I could live without you as part of my life. You have become such a good friend, more than anything else."

Her words caused her to realize that Chara was a matter far more complicated than she could understand. The "anything else" was not spoken, but she knew it could not be ignored. What would they do? Chara was a servant in her father's house. The truth was that she thought of her as a sister – a close sister.

Both girls stood quietly for a long moment, neither one wanting to mention the obvious.

"Yes, you will have to speak with your father. It is far beyond me to ever bring it up," Chara said. She, too, had concerns that haunted her thoughts. She had hidden them under many other things in her heart, for a long time. Life was not as simple as she or Athaliah thought. *Couldn't we just continue, without changing anything?*

Master Haddad busied himself with his daily responsibilities. Abel was away on a business trip for his father. The two caravans would do well together, he was sure. He had much to do while Abel was absent. Besides all his regular work, there was the wedding celebration to plan, and guests to invite. *This will be a wedding to remember*, he thought. He loved his daughter. Where had all the years gone? They passed so quickly. Only yesterday she was sitting on his knee, playing contentedly.

He saw how Athaliah went about her days in a daze. He had given orders that Chara help her as much as she could. Abel's absence affected Athaliah – not only her, but the whole family. Their hopes for their daughter were placed in the hands of this young man. *Does he know how much is expected of him? Youth! Young people don't stop to think of what their parents go through, trying to make a life for their children.* His expectations were great. Athaliah was his first child, and he intended to do right by her. She deserved that, and more. He was content in his sense that Abel was a good young man, who would love his daughter, and care for her as he always had.

"Mara, we don't know how much time we have. Abel will be away for several months, but see how the time goes past? Already, it has been almost three months. We must be ready for the wedding. I have spoken with Jacob and he seems to think that the caravan will be back before cold weather arrives. Have you spoken with the ladies of the house to make sure they know what they must do?"

"Yes, my dear. I have. They are preparing everything that can possibly be taken care of now. Of course, there are some things that can only be done later, but I believe we are ready. This is so much fun, don't you think? Just think. Our daughter is getting married."

"Women think so differently than men. I must think of expenses, and obligations and you are thinking of all the fun you will have. Then, haven't you thought about the fact that she will no longer live with us?"

"We won't lose her. I think it is right what they say, 'You won't lose a daughter. You will gain another mouth to feed.'"

"That is just what I need to hear of; more expenses."

"Yes, but I will have my daughter close, even when she lives away."

Benjamin, ever-growing, was now a handsome young man. He enjoyed his life and dedicated himself to learning. His father's business was prosperous, and it would be his in the not-too-distant future. Of course, there remained steps of preparation to be taken, before he could inherit total control, but in the meantime, he would learn. His father was proud of him, and let it be known among all his friends.

Benjamin was the delight of his parents, and the heir apparent. This gave him specific responsibilities, which he gladly accepted. He had an easy-going personality that everyone enjoyed. His father's steward often took him under his wing to teach him the fine art of doing business. Truth was foremost. Honesty, character, reliability, and trustworthiness were expected of a good businessman. This Benjamin was taught continually.

"To keep business clients, it is necessary to follow these tried-and-true principles," the steward often said. "If you treat others as you want to be treated, you will enjoy a long and prosperous livelihood." Benjamin looked for ways to implement what he learned, as often as he could.

Though he enjoyed his public life, and the attention that was his as heir apparent, darkness overshadowed his every waking moment. There were things he hid inside that he never wanted others to know. Since the tragedy of his sister's beating, he could not forgive himself. No matter what his father said, he knew he was responsible for what had happened to her. He should have been there. Had it been so, he knew in his heart that she would never have been hurt. He dreamed of it, reliving the trauma time and time again.

His mind was constantly clouded with images of Athaliah, as he brought her into the house, beaten, bloody and unconscious. His perception of life was tainted by the agony of his failure to do anything to help her. *I should have never left her alone when I returned to the house*, he thought over and over again. Night after night, he lay upon his bed crying until no tears would come, only to fall into a fitful sleep throughout the night. *Is my whole life going to be like this?*

Slowly, he became molded into a person he didn't want to be. *I am not worthy to live*, was his constant thought.

Since he was little, there was a desire to be right in whatever he did. He tried to correct himself before it became necessary for others to correct him. He did not feel that he was right, and everyone else was wrong, rather, he disliked having to be corrected by others, so he corrected himself, according to what he knew to be right.

When he was but a baby of almost one year of age, he was stricken by a cough that persisted for months. He fought to breathe between coughs and struggled to stop the uncontrollable spasms. His whooping caused his mother, and all those who attended him, to worry for his life. When they touched him, the excitement triggered the unwanted response, which caused them to worry that he might suffocate in his own body fluids. Mara gave orders that no one should touch him or excite him in any way, lest he begin coughing. At times, she cried when seeing him try to unsuccessfully expel the congestion, only to fall asleep from the effort.

Over time, he miraculously survived the trauma, but became so used to being by himself while others went about their days, that he often wondered what he had done that caused them to leave him by himself. Loneliness became his constant companion. It became the norm in his short life. He often found himself alone in his room, while others walked about outside his door. He could hear their footsteps, and see their shadows from beyond the door, while he was left to fend for himself. *What have I done to make them not want me around?* This he asked himself when it became apparent that no one seemed to care that he was alone. He didn't think that maybe it was because it was simply his bedtime, and the elders were enjoying their evening away from the children.

As he grew, he looked for affirmation from anyone that would give him attention. People often commented how likable he was, and how much he helped others by freely offering to be of help. They didn't know that he simply wanted their attention and didn't know how to ask for it. To him, loneliness was the "norm." When Athaliah treated him badly, he marked it up to *it doesn't matter, it is what I deserve.*

He worked at correcting himself when anything happened that caused others to be upset or angry with him. *Don't wait for others to correct you. Do it yourself. Don't forget and do the same thing again.* Over time, he was known as an attentive young man who had a kind heart, always helpful and aware of others' needs. He would be there with the solution before they even asked for help. But inside, he secretly wondered why others were not as ready to help when he needed them.

When Athaliah was so brutally beaten, he found it easy to assume responsibility for what had happened. In his heart he knew he caused it and could not forgive himself for his stupidity in not being present to help her when she needed him. This knowledge ate at his insides, constantly. *How can I make it up to her? There must be a way.*

Athaliah was now to be wed. It was just a matter of time. Abel would be home soon, and she would leave with him to begin her life as a married woman. With Benjamin's knowledge of the family's secret, there was little comfort for him in what should be a wonderful event for the two families. Had he known the whole truth, it might have broken him. His parents kept part of the truth well hidden, and never dared bring it up, even in their private conversations. He saw the truth in a light that others missed. *I am guilty. It is my fault.*

Mara faced each day with a smile. Not that she felt that way. Her self-imposed responsibility was to make others see the bright side of the preparations. *My daughter is to be married. I can't imagine a better young man for her than Abel.* This brought joy to her heart, and she decided that her focus was to be on this fact alone. She loved her daughter, as all mothers do, and wanted the very best in life for her. The knowledge of the "event" was her burden to carry. She must make sure Athaliah never discover what really happened. *I should have never let her go out that day, and I will protect her from knowing all that took place,* she told herself daily.

Life was sweet, as far as the servants knew. Mara took it upon herself to assure that the house be a happy home. The servants that did know of the "event" were instructed to remain quiet, and never discuss it.

Mara's thoughts often went to the past, when Athaliah was an innocent child, who was loved and cared for by everyone. The servants found it enjoyable to play with her, and she, in turn, loved their attention. There were the times she, not wishing to eat her food, tried to hide it under her chair. The dog looked for every crumb that she accidently let fall at her feet. Her actions were unnoticed for a while, but then she became careless, making it apparent what was happening. It became a game for a while, until Mom pressed her to eat her food.

Athaliah didn't always get along with Benjamin. She made life difficult for him. Her resentment of his taking her place in receiving most of the attention, previously and generously lavished upon her by the family, gave her practice in making him pay dearly.

But she was a good girl. She did love her brother, deep down. No one could deny that. She was loved by all.

Her ability with math and numbers was recognized early on, when she made a game of counting the birds that landed on the patio, "There were three birds, but one flew away. Now, there are only two," she would say in delight. "Oops, now two came back, and there are four." As she grew, her ability to think in greater sums grew, astounding all who saw her.

Mara often said she didn't know what she would do if Athaliah were not in her life. She never once thought the family would face such a tragedy as the one they had lived through.

"This should never happen to anyone," she often said to Obed. "It just isn't right. We must protect her, no matter what. No one must know what happened. She must live a normal life. This is my vow. We must keep her mind off it and try to make her forget it all."

She realized that her mind was occupied to the point of distraction, and she worked to drag her unwilling thoughts away from the source of her pain, so no one would see her inner battle. It became a full-time job. The people around her saw her battle just the same, and feigned ignorance. Her main concern was Athaliah. *She must never see me downcast. Keep a smile on your face, Mara,* she silently lectured.

Each day, Mara made sure Athaliah was calm and comfortable. Preparations had to be made for the wedding, and the two worked together to that end. It was exciting to plan such a joyous event — a once-in-a-lifetime event. Mara kept their time light and happy, making sure there was no time to reflect on the negative.

Master Haddad put himself into his work. Each day found him busily making sure his men had all they needed to fulfill their obligations. So dedicated was he, that they saw him as a micromanager. This was not normal, and everyone saw it.

In subtle ways, his life had changed. No longer was he the jovial man everyone knew him to be. He became short-tempered when occasions didn't warrant it. He worked to keep a grip on his reactions, but something ate at him deep inside, that caused a shadow over his deepest thoughts.

He was a businessman above all and went about his daily affairs with professional acumen. Though hurt inside, he made a supreme effort to assure that no one else was hurt because of him. What he didn't see was that others sensed a change but did not have a discernible answer of why. It was just an observation that couldn't be quantified—a feeling. Those who knew him pushed it aside and accepted him as they always had, but a sense, much like a faint odor that illusively wafts through the air from some unknown quarter, permeated his personal space.

Keeping secrets was difficult for him, but he was thinking of Athaliah's interests in doing so. He wanted her to live life in a manner that afforded her the freedom to express her strengths and abilities. With Abel he was sure this would be the case.

Chara kept close watch over Athaliah. Never was it mentioned that she was an indentured servant. They had become as sisters. They were always together. Chara faithfully carried out her duties with love and care. She did not see her role as that of a servant. The fact that Athaliah was to be married simply meant that she would go with her as an attendant. She tried not to think of the secret she held inside. She was trustworthy and didn't want to bring harm to Athaliah or her family. Most importantly, she loved the family, and could not see herself apart from them.

It hurt her to know that she had been the one to cause the problem by putting Athaliah in contact with Daniel. She didn't know what would happen. The fact that it did, made her know that it was her responsibility, and thus, her fault. No matter what her days were like, they were tainted by the certain knowledge that she had caused much damage. Trying to shake the feeling, and expunge her self-imposed guilt, she put herself into her work. She would, in some manner, make up for the problem she had caused.

She made sure Athaliah got out to the patio with its water fountain and beautiful flower garden. They spent time in the shade, talking of the things that interested them both. Of course, Athaliah spoke often of Abel, trying to calm her spirit, and make time pass quickly. It didn't help. Chara tried to make conversation, always avoiding anything that might bring them to speaking or even thinking about the "event." She became an expert in controlling the themes.

They spoke of married life, neither one having any real knowledge on the subject. Second-hand knowledge had to suffice. When intimacy came into the conversations it left them wondering about almost everything. They only had hearsay to rely upon, and that didn't help much. At their age, there was an abundance of speculation and conjured mental images to talk about, and they filled hours trying to do justice to the subject fancying themselves to be experts.

No matter what they did, or how happy their times together were, Chara always carried the hidden burden that constantly threatened to take her peace. She felt she would someday not be able to withstand its fury.

"Chara, how long do you think Abel will be away?" Athaliah said, one morning while preparing for the day. "I miss him so much."

"It has been a long time, to be sure. But, if you don't let your mind dwell on it, he will come riding up to the front door before you know it," Chara said.

"I know. But it is so hard to keep my mind off him."

"You are a strong person. You can do it. Hold on to your love for him but try and think of things you can do to prepare yourself for your future together. I am sure there are a lot of things you want to get done before he returns."

"You are right."

"Of course, while you are busy doing those things, there is no reason why you can't dream of him," Chara said. "I know you miss him."

"Oh, shush. Now you are just making things worse."

CHAPTER SEVEN

The Return

It had been a busy day of negotiations among the merchants. Abel decided he would walk through the city to get away from the bustle. He made his way to the city gate and saw a stairway that led to the top of the massive city wall. Its towers stood above the height of the wall by several meters, affording an even greater vantage point for the guards that stood watch day and night. The top of the wall was itself, an ample walkway. He looked down to see more caravans arriving, while others made their way out with camels laden with newly acquired merchandise. The lines seemed endless. *How can so many people and animals be in one place?*

Looking over the city, he could make out the extensive area it covered. He wondered if he could walk around the whole city before dark. At one point, he looked down to observe the beautiful life-giving water source. The artesian well appeared to boil with fresh, cool water, gushing from far below the surface. He concluded that it must be from an underground river. Life could not exist here without its constant and abundant flow. *This is marvelous, indeed.*

A few people walked in either direction, presumably doing the same as he. Each time he passed someone, he bowed slightly in acknowledgment, as was the custom. Not to do so would be considered impolite. A woman approached, looking him in the eye as she passed. He could see nothing but her eyes, but as they passed, their eyes briefly locked. After a few steps, he turned around and saw her looking back at him. She gave him a slight beckoning movement of the head, then turned away. As she walked, he knew what she meant. He allowed some distance between them and followed her. She walked with purpose. As she approached a staircase, she turned slightly to see if he was following and disappeared into the darkness of the staircase below.

"Master Abel, we have successfully bartered or sold everything we have," his steward said, one evening. "We must get our men together and give instructions for the journey home. It is time."

"Very well, tell them we will leave on the morrow. I will speak with Joab, Master Haddad's steward, to see if he and his group are ready, as well."

"Yes, Master. Do you want to let the men celebrate tonight?"

"Tell them they can choose the eating establishment of their choice, and we will all meet there after our work is done. They deserve a night of celebration and food before the long trek home."

Later, Abel met with his men. The establishment they chose was not far from their rooms. The streets were narrow and rugged, paved with stones that threatened the balance of the best of men. Years of wear had smoothed them a little, but a challenge awaited everyone who trod across them.

The men were exuberant and noisy as they gathered. Spirits were high, and laughter could be heard by everyone for a much greater distance than what Abel found comfortable. He said nothing. The evening passed, stories shared, and knee-slapping jokes passed from table to table.

"Master Joab, I am happy your group could join us tonight. Thank you for coming," Abel said, as he took a seat. "Come sit here with me and we will celebrate our success together."

"Thank you, Master Abel, for the invitation. Your father will be proud of your accomplishments, I am sure."

"That is my desire. I have done my best. I trust your time was successful as well."

A smile swept over his face. "Most assuredly—Master Haddad will be overjoyed."

The men from both groups ate and passed stories back and forth, each story a little bigger than the previous. "We will have to put a stop to the storytelling before they get so unbelievable that no one will have the strength to laugh anymore," Master Joab said, at length.

"True enough," Abel said, downing the last of his drink. "Master Joab, being the most experienced among us, would you like to give the men a few words before we disband and return to our quarters?"

Joab stood to his feet and called the men to order. "Men, this has been a lucrative venture. Now, it is time to return home. As you know, what lies ahead will be more difficult than when we came."

Looking around, giving each man a confident look, he continued. "On our return journey, we will have items of value that many would like to get their hands on. Things we have acquired from a great distance to the east. The items we brought are common to us, but much sought after by peoples in distant lands. Now we will go with things that our people covet, so, we must be alert. I have my security men, and you of the other groups know who forms the security for your group. Let's all be on alert. You are all good at what you do. Our masters need us to guard their investments with our lives. Let's make them proud—and prosperous. We do the work, but without their investments, we would have nothing. Let's give them our best. I know you will do it."

The men cheered loudly, standing to their feet.

"Don't forget to take food and drink to the men who are guarding our things. Let them know they are appreciated," Joab added, as the groups disbanded. "Now, get some sleep. The morning comes early."

"Everyone up. It is time to go. Get up you lazy camels. You have had all the fun you will get for a long while." A servant went from dorm to dorm sounding the alert. Men, eyes still shut, scrambled to their feet and dressed. There would be no time to slack. Everyone had a responsibility and stepped to it with vigor. The animals were loaded expertly, and efficiently, in record time. No one stood around looking at the others. All the men worked as though choreographed, each moving around the other, picking up here and placing there, each one making sure nothing was left to chance.

Each bundle was securely loaded and tied in place, the animals groaned and complained as the loads were adjusted. Dust arose from the ground as busy feet scurried around. Some of the workers wore tightly woven cloths over their faces to keep their nostrils clear. The only light to be had was from a few well-placed lanterns. Working in the dim light made every effort more difficult, but no one complained.

Goat skins full of life-sustaining water were strapped into place on the animals, anticipating the long distances between watering holes. The camels sniffed at the skins longingly, wanting more, even though their humps were plump and tall already.

"Abel, I will take my men out of the city first, and you and your men can follow. The guards at the gate know me and will let us out quickly," Joab said when all was ready.

"As you wish."

"Now, remember, there is a great distance between here and the next oasis. Let's pray that nothing goes wrong between here and there," Joab reminded him.

Before the sun had fully become seen over the horizon the caravans gathered at the gates, awaiting the word to proceed. Finally, the call went out, and the gates swung open. The animals strung out along the road, reluctantly making their way home.

"Let's keep the animals grouped as best we can, so no one is left behind," a man called out. "Keep an eye out, men."

Conversations were lively, but after a few miles dwindled, as the men concentrated on their routines. The sun rose in the sky, casting its rays liberally on the heat-absorbing sand, causing the workers to slow their movements. They conserved energy, moving only as much as was needed. In this way, they allowed their clothing to protect them from the excessive heat. The camels lumbered along, seemingly unaffected by the heat, knowing instinctively how to maneuver under such conditions. The horses were the most affected by it, so the riders took care not to exert them needlessly.

The road stretched high and flat, giving the travelers a view of the surrounding terrain for great distances. They seemed so small in the vast, dry sea of nothingness, that seemingly went on into infinity, in all directions. Only the most experienced among the men coolly proceeded, unaffected by the expanse ahead of them. There was nothing in the terrain around them with which to measure the true immensity of what they saw. Their progress could not be measured, only endured.

Joab moved his ride over to where Abel was riding. "Have you ever seen such a sight?" he asked.

"To be honest with you, no, I haven't."

"One walks, and only assumes one is making progress. It is depressing."

"At least we can see if anyone other than our group comes in on us," Abel commented.

"That is one advantage we have at the moment. We will have several days of this before we arrive at an area that has distinctive features. Then, we will have to be vigilant."

"How so?"

"When there is something that obscures the view, even in the most minimal way, we must expect trouble. It is hard to believe that there are people who live out here, waiting to drop in on unsuspecting travelers to steal and kill."

"What a way to make a living. They must not have much of a life."

"Oh, you would be surprised. There are men who hire hordes of bandits to take what is not theirs. That is why we can't afford to travel without men who know what to do in the event of trouble. Me, I have been assailed several times over the years, and have only lost a meager amount, everything considered," Joab said.

"I hope we don't have trouble on this trip," Abel said, under his breath.

"Look, the sun is near the horizon already. You see, time passes quickly when one's mind is distracted," Joab said. "We will have the men stop in a little while, to set up camp for the night. It may be hot during the day, but nighttime is completely different. You could freeze if you weren't prepared for the cold. I will ask the men to scout around for camel dung. This road is heavily traveled, and the animals leave not only their tracks but their dung. When dry, it burns clean and creates a lot of heat in the wee watches of the night. As you have seen, a lot of the men sit around the fires and tell stories until they fall asleep from boredom, the results of bigger-than-life stories that could never happen in real life. These men have made it an art form."

A rider came toward them fast from the front of the caravan. "Master Joab, I have seen tents on the horizon. It might be better to camp here, rather than approach them tonight. I don't know who it is. I have ordered my men to ride ahead carefully to learn what they can," the rider said.

"Thank you. I believe you are right. Give the word to camp for the night. You may go. Wait a moment." Joab looked at Abel. "Abel, this is Reuel, he oversees security for our group. Look after your men, and I will do the same. If anything comes up, I will find you later." With that the two rode off toward the others.

Night fell over the land and the stars shone so brightly that the men could see clearly, if they got away from the fires. Bed roles were laid out on the ground and sleep came fast for all but the guards of the first watch.

Morning came all too soon. In a matter of moments, the men were up, and ready to go. Food was passed around to all the men, and the camels were fed from the stores carried for them. Small amounts of water were given to each animal, especially the horses. The camels could go without for days.

Joab mounted his camel, looked to make sure the caravan was ready and gave the order to advance. The men were accustomed to carrying out their responsibilities and, given the emotion of knowing they were on the way back home, it was even easier. One by one, the animals were led onto the road, and the procession was on its way again.

After a couple of hours, they saw a caravan approaching from the west. "It must be the one we saw yesterday, so far away," Abel said, as he closed his fist and brought it to his eye. Looking through his closed fist gave him a telescope advantage, cutting excess light and bringing clarity to the images in the distance. The morning heat was not yet enough to distort what he saw.

Security men rode ahead to learn more about the men coming east. After a while, one of them returned and recommended the caravan take a tack around the oncoming group of merchants, just to be sure.

In time, the two groups came relatively close, and waved at each other as they respectively passed each other. No words were spoken between them. Caution seemed to be preferred by both groups.

It seemed as though the flat lands would never end. Abel lost count of the days. Daylight hours were hot, and the nights cold. The seemingly endless routine caused him to become bored. Not even thinking of Athaliah helped. The heat rose as they continued west.

"When we get to more rugged country, we will have to be more alert," Joab said to his men.

One day turned into two, the distance covered, stretched into a monotonously unchanging horizon of hot sand. When the men felt they could not endure any more, a scout returned from up front and shouted, "Hills. The terrain drops in a little while and gives way to washes. Stay alert men," he shouted as he approached the caravan. "Pass the word."

Almost imperceptibly, hills arose on either side of them. The road became narrow, following the bottom of gulches that wound back and forth in an unending series of curves. The men knew that these places were dangerous because there was no escape, should anyone try to attack them from above. Scouts were running ahead to keep an eye out. "So far, so good," Abel said to the nearest man.

A stretch of dunes appeared ahead. The caravan would have to wind its way in and through them. To get lost in these dunes was a distinct possibility, so experienced guides went ahead, to point the way.

"Dust storms are common here and the wind can cover the trail in the blink of an eye," Joab pointed out to Abel.

In the evening, the caravans approached an oasis. It consisted of only several date palms, and a small pool of water at their base. All else was sand and dunes. There was just enough flat land to accommodate the travelers. Soon, campfires could be seen, as the men sat around them, eating. The mood was somber. The tired travelers found it difficult to expend energy beyond simply doing their duty. It was time to rest, and sleep fell over the camp.

Up from the horizon appeared the moon, large and full. It promised light, muted as it was, and the weary travelers basked in its gentle reflection of the sun.

In the second watch, a watchman thought he heard a sound. Sitting up, he turned his good ear toward it. Again, he heard it. As he was taught, he made a clicking sound, like a cricket, and waited. From a short distance he heard a response in kind, not the same, but a variation. This let him know that whoever answered was known to him. After a short while he, again, heard a soft commotion. He heard movement from where the animals were kept.

This time, he gave the clicking sound but got no click in return. He quickly let out a loud, high-pitched sound of an alarm that resounded over the camp. In moments men were on their feet, weapons in hand. Thieves had come into camp and had the temporary advantage, but as the men from the caravans took their positions, that advantage disappeared. Anyone that was out of place became a target. Within moments, a battle was afoot. Swords were drawn and arrows flew. Men could be heard crying out in pain as the shafts met their targets. Orders were shouted as calm turned into the chaos of battle. Only experienced men could know what to do in these moments.

Abel came to his senses and stood behind one of his men. Both held swords. Around them they heard sounds of battle. Men ran from place to place, either chasing or being chased. Abel sensed movement behind him and turned in time to see a man with a sword lifted high, coming at him. Instinctively, he quickly stepped to one side and brought his sword up, thrusting it forward. He met his mark and watched as the assailant dropped at his feet.

There was no time to think. Another man was behind the first one and came running forward, screaming, sword held high. Abel's attention was on the man at his feet. His companion saw the danger. With one swift movement, he reached, grabbed Abel, and pulled him to one side. As he pulled Abel aside with one hand, he plunged his sword forward, sinking it into the chest of the attacker, dropping him with a thud at the side of his companion. The attacker was given no chance to bring his sword down on Abel. The battle was over almost as soon as it began.

Shouts were heard all over camp—shouts of victory. Men ran from place to place, securing the area. Dead bodies were dragged to a pile and counted. Twenty-two bodies lay in the sand. Three wounded men were brought front and center to be interrogated by the security team.

Only one man of Joab's company was hurt. He was on guard duty when he heard the alarm. Instinctively turning, he realized that an enemy was upon him. He dodged the blade of the sword but was scratched. Quickly, he took advantage of the forward movement of his assailant, and pulled him forward, using his momentum against him. The enemy sprawled in the dirt, having lost his balance. He was quickly dispatched.

Abel sought out Joab. "Are you alright?"

"Yes, I am well."

"What shall we do now," Abel asked, recognizing Joab's experience.

"You take your men and clean up, starting at the east end of camp. Have them drag the dead to a place off the trail. Bury them there. I will do the same. Then, we can recount the events around the campfire."

Adrenaline ran high. No one could sleep. Abel paid no attention to his emotional state. Gathering his men, he shouted orders, which were carried out immediately.

Later, the campfires were built up again, and the men sat around recounting their actions of valor.

Abel, seated by a fire, listened as the battle stories were shared. An understanding of the whole attack began to emerge. There was a group of, at least, forty men that had attacked. Half of them paid with their life.

Abel suddenly felt tired. He held his head in his hands. The realization that he had killed for the first time in his life, hit him. He felt as though he had been slammed into a wall. He was not ready for the physical reaction that swarmed over his being. The attackers were dead. *How did I do that?* He thought only of the two that he had been involved with. Sweat covered his brow. He felt the strong urge to vomit. Standing to his feet, he ran away from the fire and, relieved himself of the impulse.

"This night will be spoken of for years to come," Abel commented, later.

The men shared, with bravado, the events of that night, as they continued their journey. Heightened vigilance became the norm, as they progressed. Two more attempts were made against them, but the enemy found themselves in disarray compared to the excellent abilities of the joint caravan from Samaria.

Weeks later, the last oasis came into view. "The next stop is home," Abel said, excited. He found it difficult to stay with the caravan. In his heart, he wanted to surprise Athaliah by arriving at her door unannounced, but duty won out over his youthful impetuousness. He would have to wait another day.

That night, the men arranged themselves around the source of water and warmed themselves by welcome fires to eat and rest up for the last day's journey. The security detail was in place, and all was well. Excitement was palpable. Everyone was ready for the journey to be over. This was an expected emotion, and the more mature among them took it in stride.

The next morning, the men awoke to sounds of consternation. Several camels were obviously sick and were not eager to stand to their feet. They were the ones closest to the watering hole. No amount of urging could get them up.

Joab came to Abel and shared the news. "I don't understand it. Most of my camels are sick. Do you think someone put something in the water?"

"That is a possibility, but who would be fool enough to do such a thing? All of the animals drank from the same source."

"The guards were at their posts all night. I don't understand how this could happen. It seems to be only my animals that are affected," Joab said.

"What can I do to help, Master Joab?"

"I don't know. Maybe you and your men can go ahead and let everyone know that we will be a little late, assuming we can get the animals up and going today."

"I hate to leave you and your men here, Sir," Abel said. "We can wait with you to make sure nothing else happens."

"Thank you, but we are so close to home that no one will bother us here. Why don't you go on, and send back men with a solution? That might save time in the long run."

"Let it be so," Abel said. "I will make sure someone comes to help."

He turned to his men and told them the plan. When they were ready, they said goodbye to those staying behind and started toward Samaria. He calculated they would arrive by late afternoon.

They finally saw the city in the distance. He learned not to get too excited at this. There was still a lot of distance to cover and to think about it only served to make the journey seem longer.

Runners came into view, having been dispatched by the caravan owners to learn who was coming. Abel gave them the information they needed and watched them return up the road before them. *Everyone will be waiting for us. I will sleep in a bed tonight.*

Sitting in the saddle was hard enough when simply traveling over the desert. To have their destination in view made it harder. Abel turned to his men and encouraged them along.

"Men, we will celebrate tonight. You will be with your wives and families. Don't give up now. We are almost there" he said, so everyone could hear. He dismounted and walked the last half hour to the city gate. Walking helped get his blood circulating. His father was standing just outside the city gate.

"Welcome home, son. Come, we have the corral ready for you and the men. They can unload the goods, take inventory, and set the merchandise out for display, and be ready for the buyers in the morning. You are lucky. We get the first choice and can start to negotiate early. You made it with just enough light to see what you are doing. It will be dark soon. Come. Let the men take care of things. Your mother is waiting for you at home."

Jacob was excited to see his son and couldn't stop speaking to give him time to respond. "I am so proud of you, son. You have done it again."

Abel finally got an opportunity to speak. "Father, it is good to see you. This has been a trying journey, but you will be proud of our success."

"I will, indeed."

"How are mother and my sisters?"

"They are fine but eager to see you."

"How is Athaliah? Have you seen her?" His heart jumped as the sound of her name came out of his mouth.

"Son, it has been several days, but, yes, she and her family were over to dinner the other night. They are all eager to see you. She seems especially eager."

"Good. I don't know how I managed to make it back. I wanted to keep riding each night to get here sooner. The next thing I am going to do is take a long hot bath. My bones hurt all over."

"I have everything ready for you. I know how it is to arrive home after a long journey. You deserve a long bath, a good meal and a good night's sleep. Son, it is good to see you. Let's go home. You can tell us all about it."

"Yes, Father. I must speak with Master Haddad's people right away and let them know of Joab's delay. I will be right back," he said, as he left his father standing.

"Mother, I don't feel like staying in the house today. I think I will get some fresh air." Athaliah called Chara and asked her to accompany her into the garden. She was always able to think more clearly there. The fresh air and gentle breezes seemed to lift her spirits. Today, she needed that. It had been a long wait. Abel would be home soon, but knowledge was working against her resolve to remain calm.

"How long will he be?" she asked Chara. "I don't think I can suffer this separation any longer." Tears trickled across her cheeks.

"I know it is difficult for you," Chara said. "But you can hold on a little longer. What are your alternatives? I am sure he is thinking the same, but he must wait as well."

"Yes, but he has something to keep him busy. I have tried to keep calm, but my heart is being eaten up with worry. The longer he is away, the more I think something has happened to him."

Chara looked at her. "You are one strong girl, Athaliah. When the heart is involved, people can get mixed up. That which should be up is down, and that which is down, is up. You can be happy knowing that no news is good news. You don't have to look at the negative all the time. I am sure he is looking for ways to be strong for you. Together, even though you are both far apart, in your hearts, you are closer than ever."

Pointing to Athaliah's heart, Chara continued. "He is right here. He is close to you."

Athaliah hesitated a moment. "Chara, you help me so much." As she spoke, she saw that Chara's face was ashen. She was looking past her. Turning to see what had captured her attention, Athaliah gasped. She stood in place and burst into tears.

In a dash, she ran toward the house. There, on the patio, stood her love. She let out a scream of joy and ran toward him with all her might. Forgetting decorum, she threw herself into his waiting arms. Sobs of joy came freely, as she held him close.

Abel smiled, and held her, feeling her tears on his neck. At length, he held her at arms length, taking her face in his hands, he said, "My love, I am here at last."

"Yes, you are. Now everything is right. I missed you so much."

CHAPTER EIGHT

The Wedding

"Master Haddad, the caravan arrived late because we were detained. The animals took sick and refused to move until they felt better."

"I am glad you made it back. How are the men?"

"The men are trail weary and sore from constant exertion over months of travel but completed their tasks with forced determination. I'm sure you saw it on their faces when they arrived. With the knowledge that they had free time coming, in which to visit their families and loved ones, they forced their weary bones to move, completing their responsibilities faithfully."

"You have chosen good men, my friend," Obed said.

"We could have been home earlier," Joab said, "but the animals took sick."

"I am concerned. What do you think our losses will be?"

"It is too early to tell, but I think it might be significant. The other caravans were able to start trading much earlier than we, taking away our edge. The low morale of our men made it even more difficult. They had to push themselves just to lift

74

a finger, upon returning. The only thing that kept them going was the knowledge that the job would not be done unless they did it."

"This is unfortunate," Obed stated. "On the other hand, my future son-in-law seems to have made out alright. His father says he will finish building a house for my daughter in a short time. I must focus on that."

"You have much on your mind, Master. You have no need to worry. I will make sure all is taken care of." This was not the first time he had faced obstacles in his work.

"Thank you. You are indeed a very good friend. You give deep meaning to the ring in your ear," Obed said.

"I am fortunate to serve the best of the best, sir," Joab said.

The days passed quickly. Abel spent much of his time overseeing the final construction details of his new home, being careful not to neglect his other responsibilities as his father's business partner. In his mind's eye he could visualize the look on Athaliah's face when she would first see the house. *She will, assuredly, see the planning, and thought I have put into it for her. She will love me even more.*

Gathering the list of young men he wanted to join him in celebrating his wedding, he went about contacting them. Details came together nicely; they all gladly agreed to participate in the celebration. Each expressed the honor he felt in being chosen and thanked him for the invitation. This would be a glorious time; he just knew it. He had become a man, not just a boy, who was legally called a man at the age of twelve, but a man who was about to step into manhood with great accomplishment, Athaliah at his side. Together they would command the respect of their peers and elders alike. *Such a handsome couple we are.*

Athaliah was beside herself with joy. Her every move reflected the excitement of anticipation. All those around her eagerly joined in the preparations. She, too, had a group of young ladies who would celebrate her stepping into married life. They laughed together and spoke of great things to come for Athaliah. Life became bigger than reality, so great was their enthusiasm. Such fun it was to think of it. The elder women looked on with knowing smiles, allowing nothing to put a damper on Athaliah or her young friends. This was Athaliah's time to celebrate. Life had its own worries, but now was not the time to allow that to diminish their joy.

"I can't think of anything but Abel. Just imagine, each day brings me closer to him," Athaliah said to Chara. "I can't sleep … all I can think of is the man I love. I am so excited."

Chara listened.

"All I want to do is stretch out across the bed to think of him. And, if I go to sleep, I just want to dream of him."

"Athaliah, you must not lose sleep. What will you do if you can't stay awake when he comes in to be with you at the wedding?" Chara said. "Don't get carried away."

"I can't help it, Chara. I love him so much, I can't wait."

"But you must wait. The day will arrive before you know it. Think of him. He deserves a wife who is fully awake, and fresh in her spirit, don't you think?"

"Yes, I know you are right. But I can't stop thinking of him. You don't know what it is like. I never thought it would be like this."

"Well, you are soaring in the clouds like an eagle, but you must come back to earth. There is much to do," Chara said.

The day was finally upon them. The house was full of servants milling around, doing what they had to do in preparation. Voices could be heard giving commands. Venders arrived with final items that could only be brought in at the last hours. The bride was kept in her room, doted over by her attendants, each one giving advice, and laughing. Spirits were high.

Athaliah's mother came into the room.

"May I have a few moments with Athaliah?"

The young ladies turned and bowed. When the room was cleared, she sat beside her daughter, and smiled.

"I am so proud of you, Athaliah. You are finally here. This is your day."

Taking a small clay bottle from her pocket, she held it up for Athaliah to see.

"I have told you what must be done. Take this and do as I say."

"I know, mother."

"Be careful he doesn't see it. This is to make sure all goes well. You understand what this means. There must be no doubt in his mind. This will secure success. I love you too much to allow anything to go wrong on this night. Trust me."

"Yes, mother. I trust you. I will do as you have instructed. I know he loves me. Nothing will go wrong."

In Athaliah's mind, there was no reason why anything could go wrong. She was about to consummate her love for the man of her dreams. Since the signing of the agreement between her father and his father, they were legally married. All that was left was to consummate the agreement. *He loves me. That is enough. Mother will see.*

There was no doubt that all would go well, and that life with Abel would start glowingly.

Music filled the house. Musicians brought laughter and joy to everyone. Anticipation filled the air, bolstered by the instruments.

One young lady came to her friend. "This is so exciting, don't you think. Just think. Athaliah is getting married tonight. I can't wait. Come, let's gather some of the other girls and walk around together. We can talk to everyone we see while we wait."

"Good idea. Athaliah must be beside herself right now."

"She is the bride. I would be dying with nerves right now if I were her."

"Let's find her and give her a hug."

Athaliah was at the center of their attention and emotions ran high. This would be a day to remember. Each young lady took a turn hugging Athaliah, congratulating her.

The guests awaited the arrival of the groom and his entourage. Singing and shouts of joy resounded throughout the halls, and out into the gardens. Family and friends stood, or sat, eating and drinking to their heart's content. Conversations simultaneously filled the air, causing an increasing roar as the guests enjoyed themselves.

Candles were lit throughout the mansion, as darkness fell over the land. The proceedings would last well into the night and through the next few days. No one was worried about the time. This was a celebration of great joy. The groom and his men would soon appear, dressed for the occasion, and the anticipated gathering would become ecstatic.

"He is coming! He is coming!" a servant shouted to the crowd. All eyes turned to the door. People pushed for a better vantage point. Silence fell over them all. At length, Abel came into view. The musicians played the prescribed music, as he stood before them.

How handsome he was. Gasps could be heard as women and men, alike, beheld the sight of him. His groomsmen stood around him, protecting his space. When the music came to an appropriate place, Abel bowed.

Master Haddad approached the groom, and his attendants. Lifting his hands to quiet the guests, he said,

"Welcome to one and all. This is an honor for me. Tonight, we formally receive Abel into our family." Turning toward Abel, he took him by the forearm, formally greeting him. 'Welcome, Abel," he said as he proudly looked over the guests.

"Please, enjoy yourselves. This is a great moment. Please join with us in celebration. There will be dancing and merriment tonight. But before we continue—"

He turned to Abel and said, "Wait here." Then, he walked through the crowded room to where Athaliah sat waiting, unseen by the groom.

A drum roll was heard as he approached her. Taking her by the hand, he drew her to her feet, hugged her warmly, and placed her hand in the crook of his arm. Then, the two walked toward the groom. Applause erupted, and the guests joined the proceedings. It was a glorious moment.

A Rabi waited at Abel's side. After a few appropriate words, he said, "Abel, behold your bride. Take her by the hand."

Shouts went up, as the thrill of the moment overtook them. Abel's family, who were waiting among the crowd, came near, and joined Abel, hugging him.

When the ceremony ended, Master Haddad turned to the guests and said, "Let there be dancing. Let there be joy."

The musicians played a lively number, and the crowd joined in the dance. According to custom, all participated in the revelry. Eyes turned to the bride and groom, as they joined with the others in traditional dances. Laughter roared and no one complained. This was a night to celebrate life. Drinks flowed and hearts overflowed.

At an appropriate moment, Abel took Athaliah by the hand and disappeared through a doorway. Almost no one noticed, for they had ducked down to make their escape through their men and women-in-waiting.

The music played on. Dancing continued. Shouts of joy abounded.

Abel took Athaliah by the hand and led her to their room. He was now the man of her life. He would lead the way. She followed eagerly. All had been prepared. Athaliah was not aware of everything that had been prepared for this moment.

Abel whisked her up and stepped through the door into their bedchamber.

Closing the door, he put her down before him and looked at her lovely face. She was glowing red. "Blushing, are we? Come. Don't be afraid. Let me hold you in my arms."

He held her, as he had dreamed of doing for so long. He wanted her to be comfortable in his presence. This was not the time to be in a hurry. Love could take its time in expressing itself.

Athaliah stood before him, warmed by the confidence she read in his countenance. He led her to the bed and sat beside her. With his hand, he pushed a strand of hair from her eyes and kissed them gently. Words were not necessary. Love had its own vocabulary. A quiet gasp escaped her lips, and she melted into his arms.

This was the moment she had been waiting for and dreaming of for so long. To be loved, to know that she would not be alone, but cared for, and feel esteemed and honored by the man of her longing heart.

Gently, Abel said, "Here, let me help you with this." His hands tugged at the laces of her beautiful garment. She allowed him to proceed. The glow of the moment overtook the newness of the experience, and she forgot herself as his touch sent chills through her body. Her heart almost stopped.

He felt assured of himself, as he tenderly looked upon her loveliness. Turning to fold back the covers of the bed, he heard something fall. Glancing at his feet, he saw a small, clay bottle. Its contents spilled over the floor.

"What is this?" he asked. Understanding slowly overtook his wonder; his mind went blank. He didn't want to know what it was, but he did. His heart skipped a beat.

He felt an unfamiliar sensation overcome him. "It is blood!" He said gasping.

He could not believe what he was thinking, but it could not be ignored. *How could she do this to me? I have been faithful to her. The women at the temple and the high places don't count—they were necessary—but I am about to give my love to Athaliah. No one has stirred me as she has. But how could she do this to me? This isn't right. How could she?*

Resolve crept into his heart. *No, I will not allow her to get away with this. I was about to give her my life, but, she has totally disregarded my feelings. My honor is at stake. I will not allow her to think she can wrong me in this way. I don't deserve this.* He stood silent, thoughts racing through his mind.

Athaliah stood transfixed, not understanding what had happened. She was taken up in the moment and did not see the small clay bottle fall from her garment. Suddenly realization forced its way over her countenance. Her heart sank. The magic of the moment was broken instantly. She knew the groomsmen and her attendants were waiting below to see the blood on the bedsheets, as was the custom. This was to be proof of losing her virginity.

"What have you done?" Abel asked. Unbelief was written on his face.

"What do you mean? I have done nothing," she said.

"You are trying to cover up the truth. You have been with a man." The words came out of his mouth before he could stop them.

"No, I haven't. That is the truth," was all she could think to say.

How could this be happening to her? With her hopes and dreams now shattered, they lay at her feet. Tears welled up, and she cried deep sobs, forcibly released from deep within her soul.

Abel stood, seething with rage. *How could she treat me like this? How could she deceive me in this way? Doesn't she know who I am? No one can do this to me.* Before he could control his mouth, he shouted, "You are a harlot."

His words cut through her heart like a sharp dagger. Full realization engulfed her being. Speechless, she sobbed uncontrollably. *How can he accuse me like this? I have done nothing wrong. Oh, please, please.*

"Not even the girls at the temple would do this to me," he shouted.

Fixing her gaze upon him, she managed to sputter, "The girls at the temple—? What are you telling me? Have you been with them, and you accuse me?"

"That is completely different. I am a man. A man has needs. You are to be a pure wife, but not this."

For the first time in her young life, she saw the double standard, and it crushed her. "How can you accuse me like this? I have done nothing."

"Yes, you have, and I have the proof, right here on the floor.

Enraged, Abel opened the door and ran to the balcony. "Deception is afoot. I have been deceived. The marriage is off." he shouted to the surprised guests below. "I have been wronged. Someone is going to pay for this!"

Leaving Athaliah to grieve in her room, he ran from the house, pushing the guests aside as he went. A stunning pall fell over the surprised guests. The music stopped at once. The crowd stood, collectively stunned by what they witnessed. How could this be?

"What just happened?" The guests whispered among themselves. Unanswered questions flew through the crowd with no forthcoming answers. Bewilderment overtook the celebration.

Athaliah's attendants huddled around each other in disbelief. They could not grasp what just happened. Could it be true? Some hugged each other in stunned silence. Others cried openly, their joy suddenly turned into a sense of cruel tragedy, the pain of the emotional jolt still obscured by uncertainty.

After what seemed an eternity, Master Haddad stood before the guests.

"There must be an explanation for this sudden outbreak. Please forgive us. If you would, please allow the servants to see you out. Thank you for coming. Please, take whatever you like of the food."

Master Haddad, embarrassed and bewildered, sought to distance himself from his guests, but was stopped by Master Jacob.

"Do you know what happened? Why did my son run out shouting deception?"

"I assure you; I don't know. Please allow us to sort this out. I am sorry for the public display."

"We will demand an accounting of this from you. Our family has been disgraced this night."

The Rabi stood, silently holding the rest of a leg of lamb.

Entering Athaliah's room, Obed saw Athaliah sitting on the bed, her mother in tears beside her.

"What happened?"

Looking to the floor, he saw the clay bottle, and the blood spilled out over the floor. "No, No. What have you done?" He was looking, not at Athaliah, but Mara.

He knew exactly what had happened. A sick feeling drenched his soul and sought to steal his breath. Sitting, he was unable to say a word.

"I have been disgraced, and humiliated," he said at length.

"No, Father, I am the one humiliated this night." Athaliah said through her sobs. "Not only was I humiliated by Abel, but by my own parents. I want to know the whole truth. How could you keep the truth from me? I think I am going to be sick."

"We will not live this down, ever," Mara said. "I am to blame. I tried to do the right thing for my little girl, only to cause a complete disaster." Tears filled her eyes, and self-condemnation overtook her.

"Emotions are too high right now," Obed stated emphatically. "We will talk tomorrow after we have all had a chance to calm ourselves."

There was no sleep that night. The guests finally left. The servants went about cleaning up, not daring to inquire or speak of what had happened. It was not their place to do so. Chara could not be found, not that anyone was looking for her at the moment. She felt the weight of guilt, as though a mountain had fallen upon her, and could not allow herself to be seen by anyone. All she could do was cry, uncontrollably.

Mara stayed by Athaliah's side through the night. They both wept, arm in arm.

"Mother, I am so sad. How could everything change so quickly? At first, he treated me as I had dreamed he would, and before I knew it he called me names, and would not let me defend myself."

"Oh, my dear, I am so sorry this happened to you. It is my fault. I didn't want you to get hurt, so I thought the bottle, with its contents, would work," she said, caressing Athaliah's face.

"But what could make you uncertain?"

"My dear, there are things we have not told you about why you were sick for so long. We simply felt you were too weak to know everything."

"But I got better."

"Yes, you did, but you had scars. The type of scars you should have never had to bear. We just wanted you to move on in life as you so greatly deserve. We love you."

Mara could not bring herself to mention the details of the tragedy. There were so many unknown factors. She and Obed had agreed to never reveal the worst so that Athaliah could face life without emotional repercussions. After the events of the evening, it became apparent that they were losing the battle of silence.

PART II

CHAPTER NINE

The Lost Childhood

"Come on, Ben. You must hold it with your fingers to get it on the hook the right way. Take it in your hand and drop that cloth. It won't kill you."

"You can't tell me what to do. You are a girl," he said. Benjamin sat, fidgeting with the hook, not wanting to get his fingers dirty with the slime of the worm. The more he pressed it between his fingers, the more it thrashed about. His fear was the gush of entrails when he pushed the worm against the pointed hook. With his older sister's chiding, he forced himself to try again. This time the hook slid into the squirming fish bait.

"I did it," Benjamin shouted with delight and lifted the hook so Athaliah could see his accomplishment. His exuberance almost deafened her.

"Not so loud.   I'm sitting right next to you. You see, I do know some things. Now, put it in the water and see what you can catch. Try to hit that little pool of deep water, just there," she pointed. "You must know how to catch fish if you want to be a man," Athaliah said with emphasis on man.

Being the older child, a girl at that, was not the easiest burden for Athaliah to bear. Her younger brother, Benjamin, was a daily reminder that she was not the son her father had desired for a firstborn. This she knew because, when she was younger, she'd overheard him state it as a fact to her mother. He got her instead. To counter what she perceived to be displeasure for not having a son first, Athaliah found ways to learn, by observation, the art of being a dutiful son. Then she attempted to teach them to Benjamin. Not that she had much knowledge in that regard, but, in her mind, it helped her feel more tolerated.

She looked at him and decided to appeal to his ego. "I'll make you a deal. When I see that you need to learn something, I will tell you when we are alone. That way, everyone will think you knew it on your own, and that you are smart."

"Okay, but don't forget that I am the man here, even if I am younger than you."

"Agreed."

At 11, Athaliah was three years Benjamin's senior. She customarily watched the young men of the village when they readied their equipment for fishing. Most boys enjoyed trying to bring home dinner for their families, even though fishing involved many patient hours of sitting. Their accomplishments were a badge of honor. They all had to take part in providing, or at least, learn how it was done, if they could.

The creek, in which Athaliah and Benjamin were fishing, ran down the hillside toward the Jordan River. In the distance they could see the green palms of the valley where the two waterways met. Athaliah often wondered how the fish made it all the way up the stream, but they did, with no objection from either she or her brother. Benjamin held out his cane fishing pole and watched as the hook swung across and landed in the water near the opposite bank, just at the edge of the deep part. He could see that the current formed a small eddy. Athaliah pointed out that the fish often found places to hide near eddies. He waited a few minutes and saw the line dip into the water. The cork bobbed a couple of times and then quickly disappeared. Benjamin felt a hard tug. Athaliah was speaking to him, but he didn't hear her. Her voice became urgent.

"Pull the pole back toward you. Don't give it any slack or the fish might get off the hook." she urged.

He did so, not because he heard her, but because it seemed the natural thing to do. Gripping the pole, Benjamin walked backward to bring the fish closer. It struggled, darting back and forth. When he finally saw the fish, he couldn't contain his ecstasy.

"It's a fish," he exclaimed. "I did it. I did it."

"Don't forget what you are doing," Athaliah said. "It can still get away. Keep holding the pole tight and don't allow any slack in the line."

Athaliah reached down and took the fish out of the water and held it up for Benjamin to see.

"You did it," she said with a proud smile. "Now, take it off of the hook." She watched as he gingerly held the fish, obviously disliking the feel of it. Conquering yet another fear, Benjamin looked wide-eyed at his sister.

"Now all we need are two or three more like this one and Father will be so happy. Mom will know just how to instruct the kitchen workers to please him," he stated with pride.

Placing his catch on a holding line, he placed it back into the water to keep it alive. "Now, all we need are some more to join this one," he said, and sat to prepare the pole for another cast.

Later that afternoon, Athaliah and Benjamin proudly brought six large fish home.

Surprised, yet pleased, their mother met them at the door. "Outside you go. They must be cleaned. The servants will take care of them."

"I think it would be a good idea for Ben to clean them, Mother," Athaliah offered. "He needs to learn to do manly things."

Benjamin bristled at Athaliah.

"Don't look at me that way, Ben. You caught them. And, besides, a real man does his own cleaning."

"Thank you, Athaliah Priscilla," her mother said, "but the help will do that." Her look needed no interpretation. Even though Athaliah was the elder, it was not her place to tell her brother what to do. Girls must keep their place. Benjamin would be the person to take care of his mother when she became unable to take care of herself, assuming he outlived his father. But, for the present, mother was the one who told others what to do.

"Take the fish outside and then clean-up for dinner. We have guests coming. Your father will want both of you to be on your best behavior," their mother said. "Off with you," she said, giving each of them a symbolic swat as they passed by her.

Athaliah went to her room upstairs. From her window, she could look out over the beautiful garden behind their home. Her father was a man of means, and Athaliah enjoyed the life he provided. She knew nothing else. She assumed it was how most people lived.

Situated on the outskirts of Shechem, a city of Samaria, the neighborhood was comprised of meandering streets that followed the contours of the hills, bordered by large shade trees and clumps of flowers spread out in orderly fashion.

The homes were spacious and provided privacy due to the ample distance between them. Each house was the family dwelling of the farm owners; small social hubs with small animals which contributed to the food supply. The farms were situated around the town center, where all could go to purchase goods or trade. Master Obed ben Haddad always told the children not to give names to the animals because it would make it difficult to sacrifice or sell them when the time came to do so.

The Haddad family lived in a region where kings of olden days had lived for centuries. From time immemorial it was said that this was the "Land flowing with Milk and Honey." The kings had left their imprint on the land. Elaborate systems of irrigation, wells, and cisterns augmented the natural water supply. Not all regions were so blessed. There were arid lands not far away. A mixture of plains, forested mountains, cultivated vineyards, fruit trees, and farmlands formed a patchwork of ingenious planning and enterprise.

Athaliah gazed at the garden. A gentle breeze wafted through the window. The shutters were wide open and there were no bugs to bother her. She loved the colorful array of flowers that emitted wonderful fragrances. She felt as though she could stay like she was forever. But guests would soon be arriving – male guests.

A negative feeling washed over her as she thought about it. Athaliah was beginning to blossom. She didn't quite understand the changes that were taking place. Her mother told her she was growing into her woman's body.

"Everyone goes through this change," she explained, to teach and comfort her daughter.

A flicker of embarrassment caused her heart to flip as she thought of her mother's instructions. *Why does everyone have to look at me the way they do, especially the men?*

She knew what would happen. Her father's business associates, catching a glimpse of her, would make remarks that both confused and disturbed her:

"Time does produce some good changes."

"She is going to make the boys weep."

Athaliah would stay out of their way, glad that girls had no business to be in the same room where financial affairs were conducted.

After bathing, she brushed her long, ebony-black hair, which cascaded over her slight shoulders. At times she wished it weren't so long. It seemed to attract uncomfortable comments from the men.

Just then, her servant, Chara, knocked on the door and came in to help with her preparations. Chara was three years older than Athaliah. Though good friends, they each knew their place in life. That didn't keep them from being close.

Taking the brush from Athaliah, Chara skillfully drew the brush through her hair, making sure not to pull too hard.

"Do you know who the guests will be tonight?" the servant said.

"Some of father's business friends," Athaliah grimly replied. "At least I won't have to see them. Ben will, though. Father likes to bring him out to introduce him around because he is 'the heir.' I don't care if I'm not Ben. I don't like the way some of those men look at me."

"Well, that comes with being a female, I think," Chara volunteered. "You could just look through the lattice, unnoticed, if you are curious."

CHAPTER TEN

Daniel

The guests arrived in the cool of the evening. The gathering was expected to be more a social event among friends and associates than a business food fest. Although the food, served in abundance, never lacked to please and impress, time was needed to fully enjoy each other's company.

Master Obed ben Haddad had his hands in many business ventures. Those who knew him said he owned a business empire. Each aspect of his businesses had its steward - trusted men of integrity – who hired servants to carry out their owner's desires. This evening, these guests had recently returned home after a year of driving a camel caravan far to the east, and back. The beasts came heavily laden with goods acquired by trading for commodities that only came from exotic cultures in regions far beyond the Euphrates River.

This was a celebration of a successful venture which, after enduring many trials and unparalleled perseverance, had brought great wealth to be added to Master Haddad's holdings. He wanted to sit with the men and hear them recount the adventures in detail. This would be an evening for men. What did women know of travel or the art of negotiations? Men understood that with great risk comes great reward. Why bother women with such things? They only worry.

The house was run like a well-oiled machine. The servants knew what to do and when it should be done. As was the custom, each guest was immediately taken to a patio where their feet were washed. Then they were given a pair of clean, soft sandals to wear for the evening. Their dusty sandals were placed to the side so that when the men left, they had only to exchange their footwear and depart.

When each guest was ready, he was escorted, and seated, at his respective place around arranged tables, laden with fruits of all kinds. The host had decided that no comfort or delight would be withheld this night. Pleasantries were exchanged while servant girls carrying clay jugs made their way to each guest and poured cool wine into challises. The men made appreciative comments as they looked at their surroundings.

Most of the men knew each other; however, some were new to the business fraternity.

"I have never been in such a place. Someone will have to teach me what to do," one man said.

"Don't worry. We will teach you. It is not hard. Master Haddad is a good man and will put you at ease. You will see."

"We have worked for Master Haddad for a couple of years and are pleased to do so. From everything we see, he must command a fortune. But he is good to his workers. Not like many others. We appreciate and honor him."

The banquet patio created a sense of awe in the hearts of all visitors. Vines grew overhead, supported by an elaborate network of wood beams and lattice. Stone columns supported everything and held it in place, creating a shelter that afforded cool shade during the day and held in warmth in the evening.

Master Haddad waited a while and made his entrance in a manner that commanded the greatest attention of his guests and took his place at the head table.

Joab, the caravan's leader and Master Haddad's faithful steward, was seated at the head table. When the host approached, Joab stood to greet him.

"Master, how good it is to see you," he said as he held his arms out. They were obviously good friends as well as master and steward.

Slavery was a common practice. Not all slave owners mistreated their workers. Joab wore a ring in his ear denoting the fact that his servitude was voluntary. He could not think of doing anything else. He worked with pride, feeling that his was a vocation of honor. "How many people get to work for an honorable man such as Master Haddad?" he often said.

Turning to the table, Joab motioned to Reuel. "Do you remember Reuel, Master?"

"Yes, I most certainly do." Reuel approached and took the master's hand. "Thank you for coming tonight," Master Haddad said. A warmth that commanded respect flowed as he spoke.

"Thank you, Master. You are most gracious," Reuel said.

Another young man stood at the table, and Master Haddad said, "And who do we have here?"

"This is our assistant in charge of security," Joab answered. "Come, Daniel, and greet our master. Master, this is Daniel Aquila."

"You're in charge of security?" he asked. "You look so young."

Joab stepped to his defense. "Yes, my Master. He is young, he is a mere nineteen years of age," Joab said.

Ruggedly handsome, and appearing to have the strength of an ox, Daniel held his head high, but knew to demonstrate respect as he stood before his master. He responded to the master's outreached hand, shaking it with the same vigor the master exhibited.

"Come, let's sit." The men sat on their respective couches around the table, making themselves comfortable, following the lead of Master Haddad.

"Joab, tell me about this young man. How long has he been in our employment?"

"Oh, Master, he has been with us for this whole year," Joab said. "I needed a security leader and this one showed promise. He has lived up to my expectations, I must say," admiration showing as he spoke.

"As you know, the areas we visited this time are known for the dangers that abound along the way. Daniel was hired to keep us safe. He also brought others along. You see them over there," he gestured toward another table where several men sat talking. "They form quite a team. No one dared give us grief if they had any sense."

Servants filed in carrying platters of meats, passing through the tables, filling the plates of the awaiting guests with eye-pleasing bounty. Each was allowed to choose of the delights being offered.

While he was being served, Master Haddad looked at Daniel and asked directly, "Where does your family come from, Daniel?"

Daniel had wisely waited until being directly addressed.

"Master, I have no family, but my parents were from the Klan of Dan, north of here," he said. "I was born in Pontus, where we all lived until they returned to their father's land, when I was young."

"You say you have no family. What happened to them?"

"A gang of men raided our home and demanded money. My father gave them all he had, but they killed him and my mother anyway, because they wanted more."

"Because they wanted more," Master Haddad repeated.

"Yes, my parents gave them all they had, but the men thought they were holding out on them. I watched from a hiding place while they brutally cut both my parents down for no reason."

"This must have caused you great pain," Master Haddad said.

"I swore that no one would ever do that to me again. I had to fend for myself after their deaths, by any means necessary. My parents taught me to live honorably, still, I was angry. So, I built myself up in strength and trained in the art of war by watching the Roman soldiers as they did maneuvers nearby," he said. A spark of residual anger could be heard in his words.

"What happened to your home," Master Haddad asked.

"I lost it. I have lived in many places since then, though trying to keep out of trouble. But I have had my share of that, too."

Joab placed his hand on Daniel' shoulder and said, "Master, when I saw him, I knew he was just the man for the job. He has proven me right."

Master Haddad had come to appreciate Joab's ability to "read" people.

"As a matter of fact, all of the men on this trip did exceptionally well," Joab added. "Daniel led them well."

Looking at Daniel, he said, "Tell the master how you sent the raiders fleeing for their lives along the "Silk Road" when they ambushed us."

The master listened with interest to the exploits, enjoying every word. "Now, Reuel, tell me how the trip went from your perspective."

Reuel sat up at the sound of his name. "Master I had a wonderful time. That is to say, if one doesn't take into consideration all the troubles that presented themselves. I learned much from Daniel and his men. But, the animals, well, you know camels.

They are obstinate at best, with a mind of their own. But I was to be able to handle them. There were over fifty animals under my charge this time, and twice as many men. As the leader of the caravan, I couldn't have asked for a better crew. Of course, Joab is an excellent trail boss, which made my job much easier," Reuel rambled. "He took care of the bartering, purchases and sales, and I took care of the logistics," he added with a look toward Joab.

Master Haddad was pleased because the caravan had filled his coffers amply this trip.

"You have all done so well that I will have to pay a visit to the tax collector tomorrow," he said, feigning pain. "I congratulate you all."

The evening was spent listening to stories of bravery and exploits of valor. Master Haddad was obviously pleased as he listened. These men had risked their lives for him, and he was proud of their faithfulness under pressure.

Reaching far into the evening, the men enjoyed splendor that was normally given only to exalted guests. Master Haddad believed in keeping his workers content and feeling appreciated. His kindness paid off in many ways. The expense of the evening was well worth it.

But, before it got too late, the host called for everyone's attention. "Men, before you leave, I want to say you have made me a very proud man. Thank you for your faithfulness. My whole family and I salute you."

Athaliah, who had been watching from behind a lattice, knew this was Ben's moment to come forward. He and her mother were awaiting this moment. She gently pushed him toward his father, who waited with outstretched arms. His father received him warmly, and they both stood, facing the guests.

"Men, this is my son, Benjamin. In a few years, he will be the head of my business." He looked down at Benjamin, smiling. "I know you will work faithfully for him as you have for me. We thank you for your work." With a gleam in his eyes, he said, "This is why we pay you well."

Laughter filled the room. The men spontaneously stood in respect as Master Haddad and Benjamin faced them. Gratitude could be seen on their faces as they clapped and cheered.

Daniel, standing with the others, looked around and, by chance, was drawn to movement behind the lattice. Athaliah noticed him and froze in place. Though he could see only her eyes through the lattice, their gaze locked for a fleeting moment. Quickly, he looked away, but returned to see those eyes still looking at him. *Such beautiful eyes*, he thought.

Athaliah Priscilla, come away from the lattice, child." Athaliah could feel herself being dragged away. "You know you shouldn't be seen by the men. What is wrong with you?" Her mother didn't stop until they were well out of sight. Athaliah finally tore herself away from her mother's grasp, embarrassment creeping onto her face.

Daniel had seen the action. He saw her eyes and long, flowing black hair. He smiled as he watched them leave the patio. He did not know her name, but he knew she was his master's daughter. There was no disrespect in his heart, mostly surprise, as he viewed those eyes again and again in his mind. He had caught movement from the corner of his eye and was rewarded by unexpected beauty. *I would love to meet that young girl.*

CHAPTER ELEVEN

The Encounter

"Athaliah, get up. It is time to leave for class." Chara gently shook her shoulder. Athaliah stretched lazily in her bed and didn't open her eyes. At sixteen, she had matured beautifully. The transformation had been slow, but constant over the last five years.

"No, you can't stay in bed. We will be late," Chara urged good-naturedly.

"Sometimes, Chara, I don't know what to do with you."

"Oh, yes, I am a pain, but I have my orders. Your mother won't take it lightly if we are late."

Chara picked out a tunic for the day, while Athaliah stepped to the basin and poured water from the pitcher. She reached into the cool water and splashed her face a couple of times. With a towel, she patted her skin dry. Now, she felt awake.

"You don't realize how much your father loves you," Chara said. "Most girls don't get to study and learn as you do. Your father wants you to know how to take responsibility, so you must learn. I wish my father had done that for me," she lamented.

"I love working here with you, but there are so many things I could do if I had the training you are getting."

"I know. It's hard to wake up after a late night," Athaliah said in her defense. "I couldn't sleep with the noise going on down in the patio. I could hear them through the open window. My father always has some kind of event going on."

Athaliah studied each day until noon. She and Chara walked to the house where her tutor lived with his family. They went together for security reasons. Chara was charged with Athaliah's safety. The community was safe, and everyone knew everyone, but there was propriety to be considered. A young woman of her stature was not to be walking alone in the streets, especially now that she was becoming a woman. Athaliah couldn't understand this, but there was nothing she could do about it. She didn't mind being with Chara. They had become fast friends and greatly enjoyed each other's company.

Her father often said, "There are dangers out there. You must be careful at all times. I don't want anything to happen to you." Athaliah listened to him but had no idea what he might be worried about. Life was good. She asked herself, *why doesn't he want me to enjoy it? Doesn't he trust me?* Her thoughts were confused. With youthful impatience, she considered herself mature and desired more freedom.

The tutor had lessons prepared for her in various subjects: Reading and Writing, Mathematics, Customs, and Natural Science, even business. All were subjects her father considered important for his growing young daughter. After all, she was not the daughter of just anyone. She was his daughter. He had plans for her. He wanted the best things in life to be hers. He admired the "Virtuous Woman" spoken of by King Solomon in his collection of proverbs and envisioned Athaliah that way, virtuous and trustworthy, able to take care of her family — praised by all who knew her.

Athaliah loved reading and writing. They were her favorite pastimes. She had an inexplicable desire to know things about people and often wrote about what she discovered as she interacted with those around her. This curiosity came to her naturally.

Her mother often said it was a "gift."

Athaliah and Chara started out for her classes. The way was so familiar to her that she could have traversed it blindfolded.

"I love the trees and the shade they produce from the morning sun," she said to Chara as they walked.

The weather could get so hot that even in the shade people didn't go outside but chose to stay in the cool underground rooms in their homes and venture out after sundown. She had to go to school so there was not much she could do about it.

Chara spoke after a few minutes. "Athaliah, I would like to go to the market while you are in class if that is alright with you. That way I can get a few things done while you are busy."

"Sure, you can do that if you like. Just don't be late returning for me. I wouldn't want my father to see that you were not near me." Athaliah said.

They were friends, and Athaliah trusted Chara without reservations. After a moment, Athaliah asked, "Are you going to see someone at the market?"

"Not really. You know my aunt brings her produce to market, and I would love to say hello and get caught up with family news."

Chara was from a poor Greek family that a few years earlier had gone through rough times. Her father, not able to pay his debts, was forced to place her in the care of Master Haddad so she could work off the debt. This arrangement was not uncommon throughout the region. In this case, Chara's father knew where she was and trusted her into the hands of the Haddad family. She would be thirty years of age before the debt was fully canceled.

Master Haddad's idea was that Chara be a helper to Athaliah, as well as a friend. He was not a stern man but was precise in his dealings. He would get his money's worth in time.

The girls walked a little faster this day, due to starting late. Nearing the town, they turned down a cobblestone street. It was almost not recognizable as a street, but a path. The way was narrow and steep. Athaliah often wondered how the houses stayed in place instead of sliding down the slope. Signs of life were everywhere, with housemaids and servants going about their duties.

Reaching the tutor's house, Athaliah knocked on the door and waited. Shortly, a servant girl opened the door. "Come in Athaliah. Master says you are a little late," she said, stepping aside so the girls could enter.

Athaliah touched the prayer box fixed to the door jam and touched her fingers to her lips as she entered. This was an automatic action for her. Her family followed the traditions, as much as they could remember them. In doing so, they felt they enjoyed the blessing and protection of the All-Mighty.

Turning to Chara she said, "Be sure and return before it is time for me to leave."

"Yes, I will," she answered.

"Chara is going to visit her aunt at the market," she said to the attendant and walked into the study room. The professor greeted her. "You are late this morning, Little One." There was no rebuke in his tone.

"Your father had guests last night and I am sure you didn't sleep very well with the noise." Opening his instruction book he said, "Let's get started, shall we? Time is precious."

The morning passed quickly. Athaliah liked to study, and that helped make the time of little consequence. This day, she studied mathematics. "If you want to barter, you must know the value of the products you are selling or buying, and how to keep track of the exchanges," he often said. "Everything has value. Applied mathematics is simply a necessary practicality."

Athaliah could see herself as the woman spoken of in the book of Proverbs, who was honored as wise, prudent, and thrifty; one who took care of her family. She dreamed of one day having a family with children around her feet, and a husband that adored her.

When her classes were over, she stepped out onto the street and saw Chara leaning against the wall, waiting.

"Good, you made it back in time," she said as they began their trek homeward.

They had to be quick because her brother studied in the afternoon, and her father wanted her home before Ben left for classes. The menservants watched over and cared for him.

"I met someone today at the market," Chara confided as they walked.

"Do you mean someone other than your aunt? How is she?"

"Yes, and fine," she answered. "We were deep in conversation when I saw a man looking at me from across the market patio. He was standing behind some vendor's garments. He must have thought I couldn't see him, so he just stared at me.

"I knew I had seen him before. And, sure enough, he was the young man who had sat at your father's table that night five years ago," she said breathlessly, as they made their way up the incline. Their progress was slow. The heat made it impossible to walk fast.

"Do you mean that one who sat by Joab?"

"The very one," she said with a smile that covered her whole face.

"I remember him. What is he like? Did you speak with him?"

"Well, after a while, he saw that I had seen him, so he slowly approached my aunt's stand. He was shy … and very handsome," she said.

"He introduced himself, being sure to respectfully address my aunt first. He then asked me if I was among the girls that helped serve the tables at that event. Of course, I said I was."

"Did you know he would be there? At the market, I mean," Athaliah asked.

"No, I just wanted to see my aunt, and get news of the family," she answered. "But it was nice to see him. He seemed like a very nice young man. He is more mature, now. I thought he was interested in me, but when he asked about you, I learned his true motive for the visit. He was taking care of affairs for his boss, Joab, when he saw me speaking with my aunt. I don't remember meeting such a handsome fellow. He was very polite and thoughtful. He was cute." Scratching her head, she said, "Did I really just say that?" She found herself rambling and clapped her hand over her mouth.

"I think he would like to meet you," Chara said in a whisper.

"I am too young to meet anyone, especially a man like him. But I did think he was handsome when I saw him seated at the table. He carried himself very well, and was respectful to my father," Athaliah said.

"Well, he said he was preparing for another journey with Joab and would be gone for several months," Chara added.

"I don't know. My father would not like me to meet anyone. He is so protective. Everyone at the house watches out for me. I think my father has told the servants to protect me," Athaliah said.

"I am glad he does, Athaliah. You are a special young lady, with much to live for.

Your family loves you and wants the best for you. I wish I had a family that cared for me as yours does you. Still, Daniel would like to meet you."

She stopped and placed her hand on Athaliah's shoulder. "I sense he is a good man. He must be. He works for your father, and your father would not keep anyone around that is not honorable, do you think?"

"You actually know his name?" Athaliah asked excitedly.

"Well, of course. One can't talk with someone without knowing their name," she returned.

Daniel. His name bounced around her mind. She continued to walk in silence.

Athaliah couldn't understand her own reactions to what Chara told her. A man was interested in her. Her emotions came in conflicting waves. This was something totally unexpected. How could she feel so uncomfortable around members of the opposite sex, and at the same time feel exhilarated and drawn? Life was not as simple as it had been when she was younger. She had not met the person who would cause her to feel the emotions that separated childhood from womanhood.

That evening she and Chara spoke while preparing for the night. "Chara, I am so used to ignoring the differences between myself and the young men I have known all my life. I am a girl, and they are boys. That is just how things are. It isn't complicated."

Chara listened as she helped.

"My male friends look at me simply as another friend, I think. At least, I look at them that way. Now, I am beginning to feel something new and unfamiliar in my own reactions."

"Do you mean you feel drawn toward them?" Chara asked.

"No, and yes. I am not drawn to any particular person, but to characteristics, traits, looks, mannerisms and personalities. Is that normal? I don't know. You could call it curiosity or interest."

"Or desire?" Chara said.

"My heart feels pulled toward them in an unfamiliar, yet intriguing way."

Athaliah remembered feeling embarrassed in the beginning, because of the obvious changes that slowly took place in her body. At the same time, she liked what was happening to her. The knowledge that she was "becoming a woman" was something she had always looked forward to. Her mother spoke to her of changes, but she didn't understand how they worked.

"The day will come. You will soon become a woman," her mother said. She remembered the day when she became aware of discomfort in her lower stomach. Then she saw blood. *No. No. this can't be happening to me.* Her first reaction was fear. Panic caused her to scream. Not wanting anyone to know what was happening, she placed her hands over her mouth, but her anguish persisted. Finally, she understood she needed help.

"Mother, Mother. Come quickly. Mother, come," she screamed. *Why doesn't mother come? Doesn't she hear me?*

After what seemed hours, her mother ran into the room. "What is it, Athaliah? What happened," her mother asked in a panic.

"Mother, I don't know how to stop it," was all Athaliah could say. "Look at me. I am bleeding to death." Anguish and fear covered her face as she looked up at her mother. "Why is this happening to me?"

Her mother took her in her arms to calm her. "Come here, child, let me see. My dear girl, you have become a woman."

Her mother had tried to prepare Athaliah for this inevitable moment, but obviously, she had failed in some way, because the panic she saw in her daughter's eyes was real.

"Come, let's get you cleaned up. This is a happy day," her mother said, giving her a kiss on the forehead.

The moments that followed were embarrassing for Athaliah, but as her mother lovingly cared for her, the panic turned to understanding. Relief replaced fear.

Unbeknown to Athaliah, later that night, as Master Haddad and his wife prepared for bed. He climbed into bed, exhausted after a day of bartering and haggling with businessmen at the city gates.

"Obed, I have news," Mara said joyfully.

"Yes, what is it," he asked yawning.

Mara came around and looked directly into his face. "Our little girl has just become a woman."

"What do you mean?" he asked. "What happened? Did she...?"

"No, nothing bad has happened. She has had her first monthly."

They lay silently for a moment, while what she had said sank in. "I can't believe it. I mean, I believe it, but she is growing so fast. Soon we will have to look for a suitable mate for her. My little girl is no longer a girl, but a woman." He sat on the corner of the bed in deep thought.

"We must be cautious. Not that we haven't been doing so, but others will soon begin paying attention to her. Unwanted attention, from where I sit."

"We do have one thing on our side," Mara said.

"Yes, and what might that be?"

"The fact is that she doesn't seem to know that she is beautiful. In her mind, she is still our sweet little girl. She doesn't know anything about the world around us."

"Still," Obed said, "We must be careful. Whether she knows it or not, others do, and that can be a dangerous thing. You must tell the servants to be extra careful to protect our little girl … I mean our developing woman child. Have you spoken to Athaliah about what is to be expected of her?"

"Of course."

"This is a time of wonder and change for her, but it is also a time for added responsibility as well."

They talked for a while. Obed had lost his desire for sleep and was trying to get caught up with the events. He needed to assure himself that he would be ready for these life changes within the family.

"There was a young man interested in me, what should I do, Chara? Ignore him? Pretend he doesn't exist? Be offended at his audacity?" Why did she want to meet him? This was all so new.

Since hearing that Daniel was interested in meeting her, she found that time itself seemed to simply fly by when she thought of him. She discovered her imagination could invent endless scenarios with him as the focus. This was a new sensation. Innocently, she conjured thoughts of him sitting under a shade tree, or running across an open field, all the while turning to look at her as though she were the only girl in the world. This delighted her and produced previously unknown emotions.

Chara didn't know how to answer the questions. "Athaliah, something is different," she said. "Are you thinking about Daniel? I think you are. It is written all over your face."

"I don't know what I am thinking. I don't even know the man," deflecting a little. "I know nothing about him or his past."

"Well, you know that he works for your father," Chara said. "That should say something to you."

"You are right, if my father trusts him, I should be able to as well," Athaliah reasoned. "Joab hired him to work as head of security. Apparently, he is good at it, because he has been with the caravans for all these years.

Her thinking seemed logical to her. Chara couldn't disagree.

"Maybe I could arrange a time for you to meet. Nothing serious, just a few minutes to say hello," Chara offered.

"I don't know. What would my father say? What would my mother say? I can't take a chance. I'm so young, only sixteen." Athaliah sighed.

"Yes. But you will be seventeen in a couple of months and that is within marrying age. I can't tell you what to do, but I think it wouldn't hurt to just meet him. A lot of girls are married by the time they are your age."

"That is too serious," Athaliah protested. "I'm not thinking about doing that now. But maybe I could just meet him. My parents can't know of it, though."

"Are you sure, Athaliah?" Chara questioned hurriedly, realizing that she could be held accountable for bringing the subject up. She had no right to interfere in the family's affairs, and she knew it. Young people sometimes devise plans without the advantage of insights that come only with maturity. The meeting of two young people didn't seem too dangerous to either of the girls. What could go wrong?

"I will think about it," Athaliah said pensively. "I don't want to hurry into anything my parents might not agree to," she concluded. "Now, help me into this nightgown, Chara."

Her sleep was fitful. She dreamed of flowers in the field, swaying to a gentle breeze. While she sat looking at the beauty, movement caught her peripheral vision. Turning instantly toward the movement, Daniel came into view, his long hair blowing in the breeze. His shoulders square, exuding strength. He slowly walked toward her, reaching his hand out toward hers. His look was gentle, yet strong. He smiled confidently. She reached up to take his hand but couldn't touch it. Moving toward him, she felt as though his hand was becoming distant. She stood up, and he wasn't there. Looking around, he was nowhere to be found. Then, a noise disturbed her dream, and she awoke. A sense of loss flooded her being. *Who is making that noise?*

Hearing a whistle, Athaliah became angry. *Ben! Why can't he stay out of my dreams?* She and he had a tune they whistled when trying to locate each other. Benjamin stood at the door, whistling. Finally, unable to rouse her, he said loudly, "Athaliah, let's go. We need to leave right away." Benjamin pounded on her bedroom door. "It has been too long since we last went fishing. Move it. Let's go. The fish will stop biting if we wait any longer." he shouted through the heavy door.

"Alright, Ben, give me a minute to get dressed," Athaliah countered with determination in her voice. "Why can't you show a little patience? Why don't you get the canes and bait, instead of making so much noise? I will be right down."

Having achieved his goal, Benjamin turned to leave. "I will be outside waiting. Hurry," he said over his shoulder.

A little while later Athaliah met him at the corner of the patio. "Let's go, Ben," she said as she took part of the equipment he had gathered.

The brook was not too far from their house, and they made the distance quickly. Their father's land was vast, so there was no fear of anyone being at the creek when they arrived.

"Good," Benjamin exclaimed. "There's the spot I like. This is going to be a good day."

In a few minutes they had their canes ready, and Athaliah, out of habit, looked over to see if Benjamin had his bait properly placed on the hook. He knew how to put a worm on a hook and would get upset if she said anything to him about it, so she remained quiet.

"Well, the boy has learned," she muttered. She noticed that he had not hesitated to take the worm to bait the hook. She busied herself with her own hook.

Benjamin, thinking ahead, had asked one of the servant ladies to prepare a breakfast to carry in a basket. He and Athaliah would not go hungry. So, they could eat as they waited, poles in hand, bait on the hooks, and the strings in the water.

"Don't talk too much," Athaliah heard herself say. She couldn't help herself. "The fish shy away from unfamiliar sounds. And try to keep a low profile against the reflection in the water. Don't move too much."

"I know, I know. Leave me alone, and I will catch fish. You are the one making noise," he reprimanded.

She was his sister, and, at his age, he always had to get in the last word. The sibling rivalry seemed to be growing now that he was becoming almost as tall as she.

They were good friends, but the tension seemed to creep into their interactions of late.

Athaliah did want to have a good day with Benjamin. So, she tried to work toward that goal. She would have to take the initiative.

They sat, listening to the babbling of the water as it made its way over the rocks. It was soothing and it brought them a sense of delight. Little eddies formed in spots, which allowed the fish to rest quietly from the current.

Before long Benjamin saw his pole dip quickly. Pulling back, he set the hook and held tension on the line. He brought the line close and saw a beautiful fish at its end. This was going to be a good day. He felt it in his bones.

Athaliah took a position a little distance downstream from Benjamin and sat silently on a large stone. She was fishing, but her mind was on other things. Thoughts came to her in rapid order, producing pictures of delight in her heart. Having had no real emotional experience with young men, she wondered how her thoughts seemed to gravitate toward Daniel. Her thoughts were pleasant but disturbing at the same time. She was torn between beautiful thoughts and disturbing thoughts. It was evident to her that men now looked at her differently, for some reason. But she enjoyed thinking about them, wondering what they were like. Daniel filled her mind this day.

"Athaliah, I caught another one." Benjamin was busy pulling another fish out of the water. He now had several large fish threaded onto the holding string, which he kept in the water.

"You're not catching anything. What is wrong?" He asked.

"Don't bother me," Athaliah said. Her look added emphasis to her order. He shrugged and went back to what he was doing.

Athaliah was in another world within her mind when Benjamin whispered loudly, "Athaliah, someone is coming."

She heard him, but it didn't register. Her thoughts were pulled back to reality when she noticed movement out of the corner of her eye. Across the stream, a man came into view. She jumped, being caught off guard. Fear showed in her face as she quickly glanced at her brother, and back again, to the person standing only a few feet from her, on the opposite bank.

"Good morning, ma'am," she heard the man say. Only then did she realize who it was. Her glance softened a little, as recognition crept over her.

What was his name? She didn't have to ask that. She knew who he was. She just didn't think he would show up here.

"Daniel?" she stammered. "What are you doing here?" she said.

She couldn't believe her eyes. The two young people had not been formally introduced, and she was at a loss. Customs didn't allow for such an informal encounter between single people of the opposite sex without the express permission of the father.

"Please forgive me," Daniel said, as her shock wore off. "I don't mean to frighten you. I just wanted to say goodbye before I leave."

He stood quietly on the opposite bank. Athaliah sat, speechless. This young man had been the object of her thoughts and here he was, in the flesh, talking to her.

What should she do? Her mind raced. She sat tongue-tied until the awkwardness of the moment required her to do something. *Say something, you fool. He is looking at you.* Her mind stumbled as she tried to make a sensible utterance.

She finally blurted, "How did you…?"

At that moment she stood, her muscles reacting much faster than she realized. She lost her footing and slipped off the rock into the water, feet first. Her posterior found the bottom of the stream and stopped her fall before her head went under the water. She fought to right herself and climb out of the water, when, before she understood what was happening, Daniel was at her side, reaching for her hand. She wondered how he had gotten there so fast.

"Let me help you up," he quietly said, realizing that this was an embarrassing moment for her. He kept his composure and respectfully held his hand out until she took it.

"Do you go swimming like this often?" Daniel asked.

Athaliah was shaken, but when she heard Daniel's tender voice, all discomfort left her, and a warm sensation took its place. She allowed him to pull her out of the water onto solid ground. This was a new feeling for her. It surprised her so much that there remained no desire to do anything but look at him.

"Please, Mistress Athaliah. I didn't mean to cause you all this trouble. Please forgive me."

After a moment Athaliah reclaimed her dignity and muttered, "Not at all, it was not your fault, but mine. Just let me sit over there in the sunlight, so I can get dry." Awkward moments, such as this, were rare for her, and she felt her cheeks flush.

Daniel helped her over to where she could sit and splay her tunic. *I must keep my body covered.*

Daniel stood, looking at her from a respectful distance.

"Well, you might as well sit while I dry out," she said.

"Thank you, Miss."

Benjamin was watching from his position by the water. His expression was one of pleasant understanding.

Glancing toward Benjamin, Athaliah wanted to say, *Don't you tell anyone about this, Ben. You can't tattle to anyone.* But she held her words, her expression alone was sufficient.

106

"Don't worry," he said.

Athaliah's mind raced. How did Daniel know she was here? What could she say to him? He was so handsome…and caring. He had immediately come to her rescue. What fast reflexes he possessed. She was impressed.

Again, she said, "Why are you here? How did you know we would be here?"

Shrugging off the last question Daniel said, "I just wanted to say goodbye. I am leaving in a few days with master Joab. We will be gone several months."

"Several months," Athaliah asked. Nothing else came to her mind.

"Yes, we will be going as far as the city of Towers far beyond Persia."

"I don't know anything about that place," Athaliah confessed.

"It is on the "Silk Road" that goes to the end of the world," Daniel said.

"It goes all the way to the end of the world?"

"Yes, The City of Towers is a long way from here, but it isn't at the end of the world."

"Why is it called the Silk Road," Athaliah asked.

Daniel looked at her, not sure if she really didn't know, or if she was leading him on.

She was searching for conversation. *That was lame.*

"Merchants travel over that road, doing business with many groups of people who speak many different languages, and have strange ways of living. It is called the "Silk Road," because silk is a product that comes all the way from the end of the world and is not available here unless it is brought over by camel caravans."

"That is what my father does," Athaliah added.

"He has many workers such as I, who bring products from the East, as well as the North, West, and South."

Athaliah, not wanting to seem too knowledgeable, said, "I have heard that there is a great desert that has to be crossed in order to get to those places so far away."

"Yes, it extends far to the other side of the City of Towers," Daniel confirmed.

The conversation, though impersonal, was a means of getting to know each other. Listening, and responding, revealed subtleties of character that each was eager to learn.

"Mistress Athaliah, please forgive me for meeting you like this. I remembered you from the banquet long ago. I have wanted to meet you ever since," Daniel confessed.

Athaliah looked at him. "This is a surprise, but not an unpleasant one for me. I, too, saw you." She didn't want to say too much. He could make his own deduction. She took comfort in the knowledge that he worked for her father, so he must be in good standing.

"May I see you again, Mistress Athaliah?"

"I thought you were leaving on a trip," she said.

"Yes, I am, but there are a few days left before we must leave."

"Maybe, on our next free day, Ben and I can come fishing again. That will be next week."

"With your permission, I will be here." Having said that, he bowed toward her, and again before Benjamin, then, made himself leave. It was not his desire to do so, but he had to be prudent. In his heart, he felt pleased. Glancing back, he saw that Athaliah was watching him. *That is a good sign.*

"Ben, how many fish do you have?"

"This has been a good day. I have five fish, all of them are of good size," Benjamin answered.

"Come, then, let's go home before anyone wonders why we are so long here." She gathered up the gear she had and checked her tunic. It was dry enough that no one might suspect. If anyone should remark about it, she could always say the truth, that she fell into the water. They wouldn't need to know why. Ben must keep quiet, though.

She was pensive on the walk back home. Benjamin remained quiet as well. *What just happened?* Every move and every word of the meeting filled her thoughts. Inside, she felt an unfamiliar sensation. It felt pleasant, as though she were walking on air. She didn't dare mention this to Benjamin. He would only make fun of her. *Daniel. What a manly name.*

As they approached their home, Athaliah stopped and looked at Benjamin. "You must never tell anyone that Daniel was there today. I didn't know he was coming, but I don't want to take the chance that anyone might think I had planned it," she said.

The look on her face told Benjamin everything she was not saying.

"I won't," he promised.

In the days that followed Athaliah thought only of Daniel. There was nothing that was strong enough to keep her mind away from him. *What is the matter with me?* She wanted to know. She could not understand what was happening to her. How could she be so afraid of the way that men looked at her and at the same time want Daniel to see her? The storm of totally new, provocative emotions and feelings was so powerful that she found herself doubting her sanity. *Why am I so mixed up?*

Chara came into her room to carry out her personal chores. Athaliah had been different for several days and Chara couldn't keep from mentioning it.

"You are different, Athaliah. I am concerned. You seem to glow, but you are quiet, and I notice the change in you." She said, "What happened?"

Athaliah couldn't say anything because she didn't understand it herself. "I don't know," she blurted out at last. "I am so confused."

"You haven't been the same since I told you about that young man, Daniel. Is he the reason you are acting strange?"

"You noticed," Athaliah asked. "How could you know?"

"It isn't hard to see that your mind is far away from here. The only thing that has happened is that I told you about his desire to meet you."

"How did he know?" That was all that came out of Athaliah's mouth, as she buried her face in her hands.

"How did he know what?" Chara asked. If anything was wrong with Athaliah, she could be held accountable.

"I can't tell you."

"Athaliah, we are friends. You can tell me. Now, what do you mean by 'How did he know'?" A concerned, but worried look filled her face.

A few minutes went by, Chara made no headway in the matter. It was obvious that something was wrong.

Athaliah began to cry uncontrollably.

Seated next to her on the bed, Chara placed her arm around Athaliah's shoulders. "Come on. You don't have to cry. Just tell me all about it," she urged. Handing her a towel she said, "Here, dry your eyes."

With that Athaliah said, "I didn't know he would be there."

"Be where? Who?"

"...At the brook."

"At what brook?" Chara asked.

"I took Ben fishing the other day, and I looked up and saw someone come close on the other side of the stream. It was Daniel. He told me he only wanted to say goodbye."

"What happened that makes you cry so?" Chara nudged.

"Nothing, really, I don't know, it happened so fast. I was surprised and fell into the water. It was embarrassing. But he came over and helped me out. I don't know how he got there so fast. He was so kind, and I was a mess. He took my hand and pulled me to the dry grass. Then, he just stood, looking at me." She spat running sentences one after another, as though she had memorized every movement he had made. "But he was kind and sweet. I have never had anyone look at me like that. It turned my stomach upside-down."

"But why are you crying?" Chara asked.

"I just don't understand why I am so complicated. My feelings are like a team of wild horses, running in all directions. I can't get him out of my mind. Day and night he is the only thing I can think about. Something must be wrong with me," she cried. "I dreamed of him last night. I think I could sleep all day just so I can dream of him. I am terrible. My father is going to kill me. Please don't tell anyone what I did."

Pent-up feelings burst forth as she tried to express what was inside of her. For days she had felt the unexpressed emotions build. The tension was horrible. Now, these feelings burst out in gushes as Athaliah somehow turned them into words, surprising even herself.

"What did you do that you can't talk about?"

"Nothing." She almost screamed as the tension released itself.

"Well, all those 'wild horses' of nothing are giving you quite a ride."

"Father will kill me."

"Kill you for what? What did you do?"

"I saw a man and he was nice to me," she moaned.

"There is nothing wrong in that. Did he do anything wrong?"

"No, he was perfectly respectful – and handsome – and warm – and strong. I don't know. I just don't understand what is happening to me. He just wanted to say goodbye."

Chara looked at her with a knowing smile. "You are in love."

"How could that be? I don't even know what that means. I am too young to be in love."

"You can't get him out of your mind, right?"

"Yes."

"You can't sleep at night, thinking about him?"

"Yes."

"When you sleep, you dream of him?"

"Yes."

"You don't have an appetite?"

"Yes."

"Athaliah, you are in love." Chara laughed and squeezed her.

CHAPTER TWELVE

Smitten

Athaliah came down for breakfast the next morning, beaming. Her mother observed her for a moment.

"Child, what is wrong with you? Did you get too much sleep last night?" It was a pleasant question with no barbs in it. "You skipped in as though you have energy to spare."

"Mother, nothing is wrong. I'm just happy. Ben and I caught a lot of fish the other day, and I am thinking about taking him again on our next free day and it will be fun because I have never seen the fish like they are right now, you know, we didn't have our poles in the water any time at all, when the first one took the bait and there is nothing like the thrill of catching fish, especially if they are large," Athaliah said.

Athaliah was a bright teenager, and her mother loved the way she participated when the family was together. Obviously, the family meant a lot to her. She had always been this way. A little bit tomboyish, she filled the atmosphere with the kind of love that the family seemed to thrive on.

Her parents were very proud of her. Benjamin, of course, was the only son, and that guaranteed him a special place in the ranks, but Athaliah was charming and kind, full of life, and no one could deny it. That is what everyone loved about her. She had her bad days, like anyone else, but those were few and far between.

This day Athaliah seemed a little exaggerated. To her mother this was a good thing, so she didn't give it too much thought.

"I'm glad you like to be with your brother, Athaliah," Mara said and basked in the cheerfulness she so enjoyed in her daughter. "The two of you get along so well."

Chara looked on from where she stood, smiling silently. She was happy to see Athaliah this way. In her heart, she knew it wouldn't take the grown-ups long to put two and two together, but she would not be the one to let the secret out.

Several days passed. Athaliah dreamed of Daniel every night. One night he came to her, riding on a great white horse, its muscles powerfully exuding strength. It had a beautiful silver bridle, and a saddle made for a king. Instead of detracting from its rider, it complimented him. Together they were magnificent, moving as one. As they approached, the horse snorted, and pounded its hooves on the ground, raising clouds of dust, as the rider reined him in, stopping in front of Athaliah.

Daniel sat for a moment, looking longingly at her, then reached his hand toward her. "Come up and ride with me," he said invitingly. She accepted his invitation and was lifted onto the horse, as though she had done it a million times. Off they rode. Reaching back, he took her hands, placing them around his waist. "I don't want you to fall off the horse. Hang on."

The magnificent beast seemed to fly. With breathless speed, he raced across the fields. His movements, soft and gentle, as though he knew he carried precious cargo. He galloped with liquid grace, giving the impression that he could do so for hours on end. It was as much fun for the horse as it was for his riders.

Soon, they came to an area from which they could look over the valley below, as far as the eye could see. Daniel threw his right leg over the horse's head and dismounted, then placed his hands on Athaliah's waist, and eased her to the ground.

"Come, let's sit." He took her by the hand and led her to a rock where they talked of many things, forgetting about time.

Daniel cupped her face in his hands and looked into her eyes. Suddenly, he seemed to be thrown from her. Surprised, Athaliah struggled to understand how he could have moved so quickly. He was now in the distance, reaching out to her. She reached for him, to no avail. She awoke, almost screaming his name. "Daniel, Daniel, come back." Then, consciousness caused the scene to fade into darkness, as the morning sunlight washed over her room.

Athaliah stretched out on her bed, trying to remember each kind word Daniel had said in the dream. Unlike most dreams, this one was vivid and real. Reality and non-reality meshed into one, leaving her confused. Slowly, her mind returned her to the bedroom. It seemed so real. A heavy sense of abandonment and loss overshadowed her, like a dense fog. Why was he taken from her like that? What did it mean? In her heart, she knew Daniel was special. She didn't ever want to lose him.

"Athaliah, Athaliah." The voice forced its way into her consciousness, dragging her back to the present. It was Chara. "Breakfast is ready, and the family wants to know why you are not there," she said.

Forcing herself to move, Athaliah gathered her thoughts, put on a garment, and pushed past Chara on her way out of her room. *Why do I feel so strange?* As she made her way down to the waiting family, the strange sense of loss hung heavily over her. It seemed so real.

"There's my beautiful flower at last," Obed stated when she entered the room. "You look like a ghost has gotten you. Why are you so pale?"

Taking her place at the table, Athaliah buried her head in her hands and sat silently. Finally, taking a heavy breath, she shook herself and forced a pleasant smile. She heard her father's questions but opted not to answer right away.

"I am fine, Father," she said finally. "I just had a bad dream."

"Well, let's enjoy this new day. There is a lot to do, and I want to spend this time with the whole family," her father said warmly.

Fruit in abundance sat before them, waiting to be selected and consumed. Mother said a short prayer, invoking the Almighty's blessing, and expressed the family's gratitude. Then, she called the servants to bring the other elements of their breakfast.

"How are your classes going these days, my Little Ones?" Obed asked, looking at his two teens. He couldn't consider them children anymore and lamented how fast time had passed. It seemed to him that the only way he could understand the passage of time was by observing the changes in them.

Benjamin spoke up. "Must we talk about that, Father?"

Athaliah sat silently. Heaviness filled her heart. Try as she might, she felt no desire to participate.

"Benjamin, your education is important. Life sets before you, and you must take it by the horns. I am offering you the best education possible, so you can one

114

day help me in the business. I won't be around forever, you know," he said, looking Benjamin squarely in the eye.

"I am eager to help you, Father," Benjamin assured him. "I can't wait to grow up."

"You will, Benjamin, but in the meantime, you must apply yourself and learn. It is a privilege to enjoy the things we have, but it takes work. You can do it, I know. The family will stick together and see many good days."

"Athaliah, what is wrong," her mother inquired. "Why don't you speak? Look, you aren't eating, either."

"I don't know. It is just a feeling that came over me," she said evasively. "I know it will pass."

But she couldn't shake it. *Why does it seem so real?*

"Yes, Athaliah. I have news to share with you and the family. You have become of age, and I am looking for a good husband for you," Obed announced.

So, this is what father wanted to say. Why today of all days? Now, I will never shake this feeling. I don't want to be married to someone I don't know. Father can't make me do that." Her emotions took over, and she ran from the table in tears.

"What brought that on," her father asked. "I am looking out for her wellbeing. She must understand this. Doesn't she know that I want the best for her? She will be a good wife and mother. I know it."

He had no way of knowing the thoughts in her heart. Athaliah had just met a young man she felt she could love. *This can't be happening to me.*

"Go after her," Obed ordered, looking at Mara. "Talk some sense into her."

Running up to Athaliah's room, her mother rushed in to console her. "My little one, what is wrong. You knew that this day would come. Your father loves you as he does no one else. He wants you to be happy. This is the stuff of life. You must understand.

"Your father has set aside a great dowry for you. And, besides, he has given you an education, so you can be the best wife and mother possible. We know you. You have so much to give. Please don't fight him on this," she pleaded.

"Mother, I just can't think about this now. What if I have some ideas of my own? I want to marry for love, not to be some man's possession."

"Honey, you don't know what love is, yet. We have the best understanding of what you need to be happy. Children don't know what life brings, but we do. You will understand with time, but please let your father do what he knows is best."

"I am not a child. I have feelings. I do know my own heart. How can father know what I feel, or want?"

"Life consists of much more than feelings, Little One," her mother said, gathering Athaliah in her arms. "There is much that you have not experienced. This is why you must trust your father to do the right thing."

Athaliah's heart ached. How could love and "the right thing" be so painful? They seemed so extreme and opposed to her. There must be something she could do.

"Mother, may I be alone for a while?"

"Yes, my Love." Her mother stood. At the door, she turned to look at her daughter, tenderly. "I love you. Your father loves you. This you will understand in time."

Alone, Athaliah lost herself in thought. *I must do something*, she concluded. A plan began to form within her heart.

CHAPTER THIRTEEN

Unexpected

Athaliah awoke from a dream. It was still vivid in her mind. Daniel had again come to her. They sat by the stream, where they first talked and held hands.

Why did I wake up? I didn't want to stop dreaming.

This was the day. She planned to go fishing with Benjamin. Daniel was to meet her by the stream. Knowing that she could not go alone, she would make the best of this opportunity. *I hope Daniel doesn't forget to be there.* The thought of his name warmed her heart. *He has such a manly name*, she thought.

Gathering her things, she ran to Benjamin's door. "Come my brother, we must go fishing. We must get an early start." She hoped her insistence didn't arouse suspicion.

She must not seem too eager to leave the house.

"Okay, Athaliah," he said, as he pulled himself out of bed. "Just a moment, I am coming."

Hurriedly they gathered what they needed for the day. Their mother insisted they take time to eat something. Finally, saying goodbye to their mother and the servants in the kitchen, they headed out confidently. Athaliah brought a lunch, which she intended to share with Daniel. It would be several hours before he arrived, but she wanted to be ready. The sun was still low but climbing in the sky. Ben was a willing accomplice. He saw no harm in helping Athaliah see her new friend. It would be a harmless encounter.

He only wished he had a girlfriend to be with at the same time. After all, Daniel was leaving shortly on a long journey, and Athaliah would not see him for a long time.

A distance down the path, Benjamin stopped. "Athaliah, I forgot something. We must go back and get it."

"No, Ben, we are almost to the stream. I don't want to go back home. You go, and I will wait for you there. I will be alright. Go quickly."

This seemed logical to Benjamin. He turned and scampered toward home. "I will be right back," he shouted over his shoulder, disappearing as he ran.

Athaliah turned her thoughts to Daniel. He would be there soon. She knew it. She continued confidently. Arriving at the creek bank, she set her basket on a large rock and chose a place to wait. Pleasant thoughts ran through her mind as she contemplated Daniel's arrival.

This will be a good day.

She sat, thinking of Daniel when she heard movement behind her. As she turned, a cloth was quickly placed over her head, and she was thrown to the ground. This was so unexpected that she had no time to defend herself. What happened next became a blur.

What was happening? Why is he hurting me? She tried to scream but was struck across the face. She heard a strange voice ordering her to be silent, or she would not live long. Everything went black.

She awoke. *How did I get in my own bed? What is happening? Why do I feel so much pain all over my body?*

"Don't move, my Love," her mother whispered. "I am with you. I will take care of you."

Athaliah burst into tears. "There, there, my Love, don't cry. I am here," Mara consoled, tenderly. I am so happy you are alive."

"What happened, how long have I been asleep? Why am I in bed?" Athaliah asked at length, trying to gather her senses.

"You were hurt. Don't you remember anything?"

"No. I don't."

"You have been asleep for two weeks. We worried you would not come back to us," her mother said, eyes filling with tears.

Mara looked at Chara, "Go get the master," she said. "He will want to see Athaliah."

Word spread to all in the household, at once. Athaliah was awake. A flurry of conversations could be heard. Some spoke in whispers and others loudly.

Obed came at once. Rushing into the room, he took Athaliah in his arms, and wept. She had never seen her father cry and couldn't understand why he did so now. It seemed ages before he released her and looked into her eyes.

"My Little One, we thought we had lost you. The doctor told us that you may not come back," he sputtered.

"Why, I was just asleep, right?"

"My little one, now isn't the time to talk. We will tell you what we know, but you need to rest. You have been badly hurt." He held her hand and didn't want to let go. "Just rest for a while and get better, Honey."

Benjamin stood in the corner watching sheepishly. "This is my fault," he muttered quietly. "I should never have left her alone. What was I thinking?" Tears rolled from his eyes.

His father had accused him of endangering his sister by leaving her alone. "You should have known that you were charged with her safety," his father had said, heatedly. The reaction was swift and mindless, spoken through emotions that were raw and seeking release. The words hit the boy's heart like a lance. In the days that ensued, his father had come to Benjamin to express remorse for having spoken so harshly, but Benjamin felt the words ruminating around and around in his mind.

My father hates me. Now, as he looked at his sister in his father's arms, no words could express the loss that saturated his heart. Would she ever be the same again? Would his father ever love him as he did before? *I hate myself. I should have known better. It would have been better had I not been born.* Benjamin never needed anyone to tell him when he was wrong; he always knew it. His response to every difficult situation was to chastise himself before anyone could have the opportunity to do it. He longed to be the son his father and mother wanted, and this caused him to obey them at all costs. But he was a young man who, at times, didn't think beyond his immediate situation, if he was intensely focused. This had caused him trouble in the past. But this situation was unbearable. He had not seen the possibility of danger. He would not ever forgive himself for his lack of judgment.

His father turned to look at him. "Come, my son. Let your sister know that you love her." Not feeling inclined to do so, he held back.

He stood in place. *I can't go to her. She must hate me for what I did. When she needed me, I wasn't there.*

"Come, son," his father insisted.

With hesitant steps, he obediently approached the bed. Tears flowed from his eyes. Anguish overcame him, and he could not speak.

Athaliah had never seen Benjamin react to anything in this manner. Reaching for him, she took his hands. "Don't cry, Ben. I will get better."

No one understood the thoughts that raced through his mind. He had no words, only tears.

His mother came to him and enveloped him in her arms, "Come, son, I will hold you," she whispered, consoling him as best she could.

I can't stand here and cry. He bolted from the room. *Just run. Get away from the pain. They will hate me when they find out what I did.*

He climbed a tree in the backyard. *I feel safe here. I can look out and see what everyone is doing. I am safe here. At least they can't see me like this.*

Thoughts of condemnation, and self-loathing spread over him, as floodwaters cover the dry desert in springtime, each rush bringing brown mud gathered along the way, leaving him covered in emotional sediment, threatening to drown him with every tossing current.

"Benjamin, Benjamin, where are you. You must not act like this," his father shouted.

Approaching the tree, he looked through its branches and saw his son. "Benjamin, I know I was hard on you when I learned what had happened. I am sorry I reacted that way. I should not have said the things I said. I was afraid we would lose Athaliah."

"I am going to stand here until you come down. Please come down," his father pleaded.

"I know everyone hates me," Benjamin blurted.

"Come down, son, let's talk about this. You are not in trouble. Please, come down and tell me what is going on."

Slowly, he obeyed. Once on the ground, his father put his arms around him and led him to his room. "Here, sit on the bed, and tell me what you are thinking."

"It is my fault," Benjamin cried. "I did it. If I had been there, nothing would have happened to Athaliah. I meant to take care of her, but I didn't." Sobs came fast and his words blurred.

"Son, you did what you could. Even I would have had a difficult time carrying your sister back to the house."

"But…"

"But what?" Obed said, patiently.

Words would not come out, as though each sound stuck to his throat, choking him. "But you don't understand. I knew he was coming." Benjamin cried uncontrollably.

"What do you mean, son? Who was coming?"

"I knew he was coming."

"Let it out, son. Who was coming?"

"Daniel," Benjamin whispered. Guilt swept over him, as he uttered the name. "I should have been there, and then Athaliah would not have been hurt."

"How did you know Daniel would be there?"

"I knew, because Athaliah asked me to go with her, so she wouldn't be alone." He wanted to talk with Athaliah before he left for his journey.

"When she and I left home after breakfast, I remembered something I had left at the house. Athaliah told me to go back and get it. She would go on ahead and get set up. When I got back to the creek, I found her there. Blood was everywhere, and she would not wake up. I don't remember how I did it, but I brought her back home as fast as I could. I'm glad the sun wasn't at its highest. It would have been much hotter, and more difficult."

Controlling his anger, Obed said, "You will feel better now, son. Rest tonight and you will be better tomorrow."

121

Leaving Benjamin's room, Obed struggled with what he had learned. "I will kill that young man. No one can touch my daughter and get away with it."

"Mother, Mother, come." He called Mara and waited for her in their bedroom.

"Yes, Obed, what do you want?" she asked, entering the room.

"He did it! That young man hurt our daughter."

"Which young man are you talking about?

"It was Daniel who hurt Athaliah. Benjamin just told me that Daniel asked him to set up the meeting, so he could see Athaliah."

"But how did he know Benjamin?"

"I will find out; you can be sure of that."

CHAPTER FOURTEEN

Trauma

"How could this young man dare to meet with my daughter without my knowledge and consent? He had no right to do such a thing." The more Master Haddad thought of it, the angrier he grew.

Turmoil such as he had never felt washed over him. He was a respected businessman who had great influence within the community. He would put a swift end to that young man. *I must get justice and my just revenge. He will pay for his crime.*

Later, unable to sleep, he quietly left his bed so as not to awaken his Mara.

Making his way to the garden to sit under the stars, he notified the night watchman to have some cool wine brought out to him. It was always easier to think out there. A cool breeze wafted through the trees, making the night tolerable after an exceptionally hot summer day.

He enumerated the facts as he understood them:

Firstly, the midwife told them Athaliah had been badly beaten. That part was obvious. The swelling and bruising around her eyes and nose indicated that.

Secondly, she was savagely violated.

Third, the midwife didn't know when she would awaken.

Fourth, something must have triggered this self-preservation response.

Fifth, they were told that in cases like this, all they could do was wait and hope for the best.

Sixth, when Athaliah returned to consciousness, she could remember nothing.

These facts revealed a terrible trauma. He could only imagine the worst. His thoughts fed on themselves, fueling rage within him.

He pictured the young man touching his daughter and vowed he would pay for what he did. Long into the night his thoughts turned and churned within him, refusing him slumber. At last, in the wee hours of the morning, he lapsed into a fitful sleep.

The Roman General started his day by ordering roll call and barking orders to be passed down through the ranks. His men knew him as a hard, but just, soldier. Their respect was shown in the way they spoke of him among themselves, but murmurings were not completely unknown to them. Life was not easy for the rank-and-file soldier, and grumbling was a part of the daily "grind." Despite this, the General held his men together with an iron fist and tact that rivaled that of any popular politician.

"Permission to enter, Sir," the duty sergeant asked, as he stepped to the General's office door. "Begging your pardon Sir, there is a gentleman here requesting an audience with you. His name is Obed Haddad."

"Yes, show him in."

"General. Good day. Please forgive my intrusion. I have a request of you."

The days that followed passed slowly. "My Love, why must you cry so?" Mara asked. "You are adding to your pain."

Athaliah cried almost continually and was depressed.

"You must eat. Why don't you eat?"

"I simply can't eat. I don't know why. All I can do is cry. That's all." Something deep within her heart poured out in tears. She had no memory of the event that put her bed and had no idea of the extent of her condition. Her tears caused her head to ache, but nothing would stop them. Trauma ruled her every waking hour.

The family, and servants alike, went about their days in agony because of the situation none thought could ever happen in this house. Athaliah was everyone's pride and joy. Her pain was their pain.

Chara never left her bedside. She was so attentive that Athaliah's mother commented on her faithfulness. She even made a pallet on the floor, so she could sleep there and take care of Athaliah when she awoke screaming in panic. Unspoken was the pain Chara battled with.

I must take care of Athaliah. This is my fault. All she could think was that she had introduced Daniel to Athaliah. *I can't leave her side. Maybe in this way, I can repay her for this pain.* She was overcome with guilt.

Try as she might, Mara could not get Athaliah to eat. "I'm not hungry, Mother," she said each time.

"You must eat, my Love, or you will not get better." Concern grew into fear for her daughter. Day after day was the same.

A pall fell over the household. Hopelessness permeated the atmosphere. Everyone went about their duties with a conspicuous lack of positivity. Powerless to avoid or deny it, they simply trudged through their days.

"Poor little Athaliah will never be the same," they said. "Her life is changed forever."

Benjamin suffered in his own way, becoming silent and withdrawn. All attention was on Athaliah, which added to his desolation.

He wondered if the family would ever return to normal. He knew that he wouldn't. Life had taken a turn, thrusting him into adulthood prematurely.

If I feel this way, what must Athaliah feel? The burden he carried left him saddened beyond belief.

Master Haddad carried on with his responsibilities, attempting to cover his pain.

I can't let the family know what I am thinking. *I must be strong for them*, he reminded himself time and time again.

Mrs. Haddad sought solace, so she could cry out of the view of the family and servants.

Days passed into weeks and weeks into months. One day, Athaliah turned to Chara and said, "I think I could drink a little beef broth. I can smell it from the kitchen."

As fast as her feet would carry her, Chara ran to the kitchen and announced, "Athaliah has asked for broth. Hurry, let's get it to her."

Returning to the bedroom, she placed a bowl of broth before Athaliah. "Here, let me feed it to you. You may be too weak to hold the spoon without spilling it," she offered.

Without another word, she ladled a spoonful to Athaliah's mouth, being sure to cool it a little. "Now, isn't that good?" She whispered. Athaliah looked at her, wanting more.

"Now, be careful. You haven't had anything for some time, and your body will have to become used to it again," Chara cautioned.

At that moment Mara ran into the room. "They told me the good news. I am so glad you are hungry," she gasped, as she recouped her breath from her sudden burst of action. "This is a good day."

But, alas, her optimism was premature. Athaliah vomited what she had eaten. Chara quickly gathered the bedding and exchanged it for fresh sheets.

Their hopes faded as they worked to clean up the mess. Athaliah leaned back on her pillows and closed her eyes. "I can't eat any more right now," she whispered.

One month turned into two. The little food Athaliah was able to take in and keep down, was minimal. The family worried. She was so thin.

One morning, Chara entered Athaliah's room. She was unconscious. Something was wrong. Pulling back the covers, she saw blood. She quickly suppressed a scream by covering her mouth.

Running down the hall, she cried, "Mrs. Haddad, please come, something is wrong with Athaliah. Please hurry."

Together, they returned to the room. Mara turned the covers back to see. "Call the midwife, please," she shouted.

Athaliah lay with her eyes closed, quietly moaning, in an unconscious state.

Shortly, the midwife arrived, out of breath. "I came as soon as I heard. Let's look. Please bring some warm, clean water. Thank you."

She proceeded to clean the area of bleeding so she could see exactly what had happened. Unable to control her reaction, she froze in place. "Everyone out of the room except you, Mrs. Haddad," she ordered.

As the last person left, speaking in low tones so that Athaliah couldn't hear, she said, "She was with child."

"You mean—, what are you saying?" Mara muttered in unbelief.

"Yes, she was pregnant."

"My God," Mara cried. "How can this be? Are you sure? Why do you say she *was* pregnant?" Then understanding hit her. "I can't believe this. My little girl…"

Taking Athaliah's hand, the midwife said, "The poor girl obviously hasn't been able to really eat for some time. Her body is too weak to carry a baby. This is nature's way of protecting her. I am sorry. She just couldn't feed the baby sufficiently. In cases like this, the baby will always take what it needs, but the mother also needs sustenance. It was just aborted. This indicates the severity of the child's condition."

"This must be kept quiet," Mara said. "No one must know. Should the truth get around, no man will want her for a wife. My husband and I were planning her coming of age party. Now it is impossible. This changes everything. We must protect her."

The new reality hit her hard. She loved her daughter, but she knew that others could be vicious. Athaliah would be seen as damaged. Good men, and even not-so-good men, want to marry virgins. Though she was young, the customs of the day demanded parents to find a husband for their daughter who would provide for her throughout her life or keep her forever in their care.

"You must make sure she eats. She was feeding two, without success," the midwife said. "Now, it is even more important that she eats, or she will not survive."

Mara and Obed had deliberately stayed away from any thought of pregnancy. Now, the unthinkable was confirmed. The truth must be hidden.

Mara's reactions ran wild. *No mother wants to live through anything like this. It is a nightmare.* The family's reality was now forever changed. New considerations must now be explored. Shame would be their lot, if not handled properly.

Standing just outside Athaliah's bedroom door, Chara overheard what was said and ran to her own room, closing herself in. A sense of danger flooded her being. Guilt had been her constant companion from the moment Athaliah was brought to the house, but this pushed her over the edge.

"This is my fault," she cried into her pillow. "I am to blame. I can't carry my secret any longer," she gushed, guilt fueling her pain.

She knew the only thing she could do was to tell Master Haddad, as difficult as it might seem.

Resolved to do the right thing, Chara went to Mr. Haddad.

"Master, do you have a moment?" She asked. As soon as the words were out of her mouth, she broke into tears.

"Come in, Chara. What's wrong?"

She stood, silent.

"Girl, you are white. What is wrong?" her master insisted.

When no words came, he went to her and helped her to a chair. "Sit here. I know these weeks have been worrisome for you. Look at the way you have stayed by my Athaliah day and night, you must be absolutely worn out." He suspected she struggled because Athaliah had not gotten better.

"No, Master. Please don't be nice to me. All of this is my fault. I am so ashamed. You can beat me. I'm sorry." Again, tears overtook her and she hid her head in her hands.

"How can this be your fault? What are you talking about?"

"I didn't know things would turn out like this."

"Take a breath. Slowly tell me what you mean, Chara."

"I was the one who told Athaliah about Daniel," she cried.

"You?"

"Yes."

"How did you know that young man?" He could not bring himself to use his name.

"I met him one day at the market." Her emotions overtook her once again, robbing her of the ability to speak.

"Let's take this slowly. Start from the beginning and tell me everything."

"I walked to the tutor's home with Athaliah, as we normally do." She hesitated

128

for a moment and continued slowly.

"When we got to the house, I asked her if it would be alright to visit my aunt at the marketplace for a little while."

Once again, she hesitated to clear her mind. "I went to the market and spent a while talking with my aunt. I noticed someone looking at me from across the plaza.

"When I looked at him, he hid his face. But then, he came over to where I was and asked if I was the young lady who lived at Master Haddad's house. He had seen me as I helped serve the guests at a banquet you gave, long ago."

Obed frowned. "Go on."

"I remembered him. He sat at your table. He asked me about Athaliah and said he would like to meet her. I thought about it, and concluded that if he worked for you, he must be of good character, so I said I would see if she might be interested in meeting him."

Her words came easier now, and she continued. "On the way home, I told Athaliah about him. I told her he was interested in meeting her. She was interested in him as well. She had seen him at the banquet, and thought he was handsome, and gallant."

"Did you see him again," Master Haddad said.

"Not until the day Athaliah was hurt. I knew she was going fishing with Benjamin, so I asked her permission to see my aunt again. When I got to the marketplace my aunt was talking with him. She said he had been there for a while, speaking with her."

Chara lowered her head for a moment, took a breath, and continued.

"He confided in me that he had seen Athaliah when she was fishing with Benjamin a few days earlier. He said he and she made plans to meet that very day when the sun was at its highest. He said Athaliah was going to bring a lunch for them."

Master Haddad looked at her, "Say that again. When was he speaking with you?"

"It must have been about the third or fourth hour before the heat of the day sat in."

Master Haddad sat for a moment without saying anything further. His countenance turned pale. "My God, what have I done?" He stood, and rushed out, leaving her there to wonder what had just happened.

CHAPTER 15

The Secret

Chara stood silent, not understanding why she was left alone. "He will have me killed for sure," she muttered.

Returning to Athaliah's room, she resumed her duties. Shortly after entering the room, Athaliah returned to consciousness.

"How are you feeling, Athaliah?"

"I am trying to understand what is happening."

"Didn't anyone tell you what happened?" Making sure the door was closed, Chara took Athaliah's hand.

"I just spoke with your father. I told him this is my fault," she confessed.

"No. I can't remember anything. But, why do you say it is your fault?" Athaliah said, surprised.

"...Because I introduced you to him," she said, in a whisper.

"Who are you talking about?"

"Daniel," Chara whispered.

"That wasn't your fault; I wanted to meet him," Athaliah insisted. "I can't remember anything after what happened to me, but I can remember that."

"But look at what happened to you. I should have never consented to his meeting you."

"You mustn't say that. No one knows what happened. I didn't know him that well, but I can't believe he would hurt me."

"All of the evidence points to him, Athaliah."

"Why don't I remember anything, though? I try, but no matter what I conjure in my mind I can't remember a thing that happened at the creek. I can remember leaving the house with Ben, I remember walking alone, I remember thinking about Daniel, but everything is blank from that moment."

Chara made a quick run to the kitchen for some soup. "Maybe Athaliah can keep something down this time. She needs strength," she said to the cook.

Mara saw her and pulled her aside. "Come, my dear, we must talk."

"Yes, my Lady," following obediently.

"Athaliah can't remember anything. That means that she also doesn't know what just happened, or why. We must keep it that way. You haven't told her, have you?"

"No, my Lady, I haven't."

"Good. This can never be told to anyone. Do you understand?"

"Yes, my Lady. You can rely on me," she answered, not understanding the full reasoning behind the order.

Weeks passed. Athaliah began gaining strength, with Chara at her side. They looked at each other as sisters and were inseparable.

"Athaliah, what do you think? Would you like to try walking around a little?

"I could try," Athaliah said. Chara helped her out of the bed, and they walked across the room. "That was good, can you do more?"

"I think I could try going out to the hall," Athaliah said, her eyes looking brighter.

Her appetite returned slowly. Each day, they noticed changes in her abilities. Months had passed since the tragedy. Master Haddad was silent. He threw himself into his work, ignoring all else, but made sure to spend time with Athaliah each day. He and his wife spoke little. At night they simply said, good night, and turned away from each other. In this way a distance had grown between them.

"My dear, we can't go on like this," he said one night.

"What do you mean?

"We can't ignore each other. We could not have known this would happen. I admit I didn't react well. I don't think any father would, in a case like this," he said.

"Come here," he said, as he gathered her into his massive arms.

"I know you are hurting," he continued. "We mustn't lose each other now, not this way. I know. I am hurting, but I haven't stopped to think of how much you must be affected. I am sorry for not being here to help you through the process that has affected us all.""I want things to be better. Really, I do," she whispered. "What do you think we should do?"

"We can talk about it. Athaliah doesn't remember anything, but something did happen. I have heard rumors fluttering around the house like little birds. Some of the servants wonder why Athaliah has been so long recuperating. When I walk through the house, I sometimes hear them speaking. They become quiet as I approach. I heard what a couple of them said, and we can't assume that we can keep this secret locked away forever."

"What did they say," she asked.

"We must be careful not to give the impression that anything, other than being beaten up and severely hurt, was the cause of her illness. No one can know of the baby. I don't think Chara will ever tell anyone what she knows."

"But what did the servants say," she persisted.

"I heard the kitchen servants say that there must be more to the story. They were whispering, but I was able to hear that much. We don't want her to grow up and not have a life, do we? I have been thinking that, if a man were to be willing to help her, she could get over this."

"What are you saying?" She searched his eyes.

"What if I found someone of means to marry her?"

"But she is so young. Who would do that?"

"Yes, young, but this is not uncommon, even though it may seem so to us, as her parents. There may be someone. We must think of her. As things are now, people will become suspicious. Everyone knows she is ill, but they must not know why.

"If they knew, she would become a reproach. People won't care if it was her fault or not, she would be damaged in their eyes." His passion and fear manifested themselves as he spoke.

"I need to protect her," Mara said. "I am her mother. No one can love her as I do."

"You know I love her too, but we must consider what is best for her in society as well."

Tightening his arms around his wife, he held her close. "This is not how I thought our lives would be," he confided.

She cuddled in his arms without uttering a word. Conflicting thoughts chased one another through her mind. Much later, slumber replaced these thoughts and she fell into a troubled sleep.

CHAPTER SIXTEEN

Great Darkness

The morning after Abel left Athaliah on her wedding night, movement was detected only by mid-morning. A few of the servants were up and around, as was their duty. Obed had not slept at all. Mara stayed the night by Athaliah's side, trying to console her, to no avail. Their energy spent; they simply lay upon the bed in an exhausted stupor.

No one wanted to face the day. The whole household wanted the tragic event of the evening to just go away, like a cruel dream. But it wouldn't.

Abel ran from the house in a rage. Some of his attendants left with him. As they walked toward his father's house, conversation erupted.

"I will make them pay for what they did!" he shouted.

His companions could not understand his reaction and voiced their concern.

"Why are you doing this? She is the love of your life. What happened?"

"I found out the truth. She was unfaithful to me!" he said, stamping his feet. "No one does this to me and gets away with it!"

Arriving at his home, he dismissed his friends. "I need time to think. Go home. I can't speak any longer." Turning to enter the house, he said, "I will make them pay!"

Master Jacob arrived home with his family in tow. Confusion covered them like a dense fog. They found Abel sitting in the family area with his head in his hands.

"Son, tell us what happened," his father said.

"It is simple. She was unfaithful to me. She has been with a man. Maybe, she has been with many men. I don't know. All I know is that she brought a small bottle into our bedchamber, with the intent to deceive me into believing I was the first! But I found out in time to put an end to her plan. Can you believe it? She tried to make me believe that she was innocent!"

"My dear, I am so sorry," Sebeka said, moving to his side. "After all the planning you have done. I, too, am astonished and upset as you, my son."

"I will find a way to make them pay for this!" His anger was inconsolable, though his parents tried to comfort him.

"We will do the right thing to clear our name, son. You can be sure of this," his father said.

Athaliah awoke with a headache. It seemed everything hurt. Turning over in bed, she looked at her mother, who was still groggy.

"Mother, you slept here?" She asked, rhetorically.

"Yes, my love, I couldn't think of leaving you alone after such a shock." She reached over and gathered Athaliah in her arms. "I love you, my dear. I am sorry this has happened to you."

"I thought he loved me, mother. How could he do this to me?" Tears once again filled her eyes as she relived the horror she felt when he called her that ugly name. *Why had he called me a harlot?*

"He didn't give me a chance to speak. Not a word," she cried. "This hurts so much. I can't bear it."

Mara let her cry in her arms. What could she say that would take away the pain that still had its invasive clutches around Athaliah's heart?

"My dear, cry as long as you want. Let it wash all of the pain away. You will see that life will continue – not the same, but it will continue, and you will get over this."

"No, I will never be the same again! I don't want to be the same. I thought he loved me enough to at least listen to me. I have done nothing wrong. Obviously, there must be something I don't know." She fell quiet in thought. Sleep eluded her.

It must have to do with why she was sick for so long. Her parents had not told her any details. Now, she wondered what could have caused her mother to insist on her bringing the bottle to the chamber-bed. There were so many unanswered questions. Who attacked her at the creek? Why would someone do such a thing? Why was she so sick? Why couldn't she remember anything? What did her parents know? Did Chara know anything? What did her father know? What did Benjamin know? Everyone was suspect. *I must know what happened to me!*

"My dear, I will ask Chara to bring you some breakfast. You need to eat something to keep up your strength," Mara said.

"No, Mother. I am not hungry. I am full of questions."

"Oh, Honey, don't worry yourself with questions right now. You have suffered a great shock. Let your heart rest a little while before trying to bring up things that could only hurt you."

"What do you mean, 'things that could only hurt' me? What do you know that will hurt me?" She demanded. "What hurts me more, at the moment, is that I don't know what happened to me!"

"No, don't talk that way. You don't want more pain, do you?"

"No, I don't want more pain, but I want to know the truth. "Nothing is as painful as not knowing, mother!"

"You can't take any more truth for a while, my dear."

"Mother, I am not a little girl. Here I sit, wondering why and how my life has come to this. I have been humiliated in the cruelest of ways! I thought this was to be the happiest day of my life, only that dream was shattered with one tragic word. Mother, you must tell me what you know!"

"My dear, I can't right now." She hedged as much as she could but saw that Athaliah was becoming resolute in her insistence.

"I will send Chara in to be with you while I see to other matters. We will speak later."

Alone in her room, Athaliah lay silently fuming. Questions turned to the darkness of heart. *I will find out the truth, or I will never trust anyone again in my life. I vow I will never love anyone again. It hurts too much, if this is what love does.* Her thoughts came fast and jumbled. She felt an unknown sense of resolve overtake her. The deeper her thoughts, the worse she felt, yet her thoughts were strangely soothing. Anger arose from a deep chasm within her soul that she had previously not known to exist. She felt warm, as though cuddled in a cocoon of her own making. A seed came to life and spread its roots through her heart; unseen tentacles, intent on holding her captive to their subtle influences. "I will never allow anyone to humiliate me like this again." She said under her breath, not caring if anyone heard her.

PART III

CHAPTER SEVENTEEN

Unleashed Reactions

Chara gently opened the door and entered. The look on Athaliah's face shouted trouble. Crossing the room, Chara sat on the side of the bed and reached over to place her hand on Athaliah's shoulder.

"I am so sorry, Athaliah."

"What do you know, Chara?" Athaliah hissed.

"This has been difficult for all of us. I couldn't sleep, and I know you couldn't either," Chara whispered. "Can you tell me what happened last night?"

"Don't change this to be about me. I want to know what everyone else knows. And I want to know now."

"What do you mean?"

"I mean, what happened to me at the creek? Everything seems to have changed. My life hasn't been the same since that day at the creek."

"Why do you snap at me?" Chara knew she couldn't divulge anything. Her orders were to remain silent. Master Haddad would have her head if she told anyone what she knew, especially Athaliah.

"Athaliah, I love you like a sister. No one means as much to me as you do. I can't tell you what you want to hear."

"Yes, you can, and you will."

"No, I can't. No one knows what happened to you at the creek," she said truthfully. *She did say creek*, putting her response in the right context.

"I feel so humiliated." Athaliah sputtered. "How can I ever live this down? There is something no one is telling me."

"Athaliah, tell me what happened last night."

"Everything was going so well. He was tender and loving, and then, he heard that little vile fall to the floor, and he called me a harlot." The very thought of it caused her to cry again. This memory would haunt her for the rest of her life.

"I am not a harlot. I have never been with a man in all my life. Why would he say such a thing?"

"You know you are not that. I know you are not that," she said, not wanting to use the word. "It seems to me, that it should help to know that you were falsely accused," Chara said, in a soothing tone.

"It doesn't." The anguish she felt allowed anger to surge. "I want to know what you know. I insist, Chara. What happened to me? If you don't tell me, I will order you out of my house."

Chara didn't expect this. Apprehension and fear showing in her eyes, she said, "No, you couldn't. We are sisters."

"Yes, I can." Athaliah screamed at the top of her lungs. "Mother, come to me." She refused to be calmed until her mother came running.

"Mother, get her out of here. I don't want to see her face again—ever."

Mara looked at Chara knowingly. With a motion of the head, she told her to leave the room. "I will take care of this," she said.

Chara's head drooped and she made her way out of the room. Her emotions were scattered, and raw. She was, obviously, going to take the heat for the pain Athaliah was feeling. *If I must, I will.* Running to her room, she fell on her bed and cried.

Days passed, and the household was troubled by Athaliah's outbursts. Try as they might, her parents were unable to reason with her.

"It is as though darkness has fallen over us," Mara said, as she climbed into bed beside Obed. "I am at my wit's end. I no longer feel I can reach Athaliah. She refuses to respond to reason—of any kind."

"My dear, this is truly unfortunate. She has always been the sweetest person in our lives. No one could have asked for a better daughter. We must find a solution for her. I think we have been worried about our own reputation, instead of hers. The pain she feels is real. I have had time to ponder and think this is true: the unknown has become a slave master in her life. She has been drawn into great darkness and sees no escape. We must find a way to let her know. Then, she will understand."

"Yes, but what will we do if she doesn't?"

"It couldn't be worse than what we live with now. We can't go on like this."

A few days later, Master Haddad asked his housekeeper to bring Chara to his office. She arrived cautiously, hesitating in the doorway.

"Come in, my dear. Sit over here if you would."

Chara saw something in his face that she had never seen before. He was such a confident man in all his dealings, but his face belied his consternation.

"Chara, we have always treated you well, haven't we?"

His expression revealed unspoken pain. "I think it might be a good idea for you not to see Athaliah for a while. She is so angry that she might do something we will all regret."

Chara looked at him, troubled. "Master, you know what is best. I will do whatever you say."

"I know it seems Athaliah is putting all the blame on you because you are the easiest target. The fact is that she is furious with the whole household."

"Chara," he said, "Perhaps... Perhaps, it would be better if you went away for a while."

She didn't see this coming. To stay away from Athaliah for a while was conceivable, but to leave the house had not occurred to her.

"You are such a good worker, but I know this is difficult for you. We don't want you to suffer right along with Athaliah, for something you had no control over. There are no evildoers here, only victims. You have served us faithfully, and for that we are grateful. You and Athaliah have become close, but now she seems unable to place the bulk of the blame on anyone, but you. This makes me most sad."

Chara looked up at her master, as the realization of what he was saying sank in.

"Oh, Master, I must stay on here. What will my father do? He still owes you a great debt. I must stay and work it off, as agreed. Please, Sir."

"We must work this through. Athaliah may never be the same. But there is no reason you must be any more hurt than you have been."

Chara cried, as thoughts of abandonment overcame her. "I have come to love your family. What will you do if I am not here?"

"Come now, my dear, you have a life with your family. You will be much better with them. They will love to have you nearby. You will see."

How could things change so drastically, in such short time? Chara's thoughts scrambled within her head, leaving her confused and bewildered.

Master Haddad had not foreseen this reaction in her. Any child would jump at the chance to be with their own people.

"This is what we will do. I will take care of any financial dealings with your father, so you must not concern yourself with that. I have arranged for one of our workers to accompany you to your aunt's home. She can decide for you from there. I will send financial compensation with you for any inconvenience along the way."

Unable to do anything else, she said, "Yes, master."

The following days became unbearable. Realizing that Chara no longer came to her aid, Athaliah became more abhorrent to anyone approaching her. She allowed no attempt to console her. Conflicted within, she refused to admit her own complicity and became her own worst enemy. Her heart would not accept that, however. Blame was placed upon her parents for not having told her what she longed to know.

"Why can't you tell me the truth," she screamed.

Chara was her only friend, but she was no longer within the household. "Why did you send her away?" she demanded to know of her father.

For days he attempted to reason with her but couldn't. "My dear, you have been through so much. Why can't you simply trust us? We love you."

"No. If you loved me, you would trust me with the truth. I hate you. I hate all of you. Look at me. I will never be loved by anyone. This is your fault, father. Why did you send Chara away?"

"My love, you demanded I act. You didn't want to see her. She was innocent, but you blamed her. First, you wanted her out of your sight, and then you blame us for her absence. Can't you see the bind you put us in?"

"No, I was just angry, but I didn't want her to leave me," Athaliah shouted.

Her conflicted soul could not accept what was happening. Each action seemed to bring unexpected reactions within her heart.

She would not be consoled. All attempts to do so failed. Anguish filled the hearts of everyone around her. Darkness invaded their world.

Not knowing clearly what course of action to take, Obed and Mara huddled away from the eyes of their servants to discuss their options.

"Mara, we must find a way to console Athaliah. I have been thinking, maybe we could send her to my brother."

"How would that help?"

"He has a prosperous business and could use help keeping records. Athaliah is good at that. I think it would help her get her mind off what has happened."

"I hate to think of sending her away, for any reason, but she will not be pacified. I am at my wit's end. Maybe you are right. But I wouldn't want to impose upon your brother's kind heart, would you?"

"If she is with him and his family, maybe she can forget her pain. A change of surroundings might be just what she needs to get her mind off her problems. If she is given something that keeps her mind occupied, such as work, there would be less time for her to grovel in her sadness. It might give her purpose."

As he spoke, Obed became convinced that this should be his course of action.

"I will contact my brother right away. My dear, I shall leave in the morning to speak with him. This, I will take care of personally."

Mara turned away from him, crying. Her "baby girl" had been her life, and now she was causing so much confusion. Her mother-heart burst with grief. How had life taken such a strange, unexpected, change? It hurt her to think of Athaliah's leaving the house, but what else could be done? All she could do was cry in anguish of soul.

Two years came and went since Athaliah's arrival. Master Reuben opened his home to her without reservation, as per the request of her father. Master Reuben and his wife, Gloria, loved their niece. She arrived at their doorstep with many problems, and a tightly closed heart, defying anyone to pry it open. They saw through her conflicted spirit and overlooked what others observed at first blush. Little by little, progress was made. She became more like the girl they had known her to be in years past, but now she was a woman in her own right. Still, something deep inside her pushed others away.

Master Reuben offered her work in his business, as keeper of accounts. She seemed to enjoy having responsibility. Having something to do kept her mind off her past.

She almost never mentioned her parents. Deep anger and resentment prevented her from doing so. If her aunt and uncle ever brought them up in conversation, she shut down, or simply changed the topic. Benjamin came up often, however. She loved him. More than a brother, he was her childhood companion. She missed his smile and quick wit. He brought a smile to her face every time she thought of him. They had their spats, to be sure, but now that she could not see him, she only remembered the good times. For some reason, she could not bring herself to think of the fishing adventures, but there were many other memories she enjoyed; like the time he climbed a tree and struck a wasp nest, thinking to dislodge it and save the world from the stinging pests. His action only served to infuriate them. They flew out of their nest in a lightning flash, and stung him unmercifully, effectively motivating him to let loose of his grip, and simply drop some distance to the ground below. Just as quickly, he ran a great distance before stopping.

"I didn't know wasps could move so fast," he commentated later, through a swollen face, as he recounted his unpleasant adventure. The family laughed at him, though at first, they were concerned for his safety.

Athaliah remembered the special identifying whistle they developed to call each other. Whenever they whistled, the two knew who it was, and came to each other, while strangers had no idea of its meaning.

One day Uncle Reuben came to the door of her workplace and stood watching her at work. He admired her greatly. She was so dedicated and accomplished in her role.

"Have you finished working up the financial results of the last caravan, Athaliah? I need to make a trip to my banker," he said.

"Yes, Uncle, I have it right here," passing him a stack of parchments.

"Thank you. What would I do without you?"

She gave him a smile and turned back to her work.

"My dear, you need to take some time for yourself. Why don't you go to the special get-to-gather this evening? There will be other young people your age there. Maybe you can meet some new friends."

The thought of meeting new friends was not appealing to her. She was used to pulling away to be by herself. Life was simple, with few interruptions. Work was straightforward and understandable—uncomplicated. It didn't require being around other people. Friendships and relationships, on the other hand, were complicated and dangerous. She was not sure she wanted to venture as far as to make herself vulnerable.

"Thank you, Uncle. I will think about it, but I don't promise anything."

"Well, just give it some thought." In his heart, he knew that most young ladies of Athaliah's age were married and had children around them. Silently, he worried about her willingness to hide from the public.

At home that evening, he spoke with Gloria. "What do you think of inviting some friends over to the house for a meal?"

"Who do you have in mind," she said.

"Someone with a good-looking son, for example," he said, with a knowing smile.

"I see. You have ulterior motives."

"Would I do that?"

"Yes, you would do that," she said, playfully. "I know how you think. I know you feel it is time for Athaliah to broaden herself again. I feel the same way, but how would we do it? She is afraid of being hurt. It would be excruciating for her, even after all this time."

"A woman can't live under the roof of her family her whole life. She needs a responsible man to take care of her. This is only natural. I have no reason to want her to leave us, but as her guardians, we must concern ourselves with her best interests."

"We would have to be discreet about it. Here is an idea: she loves her work.

Is there some young man you know of that could inadvertently appear at her workplace without alerting her suspicions?"

"Now that you mention it, this is a great idea. I will search among my co-workers to find someone who can come in as a co-worker, to do a joint project. She would not suspect anything out of the ordinary. What do you think?"

"As you said, we must think of her best interest. Go to your brother and ask his advice. If he is willing, we can proceed with the idea."

Rueben traveled to his brother's city and sought him out. Finding him at the city gates, he invited him to an eatery, where they sat to enjoy a meal while they talked.

As was customary, they sat, making small talk for a while, then, Obed moved to more serious conversation.

"Reuben, this is a surprise. What brings you here? How is Athaliah? Is she well?"

"She is doing so well. She loves her work and concerns herself with little else. That is why I am here. Gloria and I have been thinking that it would be good if she broadens herself. What I mean is; we want to ask you what you would think if we were to allow her to meet some young men."

Obed was surprised, but not opposed to the suggestion. "It wouldn't be so much allow her to meet someone, as to contrive to make it happen, don't you think?"

Rueben smiled. "Yes, I suppose you are right."

Obed and Mara wanted Athaliah to have a good, well-rounded, and fulfilling life. Their pain was in knowing that she had pushed them from her life in anger.

"Is she still angry with us, Reuben?"

"We haven't seen any change in that regard. She simply doesn't want to talk about you. I know she loves you both deeply, but she is so bound by anger, that there is no way to broach the subject with her. Some day she will come around, we are sure. As you know, she is an extraordinary young lady, with so much to offer. This is why we have been led to this way of thinking. We want to be a part of the solution."

The two brothers talked at length. Obed asked many questions about Athaliah's well-being, her work and her activities, her interests. He could not help but wince at how well she was doing, knowing that he should be the father figure in her life.

"How are you and Mara holding up?" Reuben asked.

"Mara cries a lot. She doesn't even know why, at times. She breaks out in tears with no apparent cause. I try to comfort her as best I can."

"I know this is difficult for both of you. How is little Benjamin doing? She talks about him all the time."

"He is not so little anymore. He is quite the responsible young man. We are proud of him. He is now helping me in the business and shows great potential."

"Athaliah would love to know this. She worries about him. She will be delighted to know about him, but I must be discreet. She will be curious as to how I came to know about him. This, I know, makes us all uneasy."

The conversation went well into the night.

Finally, Obed said, "Come, Rueben, it is getting late, and I know you need your rest. Come stay the night at the house. Mara will love to see you. You can return home tomorrow.

❧

CHAPTER EIGHTEEN

The Discovery

Master Obed enjoyed his brother's visit but was left with a feeling of inadequacy. His inability to solve Athaliah's anger issues weighed heavily upon him. In addition, the problems at home never seemed to end. Mara was increasingly distant. Benjamin was a delight, and helped with the workload, but was obviously affected by his sister's absence. He longed to feel relief from the unwanted pressures. Being a man of stature in the community produced its own concerns. There were public expectations that never allowed for slack. His nature was not one to lend itself to that, no matter what, but the incessant nature of the social pressures became extremely burdensome.

Benjamin was a great help to his father. He immersed himself into his work with vigor. Having learned to observe every aspect of the business, he became aware of activities that presented unwanted concerns. In some way, the business was losing revenue.

Looking over the records, he noticed a pattern that disturbed him. Often, their caravans arrived late, and could not take advantage of optimal sales opportunities. The competition was great among the businessmen. In their world, it was important to maintain friendships, and hold allies close. But Benjamin observed the trend of late arrivals and lost opportunities.

Calling in his father's steward, Benjamin presented his concerns. "Master Joab, we are losing revenue because of our late arrivals. I have seen a pattern. Look at the records. What do you think?"

"You could be right. You have a good eye." Looking over the parchments, he saw that, for some time, a perceivable change in revenues was taking place. "Yes, I see what you are saying. Now that I think about it, often, we have suffered complications just before arriving home."

"Would you speak with Reuel, and ask him to be on the alert for any activities that might cause concern?" Benjamin asked.

"Yes, I will. As you say, we must get to the bottom of this. There must be something, or someone, causing these losses."

Several months passed, with no results. Then, one day, as Benjamin prepared the staging area to receive an expected caravan, Reuel appeared. "Master Benjamin, I have news."

"Yes, Reuel, what do you have?"

"As you requested, I instructed the men to observe all activities surrounding our caravans as they near home. I have found something."

"Good, let's hear it," Benjamin urged.

"One of our men was stationed to watch throughout the night at the last campsite, before arriving home. He caught a man sneaking around the animals during the third watch. He was dressed in black, and could not be seen, but by an experienced eye. Our man was able to catch him in the act of feeding our animals. By the smell of his pouch, we knew his intent was evil. Upon further investigation, we found poisonous powders in it. He was quickly bound, and we have him in custody."

"This is good news," Benjamin stated. "Where do you have him? I want to question him personally. Take me to him."

"Very well, sir, come this way."

Reuel led Benjamin through the streets to a non-descript house and knocked on the door. "We thought it might be better to keep him here, out of the way," Reuel said, as they waited. Benjamin recognized the worker who opened the door. With a quick greeting, he asked to be led to the man who was being held.

Entering a small, dark room, Benjamin saw what appeared to be a heap of clothing on the floor in the far corner. A liberal amount of straw lay beneath it. Approaching, he pulled back a portion of the clothing, and a man's face could be seen. He asked the man's name. But before the man could answer, Benjamin recognized him.

"You were at my home for the marriage festival with Abel."

The young man looked up at Benjamin with big eyes but said nothing.

"Have my men treated you well?"

There was no response.

"Come now, you must have a voice."

Benjamin quickly decided a plan of action. "I am not here to hurt you. You work for Abel, true?"

The man remained silent.

"I take your silence as affirmation."

The man said nothing.

Walking from the room, and out of hearing range, Benjamin said to his men,

"Feed him, and make him comfortable, but do not let him run away. In time he will willingly talk. Treat him well."

Benjamin left the house, having placed guards in front. He met with his father and Steward Joab.

"Father, and Master Joab, we have good news, but it might take a few days to learn just what has happened. We have a man in custody that was caught trying to feed poison to our animals. I believe he is the one who has been causing our caravans to arrive late."

"How has he accomplished this," his father asked.

"He has done in it in various ways, to avoid detection. But from what I have learned so far, I believe he is the one who has caused us delays. One way was to feed the animals poison that caused them distress, rendering them unable to travel for a time."

"Why would he do this," Steward Joab asked.

"As it turns out, he works for Abel. I recognized him as soon as I saw him."

"Say that again," His father said.

"He was in Abel's group, as a groomsman, the night of the wedding."

The elder men looked at each other.

Benjamin continued. "He has not said a word yet, but I can see a scenario emerging that causes me to believe the worst. In a few days, we will have proof."

"We can't hold him against his will," Master Haddad said. "What we do must be done correctly, or we could be in trouble, ourselves."

"Father, I have been thinking. Do you remember the case of the king of Israel who brought the warriors of his enemy in, and surprised them with a banquet? They returned home with only praise on their lips and refused to help their king fight against Israel."

"Yes."

"Well, I think we can use the same tactic here. If we give him an incentive, he will help us better than if he sees further reason to despise us."

"Very good thinking, Benjamin," Joab said.

Master Haddad could not feel prouder of Benjamin than he did at that moment. "My son, let's discuss how we are to proceed. You have done well."

Upon leaving the meeting with his father and Steward Joab, Benjamin gathered several men and headed back to the house.

The servant in charge of the house and its occupant came to the door. "Come in, Master. You are back so soon."

"Yes, we have settled on a course of action in this matter. Lead me to the room, and give us privacy, if you would," Benjamin said.

The room appeared the same as before, but now the man was seated with a plate of food in his hands.

"Now, let us talk about our situation. Start with your name."

The young man sat in silence.

"I see you will need to be incentivized. This is no problem." Coming closer, Benjamin spoke quietly, with a friendly tone.

"We know you work for Abel. So far, you are the only one in trouble. You have only two options: One: you tell us all, leaving out nothing. And two: if you do not speak, we will take this matter straight to the authorities. In that case, you will carry the complete burden of your actions. You do realize we do have proof? You were caught in the act. We have no desire to keep you in this place. As soon as you speak, you will be free to go your way."

Having heard the options, and given the passive tone in which Benjamin spoke, the man changed his attitude.

"If I tell you what you want to know, why would you need to know my name? All I need to do is confirm who I work for."

"Let me say it this way, either you tell us all, including your name, who you work for, and how long this has been going on, or we will have no choice but to take this matter to the authorities. Then, we will press for complete reimbursement of all lost revenues. Would you be able to repay us our losses?"

That seemed to register. "Alright, I will tell you. I can't afford to take the blame by myself. My name is Omar, of the house of Honan."

"Good, now you are beginning to understand the situation. Who do you work for?"

"You already know that" Omar said.

"But we want to hear you say it. We are writing everything you say on this parchment, which you will sign when we are finished." Motioning to the scribe that came with him, Benjamin told him to write.

Slowly, Omar began. "I have known Abel for many years because we were childhood friends. He asked me to work with him several years ago to supply information for him."

Benjamin looked on with interest.

"After Abel's wedding didn't work out, he asked me to do whatever I could to sabotage Master Haddad's interests. That is what I have done ever since. Abel vowed to make Master Haddad pay for what happened."

"Has anyone else helped you?"

"Yes, some of the servants of Master Jacob have helped."

Omar continued telling his story, leaving out nothing. He was so thorough that it was evident that he was telling the truth.

"Now, this is what is going to happen. We are not going to press charges on you. But, if you ever again try to do us harm, we will come after you. In the meantime, you will keep us informed of anything Abel tries to do. Agreed?"

"Yes Sir."

Benjamin led the man to the front door and said, "From now on, you will keep us informed. You know where to find us. The document you put your name to has been witnessed and duly signed. We will register it with the authorities and hold it in safe keeping. No action will be taken against you at this time. Don't let us down."

Benjamin's servants bound the man's eyes and led him away.

Armed with the knowledge of what Abel had been doing, Benjamin shared it with his father and Steward Joab. A course of action had to be decided upon that would adequately satisfy the outrage the Haddad family had suffered at his hands. They would wait for an appropriate time before acting on the matter. Obed was aware of Jacob's feelings after the wedding situation and knew there was enough guilt to go around. Only, Abel's actions were beyond the pale. Neither family had been the same after the marriage was called off.

CHAPTER NINETEEN

Co-Workers

Athaliah arrived early to work and busied herself with the accounting that awaited her. Her uncle came into the room, followed by a young man.

"Athaliah, I would like you to meet someone," he said. Turning, he motioned the young man to approach. "Athaliah, this is Jebu. Jebu, meet my niece, Athaliah."

Athaliah arose and greeted the young man with a smile, wondering why her uncle wanted her to meet him.

"Jebu works at one of our offices, in another city. He has a project, and I would like you to help him in whatever way possible. It seems there have been some discrepancies in the records in his office. He has asked us to help him learn what is happening. I am getting him set up, so maybe you could start with him tomorrow. What do you think?"

Athaliah was at a loss. This was a surprise. Politely, she said, "Yes, by all means, Uncle. It will be done as you wish."

That night, at the table, Athaliah ate quietly. Noticing her silence, Master Rueben spoke up. "Athaliah, you seem quieter than usual tonight. Is there any reason?"

Athaliah looked at her aunt, Gloria, then over to her uncle. "No, there is nothing wrong. Why?"

"You just seem quiet," Rueben said.

"Well, yes, I am thinking."

"Thinking about what?"

"I am thinking about that young man you brought into the office this morning. Am I going to have to work with him long?"

Feelings of discomfort had been chasing her all day. Why did she feel so strangely? She didn't know why she reacted as she did, but it couldn't be pushed aside. There must be a reason. She understood why she didn't want to be around men, but *why* did she feel so strongly about it? She could not grasp that. The obvious was easily admitted to by her. She had been hurt. The fact that she could not remember what had happened didn't change the fact that she lived with the results; results that had caused her to lose her husband and resent her parents. The embarrassment of her betrayal still haunted her. Maybe this was why she was nervous.

"My dear, if you are uncomfortable being around him, just let us know. The skills you have in finance could be a great help to him, but we don't want to pressure you."

Gloria looked at her, "Athaliah, you are such a sweet niece. We love you as our own daughter. There is nothing we would not do to assure your happiness."

"Thank you, Auntie. I will be alright. I just feel… odd. That is all."

The next morning Athaliah stepped into the office, ready to work. Jebu came in shortly, with a stack of parchments.

"Good morning, Athaliah. Where do you want to start?"

"Good morning, Sir. Let's see. Take a seat right over there. What can you tell me about the case? When did you first learn that something was wrong? First, would you like some water before we start?"

"I would like some water, Thank you."

He seemed nice enough. Athaliah was cordial. She called a maid and asked her to deliver water for both.

156

"We are going to be working here for a while, so if you could keep us in refreshments, we would appreciate it."

Looking back at Jebu, she spoke with a questioning gesture. Understanding her intent, Jebu said, "Well, I noticed some problems about six months ago. It was a few little differences at first, but then, the amounts grew in small increments."

"Pass me the reports from the last year if you have them. Let me look." Opening the parchments, she studied the transaction amounts, debits, and credits. As she looked them over, she took stock of the clients and products being traded, and the quantities of each.

"This will take some time," she said with a smile. "Let's not miss anything."

The day passed quickly. When her uncle poked his head through the door, she was surprised to learn that it was time to go home. Time had escaped her. Jebu was tired from searching the items she pointed out to him. But a picture was beginning to emerge in Athaliah's mind.

"Uncle Reuben, thank you. I don't know where the day went."

"You both can come back to this tomorrow," he said.

Each day she and Jebu returned to the search for the unknown factors. Athaliah had learned to be relentless when it came to figures, and her experience was beginning to produce answers, but some points were elusive, still.

Without her realizing it, her attitude was changing toward Jebu. She, surprisingly, no longer saw him as a threat. She was beginning to like him, as a person. His personality was kind and resolute. Character traits were observed as he and she interacted each day. Slowly Athaliah was changing toward him, to her surprise. Not just changing in a natural, friendly sense, but in her understanding of him as a man.

Each day Athaliah returned home with a slightly lighter emotional demeanor. Her aunt and uncle noticed the changes but said nothing. Several weeks passed and the two business partners found their work more interesting and fulfilling.

One day, Athaliah arrived to work with parchments under her arm. "Jebu, I think I am seeing a pattern. I stayed up late last night going over these. Look at this." Placing the parchments on the table, she spread them out in order.

"You buy in bulk, right? Look at these grain receipts. Here you see that a year ago you purchased these bundles of grain. This is only one instance, but I believe there are many others."

"Yes, that is correct," Jebu confirmed.

"You purchase in bulk. Look. A year ago, this batch of bulk bundles was purchased. Notice the date. Now, look over here at the same product after it was converted into this number of smaller bundles, for resale to your clients."

"Yes, I see. But what does that mean?" Jebu asked, unsure of her reasoning.

"Looking at the grain from the first receipt to final resale, you notice that this number of bundles was converted into this number of the final product."

"Yes, that I can see," he said, still unsure of what she was getting at.

"Now, look at these similar transactions, starting six months ago, and come forward." She pointed to the parchments, having placed them in chronological order. "What do you see? They are consistent each time. The amounts could be missed easily enough."

Studying the information before him, he said, "I see that these bundles we purchased and resold were similar in number to the ones from a year ago, but the number of resale bundles from six months ago, forward, is less."

"Exactly! Whoever is doing the conversions into smaller bundles is doing one of two things: They are taking out some grain and hiding it, or they are making the resale bundles larger than what they should be, thereby making the final product cheaper for the consumers."

"I don't see how anyone could get away with stealing part of the grain without being seen by other workers," Jebu said. "Why would they make the resale bundles larger than they should be? Everyone would benefit, and no one would personally save much. It would be a great risk of being found out, with little or no personal benefit."

"Well, maybe they don't realize what they are doing."

"That is possible. We do have some new workers," Jebu said.

"Let's consider another possibility," Athaliah said. "Do you have any buyers who buy from you in large quantities?"

"Yes."

"Look at the purchases and tell me who is buying most of the resale bundles."

Jebu pulled several parchments closer and studied them. "It would have to be this person."

"Good, now we are getting somewhere. Maybe that person has someone working for him within your workforce. Someone who could help him purchase more resale products for what would turn out to be a smaller price. He could, then, convert the resale bundles into the proper size, and have more bundles to sell to his clients. In this way, he makes a greater profit."

"I had not thought of such a thing." Jebu said. "Let's look at all the transactions. Maybe we can get a better overview."

In the next few days, they found a pattern of transactions, all benefiting one client.

"Now you can take this information to my uncle. He will know what to do," Athaliah said. "You might even suggest he let you do some investigation work to find the accomplice among the ranks of your workers." In her mind, Athaliah knew this would allow Jebu to stay around a while longer. She could not admit this, however. There would have to be another excuse that might suffice to keep the attention off her motives.

"We have found how the losses are taking place, but we must establish proof. We must find out who is doing this thing. As you say, that will take a little while to accomplish. Your suggestion is valid. Thank you," Jebu said.

That evening, Jebu arrived for dinner at Master Reuben's, home. This surprised Athaliah. "Uncle, this is a surprise. What is the occasion?" She asked.

"I am so pleased that Jebu has found the problem—" With a quick correction, he added, "With your help, of course. The two of you work well together."

It did not cross Athaliah's mind that her uncle had set up the whole encounter. The problem was real enough, and it just so happened, that he was able to accomplish two things at the same time, obviously delighted with himself.

"My dear, I have invited Jebu to dinner so we can all discuss our options together. Call it a working dinner."

"This is a delight, Uncle. Now that we have found the problem, when will Jebu return to his hometown?"

"Come, let's sit and talk as we enjoy our meal."

The table had been set by attentive servants. The food was a little above normal, and Athaliah concluded that Jebu was the reason. He was a trusted worker, and her uncle, obviously, wanted to celebrate him.

As the family sat for the meal, the topic of the hour concerned the problem at hand. Gloria rarely sat at business functions, but since Athaliah was present, she wanted to hear the discussion. *After all, I was a part of the planning that brought these two young people together,* she reasoned, silently.

Reuben was grateful for the job Jebu was doing. "Now that we know a few details, we must form a plan to 'smoke the culprits out,' obviously. What do you think we should do next, when you get back to your city, Jebu?"

"Master Rueben, I propose that we observe the workers we suspect of wrongdoing. I will put a few of my most trusted workers to that task. I am sure it won't take long. For good measure, I will set up some transactions that will entice the thieves into action."

The conversation went on for a while, no one noticing the passing of time. Athaliah found herself enjoying Jebu as he expounded. Her uncle was pleased as well.

Finally, seeing some of the servants were yawning, Rueben looked at Athaliah and said, "You located the problem in a short time, my dear. Thank you for that. Our losses could have been much greater without your insightful capabilities."

Athaliah smiled, noticing that all eyes were on her. "It was nothing, Uncle." In her heart, she wished Jebu didn't have to return home so soon, but knew he must, to fix the problem. "Uncle, will Jebu be coming back when he gets the situation taken care of?"

"Well, of course, my dear. I will need to know what to do next, assuming we apprehend those involved, be it one or more."

Athaliah smiled a telling smile, which Jebu didn't miss. Gloria also saw Athaliah's face and knew her plan was well on its way to completion.

Master Rueben walked Jebu to the door. "Young man, you are a great asset. Thank you for your faithfulness. Please give my regards to all the leadership in the office when you get back home. I will maintain contact through messengers. If need be, I will travel there. We will see."

"Thank you, Master Reuben. It is my pleasure. Thank you for a delightful evening. These weeks have truly been great, especially, working with Athaliah. Might I be so bold as to ask your permission to see her again?"

Without hesitation, he said, "My lad, you certainly may. She would be most pleased to see you as well, I am sure."

Several months passed. Athaliah busied herself in her work. She could not help but think of Jebu. He pushed his way into her thoughts. She wondered how it was possible to think of yet another man. She was normal in every way. As is so often the case, young women dream of marriage, and children. She was no exception. Overriding the reservations she felt in her heart, due to the hurts she had endured, she found herself pondering the possibilities of life with a man who truly loved her. She dreamed of a man who would take care of her; a man who would adore her, even with her blemishes. She dreamed of Jebu.

She didn't dare mention his name before her uncle and aunt, lest they perceive her true intentions.

One day, as she worked, a voice was heard. Someone had come into the workplace. She was sure she recognized the voice. *It is Jebu.*

Leaving her table, she ran down the steps to the lower floor, stumbling right into him, as he rounded a corner. To her horror, she fell against him, lost her balance, and ended up in his arms. Her face turned red, as she looked up into his eyes. "Please forgive, me, Jebu. I am sorry." Her embarrassment was so great that she froze speechless, mouth agape.

"The pleasure is all mine," he said, smiling down at her. "It is good to see you again." Helping her back to her feet, he bowed, gently, and turned to Master Rueben, who was standing nearby.

"Master Reuben, good day. I have come with good news."

"This is wonderful. Please, come into my office." Looking at a servant girl, he said, "Bring refreshments to my office. I am sure this young man would like to slack his thirst."

Then, looking at Athaliah, he said, "I will call you in a few moments, my Dear. Go on about your work until then."

Dispensing with the usual pleasantries, the men got directly to the matter at hand.

"Now, Jebu, what is the good news?" Master Rueben asked.

"Sir, might we close the door?"

"Yes, let's do."

"I have found the person responsible for the theft."

A smile played across Master Rueben's face. "This is good news, indeed."

"But it gets complicated, Sir."

"Tell me everything."

"After much questioning, and many threats, the man confessed to everything."

"What is the complication?"

"Well, Sir, he was working at the behest of a merchant who started purchasing items from us around the time the discrepancies began. We located the person, being careful to take a representative from the local authority. He, of course, was reluctant to speak with us, but when the legal representative explained his options, he gave us the information we needed."

"That seems to have gone easy," Reuben said.

"It was not as easy as it may seem. We had to incentivize him by speaking of prison. We had proof, as you know, and after the authority representative drew a mental example of just how prison life can be, the man quickly implicated the real person behind the theft. We pressed him for a long time, to make sure he was not trying to pass guilt onto another person, to avoid prosecution. It turned out that he really was contracted by a young merchant, by the name of Abel."

"Who is Abel?"

"He is the son of Master Jacob, a business associate of your brother, Master Obed."

"I see. This does complicate everything. Please go on."

"Well, he was hired to act as a buyer. He, then, sent one of his men to infiltrate our business. So, there was a chain of involvement to distance the real perpetrator from the thievery."

"Did you learn what this, Abel's, motives were?"

"We only have the word of the buyer, but it appears that this young man, Abel, was trying to cause pain to your brother, and financial loss to you."

"It probably cost him more money to pay these men off than what he was actually able to make on the deal," Master Rueben speculated.

"What we learned is that he had a strong desire for vengeance. He is quite a resourceful young man. He told our thief, the buyer, that he wanted certain people to suffer for what he called a 'deception' that was perpetrated against him."

Master Rueben put everything together quickly. Not knowing how much Jebu knew about Athaliah he decided not to say anything that would include her. He wanted the matter to be about the theft, and not about her.

Jebu continued, "Now, we know who was behind the theft, so what should be our next step?"

Master Reuben sat, thinking. At length, he said "I tell you what, I will go to my brother, and find out what he thinks. We will form an appropriate plan of action."

"Sir, I took the liberty to ask a scribe to record the confessions. I also asked three of the workers to serve as witnesses. They have put their names on the document, in affirmation of the facts. I have it all here."

"Well done, Jebu," he said, reaching for the parchments.

"Will you do something for me?" Master Rueben asked Jehu when he had finished looking over the documents.

"Of course, I will."

"I will leave in the morning to see my brother. Would you stay on here a few days, just to help make sure all is well? I don't know how long I will be away. We will pay for you to stay at the inn just up the street."

"I would be happy to do so," Jehu assured him.

Rueben arrived at Obed's home late the next day, having traveled as swiftly as he could. The surprise on Obed's face was genuine. "Brother, this is an unexpected pleasure. How nice to see you. Please come in, and rest."

Calling a servant, he said, "Please bring water and towels, at once, so our guest can clean the dust off from his travels." Motioning to his brother, he said, "Follow this man to the receiving room. He will make you comfortable while you freshen up. The dust on the roads is thick this time of the year. I will call the family, and have the servants prepare a room for you. Please excuse me for a moment."

Rueben followed the servant into the receiving room and sat on a comfortable couch. Several servants arrived with everything he needed to wash up, and some refreshments, as well.

Mara came into the room a little while later. "I couldn't wait to see you, Reuben. It is so nice of you to come, my brother. How are your family, and Athaliah?"

After a warm familial greeting, Rueben said, "We are all well, Mara. Athaliah is doing quite well. We are so proud of her. What can I say, she is a dear."

Benjamin walked in, not long after his mother. "Uncle Reuben, it is good to see you again."

It had not been such a long time since last seeing his nephew, but Rueben said, "Who is this handsome young man? It couldn't be Benjamin. You have gotten taller in my absence, young Benjamin. Soon you will pass me."

The conversation was brisk, as they waited to be called to the table for the evening meal. Athaliah was all Mara and Benjamin wanted to speak of. Rueben answered the direct questions as concisely as possible. He didn't want to cause her parents' concern. He expressed his delight at how well she was doing at work and did all he could to sound normal and understanding. The gap between parents and daughter still caused pain to arise within their hearts. They loved her and didn't want the separation they endured.

A servant entered and respectfully notified them that the meal was prepared and waiting. At the table the conversations continued, with many questions. The mood was cheerful, but a hint of sadness was unmistakable.

After dinner together, as was the custom, the men separated themselves from the rest of the family to speak alone.

"Rueben, what has brought you to us? Is everything alright?" Obed asked.

"I will get right to the matter. Since our last meeting, Mara and I took the liberty and arranged to have a young man meet Athaliah. It was done with utmost caution. He works for me in another city. We brought him to the office to meet her. As it turned out, he had a situation in his workplace that ended up being a perfect cover for our purposes, but that brought some troubling facts to light. He had discovered some accounting abnormalities and needed an expert to help discover what was happening. Athaliah was perfect for the job. She was able to work with him to solve the problem."

"That's my girl. She was always good with accounting."

"Well, she paid for her keep several times over with this one. You have good reason to be proud of her. She went right to work on the matter. Within a short time, she found the discrepancies, and concluded that someone was tampering with my merchandise. After studying the evidence, she and Jebu (that is his name) saw that someone was selling grain and causing us losses in the process.

"Jebu returned to his city and put a plan together to catch the person in the act of stealing from us. Several trusted workers observed the man taking wholesale bundles, and putting the contents into smaller bundles for resale, but his bundles weighed more than they should weigh. This, in effect, was giving the buyer more grain than he should have, costing us in the process. Instead of converting one bundle into twenty smaller bundles, he was converting one bundle into only fifteen. The buyer paid for only fifteen, when in truth, the contents were the equivalent of twenty normal bundles, for example, chipping away at our profits."

"It is difficult to get good help, at times."

"Well, by a process of elimination, and a preponderance of the evidence, we found that one buyer was profiting. He was the one who had put the thief up to it. When we caught the thief, he was interrogated at length. He told us everything. He had been sent to seek employment with us by his boss, the merchant.

"So, we went to the merchant and confronted him. It turned out that he had been commissioned by still another person to do the crime."

"And who was that?"

"A young merchant named Abel."

Obed's face turned ashen when he heard the name. He felt his face contort. "This is troubling, indeed," he said. For a moment he could not say anything more. Visions of the wedding night, and the trouble that ensued, filled his head.

"Rueben, this means that, by some means, Abel found Athaliah, and is trying to cause her trouble."

"If this is the case, he is doing it by indirectly coming after us. The first man we took into custody told us that his master, the merchant, was contracted by yet another man to get revenge, but he didn't know why," Rueben said. "When we found the merchant, he told us that Abel wants to cause financial hurt and pain to everyone who deceived him."

"You had nothing to do with that so-called deception, Reuben."

"Yes, but, if what you say is correct, and I have no reason to think otherwise, he found out Athaliah was living with us, and came after my business."

"Will this never end?" Obed whispered. "We recently found that he has been causing us losses, as well. He had one of his men poison our animals each time our caravans came close to home, causing us untold delays in arriving. This meant losses for us, because it allowed his caravans to arrive first, and obtain better prices."

"We both have a problem on our hands! This is more complicated than I thought," Rueben said.

"Yes. Though it is difficult, we must take this knowledge to Abel's father, at once. This can't be allowed to continue." The brothers talked well into the night.

The next day Obed and Reuben made their way to the city gate, in search of Master Jacob. Their hearts were heavy as they went, but were undaunted, due to their resolve to see the matter through. They found him seated near the gate.

"Jacob, good morning, may we have a word with you?" Obed asked.

Seeing who addressed him, Jacob sat pan-faced for a moment, not wanting to reveal his surprise. Decorum had to be maintained in this public setting. Work associates were watching.

"Obed," he finally muttered. "If we must, let us go a little distance."

They found a table located in front of an eating establishment and sat.

"Jacob, this is my brother, Ruben." Obed started.

"Good morning, sir," Jacob said, coolly.

"To what do I owe this encounter, Obed?"

"We have come upon some information that we feel you should know. I am aware of the feelings that have been between us since the unfortunate event that affected our families so deeply. We don't wish to cause you more discomfort. You are an honorable man, respected by all who know you."

Obed knew to start in this manner. It is always easier, and more productive, to offer a few accolades before mentioning anything negative.

"It is because of your reputation for honesty that we come to you today. Please forgive us for bringing our concerns to you."

The three men sat around the table, looking at each other blankly. An attendant asked what they would like to drink.

Obed said, "Please, allow me to get this."

Addressing the attendant, he said, "We would like you to bring us some hot oriental tea. Thank you."

"Jacob, it is with a heavy heart that we speak with you. It gives us no pleasure to do so." As he spoke, he was aware that he had, possibly, stepped into the subject too quickly. "What I mean to say is that it is with trepidation that we come to you."

Jacob didn't speak.

"You are a wise man. We humbly request your help."

Obed saw the softening in Jacob's countenance.

"What kind of help do you seek?"

"We have a situation that causes us grief. There is no desire to stir up trouble, but we must ask your help with a most delicate matter."

Rueben spoke up, quietly. "If you would allow me, I stumbled onto a matter that was taking place in one of my offices. It surprised us all to find that a thief was taking advantage of an opportunity to cause us financial harm."

"How does this affect me? Why do you come to me with this information?"

"Kind Sir, when we discovered who was stealing from us, we interrogated him vigorously. He confessed that someone had put him up to it. Please forgive me. He said the person's name was Abel, of the house of Jacob, the merchant."

The silence that followed could be felt.

"Are you sure this is factual? What is the man's name?"

Reaching into his carrying case, Rueben pulled out a stack of parchments.

"Here, see for yourself."

The attendant brought tea and poured it into goblets before the men. They took the opportunity to remain silent while Master Jacob studied the documents.

Looking over the content, Jacob silently read, his expression darkening with each allegation read.

"This is unbelievable. I mean, I am stunned by the allegations. Can this possibly be true?"

"As you can see, both of us have interrogated three separate people who were caught with their hands in the proverbial sweet bin. Rueben had no idea of what I had encountered here, and I was unaware of what he had found there, until last night. As you can see, it all leads to the same man who is the one behind their actions.

"Besides the two men Rueben found, I don't believe either of them knows anyone else that was involved, but Abel is named in both instances, here and at my brother's place. It must be more than a coincidence. The witnesses all heard the confessions, respectively."

"I have to say, this is unsettling, to say the least. We must get to the bottom of the matter," Jacob said, reluctantly. Resolve crept into his expression. "You have both done your research. I can't, though I would like to, deny that you have cause for concern."

"We are truly sorry, Jacob."

"This wrong must be made right," Jacob calmly said, "though it carries a troubling sting. My son, Abel, is out of town today, but he should return by tomorrow. We will get together with him at that time. I will confront him with these facts, in your presence, and see what he has to say."

"Jacob, you must know that this is not easy for us, as we are sure it is not easy for you. We are sorry to be the bearers of ill tidings," Obed said, condolence etched on his face.

"Obed, I am sorry, as well. I recognize that I have caused you pain by saying nothing to my son. It is hard to see family members hurt, and one always sides with family. Nonetheless, I have always known you to be a man of integrity. There is much I do not understand, but I will do my part to resolve this situation. You can count on me."

"Thank you, Jacob. With your leave, we will return to this location in the late hours tomorrow, to allow Abel time to arrive," Obed said.

Gathering the parchments, Rueben and Obed excused themselves.

CHAPTER TWENTY

Tragedy

Jebu kept busy around the office, making himself of use, as best he could. Having received orders not to discuss the situation with anyone, he invented a reason for being there. Athaliah, though dedicated to her work, took time to find him so she could discuss "important" matters of business. He, of course, saw through her ruse but said nothing.

"Athaliah, your uncle has asked me to be here until he returns from his business trip. Would it be alright with you if I request permission of your aunt to visit you at your home some evening?" He asked one day.

Oh, he is direct. I like that. "Well, let me ponder this request of yours." *There is no reason to be too obvious.*

"You may ask her if you like," she said, smiling modestly. She liked him. This she could not deny. Feelings of joy leaped within her chest. Simultaneously, uneasiness pushed into her mind, competing for supremacy. This she didn't understand. *Why does something so good seem to feel so dangerous?* She pushed back.

"Jebu, come over to the house after work, and you can ask her then."

"This pleases me very much," he said. "I will be there."

"Aunt Gloria, Jebu might come to visit in a while. Is that alright with you?"

"Yes, of course," she said. "Do you and he get along well together?"

"I do think we do. He is a nice young man … and single."

"Oh, I wonder what he might have in mind, Athaliah."

"Who knows? Men can't always express themselves as well as women can. We will find out soon enough," Athaliah said.

"Yes, I am sure we will. That is a good thing, don't you think, my Dear?"

Athaliah hesitated. "But, Aunt Gloria, I don't know what to think of him. On one hand, he seems to be a good man. On the other hand, I sense danger."

"You know that I see how you both are around each other. It is obvious there is something stirring between you."

"I know it is too soon to worry about this, but I just don't want to get hurt again," Athaliah confided. "I have never spoken of this, but I have a fear of being hurt."

"Is that why you have hidden yourself within your work? It is easier to work than deal with relationships. Work doesn't fight back or have opinions, but people do."

Athaliah captured the truth of that statement, for that was exactly what she was doing.

"My dear, men are not all the same. There are good men and there are bad men. Don't let your hurts get in the way of your dreams for the future. If life didn't hurt at times, we would not know to distinguish between pain and pleasure, right or wrong, love or hate. Look at me, Athaliah," she held her cheeks softly between her hands. "You must allow yourself to dream sweeter dreams. You will see that love will find you. You must find strength for your future, not relent because of your past. Dreams and aspirations create hope."

Athaliah felt tears well up in her eyes. "Aunt Gloria, you are so wise. Thank you."

Not long after, Jebu arrived at the doorstep.

Aunt Gloria had asked the staff to prepare a special meal that evening. Jebu didn't miss the implication. Now, he had to take the next step.

"I know Master Rueben is not present, but do you mind if I ask you a question, Mistress Mara?"

"Of course not, Jebu. What is your question?"

"Would you mind if I came to visit Athaliah occasionally?"

Athaliah felt her face turn red and sought to conceal the fact. Even though she knew what Jebu would ask, it sounded so real when he did. Now it wasn't only a dream, but a reality, that he would take the next step.

"Young man," she said, smiling, "Master Rueben and I have discussed the very possibility of such a question on your part, and would be pleased to grant you permission to do just that, with our blessing."

The couple found joy in spending time together. Jebu looked for thoughtful ways to surprise Athaliah with flowers, sweets, or small handcrafts each time they met. Work hours seemed to pass slowly, but afterwards, they met at the house, in the presence of Aunt Gloria, to enjoy each other's company. Athaliah was pleased at how tranquil she felt around him. Only after he left, would she feel uneasiness push its way into her heart. Taking her aunt's advice she pushed forward, thinking of the future, not the past.

Their relationship prospered over the weeks. Uncle Reuben had not returned, and Athaliah thought that was good. If he was away, she had time to be with Jebu. She began wishing that he would not return any time soon.

As planned, Obed and Reuben made their way to the eatery for the appointment. Arriving, Jacob was already standing, waiting. "Please, come in. I have a private room prepared so we can speak without interruption."

They followed him into the eating establishment, to a beautifully prepared room that was reserved for just such occasions. Businessmen often brought clients in to do business, away from the hustle and bustle of the streets.

Abel was seated on a couch in the corner. He reluctantly stood as the men arrived. He was obviously not in good humor. Unable to look Master Haddad in the eye, he half-heartedly nodded. His father introduced Master Reuben, with a similar response. Abel made no attempt to be courteous.

Ignoring his son's cold attitude, Master Jacob said, "Son, these men have something to say that concerns you."

Abel sat quietly, saying nothing.

Master Haddad started, awkwardly. "Abel, it is with great heaviness that we come to you. As your father said, this concerns you. Certain events, that affect both my brother and I, have occurred. Upon investigation, you are named as the perpetrator. Namely, you hired men to disrupt my caravans with the intent to do us financial harm. And you hired a man to actually steal from my brother. What do you say to these allegations?"

Abel sat speechless. His expression, however, told the story. "I have nothing to say. It was not I."

"Abel do not lie," his father said. "These men have proof of your wrong doing."

"They only mean to harm me by making these accusations, father."

"I was hoping that what they had to say was wrong, but by your attitude, I know they are correct. Remember, I know you, son. This is difficult for me, but I must insist on your admission of guilt in the matter."

"Master Rueben, please hand me the parchments of proof." He handed them to Abel.

He took them from his father and looked them over quickly. "These are lies." Upon that, he angrily tore them apart.

"Son, they have copies. You are digging yourself into a deep hole. Your attitude and actions betray you."

After a long silence, Abel hissed, "No one treats me like they treated me. I swore that I would make them pay, and that is what I have done. It was worth it. I only wish I could have done more."

"But why did you steal from Master Rueben?" Master Jacob asked.

"I did it because Athaliah was living with him. I wanted her to hurt as well."

"How did you find out where she was?"

"I have my ways."

"I, as your father, am implicated with you in all of this. Look at what you have done to me, son."

"They are not the upstanding people you think they are, father."

"Why do you say that?"

"If you only knew! They hire bad people to work with them. Who told them I was disrupting the caravans?"

"The parchments indicate that your friend, Omar, did that. He said that you paid him to feed poison to Master Haddad's animals to cause delays, so you would have additional advantage when arriving before them with your caravans."

Master Haddad joined in, "My chief of security caught him in the act."

"Your chief of security is a liar."

"He brought proof sufficient to establish the fact."

"Well, he is not the man you think he is, Sir."

"What do you mean by that?" Master Haddad asked.

"I learned, while we were in the City of Towers, that he did something bad to secure his position as chief of security. That is the only security your man, Reuel, offers ... security for himself. Before that, he was just a worker."

"There were other witnesses to your actions. We have established proof of wrongdoing that you hired men to do for you," Master Habdad said.

Master Haddad continued, "I had thought we could take care of this matter without involving the authorities. It appears that that is not the case. For your father's sake, why don't you admit your guilt?"

"You would take this to the authorities? Who do you think you are?" Hostility spewed forth with every word.

"Abel, listen to what you are saying. It is you who are wrong here. They are offering to remain quiet, if only you admit your wrongdoing. We have heard your motive, but not your confession. Do it for my sake. Your mother will be tremendously hurt by your actions when she learns of this."

Upon the mention of his mother, Abel broke. He could see images of her crying over him in horror. In his desire to get even with those whom he felt had wronged him, he failed to think of how his family members, especially his mother, would be affected. Reality began to sink in. In his anger, he had dishonored his family.

"Yes, father. I did it."

The three men glanced at each other and were in accord.

"As your father, I demand you make restitution for everything you have taken from these men, and their families. There is no excuse for your actions. You will calculate the advantage you gained in obtaining better sales over Master Haddad, and you will repay every bit of what you stole from Master Reuben. Your amounts must agree with, or better, the amounts they show on their records. Do you understand?"

Abel sat, with his head hanging low.

"Master Haddad, you will be hearing from us shortly. Give us a few days to work things out. I am sure it will be satisfactory. You have my word."

Master Haddad and his brother, Rueben, returned home late that evening. Mara had dinner waiting for them and called them to the table.

"I ordered the workers to prepare your favorite dish." She could see that they were elated.

"How did your meeting go, Obed?"

"It was difficult, but it concluded favorably," he answered, wearily. He had not realized how much the confrontation had affected him until he sat to eat.

Benjamin had gone to bed early, due to an early morning responsibility. *It is better that he does not know of the details.*

After eating, Obed thanked Mara for a delightful meal, and suggested that she have some refreshments brought into the study, where he and Ruben would be for a little while.

"Reuben, I just can't get something out of my head," he said, as he took a seat in the study.

"What is that Obed?"

"Abel said that Reuel is a bad person. He has worked for us for years. It is true that he was just a worker when he started. We did have another head of security before him. Something is bothering me about that."

"Whatever it is will come to you, I am sure," Rueben said.

"This has been a productive day, don't you think?" Obed asked.

174

"I am glad we don't have more of them. I would be worn out, to say the least."

"Rueben, what does Athaliah know about all of this?"

"She did the investigation that uncovered the thief."

"I am guessing that she has not put it together that we both were hit by the same person. Am I right?"

"I would say you are correct," Rueben said.

"Good. Let's make sure she doesn't hear about it. I don't know what she would do, should she find out. She has been fragile since Abel walked out on her, after making his accusation."

As he spoke, a thought hit him. *Athaliah, Abel, Reuel…* The three names came together for the first time in his mind. Then, another name pushed its way into his conscious mind: Daniel.

He had not thought of that name for years, even just now, when he mentioned to Reuben that he had another head of security before Reuel, it did not register.

That which he had previously not understood, now, suddenly, made complete sense. A lightning bolt rushed through his body, and he was as a man struck on the head by a boulder. The realization of what had happened all those years before became clear. This he was not ready for. He saw, with a new understanding that which he had missed back then. *It was not Daniel. It was Reuel.*

"Reuben, please forgive me. I must go to my room. Please, ask Mara to excuse me. Tell her I have gone up to our room." He walked away as though drunk, feeling unstable, and weak in the knees.

Sleep would not come. Try as he might, all he could think of was his little girl … and that monster who beat her senseless and took her innocence from her forever. That vile man had moved right into his life as though he deserved to live, after what he did. Thoughts of the violation danced across his mind. *My little girl was so violently beaten that she couldn't remember anything that happened to her. She was innocent.* Unwilling to accept what he saw in his mind's eye; he turned his head as though that would make the thoughts go away. He tossed, uncontrollably, on his bed.

Unbelief turned into anger. Anger swelled into rage. Rage blinded his eyes to all rational thinking. *I will kill that man.* He vowed. "I will rip him apart with my own bare hands." He heard the words come out of his mouth, and they sounded rational, even soothing.

Another realization came rushing over him; one of guilt. *What did I do? I had*

175

an innocent man pay for something he did not do. For years he had felt justified in his actions toward Daniel. Shame flooded over him. *He was an innocent man.*

Unable to sleep, he decided to correct the matter at once. Dressing quickly, he ran to the steward's quarters. "Get up and prepare my horse. Quickly, I say. Go." Not bothering to tell Mara what he was doing, he impatiently waited as the servant readied his mount. Finally, the horse was brought to him. "Tell no one of this. Only say to my wife that I have urgent business."

Reuel was not in town. He was at the stockyard with the animals, some distance down the mountain. Obed urged his horse to a gallop. Fortunately, there was a full moon to light his way. Seeing only contrasts of darkness and greater darkness, as trees and shrubs whisked past him in the night, he steered his horse as best he could. He had taken this trail many times over the years and knew it by heart. Just ahead was a wadi, or canyon, that made the trail difficult to negotiate. Winding around outcrops and jutting rocks, the trail led him slowly downward. He could make out shadows and knew which way to turn to avoid the dangers that confronted him as he flew. The horse seemed to know his way and moved smoothly around corners and across dips in the path. Well beaten and worn, the trail presented a challenge to travelers during daylight hours.

In the dark of night, under the circumstances in which Obed rode, it was only a matter of one misstep and the unthinkable could occur. In his rage, nothing mattered, but to reach Reuel. Rounding a corner, the horse saw an object before him and jumped to avoid it. The movement was so violent that the rider could not keep his balance. The horse darted quickly to the left, and Obed fell to the right. All went silent. Obed felt catapulted into a dark nothingness, with no ability to stop what was happening. He reached for anything that might slow his fall but felt himself flying as though floating; a moment later – nothing.

Mara awoke the next morning and realized that Obed was not there. Sensing that something was wrong, she sought out the house steward, Asher.

"Do you know where Master Haddad is?" she asked.

"No. He only told me to say that he had urgent business."

"Thank you," she said. There was nothing she could do but wait for him to return.

"Did he say how long he might be?"

"No, Ma'am. Only what I told you."

176

The sensation in the pit of her stomach grew. It was unusual to see him leave so early. *What business could he conduct at such an early hour? Unless he was going a great distance…*

She could not calm herself, and apprehension mounted. Mara knew her husband. This was out of character for him. When her brother-in-law came down to breakfast, she inquired of him. "Did Obed say anything to you last night?"

"What do you mean? What has happened? Is there something wrong?"

"I just know something is not right." she said. "He never leaves early, as he did today."

"He has left the house, then?"

"I must ask the steward. Excuse me for a moment."

Running to the rear of the house, she found the steward, going over the daily expense accounts. "When did the Master leave the house, do you know?"

"Yes Ma'am. It must have been around the second watch of the night."

"And, he said nothing to you about where he was going?"

"No, Ma'am."

"Did he seem his usual self?"

"No, Ma'am. He seemed to be quite agitated, and in a hurry."

Returning to the dining-room where Rueben sat at a meal, she asked, "Did he say anything to you about leaving last night?"

"No." He thought for a moment. "We were sitting in his study when he seemed to react to something. As I recall, he asked something about Athaliah, and then he said he didn't feel right about what one of the men had said earlier, at the meeting. And, then he abruptly excused himself, and left. Oh, he did ask me to let you know that he was going to his room, which I did, as you recall. That is all I know."

Around mid-morning, Reuel arrived, his horse in a lather. He greeted the steward and asked to speak with Mrs. Haddad.

"Good day, Reuel. Can I help you?" Mara said as she entered the room where he waited.

"Good day, Ma'am. I don't know what has happened, but Master Haddad's horse came into the stockyard today, without a rider."

"When did you see it?"

"It was early. I think he must have arrived before anyone was awake. What do you think it means? When I saw the horse, I thought he might have gotten away from one of the workers, but then I thought it might be best to find out, for sure."

"I fear for my husband. From what we understand, he did leave the house in the night," Mrs. Haddad said.

"Reuel, ride into town to page Master Benjamin. We need him here right away," She ordered.

"Yes, Ma'am. Right away, where will I find him?"

"He had an appointment at the grange this morning. You will most likely find him there. Go now."

Turning to Rueben, who had come out to see what he could do, Mara said, "You must help us find Obed. Organize some of the men, and ride between here and the stockyard. Oh, I hope he is not hurt. Find him, please."

Rueben ran to find Asher, who would know who was available to help. "Who can go with us to search along the road between the stockyard and here," he asked.

With short delay, the household was in a flurry of motion. The men who were present came together for instructions. Rueben stood before them.

"Master Haddad is missing. We do not know where he is. We were just told that his horse arrived at the stockyard early this morning, without him. Get whatever you need to be effective and join me here as soon as you can. Move quickly." Reuben watched as the men jumped into action. Within mere moments, they reappeared leading their horses.

"Since you know the trail better than I, go before me. Keep an eye out for anything that looks out of order. We have no idea where he might have gotten separated from his horse. Mount up."

Master Haddad was fortunate to afford a stable full of horses. This day they would be put to the test of endurance.

The men rode out. "Take notice of everything along the way. Don't be tempted to wait to explore further down the trail. Start right now, as we go along. Some can watch on the right, while the others watch on the left," Rueben instructed.

Reuben was pleased to see how dedicated the men were to the task at hand. Obviously, Master Haddad was beloved by all who worked for him.

Soon, the trail wound down, and through the wadi. The troop progressed slowly, but none saw anything that might alert them. The going was slow. "Don't be impatient. Take time to look at everything. Look for disturbances along the trail," Reuben emphasized. "This will ultimately save time."

The men arrived at the stockyard, having seen nothing untoward. "Let's go back and look better. Is there a way for some of you to reach the opposite side of the wadi so the trail may be observed from that side? In that way, the trail, and everything below it can be seen," Rueben suggested. "We must hurry. Sunlight will wane soon."

Several men offered to go to the far side of the wadi. It would take longer to reach their destination, but once there they could leave the horses, and make their way along the rim of the wadi on foot, to look down on the trail from the opposite side. The rest of the men would return up the trail and watch for indications from the men on the far side.

Master Reuben suggested that only two or three men go to the far side. "The terrain looks like it is much more difficult to negotiate on that side. One man can stay with the horses when they can't go any farther. The other two can continue to the rim. Four eyes are better than two."

As the three men hurried off, the others returned up the trail. In time, the three men could be seen making their way upward on the other side. Soon, they dismounted, and two of them continued up the rim. The distance was great, but if everyone was quiet, their voices could be heard across the expanse. Slowly, the men climbed through the canyon on both sides, searching for any possible clues. The larger group kept an eye on the trail as they ascended, taking time to look over the edge to see what lay below, while the others on the far side foraged a trail where there was no trail. The going was slow.

Nearing the midpoint of the wadi, the men on the far side shouted at the top of their lungs and made hand signals, jumping up and down as they waved their hands. Men on the trail stopped to listen.

"What are they saying," Reuben asked. "Everyone listen!"

"They seem to be pointing to an area just below us," one of the men said.

"Yes, see, they are pointing that way."

Rueben stepped as close to the edge as he could and looked down. His eyes moved back and forth, studying every feature of the wadi wall beneath him.

"There. Look down there. What do you see?"

Below them, just a small glint of color could be seen. "There, I see something." one man shouted. "It is the color of Master Haddad's cloak."

"This is what the other men are seeing from the far side. No wonder we didn't see it the first time past. It is almost invisible," another man said.

"Who has a rope in hand? Did anyone bring a rope?" Reuben asked.

"Yes, I have rope," a man shouted.

"Is it long enough to reach down there?"

"Here, let's tie the end of it around this jutting boulder. From here we can make our way down," another offered.

Working as a team, the rope was tied, and a man started letting himself down the wadi wall, slowing picking his way past obstacles, and loose rocks, as he lowered himself one cautious step at a time.

One man shouted down at him. "Do you have any water with you? Master Haddad may need a drink."

"No, I wasn't thinking of that. Pass me a skin with another rope, and I will catch it. There is a twine rope on my horse that can hold the weight of the water skin."

Shortly, he received the water skin and placed its strap over his shoulders. Lowering himself, he carefully chose each step. In what seemed like an eternity, he came into view of the body. Making his way horizontally across several outcrops, he found Master Haddad. There was no movement. He approached with caution and placed his hands on his chest. A heartbeat could be felt.

"He is alive. He is alive."

Shouts of joy erupted above him as the men rejoiced over the good news.

Master Haddad lay unconscious, wedged in a crevasse. There was no danger of his falling from there, but the man could do nothing by himself to help. Taking the water skin from his shoulder, he poured a small amount of its contents into the palm of his hand and reached it over to Master Haddad's mouth. It ran over his mouth and into his beard. No movement was detected. He checked for a pulse. "Yes," he said.

Again, he held water to Master Haddad's mouth, and he saw movement. His lips parted, and he received the life-giving moisture.

"Master Haddad do not try to move. We are here. All your men are above on the trail. We are going to get you out of here."

Looking upward, he shouted. "We are going to need a wooden frame on which to tie him, so he can be pulled up from here. We will need more rope, as well. I will stay here until you get it ready."

He could not see what took place above, but a fury of action erupted. Thinking of what was needed to move Master Haddad, Ruben said, "Someone must return to the stockyard and bring sufficient rope, and something to make the framework."

Reuel said, "There is a bed we can use for that purpose. I will go for it." Looking at another man, he said, "Come with me, and we will get what is needed."

The first rescuer sat next to Master Haddad. With nothing else to do, he searched the terrain above, and around him, for possible evacuation routes. That is when he noticed the olive tree a short distance above him. His attention was drawn to an apparent disturbance in the way the limbs were arranged. *That must be what broke his fall*, he concluded. Calculating the trajectory of the fall, it became apparent that Master Haddad had dropped through the tree, which broke his fall. "Master Haddad, that olive tree saved your life. You are a very fortunate man, indeed."

Up above, Master Benjamin arrived to where the men were standing on the trail. His horse snorted heavily with exhaustion. He had come as soon as he heard about his father. Concern showed on his face, as he pulled on the reigns. Jumping off his horse, he ran to his uncle Reuben. "What have you found? Where is my father? Is he alright?" His questions came rapidly.

Rueben brought him over to the edge of the cliff and looked down. "We found him down below. He is hurt, but still alive. We will know more when we get him up. The men are waiting for a framework on which to place him for the ascent. He must be moved with great care."

"No. This can't be happening to my father." Benjamin shouted, from pure adrenaline.

"We are doing everything we can to bring him up. Be patient, son."

The man below thought to check for broken bones and lacerations. "Forgive me, Master, but I must check to see how extensively you are hurt. I don't mean to hurt you." He checked one limb at a time. One leg was broken, and bleeding. The flow had diminished, but it didn't look good. His left arm was also broken. Master Haddad's ribs had taken a beating, as well.

Reaching for a stick from the tree above, he tore his clothing and fashioned a stint, as best he could. It took some effort to arrange Master Haddad's body so he could work. Groans of agony could not be quieted, as he did what he could as first aid. "The men will return soon with equipment to lift you away from here. Hold on, Master. Don't try to move." His voice trembled as he spoke. Obed didn't respond.

The daylight was softening when a commotion was heard above. Soon, several men made their way over the cliff and down the steep slope. A bed that had been stripped to the essentials was lowered on ropes. Now that the others had come, they placed the framework next to Master Haddad, and carefully moved him onto it. Using soft straps, they bound him as tightly as they dared without doing him more harm. "It is a good thing that he is not completely conscious," one man said.

Covering him in a blanket, the order was given to begin the ascent. Slowly, men from above pulled the ropes upward. A few groans could be heard, but progress was made. A shout of victory went up, as the bed was brought over onto the trail.

"Four of you men take the corners and walk Master up the trail. Try not to jostle him too much along the way. Trade-off if you must. I will go ahead and bring news, and call the doctor to the house," Master Reuben said.

"Master Benjamin, you can take command from here. I will go ahead, and prepare for his arrival," Master Rueben said.

The procession began its way up the trail toward home and safety. Some of the men, thinking ahead, had brought torches to light their way.

Master Reuben rode into the yard, dismounted, and quickly ran into the house. Mara arose from her chair to meet him. "How is he?" Is he alive? I have been so worried."

"Yes, my sister, Obed is alive. But he is hurt very badly. I must go for the doctor, but I wanted to bring you the news first. The men are bringing him up the trail and should be here before too long."

"Oh, thank you. Yes, please go for the doctor. You can return with him before the men get here. Take the chariot and a fresh horse. It will be faster." Looking at one of the servants, she said, "Go with Master Reuben and assist him. Show him the way to the doctor's house."

A sense of relief filled everyone in the house. All-day long they had waited, not knowing if Master Haddad was dead or alive. All they had been able to do was hope for the best and dismiss any thought of the worst.

The men eventually arrived, carrying Master Haddad on the makeshift stretcher.

Master Benjamin could be heard giving orders. "Good, men. Be careful as you take him up the steps. You have done a good job."

From time to time, he had ordered them to stop to assess his father's condition. Master Haddad now lay still and silent, as he was placed in his room. The doctor immediately asked everyone to leave the room, except for Mara and Benjamin, who insisted on being present.

Mara was relieved when she saw him brought in, but this quickly turned to concern, when she saw how broken he was.

"What do you think, doctor?"

"Allow me some time to look him over, and I will know better how to respond. At first glance, it doesn't look good. But he is alive. For that, we can be grateful."

The doctor worked over Obed with care, setting the broken bones, as best he could. Benjamin assisted him when more than two hands were needed. The patient's cuts and scrapes were cleaned and covered. "We will know more with time. Master Haddad took a tremendous fall. I am not sure how extensive his internal wounds are. From what Master Rueben told me, a tree broke his fall, possibly being what saved his life," he said as he worked in the wee hours of the morning. Mara sat waiting, having refused to move from her seat without learning of her husband's condition. Benjamin left the room.

"He is quiet for now," the doctor said. "Our next concern is infection. Let's pray it doesn't develop. I will return to cleanse the wounds and change the bandages later today. I will assess his condition then. For now, should he rouse, try to give him water. I did detect some involuntary movement. Time will tell what that might mean."

Mara sat at her husband's side, not wanting to leave him for fear that he might die. She didn't know what was worse, for him to have been killed outright, or to be hovering, as he was doing. She loved him dearly and felt the pain she knew he must be feeling. *To be unconscious is probably better for now.* From time to time, she heard him groan, and stroked his cheek to assure him of her presence.

Having to take a break, herself, she left the room briefly. Reuben was, as best he could, helping Benjamin cope with pressing responsibilities that knew no reason not to be bothersome.

"Mara how is he now?" he asked.

"He is stable for the time being. I must find Benjamin to put him at ease. Did he leave?"

"He had to take care of some pressing business, but he will return soon. He is distressed," Rueben said. "I have discussed with him the possibility of his father's inability to work for a while, at least, not until he gets better. I trust that is alright with you. Benjamin must assume his father's responsibilities, and he is doing such a good job already."

"Thank you, Reuben. That is what I want you to do, as his uncle. Thank you for helping. I am sorry you are taken away from your own responsibilities."

"Don't worry about me. I have a competent staff that can carry on in my absence, for a while. I am concerned about Athaliah. She should be notified, don't you think?"

"Yes, of course. I have been so wrapped up in the situation here that I have not thought of much else."

"Well, then, I will send a runner with the news. Consider it done."

"Thank you. You are such a help, and encouragement. I don't know what I would have done without you here to step in. I just can't understand what would cause Obed to leave that way. It weighs on me. It is out of character."

"I am sure we will find out, in time," Reuben said. "I will stay on with you and Benjamin until we know my brother is stable."

The next day the doctor returned to assess Master Haddad's condition. Upon further observation, he could not miss the steady involuntary body movements. It was worse than what he had seen the day before. Calling Mrs. Haddad, he said, "In addition to the wounds, Master Haddad seems to be suffering from what looks to me to be similar to palsy. I will keep an eye on this. If it persists, I will know more."

Mara broke into tears. "How much can he endure?"

CHAPTER TWENTY ONE

The Heart Revealed

Athaliah enjoyed Jebu's company. The two had become close friends since he had returned. Her uncle was away, and she hoped he would not return too soon. Her relationship with Jebu was delightful. Aunt Gloria was pleased, as well.

One day, she and Jebu walked in the fields near the house. Tightly growing shafts of grain formed a lovely green for some distance ahead of them. A soft breeze made the green tassels dance in seemingly liquid waves. A young chaperone walked at a distance. "Athaliah, may I ask you something?"

"Sure. What would you like to know?"

"Please don't think me forward. I am curious. Why do you live with your uncle and aunt? Do you have parents?"

A note of sadness could be detected, as she sought an adequate response.

"It is complicated." She didn't want to think of her parents because it caused her to remember her pain. In her heart, she knew the time would come when she would divulge some information if their relationship were to grow.

"I was married." She heard herself utter the words and was shocked. It was not the response she wanted to give. Not now. Not yet.

"You say, 'was married'?"

"As I said, it is complicated." Her words could not be taken back. The only option she had now was to, in some delicate way, smooth her responses.

"My husband rejected me before the ceremony was complete. I don't understand it. I thought he loved me, but he didn't."

"That is sad. Who would not love you? I am sorry for bringing it up."

Athaliah surprised herself with the response. She had guarded her secret for so long. Now, she couldn't explain why she dared mention it to Jebu.

"I am sorry. I didn't intend to tell you this."

"I'm glad you did. Athaliah, I like you a lot. In the time we've had together, I have come to appreciate you. This helps me understand you better. Really, if truth were told, I believe my feelings go much farther than 'like.' I am falling in love with you."

Athaliah couldn't believe what she was hearing. She liked Jebu, but she was not ready to hear a confession of love. *How can he love me,* was all she could think.

"I am sorry, but it is true. I have not met anyone like you. We think alike. We work well together, and the more I learn about you, the more I am sure my feelings are well-founded."

She heard his words but couldn't believe it. Yet, it caused her stomach to twitch.

They walked on in silence. Both had to become comfortable with what they had declared. Conflicting feelings vied for supremacy within Athaliah. Should she trust him? Could she trust him? *I do like him – a lot. Maybe, even more, than I am willing to admit.*

Jebu felt uneasy. *Did I overstep my bounds by telling her? What if she rejects me for presuming upon her?* Worry welled up inside him.

"Athaliah, everyone needs someone to love and care for," he said weakly. Then boldness leaped within him. "Neither of us is a child any longer. We can look at life with mature perspectives, don't you think?"

She wanted to care for him. *Why do I feel so afraid?*

"From what you told me, I think it only normal for a person, having been treated in that way, to pull away from the possibility of being hurt again."

Not wanting to seem convinced too quickly, she asked, "Do you really believe this?" Her guard was up, and it had protected her well for a long time. To let it down would not be easy.

Halting his steps, he turned to her, and said, "Athaliah. Please, let me say what I feel. I love you. Can you love me?"

She looked at him blankly.

"Just think on this. I don't want to pressure you in the least. If you don't feel the same way, I will not confine you."

CHAPTER TWENTY TWO

Change of Direction

"What did the note say?" Mara could not understand. "I sent a message by courier, so that Athaliah could come to be with her father.

Gloria sent a runner back with a troubling message. She is sorry to hear about Obed's accident but says Athaliah has disappeared. She is no longer at the house."

Mara could not believe what she heard. "What has happened? Was she there to hear of her father?"

"From all indications, no; she had left already," the courier said.

"Where would she have gone? I just don't understand why she would do that."

Fear for her daughter could not be held at bay. With tears, Mara felt shock flood over her body. First, her daughter left home. Then, her husband is hurt and may die, then, her daughter can't be found.

"Didn't she leave a note of any kind, so Gloria would know? This is unexpected behavior, don't you think? I don't know how much more I can take," she said, overwhelmed.

"I am so sorry, Mara. I am not sure why, but there is the question of a young man who works for me. He can't be found either, from what Gloria wrote in her message," Reuben said.

Mara looked at him. "A young man? What young man? I can't believe she would do this to us."

"I know all this is very troubling. What can I do to help?" he asked. "How can I be of help?"

"If you continue helping Benjamin with his responsibilities for a few days, I might be able to cover the concerns with Obed. The servants of the house know their respective responsibilities, and that is an immediate help to me."

Life had changed in one fell swoop, as though a giant broom had swished over the land, upsetting everything in its path. Master Haddad lay in bed, unable to speak or move. He might die. Athaliah could not be found. Mara removed herself and found a place to cry alone.

Reuben felt useless. How could life be changed so fast, so drastically? He walked to the patio and sat, stunned.

When Benjamin returned home, he found his uncle still seated on the patio. "Uncle, how is everything? You look troubled. Is my father all right?"

"Yes, he is stable. The doctor left us with instructions. But we received bad news from your aunt Gloria while you were in town. I sent a message by courier, so Athaliah could come be with her father, but your aunt informed me that Athaliah is gone from the house. I am sorry to have to tell you this, Benjamin. You have so much on your shoulders already."

Benjamin sat, shocked at the news. Guilt over his sister's pain was with him, as a steady companion, ever since she was hurt. Too many things were accumulating upon him. *I must be strong. My father needs me. My mother needs me. The household needs me. Athaliah needs me. I must stand, and not faint. I must be the man my father raised me to be.* Thoughts came at him like daggers, threatening to cut his heart out. *I must not fail now.*

Days passed, and the doctor kept vigil over Master Haddad's progress. It was not as he hoped it might be. "Keep him drinking water and eating. He is alert but can't speak. He seems frustrated but gives signs of understanding when we speak to him. We will know, with time, just what his limitations are. His wounds are healing. The broken bones will be better soon, but the constant movements seem to remain, and if anything, are getting worse. Always have someone with him. Speak soothingly to him when he seems uneasy." Mara made sure the doctor's orders were carried out.

CHAPTER TWENTY THREE

Life Goes On

Life settled down. The changes were accepted, for the most part. Even the most difficult of situations can be weathered if there is a will to carry on. The Haddad family, though changed, was strong and resilient. Benjamin was now at the helm. Uncle Reuben returned to his home and responsibilities, promising to keep the family informed about Athaliah, should she reappear.

Benjamin contracted an investigator to find his sister. Guilt forced him never to give up on finding her. He loved her. Thoughts of special moments and events came to him constantly. He vowed to find her. He and his mother had spoken often of her, wondering where she might be. With time they wearied of the pain they each felt at the mention of her name. Peace had to be made with their new reality. They needed repose from the heart-crushing sadness they carried inside, because of her absence. The easiest way to accomplish this was to simply remain silent. The pain only became bottled up inside of them.

In time, Master Haddad's visible wounds healed, but he could not arise from his bed. His muscles wasted away for lack of use, except for the involuntary movements; the doctor was convinced that it was palsy. Obed tried to speak but could not. His frustration was visible by all who came near him, but nothing could be done for that, except to keep him bathed and comfortable.

He knew Athaliah was lost to them. Though he tried; he could not get Benjamin to understand what he had discovered about her attacker. He wanted him to know because he was now the man of the house but could not make himself understood. This caused him constant, endless irritation.

Benjamin distanced himself from his father, to ease the constant reminder of their true situation, whenever he saw him. Life had to be faced with, or without a whole and healthy father, or a loving sister. He would keep trying to find her, and dedicated assets to accomplish that end.

Years came and went. Benjamin often wondered how time seemed to pass faster now that he was an adult, than it did when he was a child. He married a young lady he had known from youth. They now had two children. He didn't have sufficient time in a day to accomplish all that had to be done. Yet, he had the reputation of a respected businessman, loved, and admired by all who knew him. His wife, Leah, loved him and made his days worth living. His boys loved him. He rejoiced at the sight of them. They were little reflections of himself, in every way.

When he had to travel on business, he did what he always did – looked for Athaliah. He never walked in public without keeping an eye out for the remotest possibility of, someday, seeing her on a street, or in an eating establishment, or along some road.

"Leah, I must leave for several days. I have business in several cities. I don't really want to be away currently, but duty calls."

Leah never liked him to be away, but it was necessary on occasions. "My love, I will miss you. The boys will miss you, too, but we will be here when you return."

"Watch over my mother, will you? She could use some encouragement. My father is not cooperating well of late."

"Yes, my love. I will make sure to help her. And she enjoys the boys. We all will encourage her."

Benjamin gathered his equipment for travel and told his servant to take enough water for several days journey.

First, he had to travel south to Jerusalem, and then make his way to Jericho. He planned his return home by way of the valley, following the Jordan River.

Jerusalem was a bustling business center. Benjamin didn't go there unless it was necessary. The Jews didn't take well to him or his people but did business with them. To do business with Samaritans was considered a "necessary evil."

Having finished his affairs in Jerusalem, he and his servant headed down the mountain toward Jericho. The trail was busy. People walked, or rode, up and down the road, causing dust to rise at each step. Each time a foot touched the ground, a puff of dust was forced into the air, hanging there in a cloud. In the dry time of the year, this made travel uncomfortable for everyone. Benjamin covered his face with the loose end of his turban. This was customary and it was difficult to recognize anyone on the road, because of their hidden faces. The turbans effectively kept the harsh rays of the sun away from contact with the skin. Sunburn was avoided by everyone. Only the uniqueness of each traveler's attire could give away their station, or culture.

Benjamin decided to stop at a little vender on the side of the road, for a little refreshment. He took a seat under a thatched shelter at the road's edge. His workman stood at his side. To be seated with his master would not be respectful. An attendant brought them date cakes and drink. From their vantage point, travelers could be seen coming up the road from a distance in either direction. Benjamin made a game of identifying people as they passed by. "Marcos, what do you think? I say that man over there is a man of means. Do you agree?"

"Yes, Master Benjamin. I believe you are right."

"And, that person coming, he looks like a religious man."

"You could be right, Sir."

"I would say he is a Rabi. Look how proudly he carries himself."

As they watched the man pass, Benjamin saw something beyond him, lying in the middle of the road, in the distance. This caught his attention. The passerby continued to where the object was. He stopped for a moment, and then walked around it, making sure not to approach it too closely.

Soon, Benjamin noticed another man and deduced he was a Levite by the way, he was dressed. This man also stopped to look. After a short moment, he too walked around to the side of the road and went on his way. Everyone passing did the same.

Finishing their refreshment, Benjamin and Marcos continued their journey. When they neared the object in the road, they also stopped. Lying before them was a nude man, bleeding. Extensive wounds could be seen. The man's legs were obviously crippled. His cries could be heard. Benjamin looked at the man, then at his Marcos. "This lowly beggar has been hurt."

Coming close, he said, "Who did this to you?"

"A band of thieves stopped me, and took what little I had, and left me with no clothing. They beat me when I would not comply willingly."

"How long have you been here like this?" Benjamin asked.

"I don't know. I have been asking for help, but no one stops."

Turning to his helper, he said, "Marcos, come, help me lift this man on to my horse. He needs help."

Marcos obeyed. Between them, they lifted the man onto the horse. "Can you sit without falling," Benjamin asked.

"I think so, Sir. Thank you," he said, almost inaudibly.

Benjamin looked down the road, then up the road. The only place he saw was the shelter where he and Marcos had just been.

"Come, Marcos, we will inquire of the roadside vender." Coming slowly back to the attendant, Benjamin asked, "Sir, might you know if there is someplace this man can get some help?"

Looking at the beaten and bloody body seated on the horse, the man frowned, and said, "Just over the top of that ridge, on that side path," he said pointing, "is an inn. The owner might possibly tell you."

Benjamin thanked him and followed the path. Just as he was told, he came to the inn. "Marcos, would you call the man of the establishment, please?"

They waited as a man came out. "Kind Sir, this man has been robbed and beaten. I would like to ask you to attend to his needs. I will pay you for your efforts."

"It just so happens that we have a room. We can put him in the room and have him cleaned up. It appears that he needs help getting inside. Please, allow me."

"Thank you, sir," Benjamin said. "We can do it together." Between the three men, the wounded man was helped into the room.

"Let's place him over here until we can get him cleaned up," the proprietor said.

"Very well," Benjamin agreed. "I must make my way down the mountain, but I will leave these two pence with you. Should you incur greater expense, I will repay you upon my return."

Marcos said, "Master, the trip will be longer if we come back this way."

"Yes, I know. But I have the means, and this man needs our help. The All-

Mighty will be pleased. I know it."

Once the man was clean, and in bed, Benjamin shook hands with the host, and made his retreat. "Come, Marcos, we must go on our way."

The trip to Jericho seemed easy. Benjamin and Marcos talked about their adventure with the man in need. Both had a sense of accomplishment. Marcos, quietly, blessed his master for his good deed.

Within three days, their business was finished. "Marcos, it is time to go back up the mountain to see how our new friend is doing."

From the region of Jericho, they could see the road, winding its way up the mountain. As they climbed, the dust was thick. The heat of the day gave them no relief. They pushed upward. In the evening, they reached their destination and stopped for the night.

The host greeted them warmly. "Welcome. Come in. We have rooms for you."

"Thank you, Sir. How is our friend?"

"He is sleeping now, but he has made progress, though it will be some time before he can safely travel. A doctor came by after you left and attended to his needs."

"Very well, we will stay until he is able to ride."

After settling into their respective rooms, the men visited the victim. He did not remember them. In his condition upon arrival, he had responded but forgot many details.

Benjamin explained what he had been told when they came across him on the road. "Yes, now I remember. You are the ones who helped me. Thank you. Thank you both."

After a time of catching up, Marcos said, "Master Haddad, the host is calling us to the table." Whenever he and Benjamin were in public, he always used his formal name.

A rough, wooden table awaited them. A single candle provided light. Bread sat in a small basket at the center.

"Tonight, we have soup," the host said. "We call it 'the house special.' It is made up of whatever is left in the kitchen, after a long day. My wife is an exceptionally good cook, you will agree. Just wait and see."

Benjamin took a wooden spoon and stirred the soup. He was interested in what might be in it. With one small taste, he was convinced that the host was right.

194

"Upon my life, this is good. It is excellent, indeed."

"It helps to be hungry," the host said.

"Sir, might you give a bowl of soup to Marcos, here, so he can take it to our friend in the room?"

"Surely, I can." He ran to the kitchen and returned with a bowl of steaming soup.

"Here, you go, Marcos. I hope you don't mind me calling you by your proper name. Be careful. It is hot and might burn your friend."

Marcos took it carefully, and headed for the room, taking a portion of bread with him. "Do you think you can sit up a little to drink this soup? He asked the man.

"I think I can." He stacked the pillows behind his back and smoothed the blanket before him. Marcos passed him the bowl.

Marcos watched as he tried the first spoonful. "This is good. Thank you." As he placed a piece of bread into his mouth, he said, "I overheard you speaking. You called your master, 'Master Haddad.'"

"That is correct. He is Master Haddad."

"Please, go eat your own soup. I will continue here. Could you do me a favor?"

"Yes, of course I will."

"Ask your master if I might speak with him, when he finishes."

"Indeed."

Leaving the man, Marcos returned to the table. When they were finished with their meal, Marcos said, "Master Benjamin, the man in the room would like to speak with you."

"Thank you, Marcos," he said as he stood to leave.

Walking to the room, he entered, slowly. The man sat, having finished his meal. In the dim light of the candle on the side table, Benjamin could barely make out the man's face.

"How was your meal? I trust you feel better," Benjamin said.

"I enjoyed it, thank you." Then, pausing for a moment, he asked, "Is your Surname Haddad?"

"Yes, it is," Benjamin said.

"Might you be from Samaria?"

"Yes, I am."

"Please forgive my questions. You are so young. Is your father Master Obed Haddad?"

"Yes, he is," Benjamin said. "Do you know him? How else would you know to guess?"

"I knew your father. As a matter of fact, I met you – a long time ago. You were just a boy."

"This can't be. How do you know my father?"

"I used to work for him."

Benjamin could not believe what he heard. What were the odds of meeting a man like this, and discovering that there was a connection with his father?

The man held his words for a long moment. "My name … my name is Daniel, from the Klan of Dan. I used to be your father's head of security."

"That must have been a long time ago. I remember most of the workers," Benjamin said.

"It was a long time ago. I was young. Your father's steward, Joab, hired me as security chief."

"We have a chief of security. His name is Reuel. He has been with us ever since I was young."

"Yes, I knew him. He was a fine young man."

Benjamin listened and was astounded at what he heard.

"What happened? Why did you leave my father?"

"I didn't leave your father. I was doing quite well, and was received by your father and Joab, as the best security guard they had; they often made that comment."

"What happened, then? Why did you not stay with my family?"

"One day, while preparing for a long caravan trip, I was set upon by a troop of Roman guards. They carried me off to a secluded place and proceeded to beat me senseless." Daniel hesitated, pain showing in his face. "They broke my legs and arms. While they beat me, I was told not to ever come near Master Haddad or his people. One of them stomped on my hands, leaving them as you see them now. But the most humiliating thing was done to me after I fell unconscious. They took my manhood. I didn't feel the pain, until later. They left me broken and bleeding."

"But why would they do such a thing to you?"

"That is the question I have lived with for all these years. I don't know."

Benjamin looked at him, struggling to understand what he heard. "You say they broke your limbs. How did you get here?" What he meant to understand was how Daniel was able to make his way on the roads.

"I look badly broken, as I lay here. But I was broken long ago. What you see is superficial, compared to my injuries of long ago. I have made my way, with great difficulty. All I can do is beg, but I get thrown out of places because I am considered a cripple, and as such, not worthy to be among normal people. This is the inhumane treatment I have endured. But I am alive, and not dead, as the Romans intended."

"Why would someone beat you on the road, as they have, seeing you struggle to make your way?"

"I have found that some people, unable to countenance my brokenness, make sport of me, and mock me, thus, allowing themselves to feel better about their own stations in life. Others take pity on me and help. I live on the alms they provide. I can do nothing else. I lost my dignity long ago."

Benjamin staggered, within, at the sight before him. Not only because of the present pain but for the years of agony experienced by this man.

"I cannot believe, but that this chance meeting was no accident," Benjamin said, at length. Having made up his mind, he said, "I am going to take you with me."

It was Daniel's turn to be surprised. This was totally unexpected. "Master Benjamin, you would do that?"

"How do you know my name?" Benjamin asked.

"Please forgive my brazen familiarity—. As I mentioned, I knew you when you were a boy. And, if I may risk your displeasure, I remember your sister, Athaliah, as well."

Benjamin sat a moment, thinking. "Yes, you did. I remember that about you. It is all coming back to me. You were her first love."

The men talked into the night hours, unable to sleep, their excitement compelling them.

"If I may, how is Athaliah, now?" Daniel said.

Benjamin's countenance darkened. "We don't know where she is. She disappeared several years ago, and no one has been able to find her. I have contracted several men to search for her, with no results."

"I am sad to know that" Daniel said. "Please forgive me, but the memories of her have kept me alive all these years. I know I have no right to say that, but it is the truth."

"I understand, Daniel. We all love her and miss her very much."

They finally gave up, and Benjamin returned to his room, but all he could do was think of Athaliah. He missed her so much.

The following day, Benjamin asked for the doctor. "How long will it be before the patient will be well enough to travel?"

"It has been a week, and he is healing fast. I believe, if you take care, he should be able to travel the day after tomorrow. But that is the Sabbath, so he can travel after that," the doctor said. "In the meantime, keep him down, and let him up only to exercise a little each day."

"Marcos, I believe it may be easier to return home by staying on back trails, along the higher routes. The heat of the valley is overpowering right now," Benjamin said, as the three men prepared to travel. Benjamin was thinking of Daniel's safety and well-being. The trip promised to be tedious, at best. If they followed the lesser routes, they could choose their own pace.

"Daniel, you will sit on my horse. How long has it been since you have ridden a horse?"

"It has been many years, Sir."

"We will go slowly," Benjamin said. "Marcos, help me get him seated." Together they lifted Daniel onto the beast. "He is a gentle horse, and won't give you any trouble," Benjamin assured him.

Benjamin sat on Marcos' horse, while Marcos led Daniel' horse on foot. Progress was slower than normal, but that gave the men time to talk.

"Master Benjamin, is your father still alive?" Daniel said.

"Yes, he is alive. But he suffered a tragic fall several years ago and was left paraplegic. He has not spoken since but responds as best he can. The doctor thinks it is because of a hit to his head. He seems frustrated most of the time. I had to take responsibility for the business when he had the accident."

"I am sorry to hear that. He was good to me."

As the men advanced, Benjamin was pleasantly surprised to see Daniel's alertness, despite his appearance. Just one look and everyone assumed, as Benjamin had, that this "lowly beggar" was an unlearned man, who lived off the generosity of others. The fact was the opposite. Daniel displayed great knowledge and learning. He begged because of his physical limitations, and the assumptions of others. He did not speak as one relegated to the lowest of society.

Benjamin recognized his surroundings, and said, "Marcos, take the horse and run ahead. Inform the steward that I arrived and ask him to prepare for a special guest in the guest's quarters."

"Yes, Master Benjamin." Benjamin dismounted and passed the reins to Marcos, who galloped off toward home.

"It is not far, now," Benjamin said to Daniel.

"It has been such a long time since I have been here. Everything is changed, yet it remains the same." Daniel felt uneasy but kept his feelings to himself. He had been warned never to return and didn't know if that order remained. Master Benjamin treated him with respect, such as he had not known for years. This allowed him a measure of comfort, despite his misgivings.

The men arrived amid great fanfare. Leah always made a show of her love and affection when Benjamin returned from abroad. This time was no exception. The servants were abuzz with activities.

"My Love, you are home. It is so good to see you," Leah said, running to Benjamin. Hugging him tightly, she almost smothered him, holding on for a long time.

"How good it is to see you, my Dear," Benjamin said, "I have missed you and the boys."

Just then, Caleb and Little Benjamin ran up to greet him, jumping into his arms, almost knocking him over. "My boys, I have truly missed you. It is good to see you both. You are becoming young men, growing taller in my absence." he said, as he gathered them close.

He saw Leah looking at his guest. "Leah, this is our special guest, Daniel. He will be with us for a while."

Daniel remained atop the horse. Dipping his head, he greeted her, "Good to meet you, Ma'am."

Benjamin called Joab and gave him instructions. Looking at Leah, he said, "I will explain later."

Leading Daniel, still mounted, around to the guest's quarters, Joab helped him down from the horse, and into a waiting room.

The household was filled with excitement. Benjamin was glad to be home. His mother plied him with questions. Finally, she asked, "Who is the man with you? I notice he is crippled."

"Mother, His name is Daniel. He was Father's head of security many years ago. I want him treated with the utmost respect. I have come to greatly admire him. I think you will, also."

She said no more. "Mother, I want to see Father. Come with me, please." He led her to his father's room. Entering, he greeted his father. Master Haddad lay on his bed, unresponsive, unable to move, except for his eyes. The expression in his eyes expressed curiosity.

"Father, I am home. It is good to see you." Benjamin spoke to him without hesitation, fully believing that he could be understood. "Father, you will never guess who I brought home with me." He allowed a pause for dramatic effect. "His name is Daniel, of the Klan of Dan."

As he spoke the name, his father's eyes widened. They seemed to soften.

Benjamin took notice of the change. "I see you remember him. He is a good man, Father. I have been with him for several days and am convinced that my decision to bring him home is correct. I will tell you all about him, in time. When you are ready, I will present him to you. Right now, I must go to dinner with the family. Father, it is so good to see that you are gaining strength and your memory is so good."

As Benjamin left the room, he didn't see his father's tears. Obed had known for years that he was wrong to have treated Daniel as he did. For all he knew, Daniel was dead. He had not heard anything more about him since making the request of the Roman Captain. Now, he learned that Daniel was alive. This took a burden off his shoulders. *At least, I know I am not guilty of his death.* For years he had had to hold the knowledge of what he did, inside. At times, he felt he would explode. He was unable to let anyone know his thoughts. Relief welled up within him. Still, there is the matter of Reuel. *If only I could do something.*

Being a prisoner within his own body made this impossible. He lived in a world of his own; a world no one could partake in or understand.

Benjamin joined the family at the table for dinner. The servants ushered Daniel in, and seated him, making sure he was comfortable. Having been informed of his condition, they treated him as normally as possible.

Conversation erupted when the boys asked about their father's trip. He did his best to satisfy their curiosity, without disrespecting their guest. The meal was pleasantly enjoyed. Caleb watched as Daniel tried to hold his eating implement.

"Mister Daniel, do your hands hurt? If you like, I could help you."

"Thank you, little one, but I must do this by myself. To answer your question; no, they don't hurt. It is just a little different because I lack movement in them. It just takes a little more time to eat," he said.

At an opportune moment, Benjamin said, "May I have everyone's attention. Mister Daniel is our guest, and I want everyone to know that he will remain our guest as long as he desires to be here."

Turning to Daniel, he said, "You may sit at our table for as long as you wish. We owe you a great debt of appreciation." The Haddad family had not only the financial ability, but the willingness of heart, to do this. The boys were pleased.

"Our father is the best," Little Ben said, sticking his chest out.

CHAPTER TWENTY FOUR

Resolve Intensified

Benjamin doubled down on his attempts to find his sister. Bringing Daniel into his home made him think of her constantly. Memories of the past flooded back into his mind. He was determined to seek her out – if she yet lived. He didn't know. It was always easier to think of the most negative possibilities. He rebuked himself for allowing such thoughts. *I will never give up* became his silent cry of determination.

He delved deeper into his work. As an experienced businessman, he found comfort in what he did. His reputation preceded him wherever he went.

He was a devoted husband and father and was fulfilled. Leah made him know her love for him in many ways. She completed him as no other person could. Yet, Athaliah loomed in his mind, like the unforgettable sweet fragrance of spring flowers that mark a day and give it life and meaning.

The hope of finding her drove him. Every time he passed a communal well, he looked to see if she might be there. At every street, he envisioned the possibility of her coming around the corner. Many scenarios played across his mind, causing him to despair, at times. But he willed himself to be alert. *She might be at the next restaurant I visit, or at the market, or hanging out clothes to dry.* He didn't know, so he commanded himself to be alert.

Coming out of a business meeting one afternoon, after a particularly taxing negotiation with a new business associate, Benjamin walked along the street of the little, unfamiliar town. He had come to extend his enterprise into this promising community. Weary of heart, body, and soul, he walked slowly, deep in thought and wanted only to reach the quaint inn, and rest.

Unconsciously, he found it soothing to whistle. A tune he had known as a boy came to mind, and he whistled it, not really paying attention to what he was doing. It wasn't really a song, but a short tune, just a few distinctive notes. Over and over, he whistled. In some familiar way, it comforted him.

With head down, he walked, whistling, automatically looking down each street he came to. While looking down a street to his left, he almost stumbled into a person standing on his right, at the corner. Quickly excusing himself, he continued, whistling.

His thoughts were far away, in a different time, in a different place.

Further down the street, he suddenly had the distinct feeling he was being watched. A current ran through his body. Turning to look behind, he saw no one. He continued, whistling as he went, thinking only of reaching the inn.

Arriving at the entrance, he stopped to greet the inn's attendant. Out of the corner of his eye he saw a shadow pass behind him. Turning out of curiosity, he saw a woman standing silently behind him, in the doorway. He smiled and turned away. The woman didn't move, but stood, studying him. Again, he sensed that awkward feeling. Hairs on the back of his neck stood up. He turned and hesitantly said, "May I help you?"

The woman cautiously walked closer. "That tune you were whistling, what is it?" She had a veil, over her face. He could only see her eyes.

"Was I whistling?" he asked, a little surprised.

"Yes, you were."

"Oh, I guess I was. I don't know. It is just a tune from my boyhood."

"Forgive me. Did it go like this?" She whistled the tune flawlessly.

"Yes, that's it." He didn't know this woman who spoke of whistles and couldn't understand why she was curious about it.

He noticed tears flowing from her eyes. She stood in silence. Not knowing what to do, he first looked at her, and then at the attendant, whose countenance was not pleasant.

"It ... it is you," she whispered, lifting her hands to lower her veil. "Don't you recognize me?"

Benjamin stood, not knowing what to make of her.

She whistled the tune again. "We used to call each other this way, long ago. Don't you remember?"

"I remember calling my—" he stumbled, "my sister." At that moment, full recognition hit him. "Athaliah, is this really you?"

She did not wait to answer him, but threw herself into his arms, hugging him, and kissing his face. "You are so grown up. I didn't know it was you, but I heard the whistle."

Benjamin did some hugging of his own. The two stood, holding each other for a long while, not caring who saw them.

Sobs could be heard by all who passed.

"Ben, I love you. I have missed you so much."

"I have never stopped looking for you, Sister. I feared I would never see you again."

Where were they to begin? Little fragments of information were exchanged. Looking around at the gathering crowd, Benjamin said, "Come, Athaliah, I have a room. We can go there to talk. Is that alright?"

"Yes, of course. I can't get over how handsome you are. My goodness, you have grown. Yes, lead me to your room."

Looking at the attendant, Benjamin said. "This is my long-lost sister. We have a lot of catching up to do. Would you please have someone bring refreshments to my room?"

He led her to his upstairs quarters, and pulled two chairs over to the balcony, opening the double doors wide. The air was fresh, and the scenery was breathtakingly beautiful. Mountains and valleys could be seen in the distance.

"I have so many questions. Where have you been? What have you been doing?

How are you living?" Benjamin asked, in rapid succession.

Athaliah sat for a moment, as though uncertain of where to begin, or how much to reveal. Her heart was full, now that she was looking at her little brother. Little? He was now a man in his own right. She could be proud of the man he had become. Something told her it was alright to share. The shock of seeing him left her off balance, but she knew her brother was trustworthy, and words took shape in her mind.

She began slowly. "Ben, it has been so hard. You wouldn't believe what I have become. I am afraid to tell you everything, but I love you, and I know you love me."

Her heart beat heavily. Emotions came in gushes. Tears erupted, accompanied with sobs. Calming herself, she found it difficult to release the pent-up words.

"Athaliah," Benjamin said, almost in a whisper. "Just start from the beginning."

"Oh, Ben, you are going to hate me. You don't know the person I have become. I'm afraid you won't understand." Resolved to overtake her hesitation, she said, "I am so sorry. I didn't know I would end up like this. I just wanted someone to love me."

Benjamin listened intently.

"I was so hurt and embarrassed when Abel left me on my wedding night. No one knew how I felt. Rumors flew around like bats in the night. I became angry and inconsolable. I allowed my pain to cause disruption in the house. In time, as you remember, Father and Mother sent me to Uncle Reuben's home to live. Life was better there, because no one knew me, at first.

"After a couple of years, I met a young man. He worked for Uncle Reuben in another town but came to do some investigative work with me. We became friends. At first, I could not even think of becoming close with anyone, but he was so nice, and thoughtful.

"Uncle Reuben had to go away on business and left the young man in the office to oversee his affairs. That was when we began to know each other better. I let my guard down and told him I had been married. I thought it might help to slow things down a little, but it didn't bother him. I was starved for real love, and he revealed his desire for me. I let him talk me into running away to get married.

"It all seemed so exciting and reasonable. Since I had already been put away by one man and was damaged in the public's eye, I felt no one else would want me. But he did. I allowed myself to think it possible to know love, still.

"He offered to take me away, so we could make a life together. It was very exciting. That is what we did.

"At first all was wonderful. Please forgive me for what I am about to tell you. He was offended when I found that I could not let myself be intimate. I tried so hard, but I could not bring myself to do it. Night after night, he came to me. Sometimes, in the day, but I could not comfort him. Many times, I cried myself to sleep, knowing that he was fuming at my side.

"We began to fight. Little things would upset us, and days would follow without talking to each other. The world we thought we were building together fell apart. My dreams of true love and acceptance vanished. We were living a nightmare. He told me that he was the man of the house, and as such, had his rights. He forced himself on me. I would cry as he did, but that didn't stop him.

"One day, he said, 'When I was small, I watched my married brothers come to visit the family. Their wives ordered them around – all the time. I swore that when I became a man, I would be the man of my house, and my wife would not tell me what to do. I have my rights, as a man.' It didn't take long, after marrying him, for him to think he could order me to do his bidding. I wanted to love him, and have a family, but I had come to almost hate men, because of what had happened to me when I was young. My greatest anguish was due to my parents not telling me what happened. But I was left with harsh feelings toward men. I just could not override them to become submissive. I did try."

"I am so sorry, Athaliah," Benjamin said. "I have felt guilty for what happened to you. I should never have left you alone that day. I had no idea you would be hurt. Our parents never told me all that happened to you. I didn't know, but I felt it was my fault."

"No. It was not your fault. I don't remember, to this day, what happened, but it wasn't your fault."

There was a knock at the door, and Benjamin let in a servant girl with a tray of refreshments. "Thank you, miss," he said, as she left.

Returning to Athaliah he said, "What happened next?"

"There we were, two people, living in the same house, at each other's throats all the time. I wanted him to love me, but he felt I was unresponsive and frigid. It was an impossible situation. Had he just been tender with me, it might have led to a willing submission on my part, but he impatiently insisted. Every day he came into the house and took me. We were torn apart by our inner pain. He felt he had his sworn 'rights,' as the man of the house, and I had my disgust and hate for men.

"One day, he ordered me to sit on a donkey. He then, proceeded to lead the animal through town, shouting, 'I divorce this woman, I divorce this woman, I divorce this woman.' I felt terrible. There was nothing I could do, but sit there, and cry. It was so embarrassing. I had never felt so humiliated in my life. How could something that should have been beautiful, become so ugly? I was torn apart."

"What did you do, then?" Benjamin asked.

"I could not return home to my family. I would have brought shame on all of you.

"I didn't want any of you to know what I had done. It was all my fault, and I knew no one would understand. I walked to another town and begged for food and lodging. No one would help me. There was no way out of the situation I was in. A man offered me a meal if I did an intimate favor for him. From there, I had no way back. My life took a turn I never expected. Word got around. The town's men started looking for me. With the money they gave me, I found a small house on the edge of town. I hated myself for what I was doing.

"After a while, I left that place. I took the money I had gathered and made a fresh start in another town. After a while, a man offered me marriage. I thought that was more respectable than what I had been doing, so I married him. That was another mistake. I realized I had chosen the wrong man. He was bestial. I realized I had gone from bad to worse. He treated me like an animal, forcing me to partake in activities I never thought possible. I hated him, and myself, for getting involved with him. He brought other men home to be with us. When he laughed at me, one day, I left him. My heart was broken.

"All I wanted was a man, a husband, to love me, but I had lost every bit of dignity.

"You would think I had learned my lesson. I had to eat and have a place to stay. I found myself walking the streets, sleeping under any kind of shelter I could find. I went to the river to bathe by night, and wash my clothing, hoping they would dry before morning. By day, I begged. Before long, I was back doing what I had done before.

"I had a reputation around town. All the men knew me. I was torn, because I was with husbands who had their own wives and children to keep and be responsible for, but they sought me out, instead. I was so lost."

Benjamin listened, stunned by what he heard. Yet, compassion compelled him to listen further. Athaliah broke into tears and anguish of heart, as she described what had become of her life.

"Again, I ran away, thinking I could start fresh in another town. I did well for a while. I wanted to be loved, and when, yet another man offered to marry me, I jumped at the chance for stability. He was a good man. I cooked for him, kept his house, and tended his children. He was older than I, by a few years, and we got along well enough. I felt that I had found a life for myself, at last. As is so often the case, the 'wife' is the last one to learn of infidelities. I became, once again, the laughingstock of the community, when I learned that he visited any number of women in town. They all knew him. One woman finally told me that all he wanted was someone to take care of his children. No matter what I did, I always was the one being used. It was an unwanted chain around my neck.

"I left him. Before long, I was right back where I always found myself. I had habits I could not break. My thinking was twisted. All things were seen through eyes full of hate, anger, hurt, disgust, humiliation, and shame. I hated myself. Try as I might I could not wash away the stain of my guilt. I wanted to die.

"In yet another town, I tried to take my own life. I did everything wrong. I failed. I couldn't even take my own life. Everything was upside-down.

"An elderly gentleman approached me one day and spoke kindly to me. He told me he understood my circumstances. He had lost a daughter many years before and wanted to make up for her by helping me. I was at my wit's end. There was nowhere for me to go. He said he had a home where he lived by himself. He was up in years and was forthright with me. He said, 'I am too old to harm you, but I can offer you a place to live off the streets. At least you might have a measure of dignity. I have some financial means with which to help. I don't mean to offend you, but I can give you what I have, so you won't be by yourself.'

"I thought about it and decided I could not be lower than I was at the time. Anything would be better than what I had. I realized that I didn't deserve to be loved. So, I said, 'yes.'

"But I was told there would be one stipulation. I must marry him, to give the appearance of propriety. Again, I said, 'yes.'

"Are you still with him," Benjamin asked.

"No, he died. I do have the house. The money he left me lasted only for a while. He was a kind and gentle man, never wanting anything from me. It was a joy to take care of him. I had finally found a respectable life. But he died.

"What happened next was predictable. I had to return to my old pattern. I had to make a living. When you passed me on the street a while ago, I was searching for a means to that end."

"Ben, I am so sorry you must see me like this. I can't ever return to the family I have shamed so badly. Can you ever forgive me?"

Benjamin's heart went out to her, as she cried uncontrollably.

"Come here. Let me hold you. Don't cry. There is something we can do."

She looked up at him with difficulty, her eyes swollen and red.

"I have finally found you. I do understand you not wanting to burden the family with your reality. As I sit here listening to you, I feel compassion – and love. I know life has not been what you envisioned.

"There is something that comes to mind. It just so happens that I may have an answer for you. I have a friend living with me and my wife. Yes, I am married, and we have two boys. But there is a man living with us that needs help."

"How could I be of help? I don't need another man in my life."

"This man is different. He is a cripple. He is a good man. When I met him, I knew we had to do something to help him. He has lived with us, in our house, ever since. It is a long story, but what I am thinking, might just work."

"Who is this man?"

"His name is Daniel."

When she heard the name, she cried, "Oh, no, it couldn't be the Daniel I knew, could it? I never thought I would ever see him again. He left me, and I have not known anything about him since that day."

"He is the one and same."

"I can't believe it. How did you find him? There is so much I need to know. He has always been in my heart. But you say he is a cripple?"

"Well, let me think. Since you can't return home for now, maybe I could bring him to you, so you can tend to his needs. Yes, he has been crippled for many years. He was savagely beaten by Roman soldiers, who left him for dead, many years ago. When I met him, and learned who he was, the first one he asked about was you. He has never forgotten you."

"That makes me want to cry, but I am fresh out of tears. This can't be true. I have never forgotten him. But I could never look at him. I am not the person I used to be. He would never want to see me if he knew what I have become."

Benjamin hesitated a moment. "Athaliah, this is your chance to do for him as you have always wanted others to do for you. Don't let your pride get in your way. The best way to defend your heart is to make a good offense. This could work."

Athaliah didn't know what to say. "I don't believe he would want to be around me. I would be ashamed."

"He needs help. You need help. What better way to be of help to each other? Just as you don't understand all that caused you to live as you have, he has lived with as many problems, thinking his dreams will never be possible."

"How can the troubled help the troubled?"

"He used to be our father's head of security, as you know. I have taken him in and given him food and shelter for a long time. You can be a great help to him, maybe even fill in the gaps of his life."

"That is wonderful, Ben. I love you. I knew you would grow up to be a good man."

"It is settled, then. I will go to him and see what can be arranged."

Then, almost as an afterthought, Benjamin said, "There is something else you need to know. It is about Father. He suffered a serious accident several years ago and is bedridden. If you were to return home now, he might not take it well. In time, he might be able to receive you. Mother spends her time caring for him. She is well, by the way."

"I am sorry to hear this, Ben. I have caused so much trouble in the family. I can't show my face around there. I don't deserve to be called their daughter. I am sorry Father is ill."

"We can find a way to let them know about you later. But, for now, let's get you back on a proper road, and forget about all that has happened to you, shall we?"

Athaliah hugged Benjamin, tightly.

"This is what I am thinking…."

Benjamin returned home with a new lease on life. His world had changed in a flash. He had met his sister again and felt renewed. There were concerns, to be sure. Learning of Athaliah's troubles gave him the conviction that he could help her. It was in his character to do so, and he had the financial means. As the head of the family fortune, he could do anything he wanted, within reason.

Leah met him as soon as she heard of his arrival. The boys were all over him, wanting to know what he had brought them from afar. The house was a happy place that night. The servants noticed a special glow and went about their tasks with snap in their steps.

As the family finished their evening meal, Benjamin said, "It has been a good day. My trip went much better than I thought. I have good news, but I would like to speak with Daniel alone. Would the rest of the family excuse me from the table?"

"My Dear, you are the boss. Of course, you may be excused. But don't be long. We haven't seen you in days."

Benjamin gave her a loving smile. *If you only knew, my Dear.*

In the office, Benjamin helped Daniel get situated in a comfortable chair. "Daniel, I want to speak with you, because I have news you might want to hear."

"News?"

"I will get to the point. As you know, my sister, Athaliah, has been lost to the family for years. I want you to know what I have to say before I tell the rest of the family. I found her while traveling this time."

"This is a surprise. Why tell me first?"

"I have my reasons, which will become apparent in due course. I must keep confidences."

Looking to see that the door was closed, Benjamin started. "I would like to enlist your help in the matter."

"What am I able to do that would be of help?" Daniel said.

"Quite a lot, as it turns out. I will not divulge much at this time, but there is one thing I would like to ask of you. Since you came to be with us, you have been a wonderful addition to the household. It is our privilege to have you with us."

Daniel still was in awe at the way in which the whole household accepted him. They treated him as though he were special. He felt like a man again.

"I would be glad to oblige you, Master Benjamin. I can't imagine what I could do, though."

"As it turns out, Athaliah needs help. She is not the person she used to be all those years ago. She is trying to make her way back to normalcy. I think she could use some help to accomplish her goals. That is where you come in."

Curiosity was written all over Daniel's face. "What do you have in mind?"

"She has a house but has difficulty with the expenses. I would like to ask what you would think of becoming a border with her."

"Master Benjamin, you want me to live with her?"

"Yes, so to speak. She needs you in so many ways. You could be a comfort to her. I can't tell you her story; that will be left for her to tell as she becomes able. I believe you could bring hope back into her life. At least, that is my wish. What do you say?"

"This is so sudden. I am at a loss for words."

"I am sure she can watch over you, as well. She needs a purpose. She would not cause you to feel less of a man than you really are."

"Does she know about me?"

"She knows only the minimum right now. I can tell you that she became exhilarated when she heard your name. I only told her that you are crippled. What do you say?"

"If you think I can be a help for her, I say, yes. I will do as you request."

"For right now, I would like that what I have said not leave this room. The family will know that you are moving but will not be told why. You will understand in time."

"I shall do as you wish, Master Benjamin."

"As for that, please call me Benjamin. If you wish to address me as such in public, that is alright, but I look upon you as a close friend."

"Yes, Sir," Daniel said.

Leah was happy to have Benjamin back home. She always worried about him while he traveled. Normally, he traveled with at least one of his workers, but this last trip had been all alone. This night, she could have him all to herself.

"You seem to be in an extra pleasant mood tonight, my Love. Do you have a reason behind this pleasantry?"

"Leah, I have a secret to tell you. You must promise to keep it to yourself. Do I have your word?"

"My Love, do you feel you have to ask?"

"Not really. But it is important that the knowledge of what I am about to tell you not leave this room, for now."

"Well, then, my lips are sealed." Smiling, she added, "And I won't write it down for anyone to see, either."

Bringing her close to his side, he said, "I found Athaliah."

"You did what?"

"I found my sister."

"Why do you want to keep this a secret? Shouldn't your mother know?"

"I agree, but there are circumstances that make it difficult right now. We must go about this with caution, for her sake."

"Tell me all about her. And don't leave out anything," she pleaded.

The night passed in conversation. The morning light was showing over the mountains to the east before they fell to sleep.

Benjamin called a family meeting the next day and informed everyone that Daniel was going to move to another town where he would live. The news came hard for everyone. They had all come to feel he was family. Little Benjamin and Caleb especially reacted to the news. They had learned a lot from him and enjoyed his good nature.

"Mister Daniel, will you ever come back? I am going to miss you," Caleb cried. "Do you really have to go?"

"Caleb, I am going to especially miss you. You and Little Benjamin, both are great friends to me. Of course, I will come back."

"When will you leave," Mara said.

"It will be a couple of days."

Daniel didn't have much to pack. He had arrived with the clothes on his back, and now had several garments to place in a roll pack.

"Benjamin, what shall I say to Athaliah, when I see her?" He had never forgotten her. In his present condition, he was not sure how he would be received. When he last saw her, he was a gallant, young, muscular, and talented security guard, who enjoyed the respect of all who saw him. Now, he was a mangled cripple, with whom most people avoided making eye contact.

"Will she look down on me?"

"Only if you don't stand up," Benjamin said.

"Don't make fun of me," he returned, good-naturedly, taking Benjamin's obvious humor. "As you can see, I can't stand up straight."

"I know. I meant your physical condition goes unnoticed when your spirit is revealed. Your character speaks for itself."

"Thank you, Benjamin. Do you know that in all my years since my beating, no one has encouraged me as you have?"

"You forget. I was only a boy when I knew you, but, even then, I saw your character, and was delighted when Athaliah also noticed it. I know that in your heart, you are the same man I knew before."

They rode calmly on. Daniel, though familiar with horses, was not used to sitting on top of one. The going was deliberately slow.

"How much longer is it to Sychar, Benjamin? That is the name of the town Athaliah lives in, correct?"

"We will arrive this evening if all goes well. I sent a courier ahead to notify Athaliah of our pending arrival."

"Good. I am nervous."

"You should be. She hasn't seen you with a beard." Benjamin couldn't help himself. It was his way of putting Daniel at ease.

"It is not my beard I am worried about."

"I know. Just be yourself. You will see. She is eager to see you again. She may have a few questions, but I guess you have a few of your own. That makes you both even."

That evening, just as planned, they rode up in front of a small house on the outskirts of Sychar. It was not pretentious but pleasantly sufficient. Benjamin dismounted and helped Daniel off his horse. Before either of them could get to the door, it opened. There stood Athaliah, smiling.

"Ben, you are back. How good it is to see you!" She gave him a welcoming hug and turned to face Daniel. "You must be Daniel. Welcome," she said. "I have been waiting for you. Please, come in. I am sure you are both tired from your travels."

Benjamin allowed Daniel to make his way into the house before him without assisting him or bringing added attention to his obvious condition. He acted as though Daniel were completely whole. In this way, he honored him.

"I know it has been a long way, so I have prepared a good meal for you. Would you like to wash the dust off? Come this way."

She led them to a shelter behind the house, where basins of fresh water awaited them.

"While you are taking care of this, I will set the plates on the table. Feel at home, please. It is wonderful to have you here."

In a short time, the men made their way back into the living/dining room. A table was prepared and offered delicious opportunities to break their hunger.

"Thank you, Athaliah," Benjamin said, as he took his seat. Daniel, hearing her name, perked up. That name. It meant so much to him. Now he was hearing it once again in her presence. This was a moment to be remembered.

Athaliah was the perfect hostess. The men ate every morsel set before them. Soon, Benjamin knew he had to find a way to allow Daniel and Athaliah to become acquainted again.

"Athaliah, I am delighted that you have offered to board Daniel. I know you both have a lot to catch up with. Please allow me a little while to go into town and purchase a couple of items. I will return shortly."

"Yes, of course, Ben."

They were alone together for the first time in many years. Neither felt completely comfortable. Each wondered where they should begin.

"Athaliah, I want to thank you for opening your home to me as you have. It means more than you know. As you can see, not too many people have been willing to do this for me."

Athaliah sat for a moment. "Daniel, I waited for you at the creek. Did you come to see me that day?" In this question, she hoped to learn several things. The event that had changed both their lives remained a mystery to her. No one was willing to tell her what had happened, and her curiosity was overwhelming.

"I suppose when two people, such as ourselves, meet as we are now, it is only natural to start with the last time we met." He stopped for a moment and continued. "I kept my promise to meet with you at the creek, but you weren't there."

"Daniel, that was the day I was beaten."

"What do you mean?" he asked, thinking he had misunderstood her.

"I went to the creek early to prepare for our meeting. My brother had to go back to the house to get something. That was when someone attacked me. I do not remember anything about it."

"From what I remember, we had planned to meet around mid-day, right?" Daniel said.

"Yes, but I took the lunch and got there early to set up. That is all I know. I can remember nothing beyond that point. It took me months to get better. As matter of fact, I have not been the same since."

"I had no idea. Who would do something like that? This is so sad. I am sorry to know that you suffered. Had I known, I would have turned the world upside-down to find the sick perpetrator."

Daniel struggled to understand what he was hearing. Her life had been changed that day, but he had no way of knowing that.

Athaliah asked, "What happened to you. I never saw you after that day. I was unable to believe that you could have had anything to do with what happened to me."

"I left with the caravan. I could not understand why you didn't come that day.

But, sometime later, as I worked, a group of soldiers arrested me and took me away. As you can see, this is what they did to me. Look at me. I have never been the same. I have no idea why they did this. All I remember is that they warned me never to come near the Haddad family again."

He did not mention the fact that the soldiers had taken his manhood. It wasn't the time. He grieved to hear that Athaliah had suffered. The conversation continued well into the night. Benjamin intuitively stayed away, with the hope that the two could talk.

Unbeknown to either of them, their mutual healing had begun.

Benjamin returned to the house hours later. Knocking at the door, he hoped someone would still be awake. Athaliah opened the door. As he entered, she threw herself into his arms and cried. Daniel looked on as brother and sister embraced. Tears of release flowed down their cheeks.

"Ben, I had no idea," was all she could say.

He held her for the longest time. He had not been able to be with her for years, and sensed that he, also, needed this time of healing.

Finally, Athaliah pulled away and wiped her eyes. "Oh, my, look at me. I am the hostess, and my guests don't yet know where their beds are. Please forgive me."

"Sis, don't you worry. I needed that, just as you did. I love you."

"You have had a long day, and I must show you where to sleep. The house isn't large, but it is adequate. I have one room, and I have blankets to place on the floor near the fireplace. You can decide, between you, which one will take the room."

Benjamin was quick to say, "I will take the blankets by the fireplace."

Daniel tried to dissuade him, with no success. The three prepared for bed, not wanting to sleep, but knowing that they must.

They sat at breakfast and talked into the afternoon hours. They had more fun in those hours than they had experienced in years.

Benjamin finally said, "Now, what do you think of my plan? We are all adults here.

Both of you are looking for a solution to your situation. I believe you can be of mutual help to each other. What do you think?"

Athaliah and Daniel looked at each other.

Benjamin continued, "You can set parameters and conditions, according to your needs. Do you think you can do that?"

Athaliah said, "I think we can. What do you think, Daniel?"

"I, too, think we can do it."

"You both will be working, as it were, for me. I will pay you a stipend each month to amply cover your needs." Benjamin knew that Athaliah needed the wherewithal to live without falling back into her old way of life. Daniel also needed a roof over his head, and meals. Together they could find the perfect way back into society, with their heads held high.

"What will people say," Athaliah said.

"What are they saying now? You both can only climb upward from where you are now. I know you have mutual respect. That will give you a reason to honor each other and restore that which you have both lost in life. I believe you both need some hope in your lives. What do you say?"

Benjamin stayed on for two more days. Athaliah would become Daniel's hands and legs in all that he could not do. She would have a reason to live. Daniel would have a friendship, and the care he needed. It was not a perfect arrangement, but it was a start back to a normal life for them both.

CHAPTER TWENTY FIVE

The Journey Toward Healing

Their days began, neither one understanding how to relate to the other. Their lives had been spent dreaming of each other, but as they faced their new reality, uncertainty ruled. To find themselves living in the same house was a completely new set of circumstances. Though they agreed, they found that once they were alone, the world looked different.

After several months, Daniel called Athaliah to the back patio. A gentle breeze wafted through a healthy growth of wisteria that provided not only a lovely fragrance but an abundance of delightful shade as well.

"Athaliah, come sit with me. I need to say something to you. I can't imagine what it must cost you to take care of me as you do. I mean, you go out of your way to provide for my every need. I am gratefully impressed. I have not known such treatment since I was young in the house of my mother and father. I don't feel I deserve the effort you have put forth."

As he spoke, she listened without speaking.

"This is harder than I thought it would be," he continued. "Just knowing that I am now a burden gives me pause. I would give anything to be the one to take care of you."

She decided this was a good time to share her own thoughts. "Daniel, I understand your concern, but I agreed to take you in. The truth is that I need you, just as you need me. We both have been broken, each in our own way. This is not easy for me, but it is what I need. You are not a burden to me, but a blessing."

She pulled a chair over to where he sat and spoke kindly. "What bothers you most?"

"I find that, over the years, I see how much I was scared by the death of my parents. Again and again I have reviewed that loss and see how I was motivated to become a violent man. Then, after my attack by the soldiers, I couldn't help but blame others for my lack of acceptance. I see the looks and hear the sneers and off-handed remarks. The fact that I am crippled has served to make me angry; not the man I would want you to know."

"You could have been killed, as your parents were, and I would not have had the opportunity to know the man of character I believed you to be back all those years ago. I don't think I was wrong then, and I am not wrong now.

"Speaking of concerns, my fear is that you will not like the person I have become," she continued. "What are we going to do? Continue to wallow in the hurts of the past, or look for ways to understand our plight, and move on? I certainly am not the girl you once aspired to know. When I look at myself, I see that I have become so twisted over the years by my own anger and wrong thinking, that I don't really know who I was, or who I am. So, we are alike. Instead of ignoring the obvious, let's work together to find a way to reveal the character that is hidden, that has been covered up by years of wrong decisions and failed attempts to change. For my part, I will have to let go of my fears and learn to trust you. Can you learn to trust me?"

"So, I am not alone in my apprehension?" Daniel blurted. Yes, I trust you. Let's continue as friends. I will help you, as much as I can, to find your true identity. And you can help me find mine. We both will put in the effort to better ourselves. The fact of the matter is that I honor you. In doing so, I derive strength from you. I trust I do the same for you."

"Daniel, I needed to know this. I, too, honor you and have great respect for the man you are inside. Your strength empowers me to be the person you need me to be."

Slowly, they faced each day with a new expectancy.

"Athaliah, let me help you with that jug of water." Daniel reached as far up as he could and helped lower the clay jug from her shoulders. "How can you carry this so far?" he asked as he realized its weight.

"What can I say? There is no other way. The weight is not as bad as the comments of the women who gather at the well. I wish they would leave me alone. I think they feel that I am the same as I used to be and won't leave me alone about it."

"I know that must be frustrating for you. Just ignore them if you can."

"The only way would be to go out there when the other women are not present. Maybe I could go in the midday sun when everyone is avoiding the heat. But it would be very difficult."

Thinking a moment, Daniel said, "We have this area of wonderful shade here in the garden where you could sit to rest in the shade when you return from the well. I could prepare cool refreshments for you to enjoy. How would you like that?"

One day, Athaliah said, "Daniel, what do you think about the Almighty? Does he care for us at all, or are we on our own to try and better ourselves? I walked away from him years ago because I found no answer from those who believed in him."

"Now that you mention it, I too, have lost any desire to think about the Almighty. Everyone I have ever known has disappointed me – most of all the religious ones. They talk a good talk, but, I see little difference between them and the others who don't believe the Almighty at all. Yet, I still have questions," he confessed.

"There must be an answer. We are making progress. My hope is that we can find the answer to our needs as we help each other. No one understands our condition, and they can only find ways to make life more difficult for us. You are the man I have always needed in my life. That is a fact."

"And you are the woman I have always needed. You are gentle, kind, and dedicated. Thank you for that."

"It is good to feel needed, and I think the feeling is mutual," Athaliah said and kissed him on the forehead.

Since Athaliah mentioned the Almighty, Daniel felt something strange within his heart. Why mention the Creator when he already felt that his life was finally taking on meaning and he was at peace? What more could they hope for? But the peace he had felt disappeared when she brought up this topic. That night, Daniel couldn't sleep. All he could do was roll from side to side in his bed. After hours, he said in a whisper, "Almighty One, if you exist, please reveal yourself to us."

As she reflected on their circumstances, she knew there was hope for their future. She, though not as she would have dreamed of it, felt she had much of what she had ever hoped for, or desired in life – someone to respect and honor her.

Still, a persistent unconscious feeling, deep within, caused an uneasiness that would not leave. Could there be more to life? She desired to be reunited with her family but didn't know how to climb over the abyss between them.

"I will continue on; all in good time."

CHAPTER TWENTY SIX

Surprise Encounter

Athaliah came running into the house, slamming the door. "I can't believe it. She hurried into the kitchen and placed the sack of provisions on the table. "It just isn't right."

Daniel sat quietly in the living room, wondering what had caused that reaction. "What isn't right, Athaliah? What is upsetting you so?"

"Can you believe it? No less than three men stopped me on my way home and asked me to join them."

"What do you mean, join you?"

"You know. They wanted me to pleasure them. If that was not enough, they were all married."

"I am sorry you have to live with that all the time."

"Well, I learned a long time ago that men want their wives to be faithful to them, but they want all the freedom to do whatever they want when they want it. I hate men."

"Again, I am sorry."

"It isn't you who should be sorry, but them. Just because they knew me before, they think I should comply now."

"Athaliah, you have suffered at the hand of men most of your life. That makes me sad. You deserve much better in life."

"This happens all the time. I am so tired of it. Some days I just want to die."

"Then, what would I do? You have given me hope. I don't know what I would do without you. Don't say that, please."

Athaliah gave Daniel an understanding look and walked over to where he sat. "Daniel, you have given hope to me, as well. I used to do things because I was lonely, or because I needed money to live, but now, you have given me a reason to live. It doesn't make what they do any easier, though. It just reminds me of what I really am. I am a woman with a reputation. It makes me feel dirty. I have no way of freeing myself of this, no matter how much I try."

Tears dropped from her eyes as she spoke. "I live in a world of evil people. I am evil, too."

"Athaliah, sit and let's talk. I know it is difficult."

"No, there is too much to do. It is almost mid-day, and I must go to the well while the "good women" aren't there to harass me."

Daniel recognized the guilt and pain she carried and felt totally incapable of doing a thing about it. "Athaliah, this hurts me. I know you suffer. There must be some way to be free of that life."

"I don't know that that will ever be possible. I pray to the Almighty and get no answers. Oh, that it were possible. I am obviously not worthy of such help. All my life I have simply wanted someone to love and to be loved. I just don't think I will ever see the day that I will be worthy of anything different than what I have. Just let me alone with my problems. Right now, I must bring water to the house." She left quickly, slamming the door behind her.

Daniel disliked seeing her so frustrated. Since he had been with her, he saw the pattern. She went through cycles, and never knew when, or what might cause them to ruin their day. It made him feel useless and burdensome to her.

As she walked away from the house, her mind raged. *There is no justice in life. Why should I have to be the one to look for ways to not be accosted by other women along the way? They should be the ones to be shamed, they who live with husbands that care nothing for the feelings of women.*

Before long, her steps slowed, and her temper subsided. At the outskirts of town, she wound her way along the worn path toward the communal well. It was a long way to carry water. *Men should have to carry the water, so they could have some compassion in their hearts.*

Coming around the last bend, she saw the well before her. Stopping in her tracks, she said, "No. I won't put up with another man." Before her, was a man, seated at the side of the well. She felt like turning away but knew she had come too far to do that.

Coming closer, she became further enraged by the fact that the man was obviously a Jew. Determined not to back down, she approached the well without looking at him. *I will ignore him, and maybe he will not bother me.*

Taking the jug from her shoulders, she lowered it to the ground. A rope was tethered to a tree root on one end, with a wooden bucket on the other, which she could use to access the water. Going about her business, she ignored the man seated on the other side of the well. She felt his gaze but remained silent.

"Miss, could you draw water for me?"

She ignored him.

The tension thickened.

"Miss, could you draw water for me, please?"

No longer able to ignore him, she said, "How is it that you, a Jew, lower yourself to ask water of me, a Samaritan woman? Most people from your parts won't even speak to us."

The man smiled, kindness showing in his eyes. "If you recognized the gift of God and who it is that asks you for water, you would ask me for water. I would not give you just any water but living water."

"That is interesting. I see that you don't have anything with which to draw water. How could you give me water?"

"You don't know who *I am*," he said, smiling. The implication was not lost on her. The way he said, "I am" was unusual. Only God is the "I Am."

"But the well is very deep and just where would you get this 'living water'?" she asked with a not-so-disguised taunt of disbelief.

The man sat, fixed on her gaze, did not respond to her obvious attitude.

She continued, "Are you greater than our forefather Jacob who gave us this well? He, his children, and their children have drunk from it ever since, until now. There has always been such an abundant supply that even their flocks and herds have enjoyed the bounty."

"That is true enough, but whoever drinks of this water will thirst again, but whoever drinks of the water that I will give him shall never again thirst. That is because the water that I offer shall be in him a well of water springing up from within him to everlasting life. As you know, water is life. Without it no one can live."

He spoke of the "water" of the Spirit that when allowed, will enter into the person and spring forth in a fresh unending flow of life produced by a changed heart. This went right over her head.

"Well, give me some of that water you speak of so I can drink and not have to return here daily to fetch more. If your water lasts as you say, it would give me much more time to do other things."

The man laughed, not a condescending laugh, but a warm, pleasant laugh. "Go, call your husband and come back, and I will speak with the both of you of the water I offer."

Looking down, she stood in silence. Sadness crept into her eyes. She hesitated, not knowing how much she should reveal to this stranger. "You see, I … have no husband."

He took a deep breath, and said, "What you say is true. Thank you for being truthful. That shows character. You could have said anything, but down inside, you are searching for the water I offer. You have many scars within you that need healing. You have had five husbands, and the man you are with now is not your husband. You have been looking for someone to love you for many years and have been disappointed each time."

She looked at him with her mouth open in wonder. "How could you know this?"

"I have come a long way to speak with you. This is God's gift to you this day. It is true that we have never met, but your heavenly Father knows you and has a plan for your life. For you to be able to do what He wants you to do in the future, it was first necessary for you to see, and understand, the consequences of the great rebellion. This you will soon understand, and many people will be brought out of darkness into God's wonderful light."

She didn't understand the last part of what he said, because she was still taken by his previous declaration.

Wonderment filled her heart, and she smiled as her defenses dropped. "But how is this possible—? I can see that you are a prophet, but you speak in riddles." *Let's get the subject off me.* "Our fathers have worshiped in this mountain for generations, but you Jews say that Jerusalem is where people ought to worship."

"You don't understand what you worship. Your knowledge of God is based on just that – knowledge. It is not enough to know something if it never reaches your heart. Many people know about the Almighty, but that is all they have. You think that what you know is enough, but it isn't. What good is knowledge if it doesn't get down into your heart?

Oh, he is back to me.

"You have searched most of your life for something you have never found. For this reason, you have lived the consequences of seeking truth, life, and justice in all the wrong places. You did not ask to be put on the path you have followed. The men you have known mistreated you and left you thinking that no one cares. You have become convinced that you are of no value. I have come so you can meet the Truth."

As he spoke, she felt tears flow down her cheeks. Hidden pain surfaced, which she could not control. Unable to deflect his comments, she dropped to the ground by the well and cried in uncontrollable anguish of soul.

"The fact is that the day is coming when no one will say 'worship the Father at this mountain, or worship in Jerusalem.' You don't know what you worship because you think that knowing about God is enough, but there is coming a day when true worshipers will worship the Father in spirit and in truth. This will happen when God's truth reaches your heart.

"The Law of Moses only shows people that they are sinners. But its intent and purpose is to bring people to understand that they need much more than to know they are sinners – they need to know they can be forgiven and set free from their sin. There is an answer to your search."

"Oh, if I could only have this water you speak of … I want to worship in spirit and truth. I know that the Messiah, who is called the 'Christ,' will come someday. When he comes, he will teach us all things."

The man gently took her hands in his, "I am He. You are speaking with Him." To emphasize his point, he placed his hands on his chest and said, "I am the Answer you are looking for. The scriptures speak of me. I am Jesus."

As he spoke, she felt his strength, and compassion transmitted directly to her heart.

"I have come, not to judge you, but to save you, so you can have abundant life.

God is Spirit and is looking for those who will worship Him in spirit and in truth … from their hearts. This is the 'water' I offer you. You have been vulnerable since your youth. Trust has not come easy to you since you were first hurt. I have come to exchange life for your shattered dreams.

Her life flashed before her eyes. Unutterable pain of heart returned in vivid colors that could be felt. The weight of the years of turmoil and hatred flooded over her and she felt she could not bear it. Anger boiled up within her, but she could not say a word. She remembered what she had just said to Daniel. She was crushed, beaten down to nothing, unable to lift her head. Instead of her hatred toward men, she saw only her responses of anger, hatred, vengeance, disappointment, and anguish produced by unfulfilled expectations.

But this Jesus offered her life as she had never known it. Conviction flowed over her in an uncontrollable cleansing wave.

"I thought I was justified in my responses, but now I see my own heart and complicity in all I have done. I have been in a trap of my own making. I am a sinner."

"I have come to seek and to save sinners," Jesus said.

Through her tears, she managed to sputter, "Plea—" The words caught in her throat. "Plea … Please, for … give … me. I am sorry. I have been so wrong. The trap is of my own making."

"I forgive you, my dear," Jesus said.

Her understanding became clear, as the Truth spoke, and she laughed. "I feel as though a burden has been lifted off my shoulders. I can breathe."

Jesus said, "There is more; you are now living with a man because you want to help him. You have been his only means of hope. You reached out to him when no one else would.

"Do you mind if I ask your name?" Jesus said.

"My name is Athaliah."

"From this day forward, you shall be called Priscilla."

Surprised, she looked at him. "How? … How did you know?"

He waived her off with a smile. "Go and take the water you came for. Bring Daniel back with you."

"Again, how did you know? I don't know what I am doing here. I need to tell my people Who has come to our town. Wait here. I will be right back." Lifting her water jug to her shoulder, she hurried toward town.

Jesus' disciples came into view of the well when they saw him speaking with the woman. They watched as she picked up the jug and hurried past them toward town.

Peter said, "Come. Let's take the food to him. He must be hungry. Andrew, carry this," he said, passing a sack of bread to him. "Let's get on with it. He is hungry."

They approached Jesus, but not one of them asked why he was speaking with that woman. They didn't dare.

"Master, you must be hungry. Here, take this," Andrew said, passing him some bread.

"You men took your time getting provisions."

"Master," Peter said, "It is not easy to do business with Samaritans. You know how they are. We had to search for someone who would help us get the little we got."

"You must not look at them that way. When you say, 'You know how they are,' you say it with contempt. You don't know who they are inside. I have come for them."

The men looked at him, speechless.

"Don't you remember, I told you I had to come to Samaria? This is not just a chance meeting. I am come to fulfill the will of the One who sent me, and to finish His work. You watch. We are only beginning our time here."

Peter urged him, "Master, at least, take this food. You must be starving."

"I have food that you don't know of."

Looking at each other, they questioned, "Who brought him food?"

"No, my food is to do the will of the one who sent me. That is how I get my fulfillment. You all know how to calculate when the harvest is ripe, and you say, 'There still remain four months until harvest time.' But, I say, the harvest is upon us right now. It is time to reap. You are going to be doing a lot of reaping in the days to come. Get used to it."

As he spoke, a noise was heard. A crowd of both men and women was approaching from the town. They came, running, and jostling each other for position on the trail.

The crowd surrounded Jesus, everyone speaking and causing a ruckus. Jesus noticed Athaliah coming over the crest of the hill, helping a crippled man.

"She told us you were here, and we had to come to see for ourselves. Everyone knows her. When she said that she had met a man who told her everything she had ever done, we had to come and see."

Another man said, under his breath, "Yes, you are afraid the man might know that you were with her. That is why you came."

"Who are you to talk?" another man said. "You are as guilty as the rest of us."

The banter continued for a time. The disciples stood back, astounded at the sight. Everyone wanted to touch Jesus. The men pushed in, while the women stood behind.

Finally, Jesus calmed the people, and said, "Let the woman through. Come Priscilla, bring Daniel to me."

The look on everyone's faces was comical. No one could believe this stranger knew her.

"But why did he call her Priscilla?" they wondered among themselves.

"Come, Daniel. I am here to tell you that The Almighty loves you. You have struggled to get here, I know. Give me your hand. You have great faith."

Daniel reached his hand toward Jesus. Without even touching him, he felt a tingle go through his hand. It passed up his arm, and then to the rest of his body.

"Stand up straight," Jesus commanded.

Daniel effortlessly stood tall. Then, he looked at his hands in wonderment. Bending forward, he looked at his feet. For the first time in many years, he had a full range of movement.

The crowd shouted.

"This is impossible. How did you do that," they asked Jesus. "Do it to me." others said.

"I come so that you might know the power of the Almighty. He has sent me to you because He wants to heal not only your bodies but your souls."

Looking at his disciples, he said, "Help them form a line, so they won't step all over each other."

After a while, as different ones received healing, the town leaders said, "Master, you must come into town and stay with us. Don't run off."

Looking at Priscilla, one of them said, "We believe, not only because of your saying, but we have heard for ourselves. Jesus is the Christ, the Savior of the world."

Jesus spoke as he healed those in need, everyone held to his words and believed.

"Priscilla, I and my men have been invited to stay a couple of days. May I seek lodging with you and Daniel? The others will stay in other homes."

"Yes, my Lord. You are welcome in our home."

"Come, then, let us go," Jesus suggested.

The walk back to the town seemingly took a moment, the conversations along the way, riveting. The town's people were so impacted by what had happened that they could talk of nothing else.

Arriving in town, the leader said, "Master, when will you speak so that all might hear?"

"I will get settled in, and then will meet everyone in the town square."

Priscilla and Daniel led Jesus to their home, while others divided the disciples and brought them to their respective lodging places.

The disciples were new at this, but had much to say, as they were plied with questions concerning the Master.

"Come in, Master, and sit here." Priscilla was smiling as she had not smiled in a long time. Her heart was aglow. Daniel frequently touched his limbs in awe.

Soon, Jesus said, "I know you have many questions, but I want to say something of great importance. Both of you have lived arduously painful lives. This is not because God does not care for you, but so He might be glorified in you. You have a testimony to share."

"But, Lord, I have failed in everything I have ever done," Priscilla cried.

"No, failure could well be claimed by you, had you not tried at all. Yes, you have done much wrong. Sin is a deceitful thing. You have looked for love, as is only natural. But, in your hurt, you became angry and vindictive, even hateful. When Daniel came back into your life, you tried. The difference I want you to understand is that you can't succeed without the help of The Almighty, who loves you."

"But, Master, I am afraid I won't live up to your expectations. I am so weak."

"Telling someone you are afraid is not weakness, but strength. It will lead you to the way out into an entirely new life."

She bowed her head somberly.

"Time heals the pain, but it won't erase the memories of what you have done. Use these memories as a means of remembering what not to do in life. Others will need the wisdom you have acquired this day. I want you to feed your destiny, not your past. Use your past to inform others of what can happen when they give themselves to human passions and earthly wisdom. Point out to them the fact that there is life ahead of them, and that God can, and will, give them the strength to appropriate it."

Priscilla lifted her head and smiled, comprehension filling her heart.

"It doesn't matter how much has been taken from you. It is no secret to God what that is. What matters is what you do with the little you have left. Little becomes much when God is in it. You have much to give. You will find a path of dignity and purpose.

"What really counts is what you do from this day forward."

Daniel came over to Priscilla and placed his hand on her shoulder. The words they both heard were penetrating their hearts.

"Both of you have dreamed of getting back at those who did you harm. You can dream mightier dreams … dreams of victory over human failure and tragedy. It is your choice. Both of you were knocked into the dust by others, and then railed upon, and humiliated, for not being able to get up. Human compassion is lacking in the extreme. God is the one who can give you a proper perspective on life. Let Him guide you. He has healed your broken hearts. Life is full of the unknown, but you now know the one who gives life. Embrace Him."

As Jesus spoke these kind and powerful words, resolve was birthed in the two listeners.

"In the words of a prophet of old, 'go in this your strength. Have I not sent you?'"

Daniel said, "That is what the angel spoke to Gideon."

"Yes. The very fact that he had been sent became his strength. Up until now, you have not done anything extraordinary, but you will. I send you. And, again, I say you are forgiven."

"Master," Priscilla said, "we need to learn so much. May we accompany you as you teach?"

"I count on you doing just that."

They held each other closely as he spoke.

"Now, the first step will be, for you to be married. Your testimony will be established in this way among the town's people."

Daniel said, "I will go to the Rabbi at once. We will take care of this matter right now, while you are here."

After two days of public ministry and healings, and of course, a wedding, Jesus and his disciples left for Galilee.

"Master, I enjoyed the ministry time in Sychar. I have learned so much," Andrew said to Jesus as they walked.

"The people did receive us well, and the message was not lost on them. There is much to do, though. Now that we are headed north, you need to understand that a prophet is not received, or honored, in his own country. You will see. It won't always be as easy as it was in Sychar."

"Why is that?" Peter said.

"Because the people a prophet is raised around don't understand the anointing that comes to a person when he comes into his own. They remember only that he was a child and are too short-sighted to understand the workings of God. You will get the chance to see what happens when unbelief reigns."

Andrew looked back and said, "Master, that woman follows us."

"Let her be. I know what my Father is doing in her life."

From that moment, no one spoke more against her.

Jesus ministered as the Father led him. He was not the only prophet in the country. There were many prophets who went about preaching and teaching. Their respective followers listened to them and followed their sayings. But Jesus was different. The anointing of The Almighty was upon him. Men, sent by the religious leaders in Jerusalem were commissioned to follow these teachers to find out if they were legitimate or not, according to the law. They followed Jesus wherever he went, asking leading questions that might reveal some "false" teaching. Jesus did not trust these men. He knew what was in their hearts and avoided their traps.

Priscilla followed Jesus. Daniel stayed home and consented to her wish to learn more from Jesus. They would find opportunities to follow him together, but for now, Daniel stayed home to watch the house.

She listened to every word, as Jesus ministered. She didn't get in the way, but stayed in the background, helping women while their men were up close. Every day she grew in understanding. Like a sponge, she received into her life the truths she learned, putting them into practice. Never had she experienced the freedom that comes from walking in the light of a clear conscience. She heard him say, "I am the bread of life," and understood what he meant. She fed on every word he said. She paid attention to his invitation, "Come unto me all who are burdened and heavy laden, and I will give you rest." This was her lifeline to sanity. Jesus made the difference.

In each place Jesus ministered, Priscilla found lodging close so she could attend his meetings. On occasions, she returned home to be a few days with Daniel before returning to follow the ministry of the Master.

Jesus arrived in Capernaum with his disciples, after ministering in towns throughout the region. His presence was announced by those who had been healed.

"I hear that Jesus of Nazareth has come to our town," a lady said to her friend in the marketplace.

"It is true. I was healed last night. If you come with me, maybe he can help you as well."

"Why didn't you tell me?"

"I am telling you now. We can go to see him when you complete your work."

Priscilla enjoyed listening to the commentaries the people made. She glorified God with them.

A wealthy businessman invited Jesus and the disciples to supper. Though large for a family, his home was too small for the crowd that arrived when word got around that Jesus was in the house. Being sensitive to the needs of those who pressed in wanting to be healed or encouraged, Priscilla stayed on the outside, helping organize the many people who came. Hours passed, and the people kept coming.

All the while, Jesus spoke to those who were able to crowd into the house. He healed several people of various diseases, then spoke of the glory of the Kingdom of God. The night wore on. No one wanted to leave, but for the sake of those who wanted to come in, the request was made to remove all those who had already been healed.

234

Priscilla helped a man who had been healed, but who wanted to reenter. "My dear man, you have received a gift from God this night, others also want to receive help. Come, sit over here, and I will let you know what Jesus says, as I can." Pacified, the man complied.

No one saw the group of men that came by, carrying a bed. They didn't try to enter by the front door because of the throng, but went to the rear of the house, and climbed onto the roof. Inside, Jesus spoke kind words of life to all present. Dirt began falling from the ceiling. Soon, hands could be seen pulling away the roof. A hole widened in the ceiling above Jesus. He continued speaking all the while, dodging the falling fragments.

Then, a bed was slowly lowered through the roof to where Jesus stood. He stopped to watch as four men lowered a sick man by ropes to the floor.

"This is indeed impressive," he said, directing his comments to the sick man. "My son, you have friends who love and care for you. For your faith, your sins are forgiven."

A group of Pharisees gathered in the room, were offended at Jesus, and said among themselves, "Who can forgive sins? Jesus is speaking blasphemy. Only God can forgive sin!"

Jesus perceived in his spirit that they reasoned against him, and said, "Why do you say these things in your hearts? What is easier, to say to a sick person, your sins are forgiven, or to say, get up on your feet, and walk? But so you might know that the Son of Man has power on earth to forgive sins," he turned to the man on the bed, and said, "I say to you, get up, take your bed, and go home."

Immediately, the man got up, took his bed, and walked out in the sight of all. He made his way to the front door, passing people who said, "We have never seen anything like this. Look, he can walk."

On the outside, he shouted, "I can walk, I can walk."

Priscilla had been helping people who were waiting to enter the house. An elderly woman was standing to the side. "I am so tired. I can't stand any longer," she said.

Priscilla approached. "As you can see, there is no place to sit near the house. If you sit on the ground, you will be at risk of being trampled underfoot. I tell you what I will do. I will make sure the Master gets a chance to speak with you."

"Thank you my Dear," the woman said. "Could you help me walk back to my house? It is just up the street."

"Come, let's go. I am happy to help you." Taking the elderly woman by the hand, she led her away from the crowd. "Isn't it wonderful what the Master is doing?" she said, as they went. "We are witnessing the presence of God in our midst."

"Yes, it is wonderful."

Reaching the entrance to the woman's house, Priscilla gave her a hug, as she would her mother, and turned to leave. Just then, the woman said, "I am healed. Oh, I no longer have the pain I had. This is wonderful. The Master has healed me. Look at how I can move." She twirled before Priscilla, jumping into the air several times. "I have not done this for many years."

"This is wonderful. The power of God is on display right here," Priscilla said. Again, the women hugged each other. Priscilla thought of her mother. "There is a reason why God is called The Almighty, don't you think?" Priscilla said in awe. This was her first time to be so near someone who was healed – as they were healed. The presence of God was all around them, as they stood before the door, excitedly chatting about what had just happened. Joy filled their hearts.

Reluctantly, Priscilla left the woman and returned to the house. Her thoughts were of Jesus, and his power. *Truly, he is the son of God.* She walked along, sensing amazement with every step.

Back at the house, the healed man shouted. The crowd moved back, giving him space to move. "This is wonderful," he shouted, unable to quiet himself.

His companions came around to the front of the house. One of them said, "Father, you can not only walk. You can talk." Not until he said this did the healed man realize that the miracle was even greater than he expected. "Yes Benjamin, you are right, I can speak. I can speak!" The noise he made could be heard throughout the crowd. Everyone looked to see what was happening.

"Father, isn't it wonderful what God has done?" Benjamin shouted. "I knew we should come tonight. God has answered our prayers."

The men rejoiced and shouted. Benjamin thought of where they were, and said,

"Father, we must not dominate the crowd's attention like this. We are causing a scene. Let's move away, so Jesus can continue without this noise, shall we?"

Great was their joy. The power of God had fallen upon them, evidenced by the fact that Master Haddad was on his feet for the first time in years. They made their way back to the inn, not paying attention to anyone around them. None of them cared what others might think. Master Haddad was healed, and was walking, and talking.

Priscilla arrived at the house and continued helping. The people were stirring. She could hear them speaking of the man who had walked out, shouting. But her thoughts were on something else. *Jesus did say he was sending us. The woman received her healing as I hugged her. I know it was the power of God. I felt it pass through me. Did He really use me?*

The crowd dispersed, later in the night, and she made her way to an inn to rest. The next day she returned home to Daniel. For hours she talked of everything Jesus had said. "The healings were just as wonderful as what he did with us," she said. "But His words were astounding and powerful. The Spirit of God is truly upon him."

"Speaking of that, I feel as though I have been born again," Daniel said. "I am not only healed in my body, but I have been changed inside as well. I see things differently. I am a new man."

"It is interesting that you use those words. The other day I heard Jesus tell his men about someone who visited him up in Jerusalem," Priscilla said. "His name was Nicodemus. Jesus told him those very words. He said, 'Except a man is born again, he cannot understand the kingdom of God.' That must be what happened to us. We see life differently now. I heard him speak of the Spirit. It is like the wind. We can hear it, but we can't see it. It comes and goes, and no one knows from where it came, and no one knows where it goes."

"You are right. We don't see what has happened to us inside, but we do feel it. To express it as Jesus did, the Spirit of God has touched us."

At that moment, there was a knock at the door.

"Who might that be?" Daniel asked, as he stepped toward the door.

Opening, a man stood before him. "Good morning, sir, I have a message for mistress Athaliah."

Priscilla came to the door. She recognized the servant of her family.

"Mistress Athaliah, I have a message for you," he said, as he handed her a parchment.

"Won't you come in and sit a moment?" She motioned him in.

"Thank you, Ma'am. Very well."

Opening the note, Athaliah read:

Athaliah, Father requests your presence. Will you come home?

Benjamin

"Daniel, what do you think about this?" she said, handing the note to him.

As she spoke, old feelings filled her heart. She had avoided seeing her father and mother because of the guilt she carried. Rejection was a strong emotion within her. She had decided years ago that it was easier to reject them before they could reject her.

She blamed her parents for what had happened with her marriage to Abel, simply because they would not, or could not tell her everything that had befallen her. As time passed, that particular issue, though always present in her memory, didn't seem as significant as the life she had fallen into after that. The first trouble catapulted her into the second.

Another thought came to mind. *Daniel and I were just talking about the changes Jesus has made in our lives. Do I want to live in my chains of the past, or do I really want to be free? Maybe, this is God's way of cleaning up my mistakes and bringing me back to my family.*

She remembered what Jesus said to her. "It is not enough to know something if it doesn't reach your heart."

If she wanted to be free, she had to face her family – and forgive them. That would be the only way her heart could truly be changed.

"What do you think, shall we go back," Priscilla asked Daniel.

"I do believe it is the right thing to do." Benjamin had not explained all the reasons he had when he brought him to live with Priscilla, but he had a good idea.

"We will go back, then."

The servant spoke up, "Your brother, Benjamin, had me bring horses for you and Master Daniel. They are out front."

"Bring them around to the back of the house," Priscilla said. "You can pass the night with us, and we all can return in the morning."

238

CHAPTER TWENTY SEVEN

Retribution

Abel was furious after Master Haddad and his father confronted him. His plans had not worked out as he designed. His father had ordered him to pay retribution to the Haddad families. Time served to reinforce resolve within him to make them pay. There was not much he could do that would not point right back to him. A thought came to him. *I will go to the man who started the whole mess.*

When Master Haddad's caravan returned from abroad, he sought out Reuel. "I can't help but notice that you did well on this trip," he said affably.

Reuel, being aware of the trouble Abel had caused, was not eager to speak with him. "Thank you, I think. What do you want?"

Seeing Reuel's reluctance to engage him, he said, "I just want to let you know that Master Haddad is looking for you." He had no idea what Master Haddad was doing, but this lie served his purpose.

"What do you mean by that?"

"I mean, you are in danger. Master Haddad knows what you did all those years ago."

Reuel did not need to hear anymore. He had felt uneasy after Master Haddad had fallen. The rumor got around that he had left his home late at night, with something serious on his mind. No one knew why, but it stuck in Reuel's mind. The fact that Master Haddad was in bed, unable to speak, or communicate, was a comfort, but his conscience was eating at him. It had been years, and no one was the wiser.

This day, Abel brought it all back.

"What do you mean by danger?" he asked, hoping that Abel would divulge more. "How would you know, anyway?"

"That is for me to know, and for you to find out!" With that, he walked away. The seed had been sown. Now, it was just a matter of time.

Part IV

CHAPTER TWENTY EIGHT

The Return Home

Priscilla and Daniel made their way toward the Haddad estate. For her, it had been years away from her loved ones. Her anger and hatred had kept her prisoner, and as such, separated from her family. To be on her way back home gave her an odd, but good feeling. Trepidation mounted within her, as well as a sense of doing the right thing. What had made the difference? That question bounced around in her mind. The answer had to be Jesus. He was the one who affected the change in her heart. She smiled as she rode. He had indeed given her life back, and she was coming to terms with the significance and implications of it all.

Daniel rode in thought, as well. He was on top of a horse and was able to ride normally. His life had been drastically limited for so long, that he found it exhilarating to do simple things, such as what he was doing now – riding a horse. But that was not the important thing. His heart was renewed. He was a new man. After years of begging and being dismissed by others, he was now free to live.

He looked at Priscilla, and said, "Are you thinking what I am thinking?"

"What do you mean?"

"We are changed people. Neither one of us is the person we were just a short time ago. How will we face your family?"

"Oh, I see. There is so much to tell them. There is so much to ask forgiveness for. I could not have thought of being with them until Jesus came into our lives."

"It is true. Jesus did change our lives." He said.

The land became familiar to them both, as they approached, first the town, and then, the area of the Haddad holdings. Excitement grew within them.

Finally, they arrived at the entrance to the property. The house she had been born and raised in was in view. A man came running toward them, shouting, "Athaliah Priscilla. Athaliah Priscilla. My little girl has come home!"

"Father, you are running. Ben told me you were sick." Priscilla said, dismounting, as he approached. The two met and threw their arms around each other. Daniel dismounted and stood watching, tears of joy rolling down his cheeks. Soon, the others came running, and the whole family jumped and shouted for joy.

Priscilla had been away for so long that she didn't recognize Benjamin's wife, Leah, or little Ben and Caleb. Her mother arrived and hugged her tightly, tears flowing freely.

Chaos was breaking out, but before it got too far, Priscilla said, "I must ask you all to forgive me," she said, catching her breath. She felt it was time to get this off her chest. Not a moment longer would she wait to make things right. "I was wrong. I was so caught up in my anger that I caused all of you great pain. Please forgive me. I have affected your lives and caused you much pain. I am sorry."

It had been many years, but it seemed as though all of that was past, and only the present was important. The past melted away in an instant. Her action surprised even herself. She had not imagined doing what she had just done. *I have been changed.*

"Oh, Honey, we are sorry to." her mother said, laughing with deep release. "We will talk all about it, I am sure. There is so much to say."

After a while, Master Haddad said, "Come, let's move to the house. What do you say?"

This was truly a family reunion to remember.

Entering the house, Priscilla said, "Oh, Father I have forgotten someone very important to me. This is Daniel. I think you will remember him."

Daniel had contented himself in standing back to watch the reunion.

Master Haddad looked at him and took his hand. "As a matter of fact, I do remember him." Then, looking him squarely in the face, "If you are the one I think you are. I can't tell you how glad I am to see you."

Benjamin had not told the family about Daniel, or that Priscilla was living with him. He wanted that fact to come to light at the proper moment. Obviously, this was the moment. After his father's healing, there were many things to learn about what was happening.

Daniel took him by the hand, as was the greeting custom. "Yes, I am he. I used to be your chief of security, many years ago."

Master Haddad felt a flush come into his face. "Please forgive me for not being a proper host. Welcome to our home. It is truly good to see you."

Priscilla spoke, "Father, you can call him son now. Daniel is my husband." The whole family gathered around Daniel, greeting him warmly. Now it was Priscilla's turn to stand by.

At length, Priscilla said, "Father, Ben told me you were ill. What has happened?"

"You won't believe this, but Benjamin and the men carried me to Capernaum, and I met the Master."

"Well, let's hear about this. Tell me everything from the beginning." Priscilla said.

No one knew where to begin. Everyone talked, not noticing that they were talking over each other. This was a time for catching up.

Her father finally started. "I fell off my horse and was almost killed several years ago. I have not been able to speak or move from that time. There is much to share with the family."

"Forgive me, Father, how did you know to ask for me to return?" Priscilla asked.

"When I found out that Benjamin knew where you were, I asked him to send for you, so you could hear what I have to say, along with the rest of the family. When Benjamin and the men carried me to Capernaum, I was healed from head to toe. I was even healed in my spirit. I am a changed man."

He related the events of their trip.

"When was your trip to Capernaum, exactly?" Priscilla asked.

"This was just a short time back, when the Master, Jesus, was in a house preaching in Capernaum. The men let me down through the roof, so Jesus could heal me."

"Father, I can't believe it. I was there that night. I heard that a man had been let down through the roof, and was healed, but I was away for only a few moments. When I returned to the house, everyone was talking about your healing. I had no idea it was you. I was there because I am now a follower of Jesus."

"Oh, my dear, we were so close to each other. I am also a follower of Jesus. We all are followers of Jesus. He has changed our lives. All our lives."

"There is so much to share. I don't know where to start," Priscilla said. "I want to hear your story. Daniel and I can tell our story later. You continue, Father. This is wonderful."

"As I said, I have not been able to speak since I was hurt. On the way home after my healing, Benjamin and I were able to catch up on everything that happened. He has been the head of the family, and the business while I was sick. It was he who mentioned that it would be good if I could wait to share some things until you were present. I realize, only now, why he wanted me to wait. I did not know Daniel was with you. This is a welcome surprise. Welcome to the family, Daniel."

Priscilla hugged Daniel and smiled.

Obed continued. "We have been assailed for years by that young man who left you and accused us of deception. When my brother Rueben found that he was being systematically robbed by one of his workers, he came to me, because it concerned me as well.

"I learned that you, Athaliah, had a lot to do with finding out who did it."

"I? What do you mean, father?"

"Yes, you found that the thief had been stealing by falsifying the size and weight of the bundles of grain."

"I did help Jebu to find who was behind the problem, but that is all I knew. I didn't know it affected you."

"I had learned that we were also being stolen from. Putting everything together, we knew it was all being carried out by Abel. It was only when we confronted him that we learned the extent of the harm he had done to the family. It was all a plan to make us pay. During the investigation, something he said caught my attention. At home later, it all came to me, and I was furious. In the middle of the night, I decided to face the person who had done us all great harm."

Benjamin reached over to his father and said, "Father, maybe it would be better to discuss some details later, in a better setting."

"Yes, I suppose you are right. For now, all I will say is that as I was so upset, I drove my horse too hard, and he spooked at something on the trail and threw me off into the wadi. I was unconscious for a while, and only remember waking up in my own bed. I could not move or speak. That was my greatest frustration. For years I have not been able to communicate or let anyone know who I was after. Now I can."

The family listened intently. "But all was changed when Jesus came into our lives. Benjamin and I have discussed our options. We want to do right by you, Athaliah."

"What do you mean, Father?" she said.

"Well, you were upset with all of us for what had happened to you. We didn't know how to tell you the little we did know about it. The fact is that we did not know everything and thought it better not to harm you more by telling you the incomplete truth about how you were hurt. My Dear, I am so sorry for our part in your frustration and anger. I ask your forgiveness on behalf of the family."

Priscilla looked at Daniel, then her father. "Father, what did happen?"

"The question is *who* did it. That is what we didn't know until that night I was hurt. All of us had our own feelings of guilt. Your mother, Benjamin, Chara, and I felt we were guilty in the matter and could not bring ourselves to face you. We are sorry for all that happened. You have paid a great price for our wrongdoing. It was not that we wanted to do you harm, but we realize now that we should have done things differently. Please forgive us."

He broke into tears before the family. It was not a time to be shy about the feelings that had rocked the family for many years. Each one had become bound in his or her own world of guilt and shame.

"Father, Mother, Ben, I forgive you," Priscilla said. "I must ask you to forgive me, as well. I had no right to cause such pain because I was frustrated and hurt. My own feelings of guilt led me down a path of death, from which I could not return, until Jesus changed my heart."

Master Haddad said, "There is more." Looking at Daniel, he said, "By putting the details of that fateful day together, I first thought you had hurt our daughter. Now, I must ask your forgiveness. I lived for years, thinking I had done the right thing. It was not until we pressed Abel for the truth that he told us who really had done it. He had learned about what happened, and who did it, but his knowledge was incomplete. I was able to put the facts together. What happened to you was my fault. I was misguided. I asked the soldiers to arrest you. I am sorry. Please forgive me. I know I was wrong and unjust. When Benjamin brought you here to continue to heal, I wanted to tell you so, but I could not."

The family sat, stunned. Master Haddad had not discussed the matter with anyone but Benjamin. The revelation shook them, and no one knew what to say.

"Master Haddad," Daniel said slowly, "I have suffered for all these years without knowing why. I should be angry and vindictive, but I am not. The fact is that Jesus changed my life. I was bitter because I could not move around as others did, who took life for granted. I could not work. Begging became my only way to subsist, until the day Benjamin found me on the road, beaten and near death. He brought me here and gave me a place at your table. That changed all the anger and resentment I had held inside. He only knew that I had cared deeply for Athaliah and wanted to help me.

"Then, when he found her, he arranged for us to meet again. She has cared for me all this time, until Jesus healed us both. The burden we both carried was great. Athaliah had her past, and I had my crumpled-up body, and my past. Now we are married. I have no animosity against any of you. God has brought us together in this very special way. Don't you see? He cared for us all so much that He brought us back together."

The realization of what Daniel said touched the hearts of everyone, and their faces reflected it.

"I gladly forgive you for what has happened. You loved your daughter enough to care. You did what anyone would have done. I can't complain. God has healed me and given me my life back. I now have a family. That is a wonderful thing. We have each walked our own road, but God has brought us full circle."

The mood was felt by everyone. God had truly done something wonderful in their lives.

"Father," Priscilla said, at length. "There is one fact I need to mention. When I met Jesus at Jacob's well, he said I should use my middle name – Priscilla."

"Then, that is what we are going to do, Priscilla." Master Haddad said.

"In addition, I tell you what we are going to do. We are going to have a feast; a feast to celebrate God's goodness. More specifically, we are going to celebrate Jesus, and the new life we now have in Him. Our Messiah has come, indeed."

A feast of feasts was prepared. The whole family, father, mother, son, daughter, and extended family members of the household shared in glorifying the goodness of God.

CHAPTER TWENTY NINE

The Followers

Master Haddad called Benjamin to the patio. "Son, we need to talk. There is a matter I want to discuss. As you know, I have found out who did the deed that has caused so much grief. Only because Jesus has changed our lives, have I not done anything to correct it. My heart was set upon revenge for so long that it consumed me. I no longer feel the same anger or even the need for revenge, but justice must be done, for the sake of Priscilla and Daniel. They suffered the most because of the events of that day. I would like you to accompany me to the stockyards. Do you have time to do that with me today?"

"Yes, of course, Father. I can do that."

"Have a servant prepare our horses. We have some riding to do."

On the way to the stockyard, Master Haddad shared what he knew of the details.

Having spoken the whole time, the trail seemed to pass under their feet, and time flew. Before they knew it, the stockyard came into view. Entering the yard, they dismounted and walked to the main house. A servant ran out to meet them.

"Thank you," Master Haddad said, as the servant gathered the horse's reigns and walked them into the barn. "Give them water, please."

They were met by another servant as they walked into the house. "We would like to speak to Reuel," Master Haddad said, as he entered."

"Master, Reuel is not here."

"What? Has he gone to the city?"

No, sir, He is simply not here."

"What are you saying?" Master Haddad insisted.

"Sir, he left a couple of days ago and has not returned. He told no one where he was going, and we haven't seen him since. I saw him leave. It appeared that he loaded the horse well before leaving, as though going on a long trip. He seemed to be in a hurry."

"Didn't anyone ask him where he was going?" Benjamin asked.

"No, Master. We just assumed that he had been ordered to do something."

Master Haddad was visibly shaken by the news. "When he returns, send someone to me with the news at once. But do not, in any way, let him know what you are doing."

The servant bowed. "Yes, Master."

"In the meantime, you can take over his position and responsibilities. You have plenty of experience to do that. Agreed?"

"Yes sir. Thank you, Sir."

Benjamin stepped forward. "Call the workers together so I can alert them to the changes."

"Priscilla, come. We must talk," Mara said, as she led her out to the patio. "It is so good to have you back home with us. I know much has happened, but you need to know we love you. There has been a great hole in our lives since you went away." Mara wanted to say what only a mother could say to a daughter. She had lost too much time living in silence and condemnation.

"I truly am sorry for the way things turned out. We were heartbroken when we learned that you had disappeared. Let me start at the beginning: The day you were hurt, I was torn apart with grief. You were brought back to the house, and we didn't know if you would survive. All of us blamed ourselves for what happened. The fact was that we didn't know all that happened, or who had done it."

"Mother, I know it was rough on you; especially you. I don't remember that day, only that I was very ill."

"Well, in time we learned that you were with child."

"Mother, no!" Priscilla said. *Another piece of the puzzle…*

"We learned about it when you miscarried. The midwife, your father, Chara, and I were the only ones who knew. We decided to keep it a secret to allow you to lead a normal life. You know how condemning people can be. Our intentions were good, but it didn't work out as we thought."

"Oh, Mother, I didn't know—"

"I know. You couldn't remember anything of that fateful day, and little of what happened for months afterward. When you required the truth of Chara, she couldn't say anything, because she was under strict orders not to reveal the fact that you had been with child. As for the rest of the story, she was at liberty to tell you. It was not her fault, my dear."

"I am so sorry for what I did to her. I lost a good friend. The fact was that I, too, was full of guilt and shame. And when Abel accused me of deception, I snapped, and refused to be consoled."

"What you need to know now, is that your father learned who hurt you, and was on the way to apprehend him when he fell from his horse. After that, he could not speak, so the secret remained a secret until Jesus healed him. It wasn't Daniel, as he had believed, but Reuel; the very man that has been working for us all these years. He did it to get rid of Daniel and take his job. It was out of jealousy and ambition. Had we only known the truth it would have been different."

"Mother, I too have lived in my own place of torment. I became angry, to the point of lashing out at anyone who had anything to do with you or my father. When Jebu suggested we run away and get married, I did it, thinking I would get a new start and forget my past. I thought I had, at last, met a man who loved me. But the reality was that I met myself wherever we went. When he divorced me, I was shattered. From there I went further down into the dark and shameful side of life. I just wanted someone to love me."

"I am so sorry, my Sweet. We have caused you great pain."

"But Mother, look how our lives have been changed. We can't change the past but look how the Master made the difference. He brought us all back together again. I see life with different eyes. I pray I never forget what happened, so I can relate to others who have experienced the same, or worse. Mother, you are forgiven. Father is forgiven. Ben and Chara are forgiven. I am forgiven. We now have a future. I fell into a dark pit, from which I could not extract myself. I went from bad to worse. My guilt became a burden I could not carry. But then, I met Jesus at the well. He did what I could not do. I now have a future. The whole family has a future." Reaching for her mother, she hugged her and kissed her on the cheek. "I am sorry for my part in what has taken place over the years. Maybe someday, I can reveal to you all that happened, but for now, just know that I love you dearly."

Her mother held her close. "My Dear, it is so good to hold you."

Hugging her mother, she rocked her back and forth. "We are all going to learn of Him. I have been set free from my past, and I am going to stand firm in the freedom with which I have been set free."

The family enjoyed being together. Such fun it was to be in each other's company. Master Haddad was delighted to have all his family together. One day, as they sat around the table, he asked for their attention.

"I have been thinking. Do you remember the story of Hanna, who couldn't have children, but finally did, as the result of God's promise to her?"

Everyone nodded affirmatively. "Do you remember what she did? She took her son, Samuel, to the temple and gave him to the Lord's service." Again, all nodded.

"Mara and I have decided that since God has returned our daughter to us, we will offer her to the Lord with gratitude, so she can serve him as one of his flowers. Jesus has changed our lives, and Priscilla, if you are willing, we would like to support you as you and Daniel follow the Master. You can learn of him. Both of you can have total freedom to go wherever he goes and learn from him. What do you think?"

"Father, I have been thinking the very same thing. I would love to do that. I remember something that the Master said to me at the well. He said that all that happened was so I would understand the consequences of the great rebellion. I am going to learn what he meant by that. I would love to sit at His feet, as much as I can."

Daniel nodded in agreement.

"We are so grateful to him for what he did for us. When I spoke with Jesus at the well, he said I had a future, and that many people would be brought out of darkness into the light. I must learn of this light, of which he spoke. Daniel and I can learn together."

251

Turning again to Daniel, she said, "This is wonderful, don't you think, Daniel?"

"I am afraid to think of being so blessed. But, yes, it is wonderful. We will first have to ask his permission to follow him."

"I understand the number of disciples has grown recently," Benjamin interjected, "I am sure he will agree."

By asking around, it was not difficult to learn of Jesus' whereabouts. "I have heard he is preaching in a lot of towns and villages to our north. If you hurry, you will find him, I am sure. Just ask along the way," one friend told Benjamin. The news about Jesus and his performing of miracles and healings continued to spread. "From what I hear, the religious people want to kill him for healing on the Sabbath," the man said, "They are upset because he even said that he and God are one."

"Well, I believe him," Benjamin asserted, as he thanked his friend.

Returning home, Benjamin shared what he had learned. "If you prepare now, you can make your way to where Jesus is," he said to Daniel and Priscilla.

"There is more I would like to do. We are going to send a caretaker to your house in Sychar to care for it in your absence. When you have the chance, he will have the house in readiness for you."

"Ben, you think of everything. How can we ever repay you?"

"Just learn from the Master, and we will all benefit." He said, hugging her.

"Yes, the one you seek is not far from here," a man said, upon Daniel's inquiry. "He has been preaching in the synagogues. Just follow that trail, and you will find him."

Daniel and Priscilla continued their journey, eager to find the Master. They were not long in gaining sight of him. A crowd had gathered, and many milled about trying to see the healer.

"Come, Daniel, I see Peter over there. He will tell us what we should do." They dismounted and called a young man, "Will you watch our horses, young man? We will compensate you later," Daniel said.

"Yes, master. I will do as you wish. Thank you, sir."

Leaving the horses, they made their way over to where Peter was standing. When he saw them approach, he smiled and motioned them to come.

"It is so good to see you, Priscilla. This must be Daniel." He greeted Daniel warmly. "The Master is speaking now. You can stand with us here to listen. Later there will be work to do, and you both can help."

Jesus projected his voice so even the ones in the distance could hear his words.

"The harvest truly is plentiful, but the laborers are few. Pray that the Lord of the harvest will send forth laborers into his harvest. There are so many needs. Look. Look at the people. I am moved with compassion, because some of you faint, and are scattered all over, as sheep having no shepherd. You must understand that God loves you and wants to heal your hearts. Receive the words I speak, and you will be healed. The kingdom of God has come to you."

Moving among the listeners, Jesus touched them. Cries of joy erupted as the sick were healed by his touch. Some were bound by evil spirits, but all he touched left healed of their ailments. The onlookers glorified God as they observed, amazed at the sight before them.

After many hours of ministry, Jesus dismissed the crowd. That evening he called his disciples away and spoke with them. There were twelve of them in all. Notwithstanding, there were a few others who were known of him: Priscilla and Daniel among them.

"I am passing on to you the power of my Father so you can minister to the needs of the lost sheep of Israel. You must learn by doing. As I was saying earlier, the harvest is plenty. You must know how to minister. The best way is to step out in faith. You will see the power of my father in action as you obey his commands. He will teach you. At this time, don't go to the Gentiles, or into the area of the Samaritans, but go to the lost sheep of the house of Israel. You will have power against unclean spirits, to cast them out. You will heal all manner of sickness and diseases in my name."

As Priscilla listened, she knew in her heart that this was from God. There was so much she could learn by putting into action what she knew. She was not one of the twelve, but she and Daniel knew the Master had changed their lives, and they were eager to speak into other's lives. Nor was she offended by the Master's desire not to reenter Samaria. She thought of the elderly woman she had helped return to her house the night her father was healed. She thought of the power that was felt when she simply reached out to touch her. This is what Jesus meant. She also would grow in her knowledge by allowing him to manifest his power through her. She knew it was not her power, but that of God, who sought to use her for his glory.

You will heal the sick," Jesus was saying, "cleanse the lepers, raise the dead, and cast out devils. You have freely received. Freely give. Do not charge for the ministry you will do. This is what I want you to do, so you can see that my father is with you. Go forth, taking no provisions, or money. Go as you are. When you come into a town or city, ask around to find those who will receive you. Stay with them. Greet the households and receive of them. Then you can minister unto them in return.

"If anyone does not receive you, or does not wish to hear your words, just move on and do not worry about them any longer. They will wish they had listened when the time comes.

"Now, don't think it will be an easy thing to go out in my name. You see how the religious people treat me. They will treat you the same. You will be like sheep among wolves. Be wise, therefore, and prepared. Be harmless as doves, but wise as serpents. Beware of men, for they will bring you before the councils. Some of you may be beaten, or made fun of in the synagogues, or brought before governors and kings for my sake. This will work against them in the end, as a testimony of their unwillingness to hear. Don't worry about what you will say in these moments, because my father will show you what to say at the right times. You need to understand that it will not be you speaking, but my Father who will speak through you."

Priscilla and Daniel listened, absorbing every word, deep into their hearts. The disciples around them also listened intently. Many things were shared for their benefit, as Jesus spoke.

"Remember, disciples are not above their Master, nor the servant above his Lord. You will suffer just as I will suffer. But do not be afraid when you are persecuted. Just go to the next town and continue your ministry there.

"There is nothing covered that will not be revealed, or hidden, that will not be known. The things I tell you here, alone, you will spread openly among all that will hear.

"That which I share in your ears, you must shout aloud from the rooftops, for all to hear."

"Remember, you must not be afraid of those who can only harm your bodies. They cannot harm your souls. Honor him who has saved not only your bodies but your souls. He is the one everyone must respect."

Many more words Jesus spoke to his disciples that night. Words of challenge, words of hope, words of knowledge, words of power, words of promise, words of peace, words of action, words of comfort in the middle of turmoil, and words of eternal reward.

"In conclusion, know this; whoever gives a drink of cool water unto the needy, or even a little child, will indeed be rewarded. The water that we give will spring up unto eternal life because it is living water."

When Jesus finished commanding his twelve disciples, he gathered them close and prayed for each one. "Go out in teams of two. We will come together at a predetermined location. Go with my Father's blessing and power. We will meet again soon."

He selected a few disciples to accompany him and left that place to preach and teach in their cities. Priscilla and Daniel followed him wherever he went and learned of him.

Jesus preached in Chorazin and Bethsaida and surrounding areas, doing mighty works, but many people resisted him. But everywhere he went there were those who listened and received his words. The religious ones joined ranks against him, having received orders from Jerusalem to set traps for him, if they could, to establish that he was not from God. The people who were being healed and raised up to the newness of life followed him and rejoiced at his message.

Daniel and Priscilla were always nearby, following him, learning from his every word. His words were life to them, and indeed, to all those who received them. Jesus arrived in the area of Tyre and Sidon, near the coast, teaching and preaching in their synagogues. During the days, he sat in open areas, and the people clambered to watch as he healed the weak and infirm. He invited Priscilla to stand near to help the women and children who were arriving in need of help. She did so with the greatest joy. Daniel also ministered in the same way among the men. They drank in Jesus' life-giving words like sponges and grew in the knowledge of God.

As Jesus ministered along the coast of Tyre and Sidon, a large throng surrounded him, searching for ways to approach him. It was all his helpers could do to keep order among them. From somewhere in the crown a voice was heard above the others.

"Have mercy on me, Master. Please, have mercy on me."

A woman's voice became insistent and loud, over the other voices. "Oh, Lord, son of David, please have mercy on me. My daughter is grievously vexed with demons. Please help her, Lord, I ask."

Jesus kept to his message. His disciples came to him and insisted that he send her away for interrupting so loudly. "She is causing disruption, so that you can't be heard by the throng, Master," one disciple said to Jesus. "She won't be quieted."

Jesus stopped what he was doing and looked at her. "Bring her to me," he said to one of the disciples.

The woman approached, crying incessantly. Jesus said, "I am only sent to the lost sheep of the house of Israel."

She threw herself at his feet, and said, "Please, Lord. I know you are here for your own people, but please help me," she cried with anguish of heart.

Then, Jesus said something that seemed strange, to test her. "It is not right to take our children's bread and cast it to the dogs."

She did not take offense, but said, "What you say is truth, my Lord. But even insignificant little puppies eat the crumbs that fall from their master's table."

Jesus stood silently. Compassion sprang from his heart toward her. "Oh, my dear woman, you have great faith. I tell you, be it unto you, even as you desire."

Then, Jesus looked around and found Priscilla standing some distance away.

"Come, my dear, and take this woman to the side, and console her, please."

The woman still sat at Jesus' feet, crying, when Priscilla approached.

She took her by the hand to raise her up. "Come, my dear, I will help you. Come over this way."

"My daughter, she is over there."

Priscilla said, "Come, then, we will go for her, and then move away so we can talk."

The two women made their way through the crowd to where the daughter was laying. The mother tenderly lifted her daughter and carried her away from the throng. "My Love, you seem different. Does anything hurt as it did before?"

"No mother," the girl said. "I feel good. You see, I no longer move as I did before. See?"

"This is true," the mother said.

Her crying turned to laughter. "My daughter is healed. My daughter is healed. Look. She is normal again. Oh, my little one, I love you. The Master has healed you this day."

Priscilla knew at once that this was true. She joined with the mother and rejoiced.

Then, the two women looked at each other and fell silent. What they saw was totally unexpected and unbelievable. Words could not be uttered, for the emotion that overtook them was profound as they looked into each other's eyes.

"Chara, is this you?" Priscilla asked softly.

"Oh, Athaliah, it is you!"

The two fell into each other's arms and cried, this time, for joy. They stood, holding each other, and cried for the longest time. Healing took place within them as they stood there, releasing pent-up emotions that neither of them had dared to give expression to for years. Had it not been that they were a distance from the crowd, they would have caused a commotion. This was a glorious reunion.

"I can't believe it." Priscilla said at last. "You are here. This is wonderful. I have missed you so much, my sister."

"What are you doing here, Athaliah?" Chara said.

"I travel with the Master and help wherever I can. I met him when he came to my town, not long ago. He changed my life."

"Oh, there is so much to get caught up with," Chara exclaimed.

The two sat and prattled on for a long time. Chara finally stopped and presented her daughter to Priscilla. "My dear, this is my long lost friend from childhood. She is my closest friend. Her name is Athaliah."

"Nice to meet you, Ma'am," the girl said.

"It is nice to meet you, as well. I go by the name of Priscilla now. That is my middle name," she said, glancing at Chara. "And what is your name?"

"My name is Maria, Ma'am."

"That is a beautiful name," Priscilla said.

Then she said, "Where are my manners? Chara, there is someone I want you both to meet." She stood to her feet and looked over the crowd until she found who she was searching for. With a wave of her hand, she motioned him to come. He saw her and made his way through the crowd toward them. At last, he arrived.

"Daniel, I want you to meet Chara."

Chara screamed for joy. "Yes, oh, yes. Daniel, I remember you." Before she could stop herself, she said, "I am so sorry for causing you so much pain. Where have you been? How are you doing? Please forgive my informality, but I must know. There is so much I don't understand." As she spoke, a world of emotions came flooding back into her heart, and an unsolicited expression of pain washed over her, contorting her face. She had lived her years believing she was the reason for his difficulty. "But the two of you are together. How can this be?" she finally said.

"It is a long story," Daniel said. "One you will want to know."

Before he could say anything more, someone came between him and Priscilla, putting his arms around them both. "This is truly wonderful. My Father has been at work for a long time to bring you all together."

All three looked at Jesus, who stood smiling at them. "This is wonderful," he said again.

No one could speak for a moment. Finally, Priscilla said, "Master, this is my long-lost friend, Chara. You healed her daughter today."

"Yes, I know. Isn't my Father wonderful?" Then he said, "You and Daniel have served so unselfishly. I would like you to take Chara and her daughter to your home and take care of them for a while. You can catch up with me later. What do you all say?"

"Oh, yes, that would be a blessing," Priscilla said. "What do you think, Chara?" Then turning to Daniel, "What do you think?"

"I agree with it."

"I, too, think it would be wonderful, if we are not a burden," Chara chimed in.

"What do you mean? You could never be a burden. There is so much we must get caught up on."

Then, turning to the Master, Priscilla said, "Thank you ever so much. We are going to follow you for the rest of our lives. You have given us that water you speak about, and our lives will never be the same. We will thirst no more."

"Good. I will let you be on your way, then," Jesus said, and took his leave, smiling, the other disciples falling in behind him.

CHAPTER THIRTY

I Am Free!

Daniel, Priscilla, Chara, and Maria arrived at their home late a couple of evenings later. Travel weary, they dismounted, gathered their things, and made their way into the house.

"This is a beautiful house. You have made it a warm home, Priscilla," Chara said, as she walked in.

"It is not that large, but it is home. My last husband gifted it to me before he passed away."

Priscilla had spent the whole journey talking with Chara. There were so many questions; so many gaps to fill. But she had not confided all. There would be time to do that.

The housekeeper that Master Haddad had sent, was caught off guard, but managed to gather up some food items for everyone. "Thank you, Nathaniel for this provision. Did you find your quarters in the rear alright in our absence?" Daniel asked.

"Yes, Master. I have settled in, and I'm quite at home."

"Well, then, Chara, you and Maria will be staying in this room." She led them to the door, across from the reception area. It was not a large room, but welcoming, just the same. Mother and daughter would be quite comfortable there.

"It is late, and I know we are all tired, so I will bring you a jug with water and a hand bowl so you can freshen up. We will see you in the morning," Priscilla said.

The next morning the women awoke early and met at the kitchen door. "This is wonderful," Chara said. "Now I can take care of you, as is only proper."

Priscilla said, "No, you are our guest. You will not be serving us."

"Thank you, but it is only fitting that I do something to help with the concerns of the house, don't you think, Priscilla? It is going to take me a few days to get used to calling you by your second name," she said as an afterthought.

"Oh, my dear Chara, I have missed you. We must catch up on so much. As you say, there is a lot of responsibility around the house, but you must know that you are not a servant. I consider you family."

"Well, then, let's prepare something for everyone. The men will be up soon," Chara said, leading the way into the kitchen. "Where do I find everything?"

"Oh, Chara, you are incorrigible," Priscilla said, laughing. "Now, tell me how it is that you are so free."

"Do you mean do I have a husband?"

"Well, yes."

"No, I don't. Maria's father left me when he found out that I was with child. We were not married. I might as well start at the beginning.

"When I left your home, your father gave me funds for the journey home, and to take care of myself for a while. I stayed at my parent's house and worked when my father acquired jobs for me as a housekeeper. This helped them with their financial responsibilities. I was happy for a while. As happy as I could be under the circumstances. I really missed you and your family. You all treated me so well. I loved your family. Going back home was a shock at first. It was not the same as when I left home.

"I worked many jobs and became known around the area as a housemaid. One family had a son who befriended me. With time, we fell in love. I didn't think it would happen, but he was so kind to me. That is until he found out I was with child. The scandal was unbearable. I didn't want to start life that way, but I was so hurt by the guilt I felt about you. I just knew it was my fault because I was the one who helped you meet Daniel."

"But, Chara, you did nothing wrong in getting us together."

"Well, when you got hurt, I blamed myself because everyone blamed Daniel. Who else could I blame for bringing it all upon us, but myself? I made the arrangements."

"Chara, I am so sorry. I didn't know you felt that way. You might be interested in knowing that my father recently found out who really did it. Daniel was innocent."

"That is good news," Chara said. She still felt the agony of all those years ago. Continuing, she said, "When it all happened, you couldn't remember anything. You were so sick and weak that we all thought you might not survive."

"I just found out that I was with child. My mother told me when I returned to their house after many years away," Priscilla said. "How far along was I?"

"It couldn't have been more than a couple of months. You were so weak that your body could not feed the two of you. You hardly ate anything, and when you did, it came right back up. I was so afraid for you. Your parents said I must never tell anyone what happened and swore me to secrecy. I had to comply."

"I understand that, and I am sorry for making things difficult for you. I was furious. Can you ever forgive me?" Priscilla said, putting her arms around Chara.

"Oh, I interrupted your story. Please forgive me. What happened after the scandal?"

"I felt so guilty for causing your family so much pain, that I believed myself undeserving of living a good life. I was with child, and the rejection that everyone had for me only served to compound my sense of guilt. I decided to run away and hide. Of course, that didn't make things better. I found work with a family in another town that needed my help. They treated me kindly, but word got around that I was with child once the fact could not be hidden. When Marie was born, I had to do the marketing. Men began wooing me. After a while, feeling that they really liked me, I would meet them in secluded places. They only wanted one thing, and I felt used. I reasoned that it was already too late to turn back to a decent life. The family I worked for sent me away when it became clear what I was doing. The only way I had to support myself was by selling my services to whoever would have me. I am so ashamed of myself. Life was not easy. I was trapped. I found an abandoned house and made it my home."

She stopped. Tears flowed from her eyes. "I only wanted someone to love me. I mean, really love me. But all I got was used. The money only served to keep Maria from going hungry. She never knew what was happening. When I brought men to the house, she was usually sleeping."

"That must have been difficult for you," Priscilla said.

"I felt so dirty. I loved Maria and convinced myself that what I was doing was justified, because I was doing it for her. Some day she would know I did it for her, I reasoned."

"My Dear, I am so sorry you had to live that way. I know what it is like. My story is very similar. Our hurt has caused us much pain, indeed."

"When Maria took ill, and her problems became more than I could handle, I didn't know what to do. I panicked. Then, I heard about what Jesus was doing. I could not believe it at first, but I was frantic. I made the decision to find him. That was where I was when we met again."

"Chara, this is truly God's doing. I have much to share with you. I, too, needed help, when I met Jesus at Jacob's well in Sychar. He came to see me. He told me that he had come to offer me living water.

"That day, he changed our lives. He came and visited us here at this house. He healed Daniel, who had suffered a beating by the Roman soldiers long ago.

"We were not married, but Jesus suggested we change that at once. We have not been the same since that day."

At that moment, Maria poked her head around the corner. "Good morning, Mother. Good morning, Mistress Priscilla," she said with a smile. "Are you making breakfast? I am hungry."

Priscilla and Chara had become so engrossed in their conversation that they failed to make headway with the food. Quickly, they went to work.

"Good morning, Maria," Priscilla said. "We will have breakfast for you in just a little while. Come, you can help us cut the bread."

Glancing at Chara, Priscilla said, "I have something wonderful to tell you. Let's eat first, and then we can continue our conversation."

When all had eaten, Priscilla said, "Daniel, would you allow me to take a walk with Chara. We won't be long."

"Yes, of course my Dear; we will be here."

Walking into the countryside, the two resumed their conversation. "As I mentioned, I have something wonderful to share," Priscilla said. "Let's sit over there on that grass.

"I also led a troubled life; due to the guilt and shame I endured over the years. I came to hate men but had to use them to live. My heart became full of anger, hate and guilt, which led me down a path I could not return from.

"I know the rejection you speak of. Rejection can cause many reactions in us that we don't understand. I don't mean the type of rejection that pushes you away, but the kind you feel when men use you and then, make you feel dirty. The kind of rejection you feel when they think you are less than they are. The kind you feel when they use you as a toy to be pleasured by, and then shun you, or when they see you as a lesser being; the kind that causes you to lose confidence in your ability to do anything else. I mean the kind that makes you want to hide in a cave to never come out, or that makes you feel like scum, the kind that makes you think that nothing you do is good enough; the kind that makes you feel alone, even when you are in a crowd; the kind that makes you think as you get up in the morning, that you don't deserve to live–The kind that fills you with shame.

"As you, all I wanted was to be loved, but what I found were men who used and abused me. That is the kind of rejection I'm talking about. At every turn, my heart was shattered into smaller pieces, until there was nothing left of the person I once was. I didn't find myself again, until I met the Master. He put my heart back together. There was no condemnation in him toward me. He understood my plight. I was so angry and felt unmercifully bitter until I met Him.

"This is what I want to share with you: When He spoke to me that day, He offered living water. Of course, I didn't know what He meant, but as He spoke, my eyes were opened, and I saw life as I had never seen it before. I saw hope. At once, I also saw my misery, and wanted out of my pain. That is when He forgave me. All at once, I felt his forgiveness, and I cried. All I saw was my own wicked heart. I asked him to forgive me. I knew I was set free at once. It was as though I could breathe for the first time in my life.

"A burden was lifted from me. I didn't understand everything, but I saw my life change before my eyes. I felt love as I had never felt before.

"I began to follow him wherever he went. I have learned so much from him. Just the other day, I heard him say to the people, 'Come unto me, all you that labor and are heavy burdened, and I will give you rest.' Then, he went on to say, 'Take my yoke upon you, and learn of me; for I am meek and lowly in heart: and you shall find rest for your souls. My yoke is easy, and my burden is light.'

"When I heard those words, I understood what he meant when he spoke to me at the well. I now have rest. My soul is at peace.

"Chara, this is the kind of peace you can have, if you want it."

"Oh, yes, I want it. How shall I get it?"

"I have seen Jesus pray often. He speaks with the Almighty all the time. I think we can do the same. Let's say a prayer. What do you think?"

Chara nodded in affirmation.

"Alright, I will pray, and you can repeat everything I say."

With eyes looking toward heaven, Priscilla prayed for the first time in her life – and Chara with her.

"Almighty Father, I don't know what to say." Chara followed, repeating each word. "I have learned that you love me. I have sinned before you, and I ask your forgiveness. I saw love in Jesus' eyes, and know you are the same. I know you love me.

"I ask you to lift my burden and make me free to do your will. I ask you to wash me clean and give me life – that living water Jesus spoke to me about. I heard Jesus say, 'I have come to seek and to save those who are lost.' I have been lost, but you have found me.

"Save me from my sins and make me whole again. I ask this in Jesus' name."

When the two women finished, they sat with their heads bowed for a time in silence. Then, as though responding to a silent voice, they looked at each other and recognized a profound change in each other.

"I feel so different," Chara said. "I am free."

"I, too, feel it. I am free as well."

Then Chara saw a different look come over Priscilla's face. "I have never prayed like that before," Priscilla said. "How do you feel?"

"I have never done it either, but I know it is real."

Priscilla said, "I now know what we are going to do. I think Jesus wants us to speak with people of His power to save and change lives. I heard Him say that the Spirit would give us the words we need, at the right time. I am going to keep on doing this very thing. I am going to speak of salvation through Jesus, our Messiah."

They ran back to the house, their hearts full of joy and expectation. The Spirit had indeed shown them what to say, and what to do. Now, they felt the reality of what they had done. Priscilla had already given her life to Jesus, but in sharing the good news of the Messiah, she saw the impact in Chara, and recognized the power of the Almighty, in action, to change lives. She recognized the practical implication of what Jesus said would happen as the disciples walked in obedience. She remembered how the elderly woman felt the power of the Almighty when she placed her hand on her shoulder. The lady was healed, and felt it, even though Jesus had not done it personally, but through his obedient servant.

Priscilla recalled that Jesus had told the disciples not to go into Samaria, but to the lost house of Israel. Then he told her to take Chara home and take care of her in Samaria. *I am here in Samaria and see the power of God already. Maybe it is because I am from here, and the Lord wants to use me here.* It made sense within her heart. She felt confidence surge within her. *This is the leading of The Almighty.*

CHAPTER THIRTY ONE

Meetings in the House

Arriving at the house, they entered, obviously enthused about something.

"What have you been doing," Daniel asked, perplexed.

"It is God. We have learned how to communicate directly to our Father in Heaven." Priscilla said. She then proceeded to tell him and Maria how they had prayed, and how they both felt God moving within their hearts. "This is real, Daniel. We have been touched by God. I know He wants us to share what we know about Him here, among our own people."

"What do we know about God?" he said.

"Well, we know everything that Jesus has said. We have learned that He came to seek and to save those who are lost. We know that He is the Messiah. We know that He heals the sick. We know that He spoke of the baptism of John for the forgiveness of sin. Isn't that enough?"

"You are right, we don't have to speak about what we don't know, but there is a lot we already know about Jesus and His message. I heard Him speak of the Kingdom of God. He said, 'it has come to us.'" As he spoke, the same knowledge

Priscilla and Chara spoke about surged from somewhere deep within him. "We have a lot to share. There are so many people who need what we know of our Lord, the Messiah. Let's do it."

"I know what we can do. We will invite our friends around the neighborhood to our house tonight. What do you think, Daniel?"

Daniel stood to his feet and called Nathaniel. Shortly, their housekeeper appeared at the door.

"Yes, Master, what would you like?" he said.

"We are going to have visitors tonight. Would you prepare refreshments for them?"

"Yes, as you wish. I must go to the market for a few things."

"Thank you, Nathaniel."

Nathaniel disappeared through the door.

Maria said, "Mother, what can I do to help?"

"My little one, you can help by listening to everything we say. You will know what to do when the time comes," she said, running her fingers through Maria's hair. "Now, let's prepare some food for mid-day, shall we?"

An air of expectation surrounded the house. Daniel, Priscilla, Chara, Maria, and Nathaniel sensed what needed to be done, and set about doing it. Each one left the house in a different direction to meet with whomever they could and invite them to their home that evening. Priscilla took Chara and Maria with her and presented them to her neighbors. Everyone knew Priscilla. She had a reputation around town. "She is the changed woman who met Jesus at the well and returned to get all of us to meet Him," they said, after being invited to her house.

Priscilla purposefully invited only the women. Knowing that Chara was still new, and might have difficulty meeting men, she wanted to protect her from a misunderstanding on the part of the invited. In any case, it was better not to be seen talking to the men in public. "We will see you this evening," Priscilla said to each woman.

Preparations made, they sat to rest a short while. "Daniel, how did it go for you?" Priscilla said.

"I could not but wonder how easy it was to invite the men. They seemed eager to come. You have a reputation, as you know, but they all expressed how they wanted to meet 'that changed woman.' Of course, they knew me when I was crippled, and I said I wanted them to meet the one who healed me."

As evening approached, several people came to the door. "Please, come in. We are expecting you. "Nathaniel, could you lead our guests to the patio please, and make them comfortable?"

After another few moments a greater number of guests arrived. Still others followed. A few unknown individuals arrived, obviously curious, having heard of the excitement. In a town like theirs, everyone showed interest in whatever might be out of the norm.

Nathaniel shared refreshments all around. Almost all the folk knew each other and talk soon grew into a low roar. Daniel and Priscilla were happy to see so many come. At an appropriate moment, Daniel stood before the swelling crowd and requested their attention.

"I wish to thank each of you for coming here this evening. Priscilla and I have much to share with you. I know that most of you know us and, especially Priscilla…"

"Yes, we know you. But Priscilla used to be called Athaliah. What happened?" A voice came from the back of the area. Several snickers could be heard. Daniel ignored them.

"Yes, that is true. Do you remember when the Master came through town? He stayed with us, and for a couple of days, we learned a lot from Him. What we want you to know tonight is that He changed our lives. We have not been the same since that day. We have become His disciples. Many of you can testify that you were also healed by Him, correct?"

Several people raised their hands and voiced affirmation.

"We also were changed, as I said. I was a cripple and had been for many years when Priscilla took me in to care for me. We both needed Jesus for different reasons. But we had something in common that we recognized when He came into our lives. We were bound to sin and wrongdoing. Priscilla had her past, and I had mine. Our need was to be forgiven. How many of you have felt the need for forgiveness?"

A woman offered, "I know my husband needs forgiveness." Laughter erupted.

"I am not here to blame anyone tonight. We needed forgiveness, and Jesus forgave each of us. We realized He was the awaited Messiah. As such, He forgave us. We have heard Him say, 'He who is forgiven much, loves much.' I want to tell you tonight that I love much. Priscilla loves much. Not in the way she used to, but with a true love for others that compels her to share the love of Jesus, the Messiah.

"Consider my testimony. I was healed powerfully by the Master. There is no mistake about it. Some of you remember how I had so much difficulty getting around. Well, now you are looking at a man who was completely made whole in every way. Jesus did it.

"But the most important change He did in us was when He changed our hearts. We both had reasons, without numbers, why we should hate others. We were eaten up with not only hate but guilt, shame, and sin. We were sinners. It is easy to admit it now, but for years neither of us could do so. Jesus made the difference. When we saw how He loved us, we could not resist Him. He placed His hands upon us and prayed that His Father in heaven would cleanse our hearts and souls. As soon as He prayed, we felt the change that very moment. There was no denying it. Has anyone here ever experienced that kind of forgiveness?"

He waited a moment to see if anyone would respond. A voice in the rear was heard, "No, but it would be a good thing." Assent was heard through the people, as they whispered one to another, nodding their heads.

"Priscilla and I have followed Jesus for a while, and we have seen how He prays to His Father in heaven. We have found that if we pray to the Father in His name, it will be done. Jesus told his disciples, 'Whatever you ask of the Father in my name shall be done unto you.' Priscilla and I would love to pray with you tonight. You can also receive forgiveness for your sins. All it takes is a willingness to receive the gift of life that Jesus offers. That day Priscilla met Jesus at the well, He offered her living water, that if drank, would spring up unto life within her. She did receive that living water and was changed. I, too, drank of that water. It is spiritual water that can cleanse your hearts."

"Don't do any more talking, I want that water. I need to be forgiven." In the rear, a man was standing. "Please pray for me."

Daniel was surprised at the sudden outbreak. Looking toward Priscilla, he gathered his thoughts. He could see that the Holy One was at work in the hearts of his listeners.

"Of course, we will pray for you, but you can speak to Him yourselves."

Several others stood with the first man and began praying spontaneously. The eruption of voices surprised Daniel, but he flowed with it. Daniel recognized the work of the Lord that manifested and simply prayed as he had promised.

"I am free," one man said. "I can breathe. My burden is lifted ." Others followed, saying the same. Before anyone could say anything else, the crowd spontaneously erupted into joyful and reverent laughter. No one had ever felt this. No one wanted it to stop. From all quarters, the folk shared with each other what they were sensing. Daniel overheard several say, "Now I know what he meant. I am forgiven." The people were leaping and praising God, tears of joy flowing down their cheeks.

No one expected this to happen. Daniel, Priscilla, Chara, Maria, and Nathaniel stood smiling at the joy that filled the people. This was a learning moment for them—one of confirmation. Jesus was indeed working His miracles among them.

Nathaniel said, "I prayed the prayer, too. This is wonderful."

Little Maria, standing by her mother, said, "I did, too." A smile swept over her face, causing her cheeks to ache.

As the time ended, a man came to Daniel. "I am not from this town, but I would like to know if you can come to my town and speak to the people as you did tonight. Do you think that could be done? I don't want to impose."

Daniel glanced at Priscilla. With a simple look, they agreed. "Yes, we would love to do that. Come over here, and we can talk about it." The man gave instructions on how to find his house. "We will be waiting for you next week, then. I will spread the word to everyone I know. Thank you. We need what you have to give. I have never seen anything like it. God is at work here."

Without realizing it, Daniel and Priscilla had just stepped into Jesus' plan. Their lives would never be the same.

No one wanted to sleep. The house was now quiet, but emotions were high.

"This, indeed, is the work of the Almighty. Jesus truly is the Messiah, the Son of God." Daniel exclaimed. "If there was any doubt before, it is gone now."

The next few days passed quickly. Daniel and Priscilla prepared to leave for the planned meeting in the next town, as promised, and left the house with Nathaniel, Chara, and Maria.

"Be as transparent as possible, so there are no misunderstandings. If anyone comes by wanting to know more, just talk with them. Remember, you don't have to know everything. Tell them what Jesus has done for you. He will give you words," Priscilla said.

They arrived at the door of the house where the meeting was to take place, having followed instructions given them by the host. He had promised to spread the word of their arrival. Before long, there were knocks at the door. The house filled quickly. A sense of expectation could be felt by everyone present. In due course, the host stood to greet the visitors.

"Thank you for coming to this special occasion. We are pleased to have with us two disciples of Jesus. He is the one who is doing so many miracles in towns and cities up north. They have so much to say, so I will introduce them right away. This is Daniel, and Priscilla from Sychar. I met them by chance a few days ago when I was traveling through their town. Would you please share with us?" He stepped aside, motioning them forward.

"Good evening, as our gracious host has said, my name is Daniel, and my wife's name is Priscilla. I want to ask her to share how this all began in her life."

Priscilla stood looking over the group. "I want to share what happened to me. Not long ago, I found myself in a very difficult period in my life. This period was the result of many difficulties, starting many years ago. I was angry with everyone, especially men. I had a reputation all over town as a morally degenerate person. I could not get away from the jeers, sneers, or evil looks from the town's people, due to my conduct over the years. I was taking care of Daniel, who at that time was a crippled, beaten man who had suffered at the hands of Roman soldiers. We were not married but were friends since childhood. I cared for him because he was not able to take care of himself. To look at him now, it seems impossible." She glanced in his direction.

"One day, I had to go to Jacob's well for water. I always went there when no one else would be there because the women didn't like me near them. I was especially angry because several men had accosted me that day, thinking I was still doing what I had always done. As I approached the well, I saw a man seated nearby. This made me furious. I decided to get the water and leave.

"But, as I drew water, the man asked me to give him water. I ignored him. He insisted, and I could not ignore him any longer. He said something I shall never forget. He said, 'If you were to ask of me, I would give you living water. If you were to drink of it, you would never again thirst.' Of course, I didn't know what he meant. But he continued saying that this water would spring up into everlasting life. We spoke for a little while, and he told me everything I had ever done. We had never met, and I didn't know how he had come by that knowledge. He said to go call my husband and come back. I said I had no husband. Then, he said I had spoken the truth by saying I had no husband. He said I had had five husbands, and the man I currently lived with was not my husband. Of course, that got my attention.

"I said to him that only a man sent by God could know all that he knew. I wondered if he might be the Messiah we all awaited. He said, "I am He."

"Well, I ran into town and called Daniel and everyone else I could get together. I said, 'Come and see the man who has told me everything I have done in my life.' That day the whole town went out to see him. His name was Jesus.

"He came into our town and stayed a couple of days at our house. During that time, he healed Daniel and told us to get married."

Laughter rippled through the listeners.

"We began following him everywhere he preached and healed. We have seen his power. Now we have become his disciples. The most dynamic thing is that he forgave us our sin and made us whole in our hearts. No longer do we hold hatred in our hearts for all the things people have done to us. We live forgiven and free of judgment toward others. This is what Jesus has done for us.

"Jesus has said, 'come unto me, all you who are burdened and heavy laden, and I will give you rest.' He also says he has come to seek and to save the lost. Daniel and I can testify to this. It is absolutely true. Jesus sets us free when we believe in Him. He is the Messiah we have been told would come.

"Now, I ask you – all of you, would you like to be set free from the guilt of the past, and set free to live righteously from now on?"

Silence.

"How many of you know you are among those 'lost' people Jesus is seeking?"

In the rear a hand went up, then, another, and another. Soon nearly everyone there had their hands up.

"I am going to ask Daniel to pray with you. We have seen how Jesus prays to His Father. He has shown us how we, also, can pray to the Father. Jesus promised us that we will be heard when we pray to the Father in His name."

Daniel stood. "I am going to ask all who can to kneel in the presence of the Almighty." As he spoke, everyone bent to their knees. He started praying with conviction, "Almighty, and Eternal Father in heaven, we come to you this night in the name of your Son, Jesus. In His name we ask you to forgive us our sins and cleanse our hearts. Give us, we pray, that living water you speak of. Let it wash us clean and spring up unto life eternal within us."

As he spoke these words, the whole group felt as though a wind blew over them. Voices could be heard crying out to the Almighty. God was, without a doubt, touching their hearts. Praises were heard. Thanksgiving was expressed. A change was taking place in the hearts of everyone in the house. The power of God was among them. No one could stop the proceedings, nor did they wish to do so. They felt the cleansing that God was doing in their midst and praised Him.

As the celebration continued, long into the night... no one wanted to leave. Such joy, as they had never experienced, filled their hearts. God had met them in their hour of need, and everyone knew it.

A woman came to Priscilla and hugged her. It was then that Priscilla noticed that one of her feet was turned almost completely around. Then she noticed the obvious limp.

272

"I have heard that Jesus heals. Is that true?" the lady said.

"Yes, He does."

"Since you are His disciple, do you think you could pray for my foot?"

Priscilla smiled and placed her hand on the woman's shoulder. "Well, Yes, I would love to…" At that instant, the woman fell to the floor, and shouted, "Ohhhhhhh."

Priscilla reached down to help her up, and then noticed that the foot had completely turned around and was in a normal position.

"I am healed," the woman shouted. "I can walk normally. See?"

Everyone's attention was now on her. Looking around, she said, "All she did was place her hand on my shoulder. She didn't even touch my foot. I am healed." Astonishment could be heard in their voices as the people expressed their wonder.

"It was not I who healed her. It was Jesus. His power flowed through me. He is the one to be praised." Priscilla heard herself speaking but felt the same wonder as everyone else. Jesus truly was using her to not only testify of His power but to heal in His name.

After most of the people had finally left, during the last watch of the night, the host approached Daniel. "We must continue doing this. This must not be the only night of celebration. Truly the Almighty has met us here tonight. Jesus is here among us, even though He isn't here physically. We must do this again so that others may know of Jesus' saving power to change lives."

"We are in agreement," Daniel said. "Jesus meets, not only in Synagogues, but in houses everywhere He goes, so it would be befitting to do the same in His name."

Now there were two towns that had experienced the touch of Jesus' power. Daniel, being a man of action, took it upon himself to suggest what might be done to continue. Looking at the host, he said, "Priscilla and I will teach you all we know. As we learn more from Jesus, we will share it with you, so you can help others in your town. How does that sound? I see that God is working among us."

Looking at Priscilla, he said, "Jesus did send us out to teach in His name to heal and cast out demons. This is wonderful."

"I agree," Priscilla said. "We must continue."

The host said, "I will learn from you. The people need Jesus."

"Priscilla and I bless your home, in the name of Jesus. Peace be unto you."

The next step was taken. Priscilla and Daniel returned home with the knowledge that God was directing them toward a future of ministry in His name.

Master Haddad arrived home after an exceptionally long day at work. Benjamin was already sitting with Leah and the boys, enjoying some time together before supper.

"Benjamin, might I have a word with you?" he said.

"Yes, father."

"It won't take long, Leah. Benjamin will return quickly."

Father and son walked out onto the patio. "Benjamin, I heard a rumor today that has me concerned. I heard a couple of workers talking about a band of robbers that have been running around the countryside breaking into homes and stealing valuables. It is difficult enough to think men like that are in the area, but I heard one of the men say that he was in a house in another city, and hid when thieves broke in. He managed to see from his hiding place, and recognized Reuel."

"Our Reuel?" Benjamin said, surprised.

"Yes. It seems he has fallen in with some evil men. The Roman soldiers are searching for them but have not had success."

"This is a turn," Benjamin said. I must keep vigil over our place just in case he tries to come here."

"Let's keep this to ourselves. We don't want the family to be afraid. The Almighty knows I would love to catch him after what he did. He will pay for his crime someday. I no longer hate him, but there must be consequences for what he did."

"Yes, Father."

"Now, go back to Leah and the boys. They need you."

CHAPTER THIRTY TWO

Revelation
Through Tragdy

Daniel and Priscilla were busily preparing for a short trip to minister in several villages nearby, when a man came running into the house. "Master Daniel, come quickly. Please, where are you?" The man's voice trembled as he spoke.

Priscilla ran to the door. Her father's steward, Joab, stood before her. "Mistress Priscilla, you must come. They have taken Him." His voice was at the breaking point. He struggled to control it. "Please, you and Daniel must come."

Daniel ran up behind Priscilla. "Who has been taken? What are you saying?"

"The Master has been taken by the Roman soldiers, and they are going to crucify Him."

Priscilla felt her heart drop to the floor. *No. This can't be true.* "Please, Joab, come in. Sit, and tell us what has happened."

"Your father trusted no one else to bring this tragic news. He wants you to go to Jerusalem to see what is actually happening with Jesus. The last thing we heard was that He was taken before Pilate for trial."

It took a little while to fully understand the urgency put before them. "You must drop everything, and go. You may not arrive in time. Please, go," Joab said. "Your father knows you are close to the Master, and thinks you might testify on His behalf before the rulers. You must try, at least. It may be too late already, but you must try."

"Daniel," Priscilla said, "how could they do this?" The words choked in her throat. Tears flowed down her cheeks. "Don't they know that Jesus is only doing good? What has he done to them? He has done nothing but bless them in every way."

Her mind spun and anguish filled her heart as they urged their horses along. All she could think of was what evil men do against the innocent and blameless. Jesus had told them it was not His time to be taken, and they relied upon that. But, they were not ready for this.

Not knowing where to go, they decided to simply head into the city and see where the crowds were. The atmosphere that greeted them as they entered Jerusalem was unmistakable. It was as though the whole city had gone mad. They saw one of Jesus' disciples and asked where Jesus had been taken.

"He has been found guilty, and is being forced to carry a cross up to The Place of the Skull. I am headed that way."

"Thank you, we will go ahead and meet you there," Daniel said as he spurred his horse. "I don't understand how they could do this to Him."

With heavy hearts, they continued in silence, not knowing what to say to each other. Finally, they saw a great crowd ahead. "Let's leave the horses here and go through the crowd by foot," Daniel suggested.

They made their way forward, gently pushing bystanders aside as they went. Priscilla could not see through the tears that filled her eyes, and relied on Daniel to lead the way. From where they were, they could see three crosses. Coming near, they saw Mary, Martha and Lazarus, standing at the foot of the center cross. People were crying all around them. The tragedy that faced them was overwhelming. The world had gone mad. Raw hatred permeated the air. Had it been color, the atmosphere would have been black. Angry men shouted taunts at the three men hanging from the crosses. Soldiers sat around the foot of Jesus' cross, making sport of the proceedings. Above them hung the object of their hatred and disdain, all but naked, in obvious pain, yet saying nothing. Above his head was a sign that read, JESUS OF NAZARETH - THE KING OF THE JEWS.

Priscilla approached Mary and Martha and Mary, the mother of Jesus. "How long have you been standing here?"

With tears and a raspy voice, Martha said, "Too long. Look what they have done to the Master. He is innocent. We all know it, but no one will listen."

At that moment, Priscilla looked at one of the men at Jesus' side. He seemed to be saying something to Jesus. She watched as Jesus responded. Then the man on the other side of Jesus said something with a sneer, and she looked his way. Her knees went limp, and she fell to the ground. Unbelievably, she recognized the man. It was Reuel, her father's chief of security. She had not seen him for years, but recognized him right away. Her father had told her he was the man who had violated and beaten her, leaving her all but dead.

She was powerless to deflect the conflict that rushed into her soul. Before her was the Master, hanging, though innocent. With the man who had ruined her life on a cross at his side. She gasped at her own reaction. She loved the One, and hated the other. *How could this be?*

Then, Jesus looked her way, His eyes penetrating her very soul. Without saying a word, she knew He was communicating with her. It was as though He read her mind. In her innermost being, she knew Jesus had changed her heart. At that moment, she could not hate Reuel. *How strange.* Jesus had changed her heart so drastically that she was incapable of hating the man who had cost her almost everything in life. At his side was the man who had set her free of all the wrong decisions, filthy conduct, abuse of others, lustfulness, sin, and pride she was bound to for years. She no longer felt dirty and ashamed because of Him. *How can I hate Reuel after what Jesus did for me?* Her thoughts crowded through her mind, and she marveled at her own decision to forgive.

Priscilla sat where her knees had dropped her. Her life passed before her eyes. The anger pent up within her sought to break out into her conscious mind, producing one mental image after another of terrible misuse and abuse suffered over many years. She felt her head spin. Her life had been destroyed by that evil man who hung at Jesus' side. Anguish filled her heart once again — accumulated from all the years of unspoken and misunderstood events colliding into one single event — which broke her heart again as the images passed before her mind's eye. All those years of searching for answers that eluded her for so long. She covered her mouth with her hands, fearing she would scream. Then she looked up and caught His gaze and realized He understood the battle that raged within her.

Looking at Jesus, she shouted, "Thank you, Master, for giving me life." Others around her turned to look. She didn't care who looked at her. Her Savior was dying for her. He was the only one that mattered. This was so sad – and so wonderful. The dichotomy within her could not be understood. She cried for her Savior, yet praised

Him for giving her the power to forgive.

At that moment she understood what Jesus had said. "If I be lifted up, I will draw all men to myself." *He knew He would be here. He came to die. He is dying for my sin. He is paying the price of my sin against His Father.* The wonder of the revelation hit her so heavily that she could not stand. Kneeling, she cried with all her heart. "Father, I love you. I understand."

Those around her didn't know what was being transacted in her heart and mind. Daniel tried to help her to her feet, but she wanted to stay where she was. She was in communion with the Almighty. Never had such human tragedy collided with this immeasurable expression of love and hope. God in the man Christ Jesus— reconciling man to God.

Priscilla picked herself up from the ground and sought out each follower of Jesus present, and hugged them, one by one, encouraging them to believe the words of their Master. Sadness filled her heart, but the knowledge of Christ's power to save overwhelmed every glimmer of hopelessness within her.

In obvious agony, Jesus looked down upon his mother and said, "Woman, here is your son." Then, looking at John, He said, "behold, she is now your mother. Take care of her."

At midday, everyone turned when they heard Jesus say, "It is finished," and He gave up His spirit. The sky became black, and horror fell across the land. The unbelievable had happened. The Master was dead. He died a death, perpetrated in the cruelest manner, for the greatest effect, that demonstrated the absolute hatred of those responsible for it. It was the pinnacle of man's hatred toward man, and God. The darkness added to the dismay of those who stood beneath the crosses. A soldier standing at the foot of Jesus said, "Truly, this man was a righteous man. He was innocent."

Suddenly, darkness fell upon the earth, all about, from the sixth hour until the ninth hour. All sounds of nature ceased. No one dared move. The darkness was so weighty that it felt like a heavy blanket covering everything. People gasped. It was as though Satan had taken control of the world and its inhabitants.

Daniel searched for Priscilla in the place he had last seen her and held her tight. Fear tugged at their hearts as they fought to understand. Time stood still. It was surreal. Invasive evil covered them as they clung to each other. Had the enemy won? What would happen now? The conflict of this paradoxical moment flooded their hearts, but the power of Jesus and the communication that had just taken place filled them.

"Jesus won the battle for the hearts of mankind," she whispered to Daniel.

"Trust Him. He overcame the evil one."

Her heart filled with the certainty of the promises of Jesus. Still, conflict knocked at the door of her heart. She felt profound grief yet unexplainably exhilarated by the event of the cross. She understood the reason Jesus had to die. Still, sadness gripped her and threatened to overcome her emotions. The Savior wa taken away from them all. Within her spirit, she perceived the spiritual battle tha raged around them. Satan and Jesus were furiously battling in the spirit realm. Sh knew she was not the only one aware of the conflict.

As quickly as the darkness descended upon them, it vanished. Once again, lig dispelled the darkness with a mighty rush.

Daniel and Priscilla returned home heavy of heart. Conflicting emoti fought for attention and did not let them sleep. Yet, they remained aware of spiritual battle that raged around them at the cross that fateful day. It was an easy thing to forget. An overwhelming sense of profound loss threatene conquer their hearts. However, they remained faithful to the words of life J taught them; "The world hated me. It will hate you too." and found valor continue forward in faith.

But would their faith hold fast? Dark clouds already gathered just beyond horizon. Would they and the other disciples overcome the onslaught that aw them?

Hearing a knock at the door, Daniel reluctantly opened the door. "Dan and Priscilla must come. The word is all around. Jesus is no longer in the to has risen and wants to meet with His disciples!"

The beginning…